.

# THEN WE TAKE BERLIN

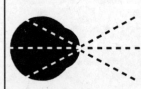

# THEN WE TAKE BERLIN

## JOHN LAWTON

**THORNDIKE PRESS**

*A part of Gale, Cengage Learning*

GALE
CENGAGE Learning

Detroit • New York • San Francisco • New Haven, Conn • Waterville, Maine • London

**LIBRARY OF CONGRESS CATALOGING-IN-PUBLICATION DATA**

Lawton, John, 1949–
    Then We Take Berlin / By John Lawton. — Large Print edition.
        pages cm. — (Thorndike Press Large Print Thriller.)
    ISBN-13: 978-1-4104-6509-2 (hardcover)
    ISBN-10: 1-4104-6509-8 (hardcover)
    1. Large type books. I. Title.
    PR6062.A938T44 2013
    823'.914—dc23                                          2013035079

Published in 2014 by arrangement with Grove/Atlantic, Inc.

Printed in the United States of America
1 2 3 4 5 6 7 18 17 16 15 14

for

Gore Vidal
1925–2012

Who helped kick me into shape.
The planet has lost its
most barbed critic.
The job of world-class pain-in-the-arse
is now vacant.

". . . Never tell all you feel, or (a better way still), feel very little . . . at any rate never have any feelings which may make you uncomfortable, or make any promises which you cannot at any required moment command and withdraw. That is the way to get on . . ."

William Makepeace Thackeray: *Vanity Fair*
1847

"Wer spricht von Siegen? Überstehen ist Alles."

Rainer Maria Rilke:
*Requiem, für Wolf Graf von Kalckreuth*
1908

"The warriors are dead. The warriors died in two world wars. Those who remain are the barterers. They know the price of

coffee and cocoa and sugar and flour in a
defeated country."

Kay Boyle: *The Lovers of Gain*
1950

■ ■ ■ ■

# I
# FIRST WE TAKE
# MANHATTAN

■ ■ ■ ■

"The city seen from the Queensboro Bridge is always the city seen for the first time, in its first wild promise of all the mystery and beauty in the world."
F. Scott Fitzgerald: *The Great Gatsby*
1925

# §1

*West Berlin:* May 1963

Christina Hélène von Raeder Burkhardt had too many names, so was known simply as Nell. She was attending the first of her twice weekly meetings with the mayor to agree an itinerary for the impending visit of President Kennedy.

"McGeorge Bundy gives me a headache."

"You don't get on with Bundy, Nell?"

"I get on very well with Bundy — one of the best —"

"Or the brightest . . ."

"Whichever . . . I get on well with him, but it does seem to me that his job is simply to say 'no.' Whatever I suggest he says cannot or should not be done."

"Such as?"

"I suggested a visit to Bernauer Straße . . . where the wall began, as it were . . . and where it claimed its first victims."

"Not a bad idea."

"Bundy won't let the president do it —

instead we get JFK's sister. She'll visit Bernauer Straße."

"We agreed to that?"

"Of course — it's better than nothing."

"Nell . . . what is it you want?"

It was a generous question. Mayor Brandt had his agenda for this visit — everyone had, from the man who swept the streets to the Chief of Police — yet still he was asking to hear hers.

"I want President Kennedy to visit *all* the Berlins — all the Berlins I know as a Berliner. Berlin new and Berlin old. I would ask that he visit the city we rebuilt . . . to look at the Kurfürstendamm as well as the Reichstag ruins. I would ask that he see and be seen. I would ask that he visit Berlin West and Berlin East."

"The East?"

"Through Checkpoint Charlie. He has every right to pass through."

"Imagine the embarrassment when he's asked to produce his passport."

"Would they dare?"

"I don't know. Nell, have you actually suggested a visit to the Soviet Sector?"

"Oh yes. Ages ago."

"And?"

"And Bundy said it would be the one idea he'd never put before Kennedy."

"The Russians never pass up a chance for a stunt. And if we did that we'd be pulling a

14

stunt too. And the only point to a stunt is not to be upstaged. Going East would give them every opportunity to upstage us. And if we don't go East . . . if we stay 'home' and peer over the wall they'll still stage something. There'll be an 'incident' of some sort. Imagine. Kennedy waves to Berliners through the Brandenburg Gate and Khrushchev waves back."

Nell smiled at the image. So often Willy Brandt cracked a joke only as a prelude to the deadly serious.

"Everything is ambivalent," Brandt was saying. "Kennedy visits a Berlin renewed and a Berlin divided. A Berlin defiant and a Berlin besieged. Everything about this visit is double-edged. Except this . . . it's going to be the biggest public spectacle Germany has seen since the Nuremburg rallies. And a Nuremburg rally is that last thing it can ever look like. The world will be watching. Nothing should remind them of the Reich. Ideally, this visit should pass without 'incident.' The world will be watching Berlin."

Incident.

*Vorkommnis.*

He'd been emphatic.

# §2

*London:* May 1963
John Wilfrid Holderness had had many

15

names. John to his parents — naturally as they had chosen the name, and indeed had had him christened so in a Stepney church in the autumn of 1927 — Wilf to his school-mates — Joe to his old RAF pals . . . and Wilderness to his women.

He would not have answered the phone that night. It was gone ten, they were in bed, they'd made love and he was sleeping it off. His wife wasn't. She answered.

She nudged him.

"Wilderness. It's Frank Spoleto."

Wilderness pretended to be asleep, but she wasn't having any of it.

She nudged him again.

"Can't be Frank," he said through a yawn. "Last I heard he went back to Washington. Tell whoever it is to fuck off."

One hand curled around the mouthpiece to muffle their voices.

"It's Frank. He's in New York, calling you person to person. It must be costing him a packet!"

"Person to person? What's that?"

"Bastard to bastard. Here, take the bloody phone!"

Spoleto's voice boomed at him, more like five feet than five thousand miles away.

"Joe. You old bugger!"

It was one of Spoleto's delights from his time in London to use anglicisms, often at the wrong moment — his confusion between twit and twat had caused many a blush.

"Frank? It's nearly midnight."

"It's ten of eleven, Joe. Clock on my desk has faces for London, Paris and New York —"

"Sounds like a bottle of cheap perfume to me, Frank."

"And there's a barman two blocks away getting ready to serve me my first martini of the weekend."

"Don't let me keep you."

Spoleto laughed loudly at this. Wilderness held the phone away from his ear.

"Joe, I need to see you."

"No problem, I'll be here."

"I need to see you in New York."

Wilderness didn't know why, but it was like a surge of adrenaline, hearing Spoleto say New York. He sat up. Switched the phone from one ear to the other, looked around for his wife, heard the sound of water running in the bathroom.

"Er . . . say again Frank."

"I need you here. I've booked you out on the one o'clock Pan Am to Idlewild on Tuesday. Tickets, and everything else you need to get here will be at the embassy on Monday morning. First class. All paid for. Hell, I even got you a room at the Gramercy."

"You couldn't afford the Waldorf?"

The only New York hotel of which he had ever heard.

17

He held the phone a moment or two after Spoleto had hung up, if only because it was never obvious with Frank when a conversation was over — it was over when Frank said it was over, no goodbyes, just his sense of an ending and the clunky silence on the line. He put the phone down, shuffled naked to the bathroom door. Tapped it gently open with his foot.

The wife sat naked on the lavatory, a wad of loo roll in her right hand, poised. Early in their marriage, six or seven years ago, he had to get over the fact that she would walk in while he pissed, and didn't give a damn if he walked in on her. He chalked it up to their different backgrounds — the public nature of a private education (hers) versus a home which knew no privacy (his) — the only door with a lock had been the loo, and the loo had been out in the yard. He'd hardly ever not had a room to himself, and only at sporadic moments in his life had he ever been in dorm or barracks, but a room he could call his own (in the sense that if you put an object down in said room, it would still be in the same place the next time you looked, in the sense that you could lock the door and not be asked why) that had been rare, that had been precious and he'd given that up to marry Judy. And given it up gladly.

She blotted herself, flushed the loo and settled in the bath.

"What did the bastard want now?"

"That's a tough one. He wants me in New York next week."

"That kind of tough I can live with. It's not as though you're a jetsetter is it? New York on expenses. Yeah — sounds really tough."

"How did you know it was on expenses?"

"Would you even be thinking about it if it weren't?"

Wilderness settled on the edge of the bath.

"I just thought . . . out of the blue after all this time . . ."

"It's three or four years isn't it? Can't be much more. The two of you came back from Helsinki together."

"I just thought . . . this wouldn't have anything to do with Alec would it?"

"Get in the bath, Wilderness. You'll feel better and you'll sleep better."

"Er . . ."

Just a grunt. Non-committal, out of nothing more than tiredness.

"Just get in. You know what you're like when you're too tired to sleep. Those nights when your legs twitch. You'll feel better. Trust me."

He slipped in at the blunt end, the rounded knobs on the taps cold against his back. Her toes found their way to his armpits. Her nipples peeked at him through the foam.

"Trusting you isn't the problem. It's trusting Frank."

19

"And my father?"

"Nah, I was just asking. Alec's been good to me — I didn't mean . . ."

"Didn't mean what? Pa's been good to you. Of course he has. But do I detect a hint of too much of a good thing?"

It was a moment to sink beneath the water and blow bubbles at her, but only Hollywood had baths big enough for that.

She took the unspoken words from his silent lips. Pushed her breasts together and made an irresistible waterfall flow between them.

"Coochie coo," she said, and he knew he was off the hook. Subject changed.

§3

He'd never flown the Atlantic before. He'd flown plenty of times. His years in the RAF had seen to that. He'd scrounged flights almost like hitching car rides. But he'd never done a long haul. It was the stuff of Sunday colour supplement advertising. "International" was a positive in the adman's world. It implied you were beyond the pettiness of nations, that you were post post-war, that you moved in a world peopled by the likes of Liz Taylor and Richard Burton, that you sat in the VIP lounge at airports, and had a bag emblazoned with the name of the airline. Things like that were coveted. It was chic to be seen with a cheap plastic holdall marked BOAC, chic-er still to be seen with the one Wilderness now had bearing the Pan Am logo.

Frank hadn't been mean with him. Whatever Frank's faults — lies, tricks, half-truths, cheapness was not one of them. First class all the way. The hostess handed him a package as soon as he took his seat, saying "A present from Mr. Spoleto."

Inside were two books and a note in Frank's hand saying, "Don't get too bored."

He looked at the titles. *The Ipcress File. King Rat.* An hour out of Heathrow he abandoned the former in favour of the latter. Too damn difficult. Fifty pages into the steamy jungle of *King Rat* he fell asleep. Woke, read another fifty and napped again. When he awoke the second time, the plane was over Newfoundland. Canada, America . . . New York.

As the Fasten Seat Belt sign came on, the man sitting next to him spoke. Overweight, balding, brimming with bonhomie, capable — Wilderness thought — of rattling on for ages. But, they'd exchanged half a dozen pleasantries over the meal several hours ago, and then the man had slept the uninterrupted sleep of a seasoned traveller sedated on free champagne and Southern Comfort.

"First time?" he asked. A question left over from the simple pleasantries that he hadn't asked first time around.

21

"Is it that obvious?"

"You get so you can tell. Just the way a guy looks around. The way he talks to the hostesses."

"Too nervous?"

"Too polite. Too grateful. We paid for all the stuff they thrust at us."

"Or," said Wilderness. "Somebody paid."

"Right. Who'd ever pay for their own ticket? Ought to be down as one of the rules in the game of life. Play it right and somebody else will always pay."

It was a disappointment. For some reason, doubtless a stupid reason, he'd expected to be able to see skyscrapers the second they stepped out of the terminal. There were none, they were way out on Long Island in a big, flat nothing. Idlewild seemed to be the right name. He strained towards the western horizon, hoping at least for a glimpse of Manhattan.

He stood next to the fat man in the queue for Checker cabs. Every one that pulled up made him feel a mile nearer to the city. A fleck of deep, warm yellow somehow just blown his way. They were at least six places away from getting a cab, when a tall, black man in a grey suit approached and asked if he were Mr. Holderness.

"Sorry to be late, sir. An accident on the expressway. Mr. Spoleto's car is waiting. We'll have you in Manhattan in no time at all."

Wilderness knew he should offer the fat man a ride, but he wanted to be selfish, to enter the city without the voice of experience jabbering in his ear. Manhattan was worth approaching in innocence. Find out for himself. He just shook his hand and said, "Thanks for the motto. I'll treasure it."

"Motto? What motto?"

"Play it right and somebody else will always pay."

"Oh that."

He was still chuckling at his own wit as the Negro picked up the suitcase and led Wilderness across the lane to a Cadillac. A big car. A ridiculous car. Low-slung, fat, covered in chrome and sporting huge rear fins. It reminded him of a beached shark. Cadillac Deville Sedan, the driver replied, when Wilderness asked.

"Frank's car?"

"Frank's car, this year. Frank's car for now."

"And next?"

"Whatever the boss takes a shine to. I driven five models in three years."

"Does Frank like to drive?"

"Naw. Frank likes to be driven."

Wilderness sat in the back, feeling he should have sat in the front, but the sense of protocol was palpable. The man drove, the man was paid to drive. The front seat was his. He doubted Frank ever sat in the front.

Manhattan loomed up so quickly it caught

him unawares. Suddenly above the one- and two-storey buildings either side of the road there it was, shining pinnacles against a western sun, the sun all but eclipsed by the spire on the Chrysler Building, a corona of light sending the skyscraper into chiaroscuro. A black spike in a red sky.

Crossing the Queensboro Bridge he was entering something akin to a dream. He'd always dreamed of cities. He'd always fallen in love with cities — mostly because he'd never known anything else. Childhood trips to the seaside had palled before he was ten — how many sandcastles can you build for some bigger kid to knock down? And rarer trips out into the Essex countryside to visit great aunts — relics from another century, all aprons and safety pins, a generation and a gender that seemed always to be dusted with flour or wiping their hands — left him awkward and speechless, blushing as his resemblance to Uncle Harold or Cousin Alfred was rattled off, baffled as they wished for him a better fate than Cousin Tom — reduced to a red mist at Ypres — or Great-Uncle Brinsley — a petty thief, an incompetent burglar, his life wasted in and out of Queen Victoria's prisons.

That was the beauty of a city. You entered anonymously. Who you were, with luck, with will, was who you could make yourself. You were not the sum parts, the flawed arithmetic of your own genealogy.

They crossed several avenues, Wilderness wound down the window trying to see the names, but they seemed to be only numbers. Then in rapid succession, they crossed Lexington, Park and swung right on Madison to pull into the kerb a dozen blocks further on.

It wasn't quite a skyscraper. It was thirty or forty floors. Bigger than anything London had to show. A long row of brass plates ran down each mock-classical column either side of the revolving door. The driver led Wilderness so quickly through the door and the lobby that he could take in next to nothing. They took the lift to the twenty-first floor, and as the doors opened a glass wall appeared, bearing the stencil "Carver, Sharma, and Dunn."

It was tempting to ask when or if Frank's name would ever appear, but he didn't.

Reception was glass and leather. Glass-topped tables, Barcelona studded leather chairs, ashtrays on stilts that spirited fag ash away like a child's spinning top at the press of a button. Furniture than defied suspension or the basic laws of physics to hang in space. It all screamed modern and it could scream all it liked. Wilderness was listening.

What screamed loudest hung on the wall, filling a space about seven feet by three between the receptionist's desk and the door to the inner sanctum. He would not have known what it was but for his wife, but then that was true of so many things. He knew what he knew because Judy told him. He had no shame about it. If she was a willing teacher he was a willing pupil and it had been that way since the day they met the best part of ten years ago.

This, and he had no doubts, was a Jackson Pollock. The kind of painting, the kind of artist to be featured on a highbrow BBC arts programme like *Monitor,* on which Judy had often worked, and to be described by the critics as cutting edge or possibly postmodern (a phrase which made no sense to Wilderness) and as "looks like something my three-year-old would do" and "what a load of old bollocks" by the general public.

Just below it on the wall was a small typed label: "Early Autumn. October 1955."

It was tempting to touch. The kind of thing that would get him thrown out of an art gallery, but this wasn't an art gallery, this was . . . whatever it was . . . Frank's office selling whatever it was Frank sold.

He ran the index and big fingers of his right hand along a spinal cord of red, a raised weal that ran almost the length of the painting.

"Tactile, isn't it?"

A very pretty young woman, in a starched white blouse and tight, grey skirt. He hadn't noticed her emerge from the inner office.

"Yes," he said. "You can almost feel the

energy he put into it, as though the muscle was kind of locked into the gesture and then into paint."

He knew he sounded a bit of a wanker, saying this, but sounding like a wanker really depended on who was listening.

She stood next to him now, blonde, a foot shorter than he was, looking up at the painting, while he looked at eye level.

"Never thought of it quite that way, but then I've never dared to touch. The temptation to pick at it like a scab would be too much. I might get fired. You won't. I'm Frank's secretary, by the way, Dorothy Shearer. And I'm here with an apology."

"Already?"

Wilderness looked directly at her for the first time, first impressions well confirmed. This one was a looker.

"I'm sorry?"

"Happens a lot with Frank. Never a deal going down, always a dozen deals going down. Now tell me he's had to nip out to a meeting and won't be back today."

"You've know Frank a long time, I take it?"

"Since Berlin. Since 1947."

"Yes, he's gone out to a meeting. He's asked that, Greg — that's your chauffeur — take you to the Gramercy. Frank will call you as soon as he's free."

Greg hefted the suitcase.

"What exactly is it Carver, Sharma, and

Dunn do?" Wilderness asked.

"Frank didn't tell you?" Dorothy Shearer replied. "I'm surprised. We're an advertising agency. You've just stepped into dreamland Mr. Holderness."

Going back to street level, Wilderness thought that it was probably where Frank was always going to end up. What better career for an excon-man than advertising? A profession dedicated to convincing you that shit is toothpaste. What kind of shit would Frank be trying to sell him now?

It was not yet six, a light spring evening. Down Park Avenue, around the helter-skelter that circumvented Grand Central, and on 42nd Street Wilderness asked Greg, "Would you pull over? I think I want to walk a while. I've had eight hours of sitting down."

Greg parked the Cadillac, swung around in the seat.

"I could take your bag to the hotel and you could walk from here, if you like."

"What are the chances of me getting lost?"

Greg pointed down Lexington.

"About zero. Just stay on Lex till it ends. Twenty blocks, not even twenty minutes."

"I can't miss it?"

"You can't."

He found himself across the street from the Chrysler, looking up as it tapered away to infinity, at a jutting silver eagle that seemed to be a mile in the sky.

He stood on the sidewalk of a new world. Hands in pockets, head back. Whatever he did next, wherever he went next, his first step would take him into dreamland.

## §4

When he'd showered and changed and gone down to the lobby to look around, the girl on reception handed him a note.

> "I'll be tied up all evening and most of the day tomorrow. Get out and see New York, kid. Remember to bring me the bill. FS."

He asked the Gramercy's doorman — a tall, stout, fifty-ish black man in a big green coat with a row of medal ribbons across the left breast that told Wilderness the man's war had been bloodier than his — how do you kill an evening in a city where being spoilt for choice left you helpless?

"What would I do? I'm a jazz man, sir. I'd find me a jazz club, hope Monk or Coltrane turn up — and I'd belly up to the bar and get my ears filled."

"Are there any within walking distance?"

"Sure. Across the square, down Third for about ten blocks. The Five Spot on St. Mark's Place. Turn left off Third and you're there. Won't take you but fifteen minutes."

Wilderness didn't think it was to his taste, but his taste was on the back burner. Neither Monk nor Coltrane turned up, but the posters on the wall told him they had on several other occasions. As Eric Dolphy alternated between flute and saxophone, between harmony and dissonance, the sound that really mattered was the voice in his head that said, "I'm in a jazz club in New York." And the voice in his head that resisted saying, "It's a long way from Whitechapel."

And then the band launched into "On Green Dolphin Street," and harmony and dissonance folded into each other and Whitechapel melted away from mind and memory leaving New York draped across his arm, whispering its seduction in his ears, in and out of the sax riffs and the drum beats.

## §5

He drifted all day. Over Fifth, across Washington Square and into Greenwich Village, the only Manhattan district he'd ever heard of apart from Harlem. He sat in coffee bars, he stood on street corners with his hands in his pockets and stared. He had lunch in an Italian restaurant at Carmine and Bleecker, drifted east again and decided to follow Broadway south just to see where it went. Where it went was down one side of Little Italy. Instinct told him to zigzag, onto Mulberry, down into Chinatown, back onto Broadway, past City Hall and out to Battery Park, the harbour and a distant view of the Statue of Liberty. He'd never imagined that it or she would be green. He found he was content with the distant view and had no desire to take a ferry out and look more closely. Proximity was not intimacy.

Around five he asked a cabdriver to take him to a book store, and found himself in the Strand at Broadway and 12th. He'd almost finished *King Rat.* He was probably never going to finish *The Ipcress File.* If Frank was going to string him out another day he'd need a book.

He checked in at the Gramercy an hour or so later. The desk clerk said a young woman was waiting for him in the bar.

"Are you sure?"

"Oh yes, sir. Asked for Mr. Holderness."

In a booth on the Lexington side of the bar sat Dorothy Shearer, sipping at a white lady and smiling up at him.

"He stood me up again, eh?"

"Yep. But look at it this way. I could have just phoned in a message. But here I am."

"And here am I."

"And we're on expenses. Manhattan, if not the world, is our oyster."

"Let's order before Frank's credit runs out."

"Unlikely, but since you ask . . . I'll have

31

another white lady."

The waiter was already at their table. They were the only people in the bar.

Wilderness ordered and asked for a scotch.

"Try harder," Dorothy said. "Push the boat out. Experiment. Have something you wouldn't have at home."

"Good point, but what?"

"Waiter, please bring my friend a whiskey sour."

She noticed the bag of books he had placed on the table.

"Show me. I can't resist knowing what people choose in book stores."

Wilderness pushed the bag in her direction. She pulled out Stendhal's *Le rouge et le noir,* a tatty Modern Library translation from the fifties.

"I don't know this book."

"I've been meaning to read it for years. An old friend once told me that if he'd read it at sixteen his life would have been totally different."

"Did you buy anything American?"

"Keep trawling."

She pulled out Kerouac's *Lonesome Traveler* and Harper Lee's *To Kill a Mockingbird.*

"Indeed you did. In fact you may well have polarised the nation in a single bag. Frank thinks all these Beats and bums are pretty much the Antichrist. America in its decadence, heading for addiction and misery and death. To say nothing of homosexuality. I doubt there's anything Frank hates more than faggots."

"And the other one?"

"Oh . . . America looks at something it's done so very very badly and . . . and manages to redeem itself. Childhood threatened, childhood challenged and somehow innocence restored. Huck Finn, revisited. The nigger didn't do it and the boogeyman at the dark end of the street really isn't the boogeyman. And the guy in that white suit is your father. We all think better of ourselves after we read it. Besides, I could believe anything Gregory Peck says. I'd vote for him for president. I'd vote for the guy in the white suit."

The waiter set down the cocktails. Wilderness sipped at his and asked her what was in it.

"Mostly they just add lemon juice to whiskey, maybe a hint of sugar."

"Pure heresy in Scotland."

"That's OK, they make it with Kentucky bourbon. Do you actually like it?"

"Oh, I could get used to it. There's a lot about New York I could get used to."

When it came to discussing a meal, each of them turned around and looked around.

"We're still the only people here," Wilderness said.

"It's Wednesday. Let's go somewhere where

it isn't Wednesday."

Outside, Dorothy's hand up for a cab, Wilderness said, "Let's take the subway. I've never been on the subway."

"Are you kidding?"

"No. It just didn't feel right. I caught one cab today and for the rest I just walked. The subway felt like it needed a guide."

She steered him over to Park Avenue. To the subway station at 23rd, the IRT Lexington Avenue local to Brooklyn Bridge. It was like whiskey sour, he could get used to it. The rattle and the roar, the pure, shrill screech of metal on metal as the train pulled into Union Square.

Walking down the side of the bridge, Wilderness began to think of New York as a city in the sky. Not simply the scale . . . more the perfection, although that was far from being precisely what he meant as he told her over dinner in a tiny restaurant boasting "the oldest bar in New York," at the corner of Water Street.

"London's far older than New York, but . . . all the bomb damage. The rubble sat around for years. I thought we'd look that way for ever. London's like a bad set of teeth. There are gaps, there are bad dental bridges just about holding on and there are rotting stumps that needed to be pulled ages ago."

"I've never been to London," she said. "And I get the feeling I'm going to have difficulty holding on to the dream."

"I'll try not to ruin it for you. But . . ."

"But you will anyway?"

He shrugged this off. It was a thought so hard-won it had to be uttered.

"Now there's new buildings — ugly, flat, featureless new buildings going up at a rate of knots. Paternoster Square, the district around St. Paul's has gone from piles of rubble to a concrete nightmare. London lives with the old barbarism of the Blitz and the new barbarism of 1960s architecture fighting it out at street level. New York . . . the old and the new seem to sit together so much better. It seems like an American talent. One we don't have back home. And I never realised New York would seem quite so old."

"You're surprised to find New York is old?"

"Nothing has surprised me more in the last two days."

"And you just fell for the bridge, right?"

"And this afternoon I fell for the Statue of Liberty, and yesterday I fell for the Chrysler . . . I walked backwards down Lexington Avenue, just so I could keep it in sight."

She giggled, a broad, beaming grin and a row of very American teeth.

"Backwards? Down Lex? You're lucky you didn't get arrested."

"I got called an 'asshole' a few times, but mostly people turned to see what I was looking at, and when they saw they lost interest.

35

As though everyone who's new in town does something like that. Gets bedazzled by one building or another."

"This sounds like the beginning of a fine romance. You and your new mistress."

"I think it is. I even fell for your office furniture."

A coy look from her, a swift hint that they both knew what they were talking about and then a turning away of the head.

"Well, if I were you I'd take Manhattan. Not sure I'd bother with the Bronx and Staten. Great rhyme, boring place. But if you really have fallen for the Brooklyn Bridge, there's only one thing to do."

"What's that?"

"We walk it. From the other side. It's a nice evening. Not too cool. But no more subways. Cabs or nothing."

Walking back across the Brooklyn Bridge at dusk consummated the affair. He took Manhattan. Manhattan as it lit up for the night, Manhattan viewed through the pointed arches of the bridge, through the fishnet mesh made by the cables — it was like peeking in through the dressing room window as a nylon stocking was being rolled up from ankle to thigh.

At the Gramercy, Dorothy let the cab go.

"Anything else I can do for you, Joe?" she asked, blatant beyond a hint.

Wilderness never wore a wedding ring. He

didn't mind signalling that he was married; he simply didn't care for jewellery on a man. The only jewellery he possessed were cuff links, and he'd bought none of those, they had all been given to him by his grandfather — stolen from he knew not whom. Right now, a wedding ring might have helped.

"I'm married," he said, knowing it sounded lame.

"So's Frank. In fact I have a Rolodex just to keep track of the ex-wives. And another for the girlfriends."

"I meant happily married."

"You think Frank isn't? Nah, forget I said that. It's unfair to him and probably to you too. Just kiss me good night and try not to blame a girl for asking."

Afterwards, alone in his room, Wilderness wondered why he had added the "happily." To say he was married was the unalterable truth. The "happily" pushed the statement not into lies, but into ambivalence. It implied permanence, which might be the case, and it implied fidelity, which had not been the case. The definition of happily married for John Holderness and Judy Jones, was that each believed in being faithful to the other and each lapsed. And why he was not lapsing this warm Wednesday night was puzzling him. She was pleasant enough, her natural nosiness appealed to him. She was a looker, perhaps a little young for him — but something felt not quite right, and the something not quite right was Frank.

# §6

The next morning Frank phoned while Wilderness was having coffee in his room.

"Sorry about last night, kid. Y'know things just ran away with me. But today is fine. Come over to the office around six when the buzz starts to go out of the place and you can hear yourself think. Steve's at his best when the office quietens down."

"Steve?"

"Steven Sharma. My partner."

"What about Carver and Dunn?"

"I bought Nat Carver out. Pays not to change the name though. And Lewis Dunn is not so much a sleeping partner as a sailing partner. Spends most of his time on his yacht in Oyster Bay. Turns up if we hit a crisis and that's about it. It's my show. I'm not just the token goy."

"What?"

"They're all Jews. Nat Carver had some Polish name so long I could never pronounce it. Steve Sharma was Thaddeus Stevens Scharmansky — jeez, you couldn't make that up if you tried, like Abe Lincoln Cohen — and Lewis's real name is Dunkelmann."

"But it's Steve I have to meet?"

"Yeah. Steve's the one who wants to hire you."

And before Wilderness could ask any more Frank was off the line.

He spent the day on the Upper West Side, visited a museum full of dinosaur skeletons, walked across Central Park to the Guggenheim, spiralled up, spiralled down, and ended up at Frank's office on the dot of six.

"A good day?" Dorothy Shearer asked.

"A great day," Wilderness replied.

"Frank'll be out in a minute. As you said, there's always a dozen deals going down with Frank."

Frank's office door was closed. Through the glass wall Wilderness could see the back of his head, lolling on the headrest of the swivel chair, a telephone cradled between his ear and his shoulder.

For all Frank had warned him about the office being noisy, it wasn't. The mechanical rattle of an electric typewriter, occasionally, like bursts of rather gentle machine-gun fire — half-heard conversations drifting by from open doors, the floating of the ad-idea. All the same the most he could hear of Frank's conversation through the thick glass wall was a muffled burr.

Dorothy said, "You and Frank go back fifteen years or more?"

"Yes."

"I like working for Frank. He's . . . well,

he's a gas . . ."

"I can hear that 'but' waiting to burst on your lips."

"Maybe it shouldn't. He's entitled to my loyalty."

"Is this where you feel you have to tell me that however affable, my old pal Frank is also a bit of a bastard?"

"It could be."

"Then stay loyal, Miss Shearer. All my adult life women have been warning me about Frank. Girlfriends, wives, even a gorgeous major in the NKVD. He is a bastard and he is a rogue. But perhaps I am too."

"No, Mr. Holderness. I don't think you are."

The door was yanked open. Frank loomed large and happy. A big grin spreading out over his fat face.

"Joe! Bang on time, kid. Gimme thirty seconds and we'll go see Steve."

Dorothy and Wilderness were looking at each other, not at him, but he didn't seem to notice.

§7

Frank led him down a long, airy corridor. One wall was almost entirely glass. The other displayed framed posters of the products Carver, Sharma, and Dunn represented.

Frank paused by "Mountain Lites — the

light, full-flavored cigarette . . . anyplace, anytime."

"Remember these?" he said. "Tasted like shit. In fact they still taste like shit. How many do you reckon we sold back in Berlin in the old days?"

The answer was not in hundreds, it was in thousands and might even top a hundred thousand. Wilderness did not reply, and walked on to the next poster.

"Rodgers & Rutgers R'n'R Coffee — the full-flavored roast."

"Do you think we sold anything that wasn't full-flavoured?"

"Fucked if I know. I never read the labels. I never read the ads. Now I write the damn things."

Wilderness moved on.

"Simply Silky Nylons — he'll simply love you in Simply Silky."

"You know Frank I think you've inadvertently set up a museum of everything we nicked, smuggled or sold on the black market. If only you had Colonel Fogg's Miniature Cigars, I think you'd have the full set."

"Nah," said Frank. "We'd still need all the butter and the sugar and the canned fish and the lipstick and the soap and you name it. Whatever fell off the back of the truck."

"Soap? 'Cadum for Madam.' Was that one of your gems, Frank? Did you write that?"

Frank laughed out loud, one of his belly-jiggling snorts.

"Wish I had, Joe. Wish I had. Guy who penned that one probably made a fortune. More than I made smuggling the damn stuff. I'd give my left arm to have written that — that and 'You can be sure of Shell.' But I just break my balls trying to find a rhyme for Rutgers."

A head appeared through the open door opposite.

"Are you two gonna reminisce all day? Or could you possibly find five minutes for business."

A small, balding, sixty-ish man in a suit that was worth triple anything Frank or Wilderness was wearing. A dark frown on his face, which dispersed like a blown cloud as a smile took over and a hand extended.

"You must be Joe. Heard a lot about you. Steven Sharma. Senior partner. But that's only to keep this bum from taking over the whole show."

"Then you have the advantage of me. I'm still a little in the dark here."

Frank lightly put an arm around each of them.

"Then let's put that right straightaway. Steve, we were just on our way to see you."

"Good. Come in, park your ass, and rest your voice. It's time Mr. Holderness and I got to know one another."

Wilderness had never worked in an office

in his life, but he knew from his wife that you could read the status in the room, and that a corner office with two views was what every pen pusher aspired to. Steve Sharma's office boasted fine views over the building opposite, a peek at the treetops of Central Park, two sofas the size of pool tables, a pool table, half a dozen original Norman Rockwell covers for the *Saturday Evening Post,* and an antique desk the best part of eight foot across. What interested Frank was the drinks cabinet.

"What can I get me?"

"Sure, help yourself, why don't you," Steve said. "And while you're helping yourself to my scotch, serve our guest."

And then to Wilderness, "Bull in a china shop, but I figure you know that? What's your poison, Joe?"

"Scotch will be fine. Ask the bull not to flood it."

"You hear that, Frank? Man who likes his scotch too much to want it drowned!"

"OK. OK. You two, lay off me."

Frank clutched three glasses of scotch between splayed fingers and set them down on the hammered brass, Indian-looking coffee table between sofas. He filled a glass dish with peanuts and then sat next to Steve, facing Wilderness, with the peanuts balanced on his knees while he scoffed.

"Joe, just one thing. You're among friends here. What gets said in this room, stays in this room? Am I right?"

"Of course," Steve said. Then, "Tell me a little about yourself Joe. Give me a taste of your . . ." and here he paused. "Résumé."

Résumé was not a word Wilderness had heard before, but its meaning was obvious. And Steve made it clear where he meant him to begin.

"Frank tells me you and he met in Berlin, after the war?"

"Yes. I was an NCO in British Intelligence."

"MI5? MI6?"

"Not at that point. I never knew what I was really in. I was a National Serviceman, doing what I was told, going where I was sent. Nominally the RAF. But I hardly saw a plane, certainly never flew one or serviced one. I was low-level intelligence — I interpreted, I translated written texts, and I eavesdropped. Occasionally they let me interrogate Germans in the hope I'd find a few Nazis."

"And did you?"

"Oh yes. No one in Berlin in 1947 was or ever had been a Nazi. Yet if you threw a stick up in the air you'd be pretty well bound to hit one when it fell back to earth."

Steve chuckled at this.

"I had languages. I was getting fluent in German and Russian by then, and I've added some Arabic, French, Turkish, and Italian since. Even a smattering of Finnish. Frank was awful at languages, but I wasn't in the same league as Frank. Frank was an officer, a captain, and unlike me he was quite certain what he was in — the Company."

"Shit. Why not rent a billboard in Times Square and paste it up in letters half a mile high?"

Steve waved Frank's faux anger away with the back of his hand.

"You said it yourself not five minutes ago, Frank. What gets said in here stays in here. But you did serve in . . . whatever the British call their Company?"

"Yes. Until a few years ago."

"And you did get to know Berlin?"

"Yes?"

"Well?"

"I was there close to two years, and I've been back on many occasions since. It changes. It changes all the time, but there's something about it that doesn't."

*"Plus ça change, plus c'est la même chose?"*

"A touch of that."

"And since you left your . . . 'Company'?"

"I've been private. What you would probably call a gumshoe."

"A good living?"

"A variably good living. Has its moments. I've worked for British Intelligence a few times since. They pay better now than they ever did when I was enlisted."

"Frank tells me you know Berlin from the ground up?"

45

Frank shot him a look across the rim of his glass. Wilderness did not know how to read it.

"More than that," Steve went on. "He tells me you know Berlin from the ground *down.*"

Now he knew.

"Why not tell me what it is you want, Steve?"

Steve paused. Wilderness did not think his question had taken the old man by surprise, but still he seemed to need to gather his thoughts.

"Frank. Freshen the drinks all round would you? Your legs are longer and younger than mine."

Frank bumbled through his bad impression of a waiter, topped them all up and refilled his dish with peanuts, which he still hogged.

With a large, untouched scotch on the rocks in his hand, Steve was ready.

"My wife has an aunt. Aunt Hannah. Hannah Schneider. Sixty-nine years old. Last of her generation in the family. Never married. She lives on her own in East Berlin. My wife Debbie is the only kin she has on earth. We'd like to get her out. To be exact — we'd like you to get her out."

Wilderness just looked at him and nodded.

"I know we've missed chances. She could have left in 1933. But millions didn't and millions died. There's no wisdom in that particular hindsight. We could have brought

46

her over any time after 1945. But we didn't. And she wouldn't. And who among us foresaw the Berlin Wall, the speed with which Khrushchev would be able to split the city?

"Of course, we've been able to make contact with one of those student groups that have dug tunnels and such — but Frank tells me the Stasi, the Vopos, whatever, are pretty wise to that now. Kids get people out through the sewers, so they weld the sewers shut. Kids drum up fake passports, so they double- and triple-check everyone at the crossings. And they are kids. I think we can use them, I think they're sincere, but they are kids. Nineteen and twenty. I think we need a man in charge who is not a kid. And I think that man is you."

"I'm flattered."

So obviously non-committal.

"I'm in no hurry. She's been stuck there for years already. A few more weeks won't kill her. Take your time. Think about it for a day or two. It's a business proposition. We're both in business. I'll meet your terms."

Wilderness hadn't mentioned any terms. But neither had Steve or Frank.

"What I'd like to avoid is incident. And this situation is fraught with possibilities. I don't want Hannah exposed to anything . . . anything . . . well, like that old lady a couple of years back who seemed to be hanging off a building right on the sector line, in some kind of insane tug of war. Half the world looking

47

up her skirt. Cop had her by the wrists, pulling her back up to the East, some guy looked like he was a fireman had her by the ankles and was trying to pull her down to the West, and she looked like she was about to fall and break her neck. I couldn't expose Hannah to that. These kids are good kids, *gerekhte* kids, but they have no . . . discretion. Their pride gets in the way of discretion. They're having too much fun not to want to boast about it. Discretion is a valuable commodity. You can get paid for discretion."

"And for knowledge."

"So . . . you bring me to the point, Joe. Frank tells me you know of tunnels under Berlin deeper than the sewers, older than the sewers?"

"I know of *a* tunnel."

"And it's possible the Reds don't?"

"It's possible. I think it might be more accurate to say they knew and have forgotten."

"But you haven't forgotten?"

"You mean could I find it again? Oh yes. It's seared into my memory. There are times I feel I spent a year of my life down there."

Steve made a circular motion with his right hand, reeling off a list as he did so.

"The butter . . . and the sugar . . . and the canned fish . . . and the lipstick . . . and the soap?"

He turned to Frank, a smile on his face. Frank grinned.

"Yeah. Me and my big mouth. What a good job I'm not paid for my discretion, eh? Of course we used it for smuggling. It's what we did. It's what everybody did. Everybody was in the black market. We were just better at it."

"And now boys, you get to smuggle a person, a human being. How much more worthwhile than sardines and soap."

Steve stood up. The conversation was over.

"If you boys will excuse me. I must get to Grand Central, or Debbie will meet every train at White Plains until I show up. Enjoy New York, Joe. It's a feast. A feast for the eye, a feast for the mind, and a feast for the belly. We'll talk again in a day or two."

Frank was still feasting on peanuts as the door closed behind Steve. He set down the empty dish, spoke through the last mouthful.

"Let's eat," he said.

# §8

They took a cab uptown. Wilderness wondered why they hadn't walked. When the cab pulled up they were no more than twenty blocks from Frank's office — but it seemed to him that Frank probably didn't walk anywhere.

He looked at the big yellow awning that spanned the pavement to meet any arriving cab in much the same colour. In sprawling italics it read "Elaine's."

"You heard of it?" Spoleto asked.

"Should I have?"

"Have I heard of Quaglino's?"

"I don't know, Frank. Have you?"

Spoleto laughed. Gave him another of the hearty slaps that Wilderness was beginning to find wearing. Frank had always done this . . . expressive bonhomie . . . hail-buddy-well-met . . . but fifteen years ago, he'd weighed a lot less. Now, there was an extra thirty pounds behind every well-meant slap on the back.

They were early. About a third of the tables taken in a large, dim, brown room, the walls covered in reproductions of Italian masters and the occasional mirror.

A young woman in her thirties, already running a little to fat, was seated at the bar, sipping a tall glass of white wine. She slipped off the stool, scarcely coming up to Spoleto's chin and hugged him.

"Frank, I was beginning to think you'd forgotten me."

"Never. I even brought an old army buddy for you to make a fuss over. Elaine, this is Joe Holderness. Elaine Kaufman . . . one of the Big Apple's success stories. Open less than a year and already you have to queue."

"Frank. I have never known you to queue for anything. All the same, any friend of Frank's . . ."

"Delighted," said Wilderness.

"Oh Frankie, you brought me an English-man!"

Now Wilderness got hugged.

"Only he has no meat on his bones. My God, do they still have rationing over there?"

A table by the wall, seated at right angles to one another, so they both faced into the room, watching as the tables slowly filled up and the room began to swell with chatter.

"Everything's good here. But whatever you have as a main course, don't miss the cannoli when it comes to *dolci.* Out of this fuckin' world."

By the time they got to *dolci,* Spoleto had run the gamut of small talk and got to what Wilderness thought might be the point.

Spoleto said, "You were kind of coy with Steve. But that I understand. We both have things that we should be discreet about even now."

"Of course."

"You didn't say how often you'd been back to Berlin."

"A lot. Most years in fact. It would be quicker if I named the years I wasn't there."

"You ever see Nell Breakheart?"

Breakheart. Always Breakheart. Would he never drop the gag and pronounce her name properly?

"No Frank, I've never seen Nell."

"When were we last there together?"

"Fifty-eight."

"So it was. My God. Time doesn't fly, it gets launched from Canaveral."

"I didn't go back at all between '48 and '51. In '56 I was stuck in Tel Aviv monitoring traffic. Absolute waste of time. I damn near quit after that."

"Monitoring Russian airwaves is never a waste of time."

"This was Suez, Frank. A total cock-up, and I wasn't monitoring Russian communications, I was monitoring yours."

"Yeah, well I guess that was pretty much the low point in the special relationship."

"From late '58 to '60 I was in Beirut. Now, that was fun. Pretending I was a stringer for *The Times* and eavesdropping on every indiscretion in the St. George's hotel bar. Getting rat-arsed with Kim Philby. Each of us pretending we didn't know. I don't know how I kept a straight face. Regular trips home, the occasional hop to Athens or Rome. Cairo or Istanbul. Didn't exactly restore my faith in the service, but it kept me on board for a couple more years. Then in '61 I was back in Berlin for the last time."

"Before or after the wall?"

"During. I flew out just a couple of days after they started putting up the barriers. In August. The British had me observe LBJ's visit firsthand. I stayed on a month or so after that. When Steve mentioned the old lady hanging off the building in Bernauer Straße to us . . . well I was there. That was September '61. I saw it happen. I saw her fall. Her name was Frieda Schulze."

"But she lived, right?"

"Oh yes, she lived. But something in me died. It was watching her dangle, both sides tugging at her. I can't translate it into precise words, but if ever there was a symbol, writ large, especially for me, that was it. It was then I knew it was all over. I went back home and put in my papers. They could hardly object. They'd called me up for two years in 1945 and got the best part of sixteen out of me."

"And since then? You glossed over that too."

"And I'll gloss over it now."

"Things ain't been so good?"

"No, they haven't."

"The low-heeled life of a gumshoe in a high-heeled country where nothing much really happens? A country where no one carries a gun, and what's a gumshoe without a gun?"

"You could put it like that."

"Divorces. You do divorces?"

"Yes. I do divorces. I'm the guy who follows the errant lovers down to Brighton at a prearranged time and catches them in the glare of a flashbulb in a seaside hotel."

"Crummy."

"I can think of worse words for it. I can

think of more accurate words for it, but yes, crummy will do."

"And yet you hesitate when Steve makes you the best offer you've had since you left the service."

Wilderness said nothing to this, waited while Spoleto waved for the check.

"You see the guys at the centre table?" Spoleto said as he counted out dollars.

"The one on the left's George Plimpton. Edits the *Paris Review*. Guy next to him is Lee Strasberg, runs the Actors Studio, y'know . . . Paul Newman, Marilyn Monroe, Eli Wallach. The guy next to him . . ."

"Is Norman Mailer. Frank, do you honestly think I wouldn't recognise Norman Mailer? His first novel came out while we were all in Berlin. I read it. Eddie Clark read it. Didn't you read it?"

"Nah. I don't want to read about the war. I never wanted to read about the war. Hell, I didn't even go to see *South Pacific*. I was probably the only guy in New York who didn't. Look over to your right. See the big feller, lots of dark hair. That's the Broadway producer Arthur Cantor, one of the big wheels on the Great White Way. And do you know the woman he's with?"

Cantor was with two women, one of whom he most certainly knew. But he sensed that Frank had not recognised her and was referring to the other.

Wilderness thought her face more than vaguely familiar — hair up, glasses, next-to-no makeup, the sense of a beauty contrivedly off-duty — but he didn't.

"C'mon. I'll introduce you. Arthur and I go way back."

Spoleto pushed back his chair and threaded his way through the tables.

Cantor got a Frank back-slap that jerked the linguine off the end of his fork.

"Arthur, long time no see."

Cantor looked as though it had not been long enough and he might just be able to do without Frank for a year or two more, but good manners got the better of him.

"Hello Frank. You know Ingrid?"

"I never had the chance."

"Ingrid, Frank Spoleto — one of Madison avenue's *shnorrers*. Frank, Ingrid Bergman."

Bergman nodded, a soft-spoken, "a pleasure" on her lips, but she was looking at Wilderness.

Spoleto slipped in quickly, "And my old English buddy, Joe Holderness."

She held out her hand for Wilderness to kiss. He was not one to resist the irresistible.

"And I believe you've met . . ."

The other woman cut Cantor off with "Clarissa Troy."

She too held out her hand, the kiss to the fingers claimed as a right, then she winked hammily at him. And still not a flicker of

55

recognition from Frank.

"We were just making plans for *The Cherry Orchard*," Cantor resumed.

"You own a cherry orchard? Jeez Artie, the things I don't know about you."

"It's a play, stupid. Clarissa's translating Chekhov for us."

"Are you in New York for long, Mr. Holderness?" Bergman asked.

She was looking right up into his eyes now. It was a moment Wilderness would have strung out for ever if he could.

"Probably not. I'll be at the Gramercy for a day or two. All rather depends on Frank."

Frank drowned out the moment.

"Say, Arthur, when am I going to get tickets for one of your plays?"

"When you pay for the last lot, Frank."

All this earned Cantor was a hearty guffaw from Spoleto. He was lucky, Wilderness thought, to be spared a second slap on the back.

Outside, under the yellow awning, Spoleto said, "I wonder what got into him. Fuckin' skinflint. He's known as one of the wittiest guys in New York."

"Perhaps you cramped his style, Frank."

"And what the fuck's a shn . . . shn . . . *shnucker*?"

"*Shnorrer*. You amaze me sometimes. How can you live in this city, work with men like

56

Steve and not know a little more Yiddish? It means cheapskate."

"Cheapskate? He called me a fuckin' cheapskate?"

"If the cap fits?"

Spoleto was on the metal kerb of the sidewalk looking out for a downtown cab.

"Let's walk a while, Frank."

"Eh, what?"

But as Wilderness led off down Second Avenue, he was bound to follow or lose him.

He zigzagged, down a couple of blocks, over a couple of blocks to Lexington. He stood on the corner and waited while Frank caught up with him.

"Jesus H. Christ, Joe. Are you trying to give me a heart attack? I haven't marched like this since I got out of the army."

"When was that exactly, Frank? When did you leave the Company?"

"Fifty-eight, about six weeks after we last met."

"Aha."

"What the fuck does 'aha' mean?"

"Frank, what are you up to?"

"I thought I was trying to offer you a job and buy you dinner."

"You could have bought me dinner two nights ago."

"I was busy."

"Bullshit. You left me to drift around New York. You left me to get to like New York, you wanted me to taste New York. And maybe I did get a taste for New York. The Bronx is up, but I skipped that. The name alone could put you off. The Battery's down and the view's great. I even rode in a hole in the ground. But that's exactly what you did Frank — you sent me out on the town. Dancing with Sinatra and Gene Kelly. And yes, I got the taste for New York — so damn good I could lick it. Then you sent your secretary round to fuck me. You dangled temptation in front of me. If Manhattan wasn't enough there was Dorothy, and if Dorothy was not enough, there was dinner at Elaine's. Tell me Frank, did you call ahead and see who had booked? Would we have gone somewhere else if Mailer and Ingrid Bergman hadn't been in tonight? Would we have gone somewhere where you could be certain I'd taste the high life, where I'd be rubbing shoulders with Hollywood stars and best-selling writers? Because that's what you've been doing. You've been dangling New York in front of me. Like a reward. One great big temptation."

"Well . . . you never could resist temptation."

"I did Frank. I was polite to Dorothy, but I sent her packing."

"Dorothy wasn't part of it. OK? Nothin' to do with it. Manhattan, what you call the high life . . . sure. Why the fuck not? But Dorothy acted on her own. You must have said something to impress her. It wasn't that damn painting in the lobby was it? Piece of fucking shit Nat Carver spent thousands of dollars of company money on. Only he and Dorothy ever liked it."

Wilderness said nothing to this.

"Tempting you with a taste of the high life? Of course I am. I'm trying to get you to see what life can be like with a little folding green in your pants pocket. I want you to take the job, for Christ's sake."

"I haven't said no yet, Frank."

"And you haven't said yes. Think about it, Joe. It's a big opportunity. A really big one. Think big. Think back to Berlin. That day in the summer of '47, when we sat round the table at the Paradise Club — the day you introduced me to Yuri — you, me, and Eddie . . . who was it said 'we have to think bigger'? Sure as hell wasn't me. You did think big, Joe, you did. How many times in '48 did you tell me not to panic? To stick with it, to sell when I should sell and buy when I should buy. Joe, you had an unerring instinct for the right thing to do in a crisis. When the Russkis were bouncing us around like we were made of fuckin' India rubber, closing this, closing that, printing money that fell apart in your fingers, trying to pay us in dogshit and sawdust, you stood your ground. Nothing intimidated you. You were the man. You were

going places, the world was your fuckin'
oyster . . . you were the man . . . but Joe,
don't tell me that life since then has gone the
way you wanted it . . . I'm the one with the
fuckin' Cadillac and an apartment on Park
Avenue. I'm the one drivin' the fuckin' Cadillac!"

Sheer bluster seemed to exhaust him for a
moment. He drew breath and resumed in a
softer tone.

"You're different. That's undeniable. You're
not the Gorblimey kid I met fifteen years ago.
There's a sophistication about you that's
more than skin-deep. But . . . I know you're
not happy, you're not satisfied, you're not
rich, you inch along with a blue-collar pride
in your own independence, when you know
damn well that without your wife's BBC salary you'd be broke, and without Alec Burne-
Jones looking out for you at every step you'd
have had no career in the service after Berlin.
And you know Joe, the real question is what
career might you have had if you'd just blown
him out, blown them all out after '48 and
taken your chances. I don't know and you
don't know. The only time in your life you
ever played safe. The only time you didn't
take a chance. All I'm saying is take one now."

Wilderness looked around him for a moment, getting his bearings by the street signs,
gazing up as he began to speak and then
levelling to look straight at Frank.

"The Gorblimey kid, eh? Frank, as you're so fond of adopting slang, let me ask you this. When was the last time you stood at the corner of Seventy-First and Lexington and had somebody knock you on your *tuchus*?"

"Joe . . . I'm not saying you blew it."

"Oh, but you are."

"OK. Maybe you blew it. Maybe you didn't. But look at it this way . . . Steve and I are giving you what so few of us ever get in life. A second chance."

"A second chance?"

"Don't make it sound like I tossed you a turd. This is big money."

"So far you haven't mentioned money. Is that because you wanted me softened up first? Receptive to your shady deal and your greenbacks?"

"Fuck you, Joe, you never asked till now. And this is twenty grand we're talking about."

It was more, so much more than Wilderness had expected. It was more than he could earn in two years. And Frank had just taken the wind out of his sails.

"You're surprised, right?"

"Yes."

"And pleased?"

"I could be."

"Joe, it says how much Steve wants his aunt out. You're the guy to do this. I've told him that all along. I told him you don't come cheap. The guys on the Brighton line might get you cheap, but this is New York. He'll pay ten grand. Guaranteed. Cash. All he wants to hear from me now is that you'll do it."

Down the avenue thirty blocks away, the western light was turning the Chrysler into a shimmer of beaten Krupp titanium, a shining spear of pure, impulsive folly a quarter of a mile high. It seemed to Wilderness that the skyscraper was female, a woman — it had to be — and she'd just winked at him. Folly to folly.

"OK. I'll do it."

"Great. Great, Absolutely fuckin' great. It'll be like old times. Berlin '48 all over again. Only this time we don't get caught!"

"You didn't get caught, Frank. I did."

# §9

He got back to the Gramercy late after another night at The Five Spot. Another note waiting for him at reception.

"I'm in the bar."

No signature.

"She's been there awhile," the desk clerk said.

Wilderness could handle one more drink with Dorothy Shearer.

It wasn't Dorothy Shearer, it was Clarissa Troy.

She'd worn well, scarcely a sign that she had aged in fifteen years, and he reckoned she must be getting on for fifty. Big eyes, big tits, and an habitual, kissable (not that he ever had) pout. All this in a five foot package — a pocket Venus.

"What do I call you?"

"Weeeellll kid, truth to tell I *am* Mrs. Troy. That really is my moniker. But you can call me Tosca — just like you used to."

"And Frank really doesn't recognise you?"

"Nope. That's got to be the third time Arthur's introduced us, and he's never so much as blinked. He's such a dumb fuck, which kinda brings me to the point. What the hell are you doing getting mixed up with Frank again?"

"It's different. This time it'll be different."

"Joe . . . for fuck's sake . . . you got caught . . . you damn near got killed. If it had been me I'd be crossing the sidewalk every time I saw Frank Spoleto heading my way."

"Trust me."

"Oh hell, kid. How much money has the bastard offered you?"

■ ■ ■ ■

# II
# ANOTHER NOVEL
# "WITHOUT A HERO"

■ ■ ■ ■

If this is a novel without a hero, at least let us lay claim to a heroine.
William Makepeace Thackeray: *Vanity Fair*
1847

# §10

*London:* May 1941

His mother died much as she had lived. In a pub. A daylight raid on London in the spring of 1941 by the Luftwaffe had taken out the Blackamoor's Head, Matlock Street, E14. It was half an hour after lunchtime closing and had the landlord closed on time, the death toll might have been less than total. When they dug through the rubble they found Lily Holderness upright at the bar, a large if dusty gin and lime in her hand, stone dead.

Her husband, Harry, was training with the Fifth Battalion of the East Kent Regiment in Wales — a survivor of Dunkirk, an event he spoke of with neither pride nor optimism. He called it his post-debacle course or "how-not-to-fuck-it-all-up-twice."

Her son, John, was thirteen. He could have been a scallywag of the streets, using parental neglect as the perfect excuse to run wild in the violent, ragged freedom of war. He was at school. He would never admit it, but he liked school. He hated teachers. One of the few things father and son would ever agree on was that the only good teacher was a dead one, but he liked learning and adored knowing. He collected knowledge without system, but imposing some sense of system was the job of universities and boys of John Holderness's class did not go to universities, and rather than a butterfly mind he might best be described as having a jackdaw mind. Not admitting any of this saved him many a playground kicking.

The first he knew of his mother's death was not when he got home to the empty flat in Maroon Street — that, after all, was the norm — but when she didn't turn up to eat the meal he had cooked her before he went to bed.

When the pubs closed — those that had survived another day in the Blitz — an ARP warden banged on the door to tell him through beery breath that his mum was dead.

He ate her portion and went back to bed, only half-wondering if his dad would be recalled from Wales, and, if he was, how best to handle the bastard.

In the morning, he dressed, ate the egg that Lily had set aside for herself, and was preparing to set off for school when his grandfather — his maternal grandfather, Abner Riley — let himself in.

"The buggers only told me an hour ago," he said.

"I'm fine, Grandad."

"No, son. No, you're not."

He sat down on the only armchair in the room, wedged between the cooker and the fireplace. Wilderness had no idea what the old man meant.

"It's the flat, d'ye see? Council-owned. They're going to want it back. And given how many poor buggers got bombed out these last six months they're going to want it back sharpish."

"But I live here. This is my home."

"Copper who banged on my door at first light this mornin' sez you was like as not goin' to a home. A hinstitution. On account as you was now a norphan. Bollox I tells him. The boy's a norphan the day they nail me down in me box. So . . . you grab your things and you come back wi' me."

Wilderness did not see how he could be an orphan while his father still lived, but knew that the verbal shorthand said how little the neighbourhood thought of his father. They could not forget him — he had thumped too many heads for that — but they might prefer to. Whilst preferable to a London County Council orphanage, the prospect of life with Abner Riley was not pleasing. Wilderness liked him more than he had liked his daughter — Lily had been an impossible person, and

71

hence impossible to like with any sustained affection — but he was a complete rogue and an habitual criminal. The great-aunts out in Essex were his sisters, the very best of a very bad bunch — better because settled, their parents having given up the gypsy life with its caravans and petty theft for a fixed abode and more serious theft about the time of the old Queen's jubilee.

" 'Ave yer much to pack, son?"

Wilderness thought his grandfather, however well meaning, had little grasp of children. It had been woman's work to men of his generation, and to their sons' generation too. He could have said he'd pack his teddy and Abner would not have batted an eyelid. Instead, he stuffed his spare trousers into a cardboard suitcase along with a shirt, the rags that passed for underwear and the socks desperate for darning. He tied the laces of his football boots together and slung them around his neck. His books he bound up with a striped elastic belt with a snake-S buckle and stuffed under one arm.

"OK," he said.

"Books, eh? You must take arter yer dad. No one on my side o' the family ever cared much for readin'. Never learnt meself. Righty-ho, we're orf."

Wilderness took a last look at the only home he had never known, and despite what he had said on the matter of "home" to

Abner, he found no remnant of home than could even aspire to meaning. Two rooms, furniture that was scarcely better than match-wood, a khazi out in the yard, a single tap above the sink, wallpaper that peeled off in the damp, mouseholes in the skirting, black patches of mold in every cold corner. Two rooms that froze in winter, only to swelter in summer.

He doubted too that Abner lived much better. He'd not been to his grandfather's house since the last row between him and Lily sometime around 1936. It was a walk of only a couple of miles. He knew it by heart, by pace, by flagstone — he'd walked over from Maroon Street, Limehouse to Sidney Street in Whitechapel a hundred times without ever knocking on Abner's door. If he passed Abner in the street, the old man — old? he was fifty-seven — would usually slip him a sixpence, ask after his mother and not listen to the boy's answer. The gang to which he intermittently belonged had taken on one of the Sidney Street gangs half a dozen times in the last three years and had the shit kicked out of them every time. This time he trod their turf with impunity, escorted by the street's hard man — Abner Riley, cracksman and burglar.

The Sidney Street house was three storeys. A narrow blade of a house standing on a plot less than fifteen feet wide. A house, not a flat. A house with some sense of decoration, some substantial, heavyweight Victorian furniture and a sense of being lived in and looked after that his last home had always seemed to lack. A woman lived here. Not a drunken, life-incapable excuse-for-a-woman like his mother, but someone who bothered from time to time. No one had ever mentioned a grandmother. For all he knew, the faeries had brought Lily one day in 1908. Or more likely Abner had stolen her — but then, why would he keep her? No, Abner had a girlfriend. It seemed unlikely, but more plausible than a lodger. Lodgers didn't go with Abner's job. Abner had a girlfriend.

"Odd, we never met, eh kid? Still can't be our fault, can it? Name's Merle. Me and yer grandad's . . . y'know . . ."

Yes. He knew.

Her name wasn't Merle. It was Mary-Ann. When she and Abner had met she had been turning tricks up West and Merle (after Merle Oberon) carried less sense of violated virginity than any combination of names that included "Mary." The fares preferred fucking a Merle to a Mary.

The boy had his own room.

His own room. His own bed. A jug of water and a basin on the stand. A pot to piss in. No more sleeping on roll-out on the kitchen floor. No more pissing in the sink. As he looked up at the moon peeping at him through two centuries of dirt caking the

74

skylight, he found himself quietly grateful to Abner for creating a level of poverty a few fractions higher than his own. Grateful, still suspicious, still scared, still baffled, but also aware of lesson one in a course of which he had no need — but he learnt it all the same — crime pays.

The funeral was apt. The church itself — St. George's-in-the-East — as blown to bollocks as any other house not so favoured by God. They'd swept the broken glass aside, made some attempt to shovel out the rubble and held what turned out to be an outdoor/indoor, roofless service in the ruins of Hawksmoor's vision, followed by a swift burial in the churchyard under a peeping May sun, with the last draught of April tugging at their hair. Abner had no hair, Merle wore one of her many wigs, and Wilderness stood hatless in an ill-fitting blazer and even iller-fitting grey flannel trousers. He'd no idea where either had come from. Abner had simply produced them on the morning of the funeral and said, "Can't see yer mum orf in rags, now can we?"

Of Herbert Henry Asquith Holderness, L/Cpl, 5th Batt., The Royal East Kents, there was no sign.

The wake was an equal absence.

Most of Lily's friends had perished in the raid that killed her, and Wilderness had long ago worked out that the only friend an alcoholic has or needs comes in a bottle.

It was left to the three of them to mourn and blame.

"I blame meself," Abner said.

"Whyzat?" from Merle.

"I spoilt the kid. Never said no to her. Not from the moment she batted her blue eyes at me. And then when her mum died, it was just 'er an' me . . . I spoilt her even more."

"Yeah, well," Merle said over her glass of stout. "Let's not spoil this one, eh?"

Abner laughed.

"Spoil 'im. I's'll thrash 'im night and day!"

It was obvious they were joking.

Harry Holderness was not.

His first act on stepping into Abner's parlour was to knock the boy across the room with the back of his hand.

Absence distorts. Wilderness had an idea of his father that was less than the reality. He'd always pictured a big man, and common sense told him that if he and Harry ever met again the man would appear proportionately smaller as he himself had grown.

But the bastard was huge. At least six two, barrel-chested, rippling with muscle and churning with rage.

"No 'ard feelings. That's just to let you know who's who."

Wilderness picked himself up off the floor, wiped the blood from his mouth. Abner, at five two and eight stone, didn't stand a chance against Harry. All the same he got between him and Wilderness with the bread knife in his hand.

"Hit him again Harry and I'll gut yer."

Harry righted one of the chairs he'd sent flying, sat down and stared at Abner.

"Don't be a silly bugger, Abner. I've killed more krauts than you've had hot mash and pies. Now, be a sweetheart and get that tart o'yours to put the kettle on. We've a lot to talk about, and I've only got a forty-eight hour pass."

Wilderness heard the pop of the gas going on in the kitchen.

Harry asked inane questions about his wife's death and funeral. Inane only because he did not seem to care about the answers. When Merle finally set a tea tray in front of him, he changed to the real subject of his visit.

"About the boy . . ."

"I'm right here, Dad, I'm in the room."

"Are you asking for another belt? Shut up. Your father is talking. About the boy, Abner."

"Wot about him Harry? You suddenly remembered he exists?"

Harry ignored this.

"Can you keep him?"

"Already am. He's got a home here."

"I'll see you right for the money. His Majesty pays me as a man with a dependant. You'll get what's due to you."

"I don't doubt it, Harry."

"The army'll do the paperwork. All I need is a letter from you, and a copy of Lil's death certificate for the Army Paymaster, then there'll be a few bob each week for you at the Post Office."

Abner didn't say he couldn't read or write. Wilderness knew he'd be doing all that for the old man from now on.

"So," Harry went on. "All that's left is what's he gonna do between now and his call-up."

"Call-up? The boy's only thirteen."

"Fourteen come August 3."

"And . . . this war ain't gonna last for ever now is it?"

"From where I stand, in a pair of size twelve army boots, Abner, I can't see no bleedin' end to it. We got our arses kicked in France. The Russkis are sticking to their devil's pact, and Uncle Sam as ever don't want to know. We're on our Jack Jones. Either Hitler invades us, or we invade him. So, I say again, what's the boy gonna do?"

"Matriculate," Wilderness said softly.

Merle flinched, and he realised she had confused matriculate with masturbate. Abner looked baffled. The word was clearly new to him. But Harry knew what he'd meant.

"What? Exams and that? You? You must be joking."

"It's what they want at school," Wilderness

78

said. "They want me to matriculate. They want me to sit the exams, and they tell me I'll pass."

"And you believe 'em? What then? College? University? Oxford? The likes of you and me don't get to go to places like Oxford, son. We leaves school and we gets ourselves a job."

He was leaning forward now, reddening in the face, looming over Wilderness like a tethered barrage balloon, blotting out the rest of the room. It was a slapping moment. If he continued to argue, Harry would hit him again. So, he argued.

"It's what I want," he said simply.

The first blow knocked him off his stool, the second, merely a spread hand against the chest, pushed Abner firmly back into his chair. Merle fled to the scullery.

Harry took off his belt, curled the buckle end around his fist and thrashed Wilderness. Every so often he'd turn to Abner and push him back down. Wilderness wished his grandfather would just leave, follow Merle and escape. Protest was pointless. The bastard was going to beat him until he ran out of energy.

Hours later. Darkness. The blackout. A couple of nightlights floating in saucers of water on the table. Wilderness examining his wounds. His ribs were black and blue. Harry had drawn blood on the back of his legs.

"I'm sorry, son," Abner said.

"Not your fault, Grandad. Not the first time and it won't be the last."

"Still it'll be an age before he's back. I shouldn't think we'll set eyes on yer dad again this side of the autumn."

"And I'm growing every day."

Merle heard innocence and childhood where there was none, and ruffled his hair.

" 'Course you are, Johnnie. Bigger every day."

"No. I meant. One day I'll be as big as him. And then I'll fuckin' kill him."

"Don't talk like that, son. He's still yer dad arter all."

# §11

Merle had not yet peaked. Wilderness had seen prostitutes outside East End pubs so raddled they could but have charged in pence for the oldest service in history. Once, inside an East End pub, in search of his wayward mother, he had seen one cross her legs and raise her shoe in such a way that the price was visible in scrawled chalk on the sole, and his suspicion came close to confirmation — 2/6d.

Merle was, as his mates would have said, a bit of a looker.

"I put a stop to that game," Abner said. "Can't be doin' with that."

Nominally, Merle worked in shops. None

for long. A Debenham and Freebody up West would give way to a Woolworth's back East and that in turn to a haberdasher's in Hoxton. Wilderness liked her Woolworth's phase the best — she'd come home with bags of stolen sweets from the confectionary counter.

But she quit Woolworth's. They'd asked her to scrape the green mould off biscuits before they were put on the counter.

"Disgustin'," she said. "Absolutely fuckin' disgustin'."

The haberdasher's paid less. Some evenings, Merle would rummage through her collection of wigs, put on a colourful dress, ply her old trade and have a blazing row with Abner when he found out. Abner was above belting Merle. He would shout and swear but he never laid a finger on her. Merle was not above throwing crockery at Abner. Her aim was terrible, and it was not safe to be in the same room.

Wilderness would retreat to his own room. Retreat to his books. The only things in the room that in any way personalised it.

# §12

Wilderness left school in July. A warm summer. He had ten days to himself before turning fourteen would thrust him into the world of work — neither child nor adult. A wet summer. The Luftwaffe had given up. The raid that killed Lily had been among the last. It wasn't clear why until the lightest night of June when Hitler invaded Russia.

He read the papers out loud to Abner. Panzers rolled across what was left of Poland, hammering at the gates of the Soviet Union. Stalin suffered a shift of meaning — now, and for years to come, he was "Uncle Joe."

"I thought it was Poland what was what we went to war on account of?" said Abner.

"It was, Grandad."

"Did we ever get there?"

"No."

"Maybe we never will."

Abner got him a job on a stall in Whitechapel Market, right in front of the Underground station. An old pal from way back who'd take Wilderness on for next to no wages and teach him how to sell cheap china seconds. Keep him off the streets by placing him firmly down on just one of them.

If it was a trade, Wilderness could not see it. Whatever there was to learn about packing and unpacking crates from Hanley or Burslem could be learnt in minutes. If there was a patter to be learnt he'd never learn it from Frankie Hodges. Frankie never took the fag from his lips long enough to make a pitch to anyone, and Wilderness soon concluded that if a patter had been required before the war, in a time of war — houses blown to smithereens, crockery reduced to confetti —

82

it was superfluous. Frankie could shift his entire stock twice over every day without so much as a "roll-up roll-up." The problem, if anything, was getting supplies in. Some Monday mornings Wilderness would unpack a single crate, the contents sold by lunchtime, and Frankie would slip him a shilling and turn him loose for the rest of the day.

Many of Wilderness's classmates were in the same age trap. Man-boys with not enough to do and not enough to spend. The East End filled up with gangs. Every bomb site became the object of a turf war, every street corner a territorial boundary. Every trespass an insult. Most of Wilderness's mates, those cowards of discretion, would avoid this by killing time in matinees at the Troxy cinema. Wilderness went to the library.

# §13

When the nights began to draw in, Abner embarked on a course of instruction. How to steal.

"I only nick what I think I can shift. I never bothers with big stuff. Attracts too much attention, and if you can fence it at all, fence'll make more'n you do and he'll bore you to death bangin' on about the risk he's taking.

"I never do a job on me own manor. Means travelling, but that's no bovver."

It was no bother because it was a major

component in what Wilderness thought of as Abner's modus operandi, and Abner as "me meffod." Abner had elected to serve King and Country in the Heavy Rescue Squad. This had distinct advantages. To be an air raid warden was almost a full time job, even when there were no air raids, for air raid wardens dealt in possibilities. It would also have tied him to his own "manor" night after night. Fire watching carried the same restrictions, with none of the power that turned so many chief wardens into little Hitlers. No one swaggered about fire watching. Heavy Rescue went where it was needed. And when there were no raids, and there had been virtually none since Lily died, a man in a Heavy Rescue dark blue blouse might have nothing to do but was free to be seen or ignored almost anywhere.

"Supposing I'm down Chelsea or up 'Ampstead? On me bike. I finds the shelter where the wardens drop in for a nightly cuppa and I sits down with 'em and has a brew up, and if anyone asks I been checkin' out some building that looks unsafe in the next borough. Sounds kosher, and as I'm in uniform I'm almost one o' them. They gets to talkin' and pretty soon I finds out who's locked up the house for the duration and buggered orf to Canada or who's just asked them to keep an eye on the place while they has a weekend in the country.

"Now . . . I suppose you think a burgliar . . ."

Abner could no more pronounce burglar
than coupon, which always resembled an ut-
terance like "cyuoopon."

". . . I suppose you think of a burgliar as a
bloke what works at dead of night, like I was
on the cover of a penny dreadful, swingin' orf
the gutters at midnight in a striped jersey wiv
a mask over me eyes."

Wilderness thought no such thing but said
nothing.

"I'm what you might call a twilight Johnnie.
I does my jobs around dusk, and in summer
often in daylight."

"A crepuscular creeper," Wilderness ventured.

"Whatever, son . . . I don't work at night.
And you know why?"

Wilderness could guess but let the old man
have his moment.

"Too many buggers about when it's dark
and not enough buggers about when it's
dark. Didn't use to be that way, but the war's
altered everything. You got coppers, always
had coppers, but now every Tom, Dick an'
Harry's in a fuckin' uniform askin' fuckin'
questions. And Joe Public stays at home for
fear of being run over in the blackout or some
such nonsense. It's so much harder to move
about. But . . . if I does a job at say five in
the arternoon . . . I just gets on a bus or goes

85

down the Underground like I was Norman Normal. Half past five is a good time to travel. You could lose Sherlock bleedin' Holmes on the London Underground at half past five of a weekday. Camden Town in rush hour? You could lose Rommel and his fuckin' Afrika Corps! Earl's Court at six? Twelve Russian Divisions try followin' you down to the Piccafuckindilly and are never seen again!"

Wilderness cut his teeth on a job in Belsize Park at 4:45 p.m. on a September afternoon in the autumn of 1941.

It was a Regency villa, bowfront — elegant ironwork, embraced by thick twists of wisteria — pale yellow paint flaking from the doors and windows, a scattering of dried blossom and browning leaves.

But it was the interior that most struck Wilderness. He had never been inside a house so well, so richly furnished, nor had his reading furnished his imagination with an inkling. Persian carpets over polished boards, wall upon wall of bookshelves, a baby grand piano on the first floor, nestling in the curve of the bay.

Abner was ready for this.

"Bedazzled, eh kid?"

"Yes, Grandad."

"Don't be. Take a look around, take it all in and then spit it all out. Get it outa yer system. You know how most toms get caught? Trying to make off with something too big and too beautiful that just happened to take his fancy and tipped the silly sod into a daydream. Or nickin' something so unique every nark in London's on the lookout for it and the first fence he tries turns him in for the reward. Third, and this is real stupid, opening the drinks cupboard, knockin' back the toffs' whisky and gin, and being caught rat-arsed on the job."

Abner had a preference for cash. Jewellery, as he told Wilderness repeatedly, was easily traced if left intact — he broke jewellery.

"You'd be surprised how many people don't trust banks — how many of 'em keep large sums of money in the house. Especially now. They . . . they want readies to be readies. If you see wot I mean, son."

A reading of the collected tales of E. W. Hornung had rightly informed Wilderness that the rich very often had safes — in walls, behind paintings, occasionally in the floor and more occasionally just standing pritch-kemp and defiant. What Mr. Hornung had not told Wilderness was that the average safe in any private house in London was old — donkey's years old and had in all probability been bought by the first rich man in the family, when the richesse was still very nouveau, and thereafter handed down with heirlooms and antiques, until, by 1941, the safe itself was an antique.

Not that a kid of six could crack them, but a kid of fourteen under instruction could.

"Anything before 1890s doable. After that, gets a bit tough. Moves up a league. They start laminating — layers of iron, layers of steel. You can't shatter steel and drilling iron is like sucking porridge up a straw. And you end up travelling with more and more tools. The light touch goes out of the job. You end up setting off like you're fighting a German division, kitted up and mob-handed. But, like I said. Plenty of old uns just waiting for the likes of you and me."

In the study at the rear of the Belsize Park villa, half hidden by the desk, was a small safe. Less than three feet high, half as wide, in a chipped green finish the colour of verdigris, bearing a brass plate — Thomas Withers & Son, West Bromwich, England. Below the plate was an off-centre handle, much resembling a pinecone, and a pivoting keyhole cover.

"I seen a lot older, but this is about 1880 summink. It ought to be a doddle."

In a workman's grip Abner carried drills, hammers, lockpicks and jemmies, and, wrapped in hessian with their stoppers tied down, two small jars, one of $H_2SO_4$ — clear, concentrated sulfuric acid, commonly known as vitriol — one of $HNO_3$ — a seventy per cent solution of reddish-yellow anhydrous nitric acid, commonly known as aqua fortis

— and an eyedropper.

"Who needs gelignite eh, son?"

Wilderness had been looking forward to gelignite, but had little expectation of it.

"I used it a few times during the Blitz, when I was trying to crack some big bugger that just wouldn't budge. But without the Jerries providing cover half London'd hear me."

Thus began Wilderness's education in cracksmanship.

He learnt rapidly how to open most makes of safe, both British and imported. The most common safe in the world was the Herring — made by the millions in the USA, but hardly much exported. The British competed with Withers and with Gores, with Milners and with Cartwrights — all of which could be found dotted around the far reaches of the Empire — while Europe's safes — Richter and Heinz or Julius Schuler, both of Hamburg, whilst much favoured by the jewellers and diamond merchants of Hatton Garden, were not often to be found in private homes.

His favourite was the Green Crocodile made by the Tiger Company. The words alone delighted him.

They came across it six weeks later. An apartment on the top floor of a building next door to Baker Street Station. They had gone in wearing overalls looking like workmen about their work. Abner's trick, his alibi, was to have a grubby piece of paper in the breast pocket of his overalls with the apartment number, a fake name and the address of the building next door written on it. If challenged, he would simply say, "Silly me. Wrong block of flats," pick up his cracksman's kit and saunter out much as he had sauntered in. They were not challenged. Most London blocks had had porters before the war, far fewer now when wages in factories paid better and most able-bodied men were in the forces.

It was beautiful.

Wilderness said so.

Out loud.

"Do I give a monkey's?" Abner replied. "What's it matter what it looks like? It's what's inside."

It was a small safe, probably custom-made for jewellery, but with luck there might be a pile of white five-pound notes inside — still referred to by Abner as "Bradburys" even though Sir John Bradbury had not put his signature to a Bank of England note these twenty years or more. Abner when flush, when cash-happy, would often refer to himself as being "out of the shit and into the Bradbury."

It was finished in deep green crocodile skin, so deep as to be almost black, fastened to the steel body with brass studs. The door had a decorative (it could hardly be functional) border in a yellow hardwood, which Wilderness, a boy for whom taxonomy was a private paradise, took to be yew or myrtle. Less than twenty inches high, it stood atop a long-legged table, ending in a burr-walnut pedestal and two carved tigers' feet in lacquered gold.

"It's beautiful."

"Shaddup and gimme the drill."

"We can't. Grandad, we can't."

They did.

Thieves there were who might have carted a safe so small back home with them and cracked it at their leisure. Abner was not one of those.

"We'd look a right pair of twats pushing this back to Whitechapel in a wheelbarrow, wouldn't we?"

A chisel ripped the lock covers from their housing, and a razor blade edged with insulating tape sliced through the green leather down to the steel.

Part of the deterrent power of a safe is the illusion of thickness and strength. The Crocodile bore the inscription "Fire and Thief Proof," which of itself might be considered an oxymoron — a word Wilderness knew and Abner didn't. A safe that appeared to be three inches of solid steel might only be half an inch thick — the lining being made up of a mix of gypsum and alum or a layer of acid-washed chalk, which, so compressed, was just about the most fire-resistant material man had invented. The purchaser of a safe had, knowingly or not, a choice — was it to be fireproof or thiefproof? For as Abner said:

"Can't be fuckin' both now can it?"

And so saying he began to drill into the steel just above the first lock. A slow process, but patience is a criminal virtue. A quarter of an hour later, when he had drilled the second, they flipped the safe onto its back.

"Lots o' brass on the outside. Bound to be a lot on the inside."

Brass locks were harder. Compared to steel an alloy like brass was hard to corrode; an ancient formula of copper and zinc, improved in recent times by the addition of tin or antimony or arsenic — all of which strengthened its resistance.

Abner opened the jar of nitric acid, filled the eyedropper, emptied it into both the drilled holes and the keyholes and said, softly "Leg it!" as noxious yellow fumes and a foaming green slime oozed from the locks.

When the air had cleared, Wilderness deployed a tool Abner had made himself — a strong L-shaped hexagonal spanner, steel with a wooden handle, not unlike a docker's hook. He inserted it into the keyholes and twisted it hard three or four times, feeling metal give as he did so. Abner flipped the safe upright, clouted the handle with a club hammer and the door flew open. Thiefproof no more.

The inside was no less beautiful than the outside.

It was like looking into a doll's house. Rows of tiny drawers with pearl handles and inlays of fine marquetry.

Abner ripped them all out in seconds — wood splintering, hinges snapping and the contents spewing out across the floor. A pearl necklace, a couple of diamond rings and — holy of holies — a roll of Bradburys tied up with red string.

Abner said, "Must be a monkey here at least," but did not stop to count. He had little interest in the jewellery. One glance at the necklace and he tossed it back on the carpet, crushed one end with the heel of his boot.

"Cultured. Rubbish."

Wilderness had picked up the rings.

"Paste?"

"Dunno. Take 'em anyway."

As they left — the diamonds in Wilderness's pocket, the money in Abner's — Wilderness looked back, a violation of one of Abner's *un*spoken rules.

The scarred and mammocked safe. Scalped and raped. The pearls crushed to dust. The dribble of acid eating into the kelim rug.

He had ruined something beautiful. He had by this act reached childhood's end — a moment which can come at any age, and at which a truth becomes inescapable . . . that what has been done cannot be undone.

He felt he had tasted sin for the first time. He felt as though he should be punished — for the last time. And he was.

# §14

Harry made a point of thrashing Wilderness every time he came home on leave, just, as he had put it, to show him who was who. Wilderness could read his mood by the sound of his footsteps in the street, by the rhythm of his knocking at the door. Rage or calm registered in every pace and every tap. He learnt that "there are strange Hells within the minds War made." Wilderness grew quickly, but never resisted. No gain in height or weight would ever have been enough to let him stand up to his father. There was the possibility Harry might kill him if he did. Wilderness would shield his face with his forearms, take what was coming to him. Abner left the house, and, as a rule, Merle would barricade herself in the bedroom or the scullery until it was all over and Wilderness tapped on the door. She would crack it open enough to see out, look at the boy, assess the bruising with a quick scan of his features and then say simply "Well?"

"He's sleeping it off," Wilderness would say.

"We could slit the bastard's throat."

"No, we couldn't, Merle. We could neither of us do that."

Then she would burst into floods of tears and be inconsolable until Abner reappeared, awash in the recognition of her own powerlessness.

"I'd understand him more if he was drunk," Abner said.

"What's to understand?" Wilderness replied. "Drunk he's as happy or as horrible as any other man. Sober . . . he'll do what he's going to do."

"He weren't always like this. Only since Dunkirk."

"And which of us is going to ask him about that?"

Abner thought about this and came to the right conclusion.

"You're growin' up a sight too quick for me, son. I can't keep up with you."

The beatings stopped when Harry's leave stopped, in the January of 1942. Wilderness had no idea where his father spent his embarkation leave, and only knew he had embarked when a postcard arrived that read, "Gone to get me knees brown, Dad," which was about as close as any serving soldier would ever get to saying he was sailing for North Africa.

Wilderness had no feelings about this news. His father had gone. He might be killed in battle. He might never be seen again. Or he could return home with whatever vicious flame burned in his brain fanned into a conflagration.

"When you say you're going to kill yer Dad, I can't help but be shocked. Yet when anyone else says it, even as a joke, you just disagree and change the subject," Abner said.

"It's my prerogative," Wilderness replied.

"Yer what?"

"My . . . privilege. It's mine and mine alone. I'm the one he's beating . . . and . . . besides, do any of us mean it? It says what we feel not what we might do. And . . . Harry's in combat. There's a half a million Jerries out in the desert who really do want to kill him."

"Like I say, son, I can't keep up with you. You and yer great big brain. Maybe you should o' done all them exams arter all."

Wilderness said nothing to this. It was too late, and "too late" was not a phrase he wanted to utter.

# §15

Abner had no time for oxyacetylene cutters. Apart from the inevitable smack of modernity — anathema to a man clinging to the last elusive vestiges of the Edwardian era — it would have altered his entire cracksman's modus operandi. It was a bulky kit and would have required him to have a van and that would have sacrificed one of his principal tenets — to be able to "have it away on yer toes."

The biggest component of Abner's kit was his Phillips Motor Hammer Impact electric-powered drill — a beast heavy enough that it was only brought out when he had cased a job and decided it was worth the effort. It could bore through steel over three-quarters of an inch thick, hammer into sheet iron, and required both of them to hold it steady.

They were back in Hampstead, on a rooftop high above Downshire Hill, only yards from Hampstead Heath. It was, against Abner's habitual practice, a job to be done in darkness — in the February of 1944 when the Luftwaffe had resumed bombing London, and provided him with cover, a blanket of night and noise to smother any sound he made.

At the south end of the heath was a station of the North London Railway Company, built to feed commuters into the City, into Broad Street, once, in the days when Victorian London was home to a million Mr. Pooters, the busiest railway station in the world. It was their getaway, a twelve-minute swaggard ride almost to their own doorstep — off the train, out the back way to vanish "on their toes" into the narrow streets of Shoreditch and to emerge home and free in Whitechapel.

London was blacked out every night. The days when people had been more at risk of being run over than bombed had long passed, as an instinctive night-awareness took over.

97

When the sirens whined Wilderness shinned up the soil stack at the back of the house, perched himself on the parapet and lowered a rope to Abner. Abner tied on the bag of tools and Wilderness hauled them to the roof. Abner followed, complaining that he was "too old for this lark." But, "this lark" had been his choice. They would not be on a rooftop with the searchlights raking the sky above them if the old man were not a hundred per cent sure of what they were after.

"Over the other side," he said, pointing with his free hand.

The top floor of the house appeared to have been turned into some sort of studio. A low-ridged glass atrium spanned the house front to back. The only way across to the far side was to walk along the parapet — a perilous nine inches, single-brick wide.

"Do we need to be over there?" Wilderness asked.

"We do. Or else it's cut a way in here and risk bringing the whole damn thing down with us."

Wilderness understood the risk. The atrium looked shaky, flaking white paint and green moss — in all probability rotten in places.

"Still we's'll manage, eh son?"

Abner crossed first. Wilderness followed slowly, inclining his head and shoulders inward to offset the weight of the drill, which otherwise threatened to unbalance him in the direction of a four-storey drop.

Once across Wilderness slung the rope around a chimney, and his grandfather climbed down one floor and slid the catch on a sash window.

The safe was a Milner List 5. Tall and tough.

Abner surmised that it dated from circa 1900 — knuckle hinges, three triple-stump fantail locks, and a sandwich door with a drill-resistant plate at its core.

The plate fell to Abner's touch, to his touch and his Phillips Motor Hammer Impact drill.

Once or twice they stopped to listen to the dull thump of bombs falling. Wilderness wondered how close they were. It sounded as far off as Hackney, but the volume was rising and the bombs crossing London manors . . . Islington, Highbury, Holloway, closer. Abner pressed on. His shoulder against the back of the drill,

"Once the all clear sounds Gawd knows who'll hear the fuckin' racket we're makin'."

But they had the door open long before the raid was over.

Wilderness packed up the drill. Abner stuffed his bag with white fivers and chuckled to himself.

"Easy money, son. Easy money."

Back on the roof, Abner handed the bag of money to Wilderness and took the drill off him.

"Let me. I'm younger than you, Grandad."

"Younger don't mean stronger. The day you can beat me in an arm wrestle . . ."

Wilderness walked the narrow parapet between the glass atrium and the drop like a man on the high wire. All but dancing. He wore the two handles of Abner's old canvas bag like shoulder straps. The money and the hand tools centred in his back for balance. He reached the other side and turned to Abner.

It was the moment before the moment when a voice in Wilderness's head would have said "home and dry."

A voice that came from the roof of the neighbouring house said, "There they are."

And the voice in Wilderness's head said "Who? Me?"

Abner was crouched down, just hoisting the drill bag onto his shoulder. He turned. A London bobby, pointy hat and all, had appeared on the rooftop and behind him was a bloke in evening dress clutching a 12-bore shotgun.

"I told you I heard something. Thieves I say, thieves!"

Wilderness froze as the barrel of the gun levelled on him.

Abner stood up, the bag now dangling from his right shoulder.

"Leg it son, he won't shoot."

Wilderness did not move. The copper was

saying something about staying where they were and being under arrest. None of it seemed to translate into meaning. It might have been Chinese for all Wilderness knew. All he could see was the gun, and all he could hear was the pulse pounding in his chest.

Abner set off along the parapet at the same dancing pace Wilderness had used. Younger was not stronger. It was nimbler. It was more agile. Abner's natural gait, limping slightly, coming down hard on the right foot was nowhere near as light or balanced as Wilderness's — and the weight of the drill on his shoulder threw him off kilter.

He was halfway across when the bag slipped to the crook of his elbow. Instinct overtook logic. Instead of letting the drill fall to earth he attempted to right it with a sudden jerk of his shoulder and the shift of weight swung the bag too far to the left, across his chest, his whole body following in a corkscrew twist with the slow inevitability of a pendulum — and tipped him through the glass roof.

His last word as he fell, roaring up through the sound of breaking glass, was "Scaaaaarper!"

Then the bang as his body hit the floor below, and the cascade of shattered glass and splintered timber as the atrium collapsed on top of him.

# §16

Wilderness found a pair of wire cutters under the wad of money. At Gospel Oak Station he snipped the lock off a bike and cycled back in the direction of Stepney. He got off and walked for a while close to Highbury Corner. Most of one side of the street was in ruins. Air raid wardens, firemen, and Heavy Rescue swarmed across the rubble. No one paid the slightest bit of notice to him. Nor did they when he abandoned the bike by the London Hospital, where ambulances swept in and out every few seconds like bees at the hive.

# §17

He lay awake, watching the night pale into day through the skylight. Around dawn it started to rain.

Abner was dead. He was certain Abner was dead. The old man would not have his identification card on him, but it would not take the police long to work out who he was.

It took till breakfast.

He sat at the kitchen table — a steel Morrison shelter to which Abner had bolted a wooden top — with a cup of tea.

Merle was asleep. He'd told her nothing. She had come in long after he had got home, another night on the game, and he'd told her nothing.

The copper at the door was not a local. He knew all of them by sight. This one was in civvies. A rain-spotted, belted macintosh and a trilby. The copper who stood behind him, buttoned to the chin, helmet clutched to his chest, was a manor face. One he knew from the streets without ever knowing his name.

"This is the home of Abner Riley?"

They knew damn well it was. As surely as they knew he was dead.

Wilderness strived for the appearance of innocence, to sound and look closer to thirteen than seventeen.

"Grandad ain't up yet."

The detective was torn between the certainty of duty, to investigate a crime, and the civility of duty, to report a death, and it seemed to Wilderness that the ambiguities of this were beyond the man. He wanted to explain and he wanted to accuse. His cheek twitched and he could not quite hold the tough-guy pose of looking him in the eye. And when he stepped in uninvited, he removed his hat.

"Anyone else at home, son?"

Wilderness had not heard Merle stir.

"What's the matter?" Wilderness asked.

"Your grandad's met with a . . ."

He was searching for a euphemism or perhaps just a small lie.

"An accident."

Wilderness reached for an equivalent fib.

"You mean the air raid? You mean he's dead?"

The detective looked at the bloke in uniform.

The bloke in uniform took the hint.

" 'Fraid he is dead, but it wasn't the raid. He died pulling a job."

At last they had got to the point. It could only be a matter of a minute or so before they asked him where he had been last night.

"Would you mind telling me where you were round about ten o'clock last night, son?"

From behind him Wilderness heard Merle say, "He was home with me."

She was propped in the doorway to her bedroom, a dressing gown pulled loosely round her, one hand holding it closed over her breasts, the other pressing a cigarette to her lips.

"Mrs. Riley?" asked the detective.

The uniform shook his head at this. Merle drew on her cigarette and didn't bother to answer.

"You're alibiing the boy?"

"Nah . . . I'd only be doing that if a crime had been committed wouldn't I? You said an accident. What accident?"

"There has been a crime. Abner Riley died . . . accidentally . . . in the act of committing a burglary."

"You don't say? My Abner was a tom? Lord love a duck."

The coppers looked at one another again. They knew.

"You're saying the boy was with you all night?"

"Yep. Once a raid starts up. I just stay put. Ain't been down a shelter since 1941. Who wants to die with strangers in a stinkin' hole in the ground. Stay put, sit it out. That's our way. Don't even sit under the table no more. We had cup of char and a bit o' toast an' Bovril, listened to the bombers and went to bed. Tucked him in meself round about eleven, didn't I, Johnnie?"

Wilderness hated the last line. It was a lie too far, a snook too cocked, but then his squirming at this could easily be read as the embarrassment of a sixteen-year-old in the presence of adults. At least she hadn't said they'd listened to the wireless, only to have them ask her to name what programmes they'd listened to.

"Now, if you haven't got any more questions, I'd appreciate being left in peace. I just lost me bloke. This is . . ." and here she paused. "A house in mourning." Emphatically, her voice rising a fraction, "A house in mourning . . . so . . . be a mensch and just fuck off will you."

They left. Wilderness had no doubts they knew, no doubts that they'd go away only to come back.

Merle lit up a second cigarette from the

stub of the first, and poured herself a cup of tea. Silent tears at the corners of her eyes.

A long exhale, a cloud of smoke and a first sip. The tears suspended in time and space, ready to roll.

"Why didn't you tell me?"

"I didn't want to say the word."

"What word?"

"Dead. That word."

"And exactly how did Abner end up dead?"

Wilderness told her. She tilted back her head while she listened, as though it were a matter of pride that a tear should not roll.

"And where," she said, still looking at the ceiling, "is the money?"

"On the roof."

Now she looked at him, tears escaping her clutch to stream down her cheeks.

"What?" she said. "Out in the bleeding rain?"

# §18

Merle took the money. Over two hundred pounds. For safekeeping, she told him. All Wilderness could hear was "keeping," and keep it she did. She kept all of Abner's loot, just as Abner had. Abner had bunged him a couple of quid every so often, but kept the bulk. It seemed to Wilderness that the old man must have built up quite a stash in his time — a successful thief, with only a fence to pay off. Rationing was a leveller, but it was clear they had lived well before the war. Well, but not high. A discreet level of consumption, attracting, whatever the rumours on the street, as little attention as possible. Abner had a decent suit, Merle some posh frocks — but the money was never flaunted. No "drinks for everybody" in the pub, no diamonds on her fingers.

All in all it seemed there must be a lot stashed away. The ill-gotten gains of all the jobs they'd pulled.

Wilderness never found it. Now it was Merle who bunged him a couple of quid every so often — and she saw he never went short, peeling notes off a roll in her handbag — but Wilderness never found the stash.

# §19

The day after Wilderness was called to a police lineup at the Leman Street nick. The bloke in evening dress who'd stood on the roof pointing a shotgun at him failed to pick him out.

Toff diffidence saved him. The sense of fair play that would not have restrained most men restrained this one.

"One has to be sure, d'ye see? Couldn't point the finger at a chap without being one hundred per cent sure. It wouldn't be cricket," he had said to the duty sergeant.

He could point a gun but not the finger?

Wilderness could not hear the sergeant's muted reply, but it was bound to be along the lines of, "But he's the old bloke's grandson. Bound to be him. Stands to reason."

And the toff had replied, audibly, "No it doesn't."

And after that all the sergeant could do was turn him loose with, "Don't think you got away with it, son. Yer card's marked."

# §20

On May Day 1945 the news broke that Hitler was dead. For weeks now "It'll be all over soon" had been a rolling cliché on the streets of London.

Wilderness thought, "I'm free. They'll never call me up now."

He had watched his schoolmates vanish into the army over the last year and more — ever since D-Day. And ever since D-Day he had thought the odds on the army claiming him to be diminishing on a daily basis.

In the spring new weapons had crashed down on London, the noisy, puttering doodlebug, the silent, devastating V2. Enough V2s and there'd be nothing left of England — but there weren't enough, it was Hitler's last roll of the dice, and when the Allied Forces overran the launch pads the raids stopped. By the end of April even the blackout restrictions had been lifted.

The neighbours were cautious.

"Hard to believe, innit? I mean to say, the buggers could be back any minute."

Merle had had none of this. She had ripped down the blackouts and thrown open the windows, clouds of dust cascading around her.

"Enough, enough of darkness and dirt. Enough of bombs. Enough of pompous little twats in tin hats. Enough is enough!"

It reminded Wilderness of scenes close to the end of *Great Expectations*. Ripping down the moth-eaten curtains that had shut out the light from Satis House for a generation.

Motes of dust danced in the late afternoon sunlight. Merle had danced with them, sweeping Wilderness along in her arms.

"It's over, bleedin' war is bleedin' over."

She hugged him, kissed him, told him again that it was over.

They'd never get him now.

A week passed in high anticipation — the national nerves stretched to breaking. Woolworth's, Bourne & Hollingsworth and Whiteleys all sold out of bunting.

May Day.

Hitler was dead.

Surely it was over now?

Germans surrendered in chunks, a division here, a division there.

Surely it was over now?

The Russians took Berlin.

Surely it was over now?

All they needed was the word.

And on May 7 the word came — the following day would be Victory in Europe Day. The Prime Minister would address the nation at 3:00. And at 3:01 the nation would erupt in a frenzy of celebration that would last until the beer ran out. And woe betide any landlord who tried to put up the towels for the night when it did.

# §21

"Not here," Merle said.

"Eh?"

"I wanna be somewhere else for this. Not sat in the street with the neighbours, wearing a paper hat and drinking warm beer from a coronation mug."

"Where then? Buckingham Palace?"

"No. Not the palace, but up West, definitely up West."

"Up West" was a concept as much as a place, and as a place it was a moveable feast — the most appropriate term imaginable for the night in question. It might begin just west of St. Paul's, but who knew where it ended? Regent Street? Park Lane? Knightsbridge? Wilderness had in a sense never been up West — he'd passed through it on trams and buses — a sensation rather like pressing your nose to the glass panes in the window of the sweet-shop — and he'd pulled a couple of jobs with Abner in Mayfair and Kensington. But been up West in the sense or walking its streets, eating in its caffs and drinking in its pubs and shopping in its shops . . . never. Harrods was just a word. Westminster Abbey a post-card. The Ritz a colonnaded facade glimpsed from the top of a number 19 bus.

"I'll take you to the Ritz," she said.

# §22

Piccadilly was a conga. A human snake that began at the circus and the boarded-up plinth on which Eros used to stand and slithered past Fortnum's, Jacksons, the Royal Academy, the Berkeley, and the Ritz to fizzle out in Green Park.

There seemed to Wilderness to be as many in uniform as in civvies, prompting the question "who is actually at the front?" which in turn prompted the question "is Harry Holderness at the front?" but that he readily dismissed.

Merle seemed content to watch. She slipped an arm through his, and they hugged the pavement rather than let the human tide sweep them up.

She seemed happy, her head bobbing against his shoulder, and — although he'd no real idea how old she was, perhaps half

Abner's age, say thirty-two or thirty-three —
"girlishly" happy.

By half past eight the sun was setting over
the palace and Green Park became ablaze
with bonfires. Londoners tore up the shelters
that had served them since the Blitz and fed
them into the flames.

Men and women danced around the fires
as though in some ancient Dionysiac — a
hint, more than a hint of impending intimacy
between strangers, encounters flashed in the
night rather than forged. To fuck but never
fuck again.

The Forces were out in force. A sailor, a
couple of RAF blokes wearing observers'
part-wings. And the Army — a couple of
Artillery gunners and a lance bombardier,
who took off their battledresses, waved them
around their heads, and let them float down
onto the flames like giant autumn leaves.

A benign policeman, a pointy-hatted London beat bobby, looked on without comment.
A large well-dressed, matronly woman caught
his eye with a wave of her brolly.

"Constable? Can this possibly be legal?"

"It is most certainly a crime to burn the
king's uniform, madam, but so long as they
none of 'em get their wedding tackle out I
shall be turning a blind eye."

Merle giggled at this, not meeting the
woman's gorgon gaze — and all but collapsed
in hysterics when the gunners stripped to

their socks, wedding tackle out, and threw every stitch of uniform into the fire.

"War is over," they yelled, echoing what Merle had said days ago, "Bleedin' war is bleedin' over."

The blind eye turned no more. The gunners set off across the park in the direction of St. James's at a bollock-bouncing trot, and the copper gave chase. The RAF observers stripped more slowly, fed their uniforms into the flames as though consigning the dead to the furnace — a gentle respect, a fond farewell to arms, at odds with the hysteria of the night. Then they turned and kissed. The matron stormed away trailing fury, complaining loudly about "the bloody queers."

Merle buried her face in his chest, he could feel her laughter in his ribs. Then she wiped her eyes and said.

"C'mon. It's past nine. Let's get to the Ritz before they sell out of champagne."

Wilderness was hesitant and she sensed this.

"Wossmatter?"

"Are we ready for this?"

"I been ready for the Ritz all my life. Puttin' on the Ritz is what I do."

"Are we even dressed right?"

Merle was in a scarlet summer frock that looked like it cost a packet. Her best patent leather handbag, with its diamante cluster on the clasp. Wilderness was in what passed for best. A light sports jacket and cavalry twill

113

trousers. Put a cravat around his neck and he just might pass for a countryman up to town for the day.

She picked up the regulation black RAF tie dropped by one of the queers.

"Slip this on and you'll be fine."

"Supposing they won't let us in?"

"I'd like to see 'em try. Tonight of all nights I'd like to see 'em try."

As they left, heading north onto Piccadilly, the naval rating was stripping, even more slowly than the RAF queers, consigning history to the flames. Ashes to ashes, dust to dust.

# §23

The crush in the bar at the Ritz was scarcely less than in the street.

Merle made him sit.

"It ain't a pub. They come to you."

And when he came, he took one look at Merle and drew too keen a conclusion.

"Excuse me, sir," he said to Wilderness, sotto voce, his back to Merle.

It was almost impulsive to look over his shoulder, and see to whom the waiter was talking, but he knew it was him and he knew what the man was going to say if not how he might phrase it.

"Your companion, sir. I understand it is a night for celebration, a waiving of the rules, but this is a respectable establishment — the most respectable in London. Certain things we cannot permit."

Not admitting he was a bookworm had saved Wilderness a kicking on many occasions as a boy. Equally effective was an ability to make his enemies laugh with mimicry. Few accents could elude his ear and tongue for long, and certainly not those of the English upper classes as personified by Ronald Colman or Robert Donat. Either would do — C. Aubrey Smith perhaps a trifle excessive.

"Sorry, old man. Don't quite catch your drift here."

The waiter coughed once into the end of a loosely clenched fist, but by then Merle had stuck out her left hand and was waving her ring finger at him.

She was wearing a wedding ring, and Wilderness could only assume she had slipped it on in the last few moments and that she carried one just to be able to pull a stunt like this.

" 'Ere, take a gander mate. What do you think this is, a bleedin' doughnut?"

The man reddened. Wilderness thought it touch and go which way he jumped now.

"My last leave," he said. "Popped the question. The old girl said yes. Now how about drinks for the pair of us? The sooner we get them the sooner my good lady and I will be on our way."

The blush deepened. He must have worked out Wilderness's age to within a year or two and might be guessing at twenty-one or twenty-two rather than seventeen, and he might deem him unlikely to be either officer or gentleman, but he wasn't going risk it. Wilderness knew he'd won this one.

"Yeah. Make mine a Tom Collins," Merle said.

"And for you, sir?"

"Oh, the same," Wilderness said, with no idea what a Tom Collins was.

"I'm afraid the lemon will be out of a bottle sir."

Ah, so it had lemon in it did it?

Wilderness smiled his assent, and the waiter vanished.

"Old hypocrite," Merle said. "He never told me he worked here."

"You mean you know him?"

"Wasn't certain till he started staring and whispering, but I think I did him a quickie in St. James's Park last February. Cold as a polar bear's bollocks and bombs wangin' down everywhere, and I pick up the only fare left on the razzle. Cheeky bugger. Of course I know him. Do you think he spotted me for a brass 'cos I look like one?"

"Well I did wonder about the handbag."

"I might just clock you with it."

A Tom Collins turned out to be mostly gin. The tipple that had ruined his mother. Gin

116

and sugar. It was little short of disgusting, but he sipped at it for Merle's sake, wishing she'd ordered champagne.

She was talking at him. "At" might be "to" as far as Merle was concerned but Wilderness could not hear her. Her words were simply bouncing off him. He could suddenly hear nothing. One of the loudest evenings of his life, the letting down of the national hair — or in many cases the national trousers — and it was like watching a silent film. Or more precisely, an effect in a talking film when they drop the sound and the observer sees only faces, and faces become grimaces magnified by the glass walls of the fish tank through which he appears to be watching.

He could think of it no other way. He was in an aquarium or in a zoo — not that he'd ever been to either — he was a scientist, they were specimens . . . *Homo anglicus,* in all his limited variety — his native grey plumage enlivened only by the deep blues of the navy and the paler blues of the RAF and the spring colours of all the posh totty on his arm. Well-heeled Englishman and Englishwoman. So remote as to be another species.

Minutes passed, perhaps a quarter of an hour, Merle still talking, and the glass shattered. Hit his eardrums with the blast of a bomb. The mass braying of assembled toffs in their mating ritual.

"Can we go now?"

" 'Course, enough is enough," she replied. "Let me summon old winkledick and pay the sod."

Walking towards home, walking to the point where they'd both get fed up and hop on a bus, she leaned her head on his arm said, "Wasn't a bad idea goin' to the Ritz was it?"

"No," he replied. "Not a bad idea at all to put on a bit of ritz. My first glimpse of the high life."

"The high life? And what do you make of it?"

"Dunno," he said honestly.

It was repellent and tempting. And he did not care to discuss temptation with her.

# §24

She took him to bed.

Reading the hesitation in his eyes, she splayed her left hand in front of him, her own eyes peeping coquettishly over the fan, a *strega* at *un ballo in maschera*. The slender gold ring still upon her finger.

"We got married on your last leave. Remember?"

That was the masquerade. They weren't real any more, they were characters in a masquerade of his own devising.

Afterwards. Passion far from spent. Looking up at the skylight. Merle stirring.

"Merle," he said. "Where's the money?"

"Wot money?"

"Our money. Mine and Grandad's."

"Safe. Don't you worry. It's safe . . ." She yawned and paused. "Safe as houses."

He said nothing to this, realising that she was not going to answer any more questions, and searched what she had said for a clue. But it was just a phrase — a common turn of phrase that offered nothing and concealed nothing.

She slid one hand across his belly.

"You're a nice shape, young Johnnie. A nice flat tum on yer. A bit more muscle on yer bones and I bet all the girls'll fancy you. Let's do it one more time. Afore I fall asleep. After all . . . we're not going to make a habit of it are we . . . ?"

Wilderness was damn certain they weren't.

"So let's do it one last time for . . . for old times' sake."

Wilderness saw in the first dawn of peace humping his grandfather's mistress, a common prostitute of the London streets, shooting the second (shared) orgasm of his life into her.

She had taken his virginity. His grandfather's mistress. He still had no idea how old she was. She took his virginity — there was no one else on earth to whom he would rather have surrendered it.

He never did find the money.

When the celebrations of Victory in Europe had dwindled to a national hangover, Wilderness was convinced he was home free. Japan had not surrendered, but it could not be long, and it could hardly be worthwhile training up anyone new and shipping them East. The voyage alone took the best part of two months.

But — the day he turned eighteen at the beginning of August a letter arrived from the War Office ordering him to register for the Forces at the local Labour Exchange.

Merle told him to do it and attract no trouble.

"Don't want no more coppers pokin' around here. They've had you marked ever since your grandad died."

He registered, and opted to join the RAF, for no better reason than that blue was preferable to brown, thinking he would, in all likelihood, never hear from them again.

The following week he received instructions to report to the RAF Recruitment Centre at Euston, a twenty-minute ride away on the London Underground. It was not his "call-up." It was some sort of exam.

Merle said, "Just do it, kid. Don't ask for no more attention. Like the man said, yer card's marked. Besides, nothin' ter lose. Not after them big bombs on Japan. War's all over bar the shouting. And you was always good at exams."

He was good at exams. And all this one seemed to be was some sort of crude test of his intelligence. A matter of not banging a square peg in a round hole. A doddle.

Then the shouting — August 15, 1945 — Victory over Japan, and a piss-up in the streets to beat all piss-ups, and it was, as she had said, "all over."

About a month passed — Britain adjusted painfully, if at all, to life under Labour government, life in the nuclear age, and life at peace.

Then Wilderness received his call-up papers. A travel warrant to get him from St. Pancras Station to RAF Cardington in Bedfordshire and a postal order for four shillings. Two days' pay in advance.

"Oh fuck."

Merle took the letter from him.

" 'Ere. You're now Aircraftman 2nd Class Holderness, J. of the RAF Regiment."

"Oh fuck."

"Oh fuck indeed."

There was a telling pause as she lit up a fag. Merle striving hard to look as though she was thinking.

"You know I've always urged you to keep your nose clean? You know, ever since Abner . . . you know . . . Well this is different. I wouldn't blame you if you did a runner.

121

Really I wouldn't. The bloody war's over. They're demobbing blokes already. For all we know yer dad's on his way back right now. What can they possibly want with a skinny bugger like you?"

"No," said Wilderness. "They've got me. Nowhere to run to. They've got me by the balls. And I think it pays to know when they've got you by the balls."

"What you gonna do? Join up, keep yer head down and yer nose clean and hope trouble just passes you by?"

"Well I can try," Wilderness said.

"Fat chance, kiddo. Fat chance."

The sole consolation in this was that if his father was on his way home, back home from God only knew where, perhaps to be on an RAF station somewhere, anywhere where Harry wasn't, might be no bad thing.

"Fat chance," she said again, leaving the phrase echoing around in Wilderness's mind.

# §26

RAF Cardington seemed to take up about half of Bedfordshire. Wilderness was there for five days.

He had his hair cut to regulation RAF length ("Get yer 'air cut! You bunch of fuckin' pansies!") — length and regulation being about as close to an oxymoron as possible — was issued with a best and a working uniform, a "cheese-cutter" forage cap ("Stick it to yer 'ead with Brylcreem!"), shoes as well as boots ("This ain't the bleedin' army — we don't live in fuckin' boots.") assigned a number ("Learn to recite it in yer sleep! You can forget yer own name, but never forget yer number!"), and told to stamp the number into his personal cutlery ("Knife, fork an' spoon, nerks fer the use of. Get 'ammerin!"). The uniform could have fitted better, as with every pair of trousers Wilderness had owned since he was thirteen they were too short in the leg. ("You're a big bugger ain'tya!"). And he ate five days' worth of bangers and mash, rendered soggy by the limp, dripping grey cabbage piled onto the plate. RAF Cardington seemed to smell of cabbage constantly. Later in life, he had only to catch a whiff of boiling cabbage to see Cardington for a split second in the mind's eye.

The low point was posting home all his civilian clothes. Nothing, not the brutal haircut, the mindless shouting or the appalling food brought home quite so sharply that they had "got" him. He stuck a note to Merle in the package. "Trying to keep me head down and me nose clean. Don't bet on it. Jx"

None of this seemed crucial. What was crucial was the careers hut.

"Right. You gotta pick. What do you want to be?"

Wilderness had replied that he would like

to be a pilot.

"Nah, clerk, cobbler, barber, mechanic, cook, driver an' blah blah blah."

"No, really. I'd like to be a pilot."

The flight sergeant had laughed at this.

"No chance, son. Not for likes of you. Pick a trade. Wot was you in Civvy Street?"

He could hardly say thief.

"OK, how about driver?"

"Can you drive?"

"Not yet."

"We got a word for drivers wot can't drive. It's clerk."

He left Cardington a clerk, with a recommendation that he train as a driver — if a vacancy arose. They had got him, and chained him to a desk.

# §27

Cardington dispersed its recruits on the sixth day. From Cornwall to Aberdeen, from Pembroke to Suffolk. Wilderness, along with half a dozen new recruits, was posted to RAF Ravenhoe in Essex for basic training. Until the peace Wellingtons had flown out of Ravenhoe to bomb Germany. Now they ferried men and equipment, and half the base was given over to training.

The school cliché had always been that the fat kid who could not tie shoelaces was always last in a race and never to be trusted in goal.

Sandy Birch was not fat. He was a skinny redhead who looked less eighteen than fifteen. You would never trust him in goal, he could not tie his shoelaces, nor could he dress on time or shave to a sufficient standard to please the NCOs. He laid out his kit on his half-made bed in a fashion that could only be described as chaotic and graced his first parade with patches of bog paper sticking to his cheeks, crisping with brown stains as the blood dried.

As such he was poison to the RAF corporals charged with licking civilians into the shape of airmen. They ate him all the same.

Wilderness had spotted him as long ago as day two at Cardington, when he had managed to drop most of the kit he had been issued, his personal knife, fork and spoon clattering down with his enamelled tin mug.

Their first pre-breakfast, post-ablution parade at Ravenhoe: 7 a.m., all in working blues — a second-best uniform, designed to get dirty — and boots.

The bog paper was a red rag to a bull. Corporal Turpin passed Wilderness with a glance, stopped and stared at Birch's face, then let his eyes roll down the length of the boy's body, to his boots. Each boot had twenty-two lace holes. Birch had missed a good half dozen on each boot.

"Jesus H. Christ. What are you, boy?"

Birch rattled off his name and number.

125

"No, that's who you are. I asked what you are? Now, what in God's name are you?"

"Please, Corporal, don't know Corporal."

"Then I's'll have to tell you. You Birch are a twat. What are you Birch?"

"A twat," said Birch.

"Sorry, Birch. I must be a bit mutt an' jeff this morning. I didn't hear you."

"A twat." Birch said more loudly.

So far Turpin had not raised his voice, but Wilderness readily deduced it was a weapon held in reserve.

"WHAT THE FUCK ARE YOU?"

Birch went red, his cheeks blew out as though he might burst, then he yelled as loud as he could.

"I AM A TWAT!"

Turpin resumed a normal volume.

"No, no, no. . . . 'I am a twat, Corporal.' "

"I AM A TWAT, CORPORAL!"

"Thank you Birch. You are indeed a twat."

Wilderness had said nothing. Further down the line, his newfound comrades were grinning and sniggering. Wilderness said nothing. But, any English school will teach you that silence is not the same thing as innocence. Turpin stepped back to him. It reminded him of those moments when a teacher could seize upon the merest expression and decide it was insolence. Wilderness had never been able to work out what insolence was. It defied definition and was so bound up in matters of rank

126

and status as to require an entire chapter in any manual of etiquette. However blank the face, the offended party would profess to read a message in it — invariably it would be found insolent. And Wilderness had long ago concluded that only the insecure bastards hovering one rung above bottom ever bothered with insolence — it marked out the losers in life that they could be so readily offended by silence.

"And you. You lanky bastard. What's your game?"

Wilderness recited his name and number.

"Could it be, Holderness, that you are a smart alec?"

Wilderness said nothing.

"Answer me, son. Are you a smart alec?"

"Oh yes, Corporal. Smart as they come. Smarter than you by a plank and a half."

Wilderness wasn't wholly sure why he'd said this, but had time to reflect as he doubled up under a fist to the solar plexus.

"IF THERE'S ONE THING I HATE MORE THAN A FUCKING TWAT IT'S A FUCKING SMART ALEC! ONE MORE FUCKING CRACK, ONE MORE SNOTTY FUCKING LOOK OUT OF YOU SON AND I'LL HAVE YOU ON FUCKING JANKERS!"

# §28

Jankers was universal British forces slang for punishment, usually following a charge of insubordination. It did not require a court-martial.

Jankers duly followed. Wilderness failed to salute a pilot officer, who sent for Flight Sergeant Mills, who shouted at him and rushed him in front of the flight lieutenant, no one of higher rank being available or interested. Wilderness scrubbed lavatories with a toothbrush for a weekend.

Not long afterwards, on morning parade, he laughed at something a chap in the row behind had muttered about Corporal Turpin's mother. Turpin exploded into a practised routine of "Twat," "Fucking twat," and "Smart-alec wankers." He sent for Flight Sergeant Downes, who sent for the flight lieutenant, who could not conceal his boredom with all of them.

"Is this really necessary, Flight?"

"Rank insubordination, sah!"

"Do you have to be quite so loud."

"Sah!"

"Call the man a fool and have done, Flight."

"No, sah! King's Regulations clearly state —"

"Flight Sergeant, do not start quoting me King's Regulations. If you want to punish this man, punish him. I don't know . . . have him whitewash the coke heap . . . polish the lino . . . something like that. But for Christ's sake stop shouting."

Wilderness whitewashed coke, and when he had whitewashed it Downes and Mills had him hose it down and do it again. After three days he was whitewashing it by torchlight. Small incident followed on small incident. More bogs to scrub, more coke to whitewash. And the added pleasure of putting a shine upon linoleum floors that already shone. He spent a total of six nights in the glasshouse for minor misdemeanours. They had him marked as a troublemaker.

Along the way he learnt what he had to about marching, cleaning a Lee Enfield .303 (but not actually firing one), the boundless joys of blanco and stamping his feet. It wasn't enjoyable, but it was tolerable. For some reason planes — surely the raison d'être of the RAF — had not yet come into it. Nor had clerking, nor had the prospect of driving.

What changed things for ever, and most certainly for better, was the cunt.

Yet again they were on parade. Wilderness bored out of his brain, Flight Sergeant Downes shouting orders, Corporals Turpin and Bodell enforcing them, checking that thumbs aligned with the seams of trousers, that feet were splayed at the regulation RAF angle, that heels banged down with the requisite force.

They got as far as Birch.

Today he was not bleeding, but his shirt protruded beneath his blouse and his boot-laces resembled a cat's cradle made by a three-year-old.

Turpin kicked at his feet.

"What are you Birch?"

Birch knew the routine.

"I am a fucking twat, Corporal."

"No, no, no, no . . . laddie. That was last week. You have slipped down the slippery slope of sloppiness since then. Birch, you are a cunt."

Birch said nothing, reddened in the face.

"What are you, Birch?"

"No, corp. I can't say that. Not that word."

Turpin screamed, "YOU ARE A CUNT. WHAT ARE YOU BIRCH?"

Birch said nothing, turned his head towards Wilderness to avert his eyes from Turpin's glare.

Turpin seized him by the chin, turned his head back and an inch from his face yelled, "SAY IT! YOU ARE A CUNT!"

Birch wet himself, a hissing sound of escaping urine, a rapidly spreading wet patch discolouring his best blues, and a splash of orange piss bursting over his shoes and onto Turpin's. Turpin all but jumped backwards.

"Jesus H. Christ. I do not fuckin' believe it."

As he raised his arm to hit Birch, Wilderness blocked it.

"Hit him and I'll deck you."

Wilderness was at least six inches taller than Turpin. Turpin looked up in disbelief, not trusting his own ears.

"Come on, Sandy. Let's get you cleaned up."

He led Birch out of line and across the parade ground in the direction of their hut.

Bodell intercepted, positioning himself in front of Wilderness. Downes stood motionless a way off, swagger stick tucked under his arm. Turpin began to yell, so loudly Wilderness could not make out what he was saying.

Bodell was no bigger than Turpin. Five foot six of gutless obedience.

Wilderness said, "Step aside, Corporal. This won't take long and then we'll both be back on parade."

Bodell seemed to have a verbal fit, "Wuuh worra wuuh worra wuuh."

Wilderness shoved him aside, the palm of his hand flat against his chest.

It was then that Downes's voice boomed out, "Arrest that man!"

# §29

This bloke wasn't RAF he was Army, a half-colonel in the Guards. As a boy Wilderness had collected the cards that came free inside packets of cigarettes — he'd had a full set of

131

English Automobiles, most of British But-
terflies and all but three of HM Forces
Uniforms. According to his fag cards, this
bloke was in the Coldstream Guards — the
buttons on his tunic grouped in pairs.

Wilderness wondered why he was getting a
bollocking from the army. Was the RAF not
capable of slinging him back in the glasshouse
one more time without calling in the troops?

A corporal he'd never met before had
barked him in, all the hup-to, left-right, left-
right bollocks, slamming down his feet and
expecting Wilderness to do the same. Wilderness went through the motions, out of step,
out of time and no doubt far too quietly for
the barker.

The colonel was bent over papers. Looked
up once to say, "Thank you Corporal. You
can go now."

More stomping. Turning on his heel as
though powered by clockwork. But then that
was their trouble with NCOs. They really
were clockwork.

More than a minute passed. The colonel
looked up again, pushed his sheaf of papers
away from him and pointed at the chair opposite.

"You might as well sit. I'm sure you're less
trouble sitting down."

It seemed to Wilderness like an invitation.
He took it.

"I don't think I'm ever trouble."

"Really? You don't say? Aircraftman Holderness, I've just read a dozen pages about you — all but three of them complaints. Complaints from Corporal Turpin, complaints from Corporal Bodell, complaints from Flight Sergeant Mills, complaints from Flight Sergeant Downes — all endorsed by Flight Lieutenant Cooper. Not trouble? Holderness, they think you're a pain in the arse!"

"That's 'cos they're a bunch of fucking twats."

There was a momentary pause, the merest flinch on the colonel's part.

"A bunch of fucking twats, *sir.*"

"Of course. Sorry. A bunch of fucking twats, *sir.*"

"Let's get one thing clear. I'm not a fucking twat, and if you talk to me like a fucking twat I've enough authority to bung you back in the glasshouse and throw away the key."

"Yes, sir."

"Good — now we understand one another, let's backtrack and get to the introductions. I'm Lieutenant Colonel Burne-Jones. And I can save your bacon if you let me."

Burne-Jones. A hyphenated Englishman. That went with the rank and the regiment and the pencil-line moustache. If he stood he'd be six two and ramrod straight . . . but then so would Wilderness.

"I'm listening."

Burne-Jones held up the top three pages of

the papers in his right hand.

"You remember this?"

Wilderness didn't.

"It's the test you sat in London last August. It's known as an IQ test. Now, do you know what that stands for?"

Wilderness remembered it now. Word games and pattern recognition. Matching up identical triangles. Juggling rhomboids and trapezoids. The square peg and the round hole. Only an idiot could fail it. He'd thought nothing of it at the time. Just call-up bollocks. It went with the ill-fitting uniform and the beetle-crusher shoes.

"Intelligence Quota?" he ventured.

"Close. Intelligence Quotient. It's a way of measuring intelligence. Assigning a score to it. Would you be interested to know yours?"

"If I say no I go back to chokey?"

"Yes."

"Then I'm all ears."

"One hundred and sixty-nine."

"Big is it?"

"Well, it's bigger than mine. In fact it's bigger than most."

"Bigger than yours? Then maybe I should be the officer?"

"That's right, Holderness, push your luck. I do hope you like bread and water."

"Excuse me, sir. Cheek is a way of life where I come from. Almost a language in itself. It has its own rules and syntax. My point is it must mean something, it must change something or you wouldn't be telling me."

The shift from cockney lout to articulate individual gave Burne-Jones another little pause. An effect Wilderness relished. It was like swapping masks at the ball.

"Quite. It does. It means I'm not going to let you go on square bashing. It would be a waste of everybody's time. You're moving to my operation."

"What? The Guards?"

"Regiments are meaningless. You'll be a trainee for a while, in fact for six months at least. If you pass you'll be in an Intelligence unit, and for the time being that's all you need to know about it. You'll still be in the RAF for purposes of pay and uniform, but effectively not. You need never go on parade again, no one will put you through a crack of dawn kit inspection. You'll answer to me. And I'll tell you now, you make trouble, you fuck up . . . I'll just send you back here for the bunch of twats to pick over your bones."

No was not an option. Technically, in shoving Bodell aside Wilderness had struck an NCO. He'd spent the last four days in the glasshouse. He knew he was looking at six months in a military prison.

"Fine, sir. Where do you want me?"

"Cambridge. Queen's College. You'll be learning Russian and German."

# §30

Much to his surprise this transfer — which
Wilderness saw as something between being
booted out and being rescued — was regarded by the RAF as just another posting.
He was paid up to date — an unprincely two
pounds and six shillings — and he was allowed forty-eight hours embarkation leave.

He avoided Turpin and Bodell, since it
seemed obvious that they would resent his
dodging the glasshouse, would therefore have
it in for him and be looking for one last way
to take a poke — and whilst it was tempting
to make up his bed by numbers, lay out his
kit to a grid and then unzip and piss all over
the lot, it was a temptation readily resisted.

He spent a quiet, sad weekend back in
Sidney Street — Merle poised wistfully in
front of a cold cup of tea lamenting the
downturn in trade since peace broke out —
walked the streets of the old manor in search
of faces he knew, concluded that everyone
he'd ever known, every kid and every scallywag, was now in uniform and elsewhere, and
boarded a Cambridge train at Liverpool
Street Station two days later, not glad to be
there, or anywhere, but feeling that he was
nowhere, and hoping this sensation would
not last.

Much more to his surprise Burne-Jones met

him off the London train at Cambridge Station.

"You thought I wouldn't show up?" Wilderness asked.

"Nothing of the kind. And don't look a gift horse in the mouth. Or in this case a gift MG in the radiator."

Wilderness had never thought much about cars. They had always been beyond his reach. He knew no one who owned a car. He'd never even been in a London taxi. He'd not yet learnt to drive. But if he did, when he did, this, a neat little open-topped 1938 MG two-seater, was what he'd like to own.

"Sling your kit bag in the back."

Driving up Hills Road towards Parker's Piece, Burne-Jones said, "You're in digs a couple of streets from here. There'll be no room in college, what with dozens of chaps returning to pick up the degrees they put on hold during the war. But you'll be fine. Besides, you get a taste of living in hall and it could spoil you for life."

"Maybe I'm ready to be spoiled. Very few opportunities to get spoiled have come my way."

"My point exactly. You're vulnerable. Seducible by easy living. And if you get seduced . . . you're no bloody good to me."

Wilderness handed over his kit bag to his new landlady — an aproned, tiny, floury, cockney woman called Mrs. Wissit, who looked not unlike his great-aunts and who did not look likely to seduce him — and dashed back to the car.

"We'll go into college. I'll introduce you to a few people I know."

"You went to Cambridge yourself?"

"Yes. Magdalene. 1920 to 1923, and again in 1926 for my master's. Hasn't changed much. I'll show you around. There'll be about a dozen other chaps doing the crash course with you. And if you could try to remember ranks for the rest of the afternoon, mine included, I'm sure we'll all get along pretty well. Just say sir from time to time, on the basis that everyone you meet today, whether in civvies or in uniform, will probably outrank you."

"I'll do my best."

"Just try, Holderness. Just fucking try!"

# §31

Wilderness became aware of the phenomenon of town and gown, and equally aware that he was neither. He mixed with undergraduates without being one of them, and while though he wasn't exactly town, he never wore a gown, he wore his RAF uniform. He was one of twelve students of Russian and German assigned to a short-term course by His Majesty's Forces. Two RAF, four Royal Navy, two of whom were the same age as Wilderness but not the same class, and were newly-commissioned sub-lieutenants — that is green whilst being blue — and six soldiers, two of whom were NCOs in their mid-twenties, far from green, who had seen combat in the war and elected to stay on with Burne-Jones's unit. They also elected to have nothing but contempt for the "kids," officers or other ranks, who had not taken part in the war, and that was everyone else on the course. In between the active and the inactive, but receiving no less contempt was a fat artillery bombardier with a broad Birmingham accent, and a demeanour of contained misery, who had been called up in 1942 and had spent the entire war in England as a driver.

"Even rationing doesn't make me thin. I reckon they did me a favour. Too fat to be fit. Basic training was a total bloody nightmare. Jump this, jump that. I look like Porky Pig and they wanted me to be Road Runner. So I got trained as a driver. Jeeps, staff cars . . . driving officers and nobs. I drove Anthony Eden across London once during a V-1 raid."

Wilderness wondered if this was Bombardier Clark's way of saying he had done his bit. He didn't care if he had or not.

"Could you teach me to drive?"

"O' course. But we haven't got a car."

"You leave that to me."

However superior the NCOs felt, it was

Clark and Wilderness who shone at languages. In weekly tests of what they had learnt, Wilderness came top and Clark invariably second, followed by the two navy sub lieutenants and everyone else an also-ran. It narked the NCOs, but not half as much as Wilderness's inability to respect them, their rank or their experience.

On one of his occasional, unannounced spot checks — roaring up in his MG, a dozen belt-fed machine-gun questions rattled off — Burne-Jones found Wilderness bruised, scabby, and with an Elastoplast over one eyebrow.

"What happened?"

Wilderness would not tell him that the two infantry corporals had given him a kicking for his cheek, but Burne-Jones was no fool and readily deduced it.

"You want to report this?"

"Of course not. You think I can't handle a pair of fucking twats?"

"Holderness, is everyone in a uniform a fucking twat to you?"

"No. Just the NCOs, and to prove it you can have a sir at the end of this sentence, sir."

"I hope I don't come to regret you Holderness, I really do."

"I'm good at this, you won't have any reason to regret it."

"Quite."

One of those non-committal toff words that Wilderness was adjusting to — it was less than meaning, more than punctuation.

"I'm not only good. I'm the best you got right now."

"That I can't deny. Top of the form. But is there a point to you telling me this?"

"Yeah. The quid quo . . . quid . . ."

"Quid pro quo. Nice try, Holderness."

"I want something in return."

"We don't make deals."

"It isn't much. In fact it'll cost you nothing."

Burne-Jones could have walked away at any moment. He didn't. His look said "try me."

"Birch," said Wilderness.

"What?"

"Aircraftman Alexander Birch. The kid who pissed himself on parade."

"Ah, yes I do indeed recall."

"I want him out."

"Meaning?"

"He's still back in Essex doing his basic training, while I'm here leading the life of Riley. I want him out."

"I've no use for him, Holderness. You were the only one who met the IQ requirements."

"I'm not talking about that. What I mean is I want him out of the RAF. Away from those tosspots who'll drive him to suicide before his ten weeks are up. Get him discharged. Medically unfit."

141

"But he was passed fit or he wouldn't be in the bloody RAF."

"Then un-pass him."

"He's got two years to serve, just like everyone else."

"You can do it."

"It's not that easy."

"Never said it was. But if it were impossible you'd have said impossible."

"Two years, Holderness."

"Fine. If the king can't spare 'em, I'll serve his two bleedin' years. You can sign me up till 1949."

"You're not joking?"

"Just get him out and back in civvies before those fuckers kill him."

"Was he charged after the piss incident?"

"No. They blamed me for everything."

"Jankers?"

"All they could pile on I'd imagine, but no formal charges."

"Alright, you have a deal. And you tell no one. Mr. Birch will be back in Civvy Street by the end of the week."

"Thank you sir. You are a gentleman . . . and I am a scholar."

The grin was too much for Burne-Jones.

"Don't push it, Holderness. And don't let altruism ruin you. Or you'll be no bloody use to me."

Burne-Jones got back in his MG. Wilderness went in search of a dictionary and

142

looked up "altruism." It was not something he thought would trouble him much.

# §32

It was tempting to be a schoolboy and slip laxative into the cocoa of the two infantry corporals or to let down the tyres of their ubiquitous Cambridge bikes, but it went against the grain of everything he had learnt from his grandfather, chiefly that vengeance could and should be tempered with profit.

It was easy enough to find out where they boarded, and almost as easy to slip in when no one was home and rob them of everything worth stealing. Two burglaries in a single wet afternoon while both corporals were stuck in remedial German grammar would point the finger squarely at him, so he chose the digs of the bigger, nastier of the two and netted seven pounds seven and sixpence in cash, a pair of gold cuff links, a silver cigarette case and several back issues of *Men Only*. It felt odd, like practising an instrument after months of neglect — a strange tingling in the fingertips as though they itched not for the easy pickings of petty theft, but for a safe.

On his next trip to London he sold the gold and silver to Abner's fence and on his return took Clark out for an off-the-ration meal at one of the city's better restaurants. Much to the bafflement of the waiters they conducted their entire conversation in two languages. Clark would speak in German, and Wilderness was obliged to respond to whatever he said in Russian. And vice versa.

"Мне кажется, что если мы не были в форме, они уже позвонили бы Полиции." Wilderness said.

*"Verdammt richtig."* Clark replied.

Wilderness switched to English over the coffee, not yet feeling he could string out every vital thought at its proper speed in any foreign language.

"I've never eaten in a restaurant before."

"I can tell," said Clark.

"Not counting chippies of course."

"I have. When I was a War Office driver, the back pay used to pile up by dribs and drabs and about once a month a few of us would go up West and have a bit of a blowout. It's what got me interested in languages, reading menus in French."

"Like what?"

*"Filet mignon."*

"What does that mean?"

"Steak, posh steak."

*"Et pommes dauphinoises."*

"You got me there, Eddie."

"Spuds in milk."

"Sounds awful."

"It's not."

"Y'know. One day, I'm going to go into one of those posh restaurants and eat my way through the menu."

"Literally?"

"Nah . . . but have anything, absolutely anything I want."

Clark paused, drew breath.

"You've never really lived have you, Joe?"

"I'm eighteen and a half, Eddie. How much living do you want me to have done?"

"I'm only twenty-three meself. What I mean is England isn't one world, it's several. Let's not kid ourselves that because we're on first-name terms with a couple of navy sub-lieutenants and the colonel's not above using our first names when it suits him, that us and them live in the same world. We don't. Going up West was a wartime treat. It would have been unpatriotic for any restaurant to have been snotty with us, but the war's over. English snottiness will be back in spades. And we'll be down the chippie."

"I say, waiter, cod and chips twice with an extra helping of mushy peas and a saveloy. Pip pip!"

Clark giggled.

"How do you do that? You sound just like Burne-Jones."

"Ain't difficult Eddie, and if all it takes to pass for a toff is sounding like one and looking like one . . . well . . . their world is ours for the taking isn't it? A bit of ventriloquism and a decent tailor and it's ours."

"I'm not sure I want it."

"I do. I want the bleedin' lot. I wants what's mine, and if some other tosser's got it I want what's his too."

"For a chit of a kid, you certainly scare me sometimes, Joe."

# §33

Wilderness had no idea why or how a serving officer might come to pawn his uniform, but at the back of a dusty, cobwebbed window in a pawn shop in the Mile End Road there hung the jacket and trousers of what his fag cards (buttons grouped in fives, ludicrously embossed with leeks) told him was a second lieutenant in the Welsh Guards.

Wilderness asked.

"Yeah, I remember him. Three sheets to the fuckin' wind 'e was. One day in, I reckon it was January 1943. Said he'd come on leave without evening dress and could he swap his uniform for a full DJ and dickie until Monday morning. Well, I got five bob off him up front, 'cos if he never come back I was stuck with the bleedin' thing wasn't I? And he never did. Not seen him again from that day to this. Either he was so pissed he forgot where the shop was, and if he weren't pissed and lost, what was he doin' in the bleedin' Mile End Road in the first place? . . . or he copped it. Either way I got stuck with his uniform."

"Two quid," said Wilderness.

"Three," said the pawnbroker. "This ain't tat. This is the proper clobber. Gieves and Hawkes. Savile Row tailors they are."

"Two pound ten."

"Done, but yer robbin' me blind, son."

Looking in Merle's full-length mirror on the front of her wardrobe he thought, "Not bad. Bit shorter than me, a bit fuller."

Merle said, "Nobody looks at your feet. The length don't matter. Tighten your belt and the tum'll be OK. What people look at is your face. If you're going to pull off the stunt I think you're going to then what you need is a proper haircut — and I don't mean the ninepenny barber down the road. I mean a proper job. Half a dollar up West."

In an alley off Jermyn Street, he strangled his vowels, got a haircut for half a crown — a ludicrous sum of money, but the trick, he knew, was to suppress all sense of the ludicrous — and took himself for tea at the Café Royal.

Café Royal was nothing more to him than a name. He'd never been there. He had no idea if royalty might be there. One of his childhood heroes was forever eating there, but A. J. Raffles was fictional. He'd no idea what would be on the menu, but assumed that at four o'clock they would probably be serving tea and cake. All he had to do was catch his dropped aitches before they hit the carpet.

It was a caff. Just a caff. A caff glorified by

waiters dressed like penguins, by a lick of paint and a clean cloth on every table, but a caff.

He was shown to a table with a degree of obsequiousness unknown in the Mile End Road — and over Assam and Battenberg pretended to read the *Daily Express* while looking at and listening to everything around him.

It reminded him of going out on jobs with Abner. He was peeking into other rooms and other lives. It was the same feeling he got creeping around in some rich woman's bedroom. Every sight, every scent was fascinating. The real difference was not in his visibility — he was surely almost as invisible at four in the afternoon under electric chandeliers as he had been in the crepuscular light by which Abner worked. The real difference was he had not snuck in through a window or shinned down a soil stack, he had walked in through the revolving door. It wasn't his world, it might never be his world, but it was just a game, a game of manners and illusions and deceptions, and at that a game he could play. Raffles got away with everything. He could be as fake as Raffles, and get away with everything.

# §34

Eddie Clark did not agree.

"You stupid bugger. Masquerading as an officer. It's a court-martial offence!"

"So?"

"Supposing you'd been rumbled?"

"I wasn't. I remembered to tip the waiter. I got a cab to King's Cross. Tipped the cabbie. Once I was on the train I nipped in the bog and changed back into my RAF togs. Nobody rumbled me. In fact I've found only one thing not to like about being a toff."

"And what might that be?"

"All this tipping lark. Never had to do that before. But then I've never had tea at the Café Royal or ridden in a cab before."

"And your point is?"

"My point? My point . . . my point is it's our world Eddie, not theirs."

# §35

The first car they stole was a 1937 Crossley 26/90. A plain four-door model with no exotic, athletic ornament on the radiator cap — as though Crossley Motors had anticipated the austerity to come.

"We don't want to attract too much attention, now do we?"

"Joe — I don't want to attract any attention. I'm not past a bit of coupon fiddling, but I've never nicked anything in my life."

"We aren't stealing it, Eddie."

"How do you reckon that?"

" 'Cos if there's no one about when we've finished, I'll put it back where we found it. And if you have any of those hooky petrol coupons about your person we'll even put a gallon in the tank for him. Now I'm going to head out in the direction of Trumpington, you just tell me when I do something wrong."

Eddie told him not to crunch the gears, to ease his foot off the clutch not just let go of it, to make more use of the mirrors.

"You're not half bad for a beginner," he said. "Get some miles in and you'll pass."

The coast being clear, Wilderness parked the car back where he had found it. As they walked away, he taught Eddie a thing or two.

"Never look over your shoulder. It's a dead giveaway."

"Whatever you say. But . . ."

"Yeah? What?"

"Are we going to go on nicking cars?"

"Don't see why not. Nobody loses. Bloke who owns the Crossley made half a gallon of petrol and still has all his coupons."

"Then, next time, would you nick something a bit smaller."

Two days later, they had arranged to meet by Jesus Green. Clark stood watching as Wilderness roared up in a 1938 MG.

150

"This small enough?"

"But . . . but . . . that's Burne-Jones's car."

All the way to Newmarket, Eddie said nothing.

On the way back he said, "You're still not using your mirrors and you stay in third too long."

Then he said, "Do you do things like this just because you can?"

"Not quite with you there, Eddie."

"I mean — what are you trying to prove? You could have nicked any car. You didn't have to nick Burne-Jones's."

He insisted on getting out at Parker's Piece, well short of the city centre, well short of Queens.

"Y'know Joe . . . I think I'll get shot if I stick with you."

# §36

About a week later, Burne-Jones called Wilderness to a meeting in rooms at Queens.

"You're doing very well. In fact too well."

"How do make that out?"

"You're ahead of the class. I am told that the pace at which you learn is forcing the tutors to speed up and that isn't working out for the rest of them. Hence I've arranged more private tuition for you. Native Russian speaker. Probably the best tutor in the business. Think of it as your finishing school. It'll mean you going up to London twice a week, but I doubt that'll be a hardship for you. Tuesdays and Fridays from now on."

Burne-Jones fished around in his pockets, found a battered, dog-eared calling card and handed it to Wilderness.

Wilderness looked at it.

Countess Rada Lyubova
99 Douro Mansions
Cornwall Gardens
London SW7
Tel: Knightsbridge 349

"Not your neck o' the woods I suppose?"

"I might have seen it from the top of a bus. Where is it exactly?"

"Sort of between the Albert Hall and Earl's Court."

Ah — he knew now. He and Abner had pulled a couple of jobs in Earl's Court.

"This Friday? Like tomorrow?"

"Yes, Holderness, tomorrow. Just gives you time to fit in another driving lesson."

Wilderness stared at him and said nothing.

Burne-Jones threw him the car keys. Wilderness almost dropped them, clutching them to his blouse with one hand.

"I'd prefer it if you didn't hot wire my car, and if you could see your way clear to making it two gallons of petrol this time I'd be most appreciative."

Wilderness looked at the piece of paper again.

"Countess? What do I call her?"

"You'll think of something. Either that or she'll tell you. But it's what you tell her that matters. She is a Russian. Don't ever forget it. And I've never been quite sure whose side she bats for. So you tell her nothing you don't have to. Not the names of your fellow students. Nothing. Not the size of your feet. Nothing. Do you understand me, Holderness?"

§37

Cornwall Gardens was like an island shrouded in mist. If you didn't seek it out you'd never stumble on it, tucked away as it was between Victorian extravaganzas — the Albert Hall, the museums — and Victorian practicalities — the curve of the Circle line as it cut its way from Kensington High Street to Gloucester Road.

He could scarcely believe anywhere in central London could be so quiet, so utterly devoid of traffic, only a hundred yards from the Cromwell Road.

Douro Mansions was a large and rather dirty redbrick building sitting next to the railway cutting. A hydraulic lift hoisted him up to the ninth floor, with a smooth motion, silent but for the gentle hiss of water under pressure.

When he rang the bell a small face peered around the door.

"Ah you must be Alec's boy. Aircraftman Wilderness?"

A small woman, with masses of thick, black curls — the high cheekbones and fine lines of a fading beauty.

"Er . . . that's Holderness."

"Quite so, quite so dear boy. Wilderness. I haff been expecting you. Come in, come in."

She left him standing in the open doorway, and, leaning on a walking stick, bustled away to the end of a dim corridor. As he followed he could just make out the dozens of framed photographs that lined the walls — peeling strips of passe-partout, cracked glass, and clinging cobwebs.

She flicked on the overhead light. He could see her clearly now. No more than five foot two, slim, lithe even, but leaning heavily on the duck-head handle of her walking stick.

She met his gaze.

"No, I am not totally increpid, young man. I simply twisted my ankle on the threshold at Derry & Toms department store the day before yesterday."

Increpid? Why not?

"Perhaps I can sue them? Are you familiar with the law?"

"Only in so far as I break it now and then."

She smiled at this. For a moment he

154

thought she might laugh, but it was a bubble that never quite broke the meniscus. He could only guess at her age. She could be anywhere between forty and sixty. He was careless about middle age. Ignorant of middle age. Merle was the oldest person he knew. The countess was not of his era and he had no idea which hers had been. Had she been a girl at the turn of the century? On the eve of the Great War? A Russian beauty to drive the young men wild?

"Husbands," she said, seemingly apropos of nothing.

Then he realised, the photographs. They couldn't all be her husbands. No one could marry that often.

She tapped lightly with her free hand on the one nearest Wilderness's chest.

"My first. Leonid Andreyevich Lyubov. Ten thousand acres and a castle in Estonia. Shot himself in 1915. Couldn't wait for a revolution any longer. Silly bugger."

Her hand moved like a knight advancing on a chess board, across and down.

"My second. Piotr Ilyich Zakrevsky. Composer of romantic symphonies that were thirty years out of date before the ink was dry on the stave. Taken in the flu pandemic at the end of the Great War."

Pawn takes pawn.

"Fyodor Ivanovich Ranevsky. A colonel in the Red Army. Loyal to Trotsky. I left him after six weeks. I never knew what fate befell him after 1924. I asked, of course I asked. Letter after letter. Stalin even replied to one. I had him declared legally dead in 1932, so I could marry my fourth . . ."

Straight up almost to the picture rail — rook to bishop 4, her arm stretching out.

"Graf Klaus von Rittenberg. Another ten thousand acres, another castle, but of course he'd abandoned both in East Prussia years before I met him. Died on me. Just before the last war started. Just as well. A German in London. You English would haff locked him up I daresay — Klaus would haff hated being locked up. I didn't haff the heart for any more husbanding after that. There was the odd candidate, but as you can see I am grown old."

So, she was a German countess. He'd never met a countess before, of any nationality.

She led him into her parlour — a room lined with books, books in shelves, books stacked on tables, books in piles on the floor, and dust everywhere.

She pointed to a large, empty birdcage.

"I also haff no heart for parrots any more. The one before was an artist, could recite almost whole sentences. 'Half a league, Half a league . . .' but then he'd stop. This last was a lazy bugger . . . he'd copy the creaking door or a fart, but he wouldn't say a damn word. So tiresome. Really I was quite glad when he fell off his perch. Now, Alec tells me you are learning Russian?"

"And German."

"Very well, from now until you leave we shall talk in one or the other but not in English. That is the rule. *Verstehen Sie?*"

# §38

Naturally averse to rules of any kind, much to his own surprise, he found Rada's rules acceptable and easy.

He had no idea how to address a countess.

"Call me Rada."

He longed to be out of uniform.

"Wait till the suit you own is better than the uniform the king supplied for free. We both work for him, after all."

On his second visit, the following Tuesday, he found her on the floor, the duck-head walking stick discarded, clipping articles from newspapers with pinking shears. Not the ideal tool, but clearly what she had to hand. They left the clippings with serrated edges. Part news, part history, part dress pattern.

"What are you doing?" he had asked, as the rules demanded, in German. *"Was machen Sie?"*

"Making history," she replied. "In so far as the keeping of the record is the making. Others act. I record. I comment. I rage. I kick against the pricks."

"Sorry, I don't follow."

She prised herself off the floor. Surprisingly supple now the ankle had healed. She led him to the longest wall, the one without a window. A room-wide rack of books and folders.

"How old did you say you were?"

"I didn't, but I'm almost nineteen."

"A boy."

"No. A National Service*man.*"

"Quite so, *un ragazzo.* And you know nothing."

"I know things you don't know."

"Such as?"

"Such as how to open the wall safe you have hidden behind that awful oil painting of some old bloke."

Her head turned to the portrait. He thought she might take offence, but she was smiling.

"My great-uncle Nikolai. How can you tell there is a safe?"

"You hinged the picture at the right hand side. It hangs very differently from the way it would if it were on a wire and a central hook. I spotted it at once."

"Ah. No matter. You see . . . my files. I have clipped the papers since I first arrived here nearly twenty-five years ago. They hold . . . they hold whatever takes my fancy. And that is the wrong word. Most certainly the wrong word. But they are things of which, I say again, you know nothing."

"Am I to blame?"

"Of course not, *ragazzo*. But . . . but . . ."

She pulled at one of the thin cardboard folders, and half a dozen tumbled to the floor.

'Appeasement.'

'The Rhineland.'

'Armageddon.'

'Hitler.'

"Take them, take any, take them all."

"I thought I was here to learn Russian."

"You are here to learn. Does it really matter what?"

"I don't know."

"Then trust me. You are a natural at Russian. And German too for that matter. You don't need me to teach you languages. A quick polish here, a bit of dusting there. A tweak or two at your accent. You will be of much more use to Alec if you know the world as well."

"Alec?"

"Colonel Burne-Jones."

# §39

Later. In bed, at Mrs. Wissit's boardinghouse, he read the file named "Armageddon." It was everything Rada had ever found on the atomic bomb. Indeed, she had been prescient. Long before the bomb had been much more than a fantasy she had clipped the papers in three or four languages — anything she could find on the meetings of obscure physicists at conferences across Europe at which they discussed the atom and its fission at a purely theoretical level. He made a start on French ("Make what use of that you will, Alec") and learnt the names of Niels Bohr, Otto Hahn, Lise Meitner, and Werner Heisenberg. It settled in a sedimentary layer of the mind, compressing slowly into meaning. None of it quite made sense, and none of it would ever quite be wasted. And suddenly it all jerked to the moment, as though kicked into life, as the clippings came almost up to the present and recorded the bombs that had fallen on Japan . . . and the names were names like Robert Oppenheimer, Edward Teller, and Karel Szabo.

## §40

His supposed practice in German and Russian now became a test of how well he could hold his own on current affairs, history, and the arts, in several languages. They would often begin with something close to absurd — she would have him translate an episode of *Tintin,* a page from *Dead Souls,* or the entire menu she'd saved from Quaglino's one night in 1936 . . . *potages, poissons, légumes . . .* there were more ways fish could be cooked than he'd ever imagined in a Mile End chippie . . . *Dieppoise, czarine, meunière.* But that was the point — things he had never imagined. And then they'd dissect the century.

As the days grew longer he stayed later at Cornwall Gardens, often rushing to the Piccadilly Line to arrive at King's Cross or Liverpool Street in time for the last train of the night.

She would talk to him about anything and everything. The people in Petrograd. The weather in Warsaw. The food in Florence . . . the beer in Milwaukee.

How she had danced with Kaiser Bill in 1912 . . . "more charm than you might imagine."

How she had dodged anarchists in Moscow in 1918 . . . "monsters who killed for pleasure."

How she had fled the Bolshevik Cheka . . . "rough justice that became an institution."

How she had turned back at the British lines near Archangel . . . "such folly."

How she had crossed Siberia with the remnants of the Czech Legion . . . "not many ever saw home again."

How she had found herself caught between the Japanese, the Americans, and even the Italians at Vladivostok in 1920 . . . "poor buggers stranded in a land without tomatoes."

How an American infantry major had taken her back to San Francisco with him . . . "I might have married him but for the uncertain fate of my third husband."

How she had landed in England, far from penniless, in 1923 . . . "but money isn't everything."

How she had been wooed by H. G. Wells in 1925 . . . "he loves to talk, usually about himself."

How she had plunged into London society . . . "such a fuss."

How she had danced with the Prince of Wales . . . "such a bore."

How she had slapped von Ribbentropp's face at a reception in 1937 . . . "such a pig."

He stayed later.

On one occasion he slept on the sofa.

"Let us not make a habit of this. I see no reason to let anyone of your age catch me in my dressing gown."

It had been his bad luck, the next morning, to meet Burne-Jones leaving King's Cross as he was entering.

Burne-Jones had said, "Anything I should know about?"

And Wilderness had replied, "How do I know what you think you need to know?"

§41

Late in June, after an evening discussing the crisis in Greece, the demise of the League of Nations, and a recipe for *Oeufs Balzac* (truffle and ox tongue), she had led him out onto the tiny, west-facing terrace. Just big enough for

162

a small table, a couple of chairs and a row of dead plants in terracotta pots. They had watched the sun set over Kensington, making a chiaroscuro of the plain backs behind the ornately fronted Art Deco department stores on the High Street, Pontings, Barker's, Derry & Toms — a reddening sky across all the boroughs beyond that he never quite knew the names of and had never visited — and they had sipped champagne and nibbled on warm toast and chilled caviar. The champagne was off the ration, the caviar probably counted as fish on the coupon — no more or less than cod or kippers — God only knew where she got hold of ice — and the bread wasn't rationed either, though there were rumours that it might be soon. He liked neither fish nor fizz. It was just another recipe, another part of the glossary. No more than a practical test. No more or less than *Tintin* or another egg recipe. As with so many toff things he faked the pleasure and wondered at the cost. Chips and a saveloy, pip pip!

"I could watch sunset all day," she said. "I haff seen sunsets over the Atlas Mountains in North Africa, I haff seen sunsets over the myriad lakes of Finland, and through the giant redwoods of California."

"I never much bothered, meself. Sunset over the East India Dock Road doesn't have the same ring to it. Besides you can't watch them all day. There's only one a day."

163

"On this planet. Who knows about other planets? Perhaps there really is a planet somewhere out there on which one can watch the sun set forty-four times."

"Forty-four? How do you reckon that?"

"Oh . . . one would haff to keep moving the chair of course."

He giggled, snorted champagne, felt the rush of bubbles down his nose.

"And for all that, for all those places . . . a sunset still reminds me of home. And there is no earthly reason why it should."

"Do you miss Russia?"

"Of course."

"Do you wish you could go back?"

"Now you're just being stupid."

"I don't miss Stepney."

"Well . . . not yet anyway . . . but you will. Meanwhile . . . what is the place of birth but a jumping-off point?"

"A what?"

"You are a boy . . . a better-educated boy than when we met, of that I shall flatter myself . . . but a boy. You will miss nothing for a long time to come . . . but one day you will be so far from Stepney . . . physically, morally perhaps, that you will look back at it and wonder how you ever got from there to wherever you are in . . . I pluck a date from the air . . . 1963 . . . an impossible figure . . . only H.G. or Verne could ever conceive of such a time . . . men on the moon . . . a war of the worlds . . . and you will look back . . . believe me you will . . . the physical distance will mean nothing, the moral distance may, but the emotional distance and the passing of time will rip through you like hawk and hand-saw."

She downed half a glass of Veuve Clicquot. A silence he would not fill. No glib remark about the East India Dock Road would do.

"But," she resumed, "if you weren't looking at the sunset or gazing at the stars, what were you doing, Wilderness, looking at the gutter?"

She had forcefully changed tack on him, swung the subject away from herself, away from the tears that had formed in the corners of her eyes but would not roll.

"Not especially," he said, looking down into the bubbles of his champagne, then lifting his eyes past her and staring westward. "Standing in it some of the time, for sure. But mostly I looked at the streets, the people in the streets, and when I wasn't looking at the streets I had me nose in a book. I was . . . I was . . . a . . ."

He looked at her now. The tears had vanished. They might never have been there at all.

"A word child?"

"Yeah. That'll do. That's exactly what I was. A word child. It's what I am. A child of language . . . a word child."

"Of course you are. That is why Burne-Jones chose you."

"Is it? Chose me for what?"

Rada had a way of not answering any question she didn't want to answer. The dark eyes might smile at him, but the lips would move only to change the subject.

"He tells me you have signed on for another two years."

"Yeah, well. He won't hold me to that. He'll have had enough of me after two years' National Service."

But she was shaking her head.

"Oh no, oh no no no."

She made him wait as she downed another half-glass of Veuve Clicquot.

"He has you. He means to keep you."

"Bugger."

"You might have realised that the moment he sent you to me."

A little after eleven she bundled him towards the door, shoved another couple of folders under his arm — "FDR — The Tennessee Valley Authority," "The Death of Leon Trotsky." The short excursion to watch the sunset had made him duck through the rarely opened French window, and he had cobwebs in his hair. She stood on tiptoe, brushed them away and as her fingers ran across his cheek she, who had seemed always to avoid touching, had kissed him on the cheek. The only time she ever did so.

"Rada, what did he choose me for?"

"Спокойной ночи (Good night) Wilderness. It is time for candlewick and cold cream."

# §42

One day, later in that same summer of 1946, a letter arrived at his digs by the second post of the day. It was from his father, contained no return address, and was easily the longest communication of any kind that he had ever received from the man — and the first in four years. Wilderness knew where the regiment had been. He'd been able to follow the course of the war and the regiment's part in it in the newspapers. His father had fought under General Montgomery and helped defeat Rommel, had landed in Sicily, fought up the spine of Italy, through the South Tyrol and into Austria, where he had met up with the Russians or the Americans or both. And only the absence of any letter from the War Office informing him of his father's death gave him reason to think the old man had survived all this. But he had, and here was the final proof scrawled in pencil on lined paper.

Son, I'm due for me demob. Back in Blighty. If you can get away meet me at noon on Saturday. You remember that last holiday me and your Mum took you on before the war? It was 1937 or maybe 1938, we went to stay with your Great-Uncle Ted in Felixstowe, and one day we caught a ferry over the river and walked out along this shingle beach all the way to that martello tower they got out there. I reckon it was called Bawtsey or Battsey or something like. Anyway meet me there.

Dad.

It was Bawdsey beach, and it had been 1936.

Come Saturday, Wilderness caught an early train from Cambridge to Ipswich. In Ipswich he changed for a train to Woodbridge and in Woodbridge he stole a bicycle.

The ride was six or seven miles, and he arrived at the beach pretty well on the dot of noon. Riding a bicycle on shingle is impossible, so he propped it against a groyne and set off on foot for the tower and what he perceived to be a human speck at the water's edge.

Closer, the speck was clearly his father. Closer still, it was his father stark naked, staring out to sea, his khaki uniform a neat, orderly, barrack-room stack at his feet, even down to the crowning effect of the tin hat and the black boots splayed at forty-five degrees. Closer still and Wilderness could see that all his father was wearing were his army dog tags — two small pressed discs, each about the size of a florin, on a green string around his neck.

"Well," Harry said. "Here's a how de do."

It was the sort of thing he would have said to his son ten or twelve years ago — a nonsense phrase for a small boy who strived for literal meanings to puzzle over.

Wilderness looked at his father. He could not recall that he had ever seen him naked, and certainly the man had no sense that he was. The coast of the North Sea is never warm, and for all the beauty of its beaches it is a hardy soul that strips off there on any day. Harry's skin rose up in an alpine terrain of goose pimples, and the muscles in his chest twitched involuntarily. His genitals had contracted to an olive perched atop a walnut. But it was the scars that drew the eye. A brown, bronzed body, taut with muscle, and punctuated by scars.

Across his left arm and left thigh ran raised, paler welts where bullets had skimmed his flesh. Wilderness could imagine him being bandaged up in a field hospital and stood down for a week. On his right thigh was a moon crater where shrapnel had been dug out. Where had that happened? How long had he been hospitalised with a wound as nasty as that? What was a man his age — still under forty by Wilderness's reckoning, but an "uncle" in infantry terms — doing in the front line?

"Yes," he replied. "A bit of a how de do."

"I'm glad you could make it son. We haven't a lot of time."

"Haven't we?"

Harry nodded, a tilt of the head seaward.

"Doesn't do to hang about. I mean to say, once your mind's made up it's made up, innit?"

"I suppose not."

"And there's not a lot to be said."

He paused. It seemed to Wilderness that he was waiting on him, and looking at him without quite seeing him.

"But if I don't say 'em now . . . well. I know it's been tough for you."

Indeed it had. Abner's conviction that Harry had been "a nutter since Dunkirk" was a portion of the truth. Harry had always been a nutter who expressed his emotions with his fists. Dunkirk had simply made him a worse nutter. Shell shock, that old phrase from the last war, did not begin to explain Harry Holderness.

"And," he went on. "What's the bleedin' point of sayin' sorry. What's done is done. So I thought, I should just say goodbye, wish you all the best and hope you make a better job of this life thing than I could."

"Thanks," Wilderness said.

"So . . . I'll be off now. It's good to see yer, and you look a treat in that uniform. RAF, who would have thought it, eh? You're a big lad, you just ain't filled out yet. But you will."

Wilderness was not a copy of his father. As tall, he'd never be as broad. Nor did he have his father's wispy red hair or his dazzling, bright blue, crazy eyes. The eyes that now looked into his.

He was holding out his hand.

"Shake, son?"

Wilderness shook his hand. A more formal parting than he ever would have imagined, and watched as Harry walked out into the North Sea. It evoked the old classroom puzzle. How do you know the earth is round? Because of the way a ship vanishes over the horizon. Wilderness watched Harry until he vanished. And then he stood and stared a while longer in no anticipation of his re-appearance — just to be sure that he had finally gone.

Then he turned to the pile his father had left on the beach.

The boots had no name in them and were two sizes too big. They could be left for some lucky beachcomber.

In the pockets of the blouse he found a packet of Craven "A" cigarettes, with nine still in it, his father's ration book, ID card, and more than fifty pounds in notes. He had, clearly, picked up his back pay and demob gratuity before setting off for Bawdsey — fourteen shillings for every month served was a pittance, but over five years and more it slowly mounted up. In the trouser pockets, twelve shillings and eightpence in change. The last item was a brown paper parcel. He tore it open and found a crushed trilby hat and a shapeless demob suit, pale grey with a thin blue stripe and in the inside pocket of the suit, the War Office documents issued by the demobilisation centre in Wembley formally discharging his father from the Army. Neither the blouse nor the jacket had a name in it. But on the front of the blouse was a row of ribbons, and it seemed to Wilderness that they could be read as a language, that there was a hidden syntax to the strip of reds and blues and greens, whereby an informed person could read the history of Harry Holderness's war and hence, sooner or later, know that these colours had belonged to Harry Holderness. A man's war in a colour palette. A neat and simple semaphore. The strip came away in his hand with a gentle tug, and he tucked it into his trouser pocket. The rest he left. Walked back to the bicycle with the brown paper parcel under his arm.

Wilderness put the bike back where he had found it and boarded the next train for Liverpool Street, London. From there a short hop on the Metropolitan Line (Hammersmith and City branch) took him to Whitechapel Underground, a matter of yards from the house in Sidney Street in which Merle still lived. But he passed the end of

Sidney Street, walked on past the Blind Beggar and the Gaumont cinema to a grimy shop-front on the other side of the Mile End road — "Abel Jakobson Tailor, formerly Minsky & Jakobson est. 1904."

With any luck the irascible Mr. Jakobson would be at home on a Saturday afternoon, or down the Catford dog track, and the premises manned by his diligent, civilised partner, Mr. Hummel — or as Wilderness had known him since he was a boy, Vienna Joe.

"Ah, Johnnie Holderness, looking every inch the hero in his RAF uniform."

"Hello, Mr. Hummel. I was hoping you'd be here. I got a bit of a job for you. I mean, a paying job."

"No problem. I long ago gave up any notion of a Sabbath. Indeed, I have been wondering for a while now which of you street urchins would be the first to knock at our door in search of their first bespoke suit. I am glad it is you, Johnnie. It is a significant *rite de passage*."

"That's not quite what I meant, Mr. Hummel."

Wilderness unwrapped the demob suit. Laid it out on the cutting table.

"Could you tailor this to fit me?"

Hummel turned the suit over in hands, rubbed the fabric between finger and thumb, turned down his mouth at the corners.

"Is it worth the effort?" he asked.

"I don't know. I never owned a suit."

"That's no reason to look like a *shlump*. How much money you got?"

"Enough I reckon."

"Spoken like a cockney miser. Follow me."

Hummel led him over to a hanging rail. Took off the cover and pulled out a single-breasted suit in a plain, dark blue.

"This I made for Captain Gibson of the Sherwood Foresters. In the May of '44. It has hung here in its wrapper these last two years. The poor captain was killed in Normandy before he could collect. Naturally, I wrote to his widow. The suit after all was paid for. But I never received a reply. Captain Gibson was your size. I'd be a poor excuse for a tailor if I could not see that."

"What even without measuring me?"

"I don't need a tape measure, Johnnie. Just try the suit."

Wilderness admired himself in the mirror, his mind juggling clichés . . . a second skin . . . like a glove . . . and comparisons . . . like Cary Grant, like Fred Astaire. The late captain and he had been cast in the same mould.

"How much?"

"Nothing. As I said, the suit is paid for."

"But . . . but it's a much better suit than the one I brought in."

"Such understatement, Johnnie. It is an infinitely better suit than your demob sack. If

I ever talk Billy into opening up in the West End this suit would cost . . . forty-five guineas. That's what Kilgour and French or Henry Poole would charge in Savile Row this very day."

"Fuck me."

*"Genau."*

"Mr. Hummel, if you are, as I think you are, offering to give me this suit, why did you ask how much money I had?"

"Why? Because for two pounds ten shillings I will recut your RAF uniform so that it fits you as well as this suit. You will be the best dressed basher on the square."

"I don't do square bashin' Mr. H. I'm an egghead these days."

Wilderness left his uniform, strolled into Sidney Street wearing his Gibson suit, looking, as Merle told him, like a million dollars.

Lunchtime Monday, he put on his tailored RAF uniform, felt like two million dollars, paid Hummel, and caught the next train back to Cambridge.

He had not told Merle or Hummel about Harry. It would be more than a year before he would tell anyone.

# §43

It was about three months later. Towards the end of October. He let himself into the flat in Cornwall Gardens and called out Rada's name. It was his intention, his desire, to surprise her. Wearing his Gibson suit rather than his uniform for the first time. The suit the king had not bought.

She did not answer. No "Chust a minute, dollink." No "Put the kettle on, *ragazzo.*"

She was sitting upright in her armchair, her chin resting on her chest, a book open on her knees, a folded page of unlined paper wedged into the spine. He read her last words, surprised to find they were addressed to him.

Wilderness, chéri — "Quand tu regarderas le ciel, la nuit, puisque j'habiterai dans l'une d'elles, puisque je rirai dans l'une d'elles, alors ce sera pour toi comme si riaient toutes les étoiles." . . . au revoir, Rada.

He picked up the book to look at the title. What had she chosen to read in the moment of her death? A fairy tale, of sorts: *Le petit prince* by Antoine de Saint-Exupéry.

He lifted her chin.

She was not yet in rigor, and he smelt the scent of almonds on her lips. He did not know how he knew this meant that Rada had taken cyanide, and could only ascribe it to Hollywood films seen on matinees at the Troxy cinema — but he knew she was dead. He did not know where she might obtain cyanide — but he knew she was dead.

He could see the grey roots to her hair. If he had noticed them before, he had blotted them from sight and from memory. Rada had not been old until now. Rada had been ageless until now. If she'd worn a wig . . . he would have noticed . . . Merle's atrocious collection of wigs for her nights on the game had made him aware of wigs . . . but now he saw that dead Rada was old Rada. The years had not slipped away, they had accumulated, the twentieth century had fallen on her in a single coup. The Great War, the Russian revolutions, the death and disease that had followed in the wake, the starvation years of the twenties and thirties, the coming of the Nazis . . . death camps, gulags, total war . . . a continent of refugees . . . ragged, battered humanity on the move . . . everything that had wiped out her generation . . . for whom to grow old was a rarity. The survivors were few. Her false teeth had slipped in her jaw.

She was not yet in rigor. He slipped the teeth back into place.

He looked at the wall safe. It was shut. He looked at the rings on her fingers, at the tangle of necklaces trailing out of a drawer in her rolltop desk. He smelt a faint scent of burning. Looked in the fireplace. A cascading pile of fine, feathery ash, as though she had burnt letters or papers. There'd been no crime here but the obvious one. And all his instincts told him not to get involved.

177

He took out his handkerchief — a linen one, one of half a dozen she had given him on his birthday only a couple of months ago — and wiped everything he thought he had touched. He picked up the book, stuck it in his pocket, closed the door behind him, wiped the doorknob and went back to his digs in Cambridge.

He told no one.

Lying on the bed, he read *Le petit prince* at a single sitting.

He learnt of the forty-four sunsets, and . . .

Quand tu regarderas le ciel, la nuit, puisque j'habiterai dans l'une d'elles, puisque je rirai dans l'une d'elles, alors ce sera pour toi comme si riaient toutes les étoiles.

He put the book on the shelf with the folders she had given him in ones and twos and half dozens. He had forty-eight. His private university. He would never part with any of them.

He told no one.

Not Eddie.

Eddie had been posted in August.

Not Burne-Jones.

Burne-Jones told him.

The next morning Mrs. Wissit called him to the hall, where the telephone sat in exile from the warmth of the kitchen, as though it might emit rays and curdle the milk or rot the brain.

"Were you due for a session with Rada yesterday?"

"Yes. But, I was coughing fit to bust, so I put it off. I'll be going up later today instead."

"You told her this?"

"No. She hated the phone. Always said if I couldn't make it just to show up the next day."

He hoped that sounded believable.

"Joe — she died yesterday. Looks like suicide, but you never know."

"Then I won't be going."

"Yes. Come up to town. I'm there now. In her apartment. I need you to do something for me."

# §44

There was a London bobby on the door of the block and another at the door of the flat. Both just said "Mr. Holderness?" and waved him in.

The body had been removed.

Someone had raked through the ashes in the fireplace.

Burne-Jones was sifting through the papers that remained on Rada's desk.

"Good of you to come," he said. As if Wilderness had any choice.

The painting in front of the wall safe that had so scarcely disguised it was open. The safe wasn't.

"Can you open that?"

Wilderness looked at the safe. Then he looked at Burne-Jones.

"Tell me. Is there anything you don't know about me?"

"Can you do it or not?"

Of course he could do it. It was rather small wall-mounted Cyrus Price, operating on a combination. Half the defence was in its concealment. The door and the tumblers would be simple.

"Yes I can do it. Give me five minutes of silence and I'll have it open."

"Good, because —"

"I mean, silence. You have to shut up, and you have to stop rustling papers."

"Alright."

Burne-Jones sat down. Folded his arms. A child under sufferance. Instantly bored, he then picked up a book off the nearest pile and began to leaf through it.

Wilderness took a tumbler from the kitchen and pressed it to the safe door with his ear. It took him less than five minutes. As he swung the door open Burne-Jones got up. Snapped the book shut, as though pointedly breaking the silence, and stuffed it in his jacket pocket — just as Wilderness had done only yesterday.

"A souvenir of Rada. *Le rouge et le noir* by Stendhal. Read it when I was about twenty-five. If I'd read it at sixteen I rather think my life would have been utterly different. Now, is there anything in there?"

Wilderness passed him a fat sheaf of papers.

"No jewellery or anything like that?"

"That was all in her desk. She didn't seem to care much about it. But."

"But what?"

"But . . . you're not interested in jewellery in the first place . . . and there's a false panel at the back. Easy trick on the manufacturer's part. You get the door open, make off with what you find and don't think there might be a second compartment."

Wilderness took out his penknife and prised off the back panel.

"Letters."

"Letters?"

"See for yourself."

Wilderness handed over a bundle bound up in black twine. Burne-Jones turned it over in his hands. Riffled the letters like cards and stopped about halfway through.

"Good Lord. Just look at these. Half a dozen of them. The edges of the envelopes, sewn up in cotton like the hem of a dress, and then sealing wax . . . talk about belt and braces. Never seen anything like it. Someone didn't want these read by anyone but the person they're addressed to."

He threw them all back to Wilderness, sat down again, bent over the first pile of papers. Flicking rapidly through them.

"Are you looking for anything in particular?"

"I've no idea what I'm looking for. She left no note . . . so . . ."

Wilderness sat down and looked at his much smaller share of the loot. They were all letters, complete with envelopes, stamps and postmarks and all from well before the war. Some more than thirty years old. The foreign stamps were those he had collected as a boy . . . Germany: Weimar stamps in millions of marks, Nazi stamps with Hitler's face in shitty brown . . . Russia: Tsarist stamps with the imperial eagle, Soviet stamps crudely overprinted to cope with inflation . . . France: stamps with revolutionary maidens in flowing dresses looking as though they had stepped straight from the barricades in a Delacroix painting. It was how he had learnt geography . . . and it was now how he learnt history, as Rada had lived it.

He opened one, delicately sliding his fingers between the slit threads and the paper, watching a brittle flake of red sealing wax break off and fall to the floor.

"Sorrento. November 22, 1924." The paper dull, the ink faded, the Cyrillic handwriting precise as its era and devoid of modern scrawl — 'Дорогой Радочке.'

He opened a second.

"Tripoli. January 10, 1936." Another precise hand, a geometric regularity, almost a typeface in itself — "Rada, chérie, j'ai tant de choses à te dire . . . le sable, les étoiles . . ."

"Anything?" Burne-Jones said, still not looking up.

"Anything like what?"

"Anything that might explain her death or might tell me one way or the other who Rada really worked for. I said I was never certain. I'd be delighted to find out it was us."

"So, what am I looking for? An uncashed cheque from Joe Stalin?"

"Cut the flippancy."

"No," said Wilderness. "Nothing like that. They're love letters."

She had saved the love letters and she had burned what? If Burne-Jones would not utter this, nor would he.

Burne-Jones looked up.

"What? Hidden at the back? Love letters? Love letters from whom?"

Burne-Jones seemed genuinely surprised, almost incredulous, as though an unimagined side of her nature was unfolding before him. Wilderness was not surprised. The facts were new, not the feeling.

"Well," he said. "This one's from Maxim Gorky . . ."

"Ah . . . makes sense, I suppose. She knew Stalin, she knew Stravinsky. She'd know Gorky as well, wouldn't she?"

"And this is from Antoine de Saint-Exupéry."

"Who's he?"

"Another writer." Wilderness said, feeling for the first time that he knew something Burne-Jones didn't. "They were both writers."

# §45

*The British Zone,* Germany: Spring 1945

When the Führer announced the formation of the Volkssturm in October 1944, Max Burkhardt said, "That's it. He's calling up old men and boys. We're fucked now." He might have added "cripples too" as he, born with a club foot and hence lame for life, found himself pressed into service in the Volkssturm at the beginning of November.

Shortly before Christmas, convinced that Germany would lose the war and that Berlin would fall to the Russians, who had already entered Slovakia and were at the gates of Warsaw, if Warsaw had any gates left after the SS had finished with it, Max's wife, Marie Burkhardt, sent their fifteen-year-old daughter Hélène west to live with Great-Uncle Klaus, the elder brother of her late mother, in a village a few miles north of Celle, a mile or so off the road to Bergen, in Lower Saxony.

21 Pfefferstraße,
Charlottenburg,
Berlin
17 XII 1944

. . . She is a bright child, she loves to learn — but an innocent, so trusting I fear that her life will be one in which others take advantage of her. But she is brave. She has stamped her little foot and stood up for what she thinks is right, however wrong she might be, since she first learnt to talk. Take good care of her Klaus and she will be all the reward you could ever ask for.

Your loving niece,<br>Marie

ps Beware of her "po" face. It's her biggest, perhaps her only failing.

Nell Burkhardt had spent the war in Berlin. Berlin was all she knew. She had no wish to leave. When the city Hitler had told his people would never be bombed was bombed late in 1940, the Nazis responded with typical efficiency with the *Kinderlandverschickung* — a scheme more aptly and more curtly named "evacuation" by the British. Berlin's children would, effectively, be deported to rural homes and specially built camps. Nell was eleven. She had no wish to leave, and her parents — Marie, a former university tutor and Maximilian, a civil engineer for the City of Berlin — easily evaded the rules by telling the medical examiner that Nell wet the bed each night. They might just as well have said she had bubonic plague or was Jewish. Her name was off the list. She would live or die in her own wet bed.

By 1944 everything had changed. The RAF had sent bombers over in wave upon wave of hundreds of aircraft, and while the death toll was low, and Berlin had not burned like a Roman candle or, more aptly, like Hamburg, the damage to the city had been vast. Besides, the RAF and the USAF were as nothing — the tide of the war in the East had turned at Stalingrad and only a fool would think the Slavic horde would not be the first to march down Unter den Linden. So when her mother put her on a train to Celle, Nell complied. A small fawn knapsack with red leather straps contained almost all she would ever keep from her childhood.

Great-Uncle Klaus met her at the station with a pony and trap. She had seen him only once before, sometime in the midthirties, and while she had changed to the point where it might have made sense to wear a label, he had not — conspicuous by the fulsomeness of his moustache, the look of a man a generation or more out of date. Modernity an age he would never come to know.

Nell had no real idea how old Klaus was,

and guessed at seventy. He had fought in the last war, and according to her mother had been middle-aged even then. He had come back from the Western Front, from the Second Battle of the Marne, a disappointed though hardly broken man, adorned with *Eiserne Kreuze* first and second class, had raised pigs in the gentlemanly manner and done his best to ignore politics, and with it history. The weather forecast mattered more to him than any speech Adolf Hitler could ever make.

Great-Uncle Klaus, being childless, had no vocabulary with which to talk to a fifteen-year-old. He sidestepped the obligation to send her to school, declined to enrol her in the local *BdM,* and offered her free access to his library — and whilst in most houses this might mean a shelf of forty or fifty books, in his it meant a room dedicated to reading, containing ten thousand books, in which Nell could continue her education on her own — ten thousand books which, she rapidly concluded, Klaus had inherited and never opened, so honed were his interests. She blew off the dust, and took a paper knife to uncut pages.

Klaus had taught himself to cook after all his household staff were directed into war work in 1941, and once the evening meal was served would engage her in conversation about the only things that seemed to interest him — Shakespeare, Beethoven, Mahler, and pigs. She knew next to nothing about the last three of these and was happy to learn. When the meal was over, often as not, the old man would wind up the gramophone and play records . . . Bruno Walter conducting Mahler's Ninth, Artur Schnabel playing Beethoven piano sonatas. And afterwards, a finger pressed to his lips and a gentle "ssshhh," he would tune the radio set in to the BBC.

Nell passed the most austere Christmas of her life, and had no complaints. Letters arrived from her mother, but no presents —

"There is nothing left to buy in Berlin except Berlin itself."

And in January she turned sixteen and passed the most austere birthday of her life.

When the thaw came, late in March, a vast plume of smoke appeared in the sky a few miles to the north, black, turning grey, and a sickly-sweet smell of cooking fat hung over the house.

"What is it?" she asked.

Klaus stood on the threshold, his eyes fixed on the plume of smoke.

"The camp," he said.

"Camp? What camp?"

He turned and went inside. Nell followed.

A soundless, invisible stamping of the little foot.

"What camp? A *Kinder* camp? A prisoner of war camp?"

He sat at the dinner table.

"You have not heard?"

"Heard what?"

"And I have not told you. Remiss of me perhaps, but I had rather you had not known, and now it seems you must. A concentration camp. A camp into which the Nazis throw people in order to forget about them — the biggest oubliette in the world — a concentration camp that exceeds even the Nazi imagination. And, if what I am told in the town is true, they have been shipping in prisoners from the east, from other camps, for months now . . . Poles, Russians, Jugoslavians . . . Dutch, French, and Belgians that have shuttled back and forth across the Reich. Just so the Russians capture empty camps and free no one — and this one, Bergen-Belsen, overflows until it bursts."

"And the burning and the smell?"

"I fear they are burning the dead. Of whom there may well be thousands."

That night, as ever, they listened to the BBC and she learnt that the Russians were only a few kilometres from Berlin and that the distant booming that had peppered the sky for days now was the advance of the British.

It was about three weeks later; she stepped out into the sparse sunshine of an April

189

morning. Crisp, scentless air. There had been no more bonfires of the dead. She had asked questions in the town — no one but Klaus seemed to know anything about the camp — indeed the grocer had turned her out of his shop for daring to ask and upsetting his customers, and the burgomeister, another veteran of the last English war and an old friend of Klaus, had told her it was "nothing you should worry about." It seemed to her that the only words missing from his evasion had been "pretty little head."

Klaus had shot his dog in 1943. The dog was old, and he would have hated to see her starve to death. Since then the kennel had stood empty, halfway down the track between the road and the house — its felt roof peeling back and its timbers rotting.

As she approached a hand stuck out of the arch and a guttural voice said, *"Gib mir Tabak."*

She hesitated; the voice spoke again, *"Gib mir Tabak."*

She knelt down. The hand extended from a ragged cotton sleeve of dirty white with blue stripes. Where the roofing felt had parted a thin shaft of sunlight cut across the face of a gaunt unshaven man, hunched up with his knees against his chest. She could name every bone in the hand that held itself out to her, phalanx, carpal, metacarpal — it was less a limb than an anatomical drawing. Bone merely sheathed in skin.

*"Gib mir Tabak."*

She ran to the house. Klaus did not smoke cigarettes. She found a pipe and tobacco and matches.

A second arrangement of bones emerged to grasp the pipe, the first tamped in tobacco and struck the match, then both withdrew into the kennel and a cloud passed across the face of the sun, the stripe of light vanished, and only a wisp of fragrant smoke drifting out showed where the man was.

Later she and Klaus split their rations three ways and she put a portion of their evening meal out on a plate, just as she would in giving leftovers to a dog.

"He must have escaped," Klaus said simply.

The next morning she approached with bread and apple jam and ersatz coffee made from roasted acorns. Last night's plate was empty, but next to it a pile of vomit.

*"Gib mir Tabak."*

A British jeep roared by.

*"Gib mir Tabak."*

The jeep pulled up sharply and reversed.

*"Gib mir Tabak."*

Two men got out. A corporal-driver who stood by the car and a captain who approached her.

*"Gib mir Tabak."*

The captain had the initials R.A.M.C. on a band sewn onto each shoulder, atop a large and curious serpent symbol. He looked at the hand, he looked at the house, he looked at her.

"Do you live here?"

Accurate, if oddly accented German.

"With my uncle. An old man."

He knelt down, peered into the dog kennel.

*"Gib mir Tabak."*

"How long has he been here?"

"Since this time yesterday."

"He must have escaped. The Wehrmacht have gone. There's just a few SS left now. He must have just slipped out. I'll have to take him back."

"But . . ."

"But what?"

"The Wehrmacht have gone. You just said so. They have surrendered. There is no need to take him back."

"Oh no, my dear. Not a surrender, just a truce. We took the camp without a shot fired, that was the deal. He has escaped from us not them. I can't let him go or let any of the prisoners go. Typhus, you see. It could spread like a forest fire."

He knelt down again.

"Come on, old chap, we'll soon have you fixed up."

What came back was gibberish to him.

"Oh hell."

Nell said, "I think the only German he knows is how to ask for tobacco. He answered you in Polish."

*"Gib mir Tabak."*

"And at least let me get him some."

She dashed into the house, came back with a fat pinch of Klaus's tobacco. Both hands appeared, the tamping down and the lighting up.

"You speak Polish?"

"Yes."

"Well . . . see if you can't coax him out."

Before she could say a word a big British Army truck came up the road from Celle and stopped by the jeep. A short fat Army major climbed down from the cab. The captain saluted, after a fashion.

"What's going on here?"

The captain explained and when he had finished the major turned and bellowed at the truck.

"Jones! McKay! Crawley! On the double!"

Three enlisted men came running.

"Get this bugger on the truck. Now!"

Then he turned to Nell.

"You too, and anyone else who lives here. Crawley, round 'em up."

The first two men lifted the roof off the dog kennel, then they lifted out the skeletal man clamped on the end of Klaus's pipe. He made no move to cooperate, said nothing, and blew smoke. It seemed to Nell he was weightless and if the soldiers let go he might drift off into air as lightly as his puffs of smoke. The third soldier emerged from the house, gently propelling Klaus along with the flat of his hand against his back.

He slung his rifle, slipped his free hand around Nell's upper arm and escorted them both to the back of the truck. The skeletal man sat on the edge by the tailgate, still hunched up, bony chin resting on bony knees, drawing on the now lifeless pipe. Klaus reached into his pocket and handed him more matches. The crab hands flicked one into life.

As the tailgate swung up another truck drew up next to them. While the drivers talked, across the gap, Nell saw the burgomeister, wedged in between the grocer and the man who ran the pharmacy. He turned away from her gaze. She looked around. The two trucks held perhaps forty or fifty locals — sullen, resentful, or merely perplexed — and the skeletal man, who was none of these. She could see him clearly for the first time now, skin the colour of parchment, stretched across the cheekbones as tight as timpani, and as the truck jerked into life she fell down next to him and found herself looking into eyes that did not look back.

# §46

The small convoy of two trucks and a jeep arrived at the gates of Bergen-Belsen in a matter of minutes. The jeep led, and the truck carrying the burgomeister, the pharmacist, the grocer and, it seemed, every other district notable, overtook them as the first truck stopped to unload the prisoner. Two Tommies lifted him down, his teeth still clenched around the pipe, his limbs still tucked into his chest and sides as though minimising his place in the world.

When they set him down Nell thought he might unwind like a watch spring, but he stayed hunched, sucking on the last of Great-Uncle Klaus's tobacco.

She jumped down, the Tommies seemed not to notice her as they banged the tailgate shut and drove on another hundred metres.

Nell looked around her, lifted her eyes from this lone, troubling individual to the scene in which she had landed. She was washed ashore, driftwood bobbing at the edge of an unknown world, flotsam in a lagoon of barbed wire, marooned upon the dark side of the moon. He was not a lone individual, he was one of thousands.

Everywhere she looked living skeletons squatted, naked and half naked, everywhere she looked vacant eyes looked at nothing, everywhere she looked men, women, and children lay prone as sleeping dogs or hunkered down to shit where they were. And beyond them the dead, body piled upon body as they had been tossed out and tossed aside — rat-gnawed limbs, bird-pecked eyes and

195

the concave stomachs of the starved.

She followed the trail in the dust left by the trucks, past wooden huts onto a flat parade ground. It resembled a grotesque jamboree. The British had provided tents, and the prisoners had lit campfires — fires by the dozen, fires by the hundred. A thousand billycans of boiling water. She picked her way across in a haze of smoke and steam.

She peered into one of the huts. The smell hit her like a blow to the gut — death and shit and decay. The full blast of the corruption that wafted and faded all the way to Celle when the wind was southerly. An abattoir could not smell as bad as this. It was as though she had plucked the lid off the dustbin and come across a nest of maggots in stinking meat — but the meat was human flesh and the living and the dead lay side by side.

The old men were just in front of her, poked and prodded forward by the British. A shuffling line of the stout and the respectable, all dressed for the occasion. Old men in winter woollen overcoats, clutching their felt hats to their chests as though they might be entering a church, old men herded along like sheep. But sheep were never so silent.

She picked her way between them until she found Klaus. As she touched him on the arm to let him know she was there, a diesel engine started up with a roar and Klaus turned and pressed her head to his chest blocking her view.

"Don't," he said.

But she squirmed free. Ducked underneath his restraining arm. Found herself on the edge of a pit some two metres deep and twenty long, in which the dead were strewn in their hundreds. And on the far side a British sergeant, a scarf across his nose and mouth, drove a bulldozer forward to topple more bodies in, a Gordian knot of arms and legs cascading down to add another layer. Humanity shovelled up and tipped like garbage. Dogs did not die this way.

Behind her the pharmacist was crying, the grocer was throwing up, and Klaus's hand rested upon her shoulders, his fingers digging hard into her collarbone, less restraining her than himself.

The Tommies made them watch as the bulldozer did its work, the pit was filled with corpses and the first scoop of soil tipped back on top of them. A grave for the great unknown.

Then a whistle blew and the engine stopped. A rumble that dwindled to nothing and left a piercing silence. A bucket of earth poised in mid-air ready to fall. The British major stood on the far side, across a gulf as wide as evolution itself, and began yelling something at them all in mechanical German, reading it off a sheet of paper, something formal, a headmaster's reprimand, almost a lecture — but she neither saw nor heard.

Suddenly it was over. Whatever purpose had brought them there was fulfilled and half a dozen Tommies came along, badgering them in English and reinforcing their words with nudges from rifle butts and the one German phrase they all appeared to know.

*"Schnell. Schnell. Macht schnell."*

Again they missed her. Either they hadn't seen her or they didn't associate her with the old men, or any child was taken to be an inmate. It seemed to her that she must wear some cloak of invisibility like a creature in a Brothers Grimm tale.

She stared into the pit. As though she might will the dead to move and show they were not dead. As though a hand might yet rise up for rescue. Some instinct made her want to count them, but it was absurd — a tangled skein of limbs, slack, nacreous skin and featureless faces, a merging of individual bodies into a composite dead flesh. Extreme emaciation produced effects she had never had cause to imagine. Human beings reduced to sticks — the difference between thighs and calves eliminated as legs, and arms, shrank to the straight lines of geometry, the human curve disappearing, punctuated only by the bulbous knots of knees and elbows, and the gaping anus — the fixed shutter, the dark lens, as though it had opened only to expel life and admit death.

An April breeze had caught the ubiquitous dust, whipping it up into eddies, settling it on the dead like frosting.

A line from school English lessons — all those weeks spent translating the metaphysical poets — rolled around in her mind: "The grave's a fine and private place . . ."

This wasn't.

A hand on her arm. Slowly she turned.

It was the English captain who had first approached her an hour, a year, a lifetime ago.

"Look . . . I'm sorry. I didn't know Major Thomas was going to do that. The old men, well . . . perhaps they had to see this, but I would not have exposed you to this for the world."

"I'm not a child."

"I think perhaps you are. What are you? Fifteen?"

"Eighteen," she lied. "And I could be of use to you."

"How so? Do you have medical training? I have fifty thousand patients. I could use all the nurses I can get."

"No. I have no training of any kind."

"Then I don't see what use you'd be —"

"Please!"

She didn't stamp her foot. She waited until she saw compliance in his eyes.

"You're English . . . and you speak German? Perhaps some French?"

"No . . . I speak next to no French."

"These people . . . these people that the Ger. . . . that *we* have put here . . . they are French, Poles, Russians, Jugoslavians . . . I speak more of their languages than you do."

"Russian? You speak Russian?"

"Better than my Polish. And my French and English are fluent. I can help you do what you are going to do."

"And what is it you think we are going to do?"

"Put them back together again."

Whatever it was he was going to say she had stopped him in his tracks, the words half formed on his lips froze into silence. He turned away from the pit, took a couple of steps, turned back with the bodies beyond his line of sight.

"Put them back together again? Jesus Christ."

"Believe me. I can help."

"I'm sure you can. Russian? Polish? No one on my staff speaks either."

"It's what I am. A child of language . . . a word child."

He looked off into the middle distance, to a group of the motionless living, squatting on the ground as her skeletal man had squatted in the dog kennel. Then he looked back at her. She could almost hear the sigh he would not let out.

"Alright, word child. Report to the main

gate. Eight o'clock tomorrow. Ask for me. Nicolas Dekker of the Royal Army Medical Corps — and I'm not English, I'm Dutch."

On her way back to the main gate she came across her skeletal man, squatting exactly where the Tommies had set him down when they lifted him from the truck, dust settling upon him, on the living as on the dead. She doubted he had moved a millimetre. His pipe had gone out. Without the pipe would she have known him? He was all but indistinguishable from every other skeletal man. The identities of the living had blurred, the flesh of the dead had merged. He heard her approach, but did not look up. The hand simply extended in her direction, his gaze elsewhere, infinity, oblivion, locked on to some inner vision, and all he said was, *"Gib mir Tabak."*

# §47

When she got home the front door was wide open and the house silent. The British had taken every mattress in the house and most of the bedding.

Klaus was in the garden, digging. It was almost time to plant potatoes. He was out there most of the day and returned only an hour before dusk. He prepared a meal of mashed turnips and bacon, said nothing at all in the cooking of it and next to nothing in the eating.

Afterwards, there was no music, no BBC.

She had a thousand questions that came down to one question, and she did not ask it because she knew he would not answer.

*"Wer sind wir, was sind wir?"*

Who are we? What are we?

# §48

Dekker asked her to roll up her sleeve.

"We're losing hundreds to malnutrition every day. They can't keep down what we give them. If we don't get it right, thousands will die. After that the biggest threat is typhus. You won't starve to death. You're skinny but you're healthy. But typhus will take the strong as well as the weak. And we have typhus rampant — you've surely smelt it, that stench of boiling peas. Like winter in an Amsterdam café. *Erwtensoep* and pumpernickel."

She watched the needle sink into her upper arm.

To speak might stop her crying.

"We were rationed too."

"We?"

"My family. Mother, Father, me. Berlin was rationed."

"Don't talk to me about rationing. Rationing isn't hunger. And whilst you may not have known it the Wehrmacht stripped Poland and the Ukraine to feed Berlin."

He dropped the needle into a steel kidney

dish and stuck Elastoplast on her arm.

"I'm putting you in with the German nurses. They're awkward buggers, but they're fitter and, dammit, they're saner than the inmate nurses we've found. But they speak nothing but German and their attitude has got to change. Interpret for them. Get between their denial and the patient's fear."

"Denial?"

"They don't believe their own eyes. They don't believe what Germany has done. Any more than those old men yesterday. They probably thought rationing was starvation too. And the patients trust no one speaking German. Why would they?"

# §49

The German nurses were crisp, confident, and contemptuous. They had arrived from another world, one that was clean and starched. They could not have scared Nell more if they had carried guns. Clearly, they felt she was superfluous. They'd get through to the inmates without her help. Dekker told them they wouldn't, shouted down the protests of "she's just a child" and "it's unprofessional."

"You know what unprofessional means? It means you don't like what I'm asking you to do. You know what this uniform and these three pips mean? It means you bloody well

203

do it anyway!"

One of the first tasks was to try to inject a ward of Polish women against typhus.

Most of them were just a day away from the filth of the huts they had been found in — hours before they had been hosed down and scrubbed in the makeshift showers, those with lice had been shaved, and, as far as was possible, they had been clothed, although in most cases this amounted to no more than a clean blanket to drape around their shoulders.

The sight of German nurses in Wehrmacht uniforms widened Polish eyes. The women seemed to flatten themselves against the wall, as though they would pass through it like wraiths.

Nell explained what was happening to the first woman they approached, but at the sight of a hypodermic needle her reaction was to scuttle into a corner, to make herself as small as possible and to pull her blanket over her head.

Nell caught a muttered *Strauß* (ostrich) from one of the nurses. And the nurse, flourishing the hypodermic like Lady Macbeth's dagger, moved on to the next bed and told the next patient, in uncompromising German, that she hoped she would be *vernünftig*.

Sensible. Not a word Nell had found much use for since the day she found her *Tabak* man in the dog kennel. She translated all the same.

This woman was no ostrich. She knocked both hypodermic and kidney dish flying and leapt from her bed to the next and from the next to the next, and in a dozen leaps to the far corner, pursued by all the nurses.

All the other women in the room fled screaming, flocking like birds, as far away from the nurses as they could get.

Nell shoved her way to the front, trying to get between the Germans and their reluctant patient.

"Please, leave this to me."

"Ridiculous. Chit of a girl."

They paused, all the same.

Nell turned to the woman defending her corner. Knelt down.

"Trust me. It's harmless. It's for your own good."

She seized Nell's head between her hands.

"Don't let them touch me. The SS. Auschwitz. They injected benzene to make us burn better."

Nell prised herself free, the woman's fingers like twigs in her hands, and faced up to the nearest nurse clutching a hypodermic.

"We can't do this. They won't have it."

"We are the nurses, you are just an interpreter, stand aside."

"They won't let you do it. In Auschwitz . . . in Auschwitz they were injected with benzene so that their bodies would burn better."

"That is nonsense!"

"It may be nonsense but it's what she's saying. We don't know what they've been through. But it all comes down to the same thing. They are terrified of needles and they're terrified of you!"

Nell saw the nurse flinch and crouch and turned to see what she had seen. A tin plate, thrown like a discus, sliced through the air and into Nell's cheek. She felt the warm blood washing down her face, clapped a hand to the cut and fled.

# §50

It was a deep cut, but Dekker was reluctant to stitch.

"You'll be scarred for life, I'm afraid, but it will be a neater scar without stitches. With any luck I can tape you tight enough for it to heal properly."

When he'd finished he held up a scratched, stainless steel mirror for her to look in. She looked like an Apache in war paint — a broad white stripe that started on the side of her nose and travelled left to end just under the corner of her eye. Scarred for life. Such a telling phrase.

"My war wound," she said.

"Well . . . your visible war wound. You did the right thing, you know, running when you did. They ripped the clothes off their backs."

"What?"

"You were just the first casualty. The Polish women damn near stripped those nurses naked. But there is a plus side. Perhaps they'll listen now. Perhaps they'll start realising their patients are human."

"Will they carry on with injections?"

"They have to or we'll have an epidemic on our hands. All depends on their attitude, how they go about it."

"What about what the Polish woman told me, about Auschwitz and benzene?"

"Might be true. Might not. There's one bugger we have locked up right here, rumoured to have injected his victims with creosote. Who knows what went on at Auschwitz? Who knows what they were injected with? God knows, it would hardly make a difference. Human flesh burns pretty well."

"And Auschwitz. What is Auschwitz?"

# §51

Approaching the main gate she found her *Tabak* man. He had moved she was almost sure, but he had resumed the same position — and he'd found another source of tobacco and was puffing on Klaus's pipe. He was, the last two days had taught her, one of the "healthy" ones. She doubted he weighed much more than fifty kilos, but that was health by Belsen standards.

She crouched down, copied the posture, tried to look beneath the tilted brow.

"*Pamitasz mnie. To ja, dziewczyna z tytoniem.*"

You remember me. I'm tobacco girl.

The head lifted. The light not yet on behind the eyes.

"*Nazywam si Nell. Nell Burkhardt. Jestem Berliner. Jak masz na imi?*"

My name is Nell. Nell Burkhardt. I'm a Berliner. What is your name?

The merest flicker. For the first time he seemed to know what was beyond the reach of his hand, to what he reached out, to be able to see the person he had heard and never looked at.

"*Tabak?*"

"Yes. *Tabak.*"

"Berlin?"

"Berlin."

Now he looked directly at her for the first time.

"*Jestem* . . . Kraków," he said.

Then his head tilted, he drew on the pipe and said no more.

She waited, hoping that her silent determination might draw more from him. Minutes passed, the pipe smoked out, the head lifted.

"*Jestem . . . byłam . . . nikim . . . mniej ni nikim . . . jestem . . . niczym.*"

I am . . . I was . . . nobody . . . less than

nobody . . . I am . . . nothing.

*"Nikt nie jest niczym. Nawet pies ma imi."*

No one is nothing. Even a dog has a name.

*"Jestem mniej ni niczym . . . mniej ni psem."*

I am less than nobody . . . less than a dog.

# §52

In the morning she asked Klaus for more tobacco. As she passed the main gate, the same hunched figure, the same hand extended, the same head bowed.

*"Dziewczyna z Berlina. Gib mir Tabak."*

She found Dekker.

He said, "I can't put you back in with the German nurses. I really don't want to take that risk."

She said, "I have found something better to do. You're treating people whose names you don't even know. Give me access to the records, the papers, the card indexes, whatever system the SS had. Let us give them back their names."

"The buggers burnt the lot."

"So the only way we have of finding out anything at all about anyone is to ask them?"

"And you're going to be the one to ask, is that it?"

"If you let me."

Dekker did what he always did, looked away, took his eyes off her, took in some object in the middle distance and made up his mind without the persuasive glare of her gaze. He picked up an RAMC battledress. Tossed it across the desk to her.

"It'll be as well if they don't think of you as German. Put this on. It's the smallest I could find. You may look daft wearing it with a skirt but no dafter than any other ragamuffin in the camp. And it may just protect you from another attack. See the stores NCO, Staff Sergeant Cox, ask for pen, paper, cards, whatever you need or more precisely whatever he can spare. When we can we'll set you up with a desk somewhere. But you can't do this on your own. We really could use some sort of record, but it'll only stand a chance if we have nurses and the med students involved. That will take a while. A few days at least. We're moving people out haphazardly. I'd prefer to take the sickest first, but it just isn't possible. It's selective, and a selection will be about as welcome as an injection. Meanwhile what we have is a mixture. The walking "healthy" — that is anyone who can stand unaided — and the chronic. Start with a "healthy." Someone who's fit enough to talk. See what it yields. See what you can do for him or her. For all we know you may be the first person to ask anything of them in months. Even if we don't get answers, your asking may be worthwhile. Implant the idea that they matter to someone. And if they do answer, get what you can, in particular get medical history. Operations, permanent conditions, immunisation. I'll give you a checklist to tick off. I suggest two of everything. One card for us, one for them. Give them the second card and hope they don't lose it. For a while, possibly for months, it may be the only identity card they have."

He stopped as suddenly as he had begun. Drawing breath. Hitting the buffers.

"That's quite a speech," Nell said.

Dekker was smiling now. "I was improvising. It's quite an idea. It may not work, but it's quite an idea. And I have to ask you . . . why?"

It was her turn to pause. She knew what she wished to tell him, but it had to be precise.

"Having been nothing, they wish to be someone," she said.

"Yes," Dekker replied, "I suppose they would."

"These are people who have families . . . brothers . . . sisters . . . children . . ."

"Nell — the tense of what you say may be your biggest mistake. These are people who *had* families, who *had* brothers, sisters, parents, children. These are the survivors. The rest are probably dead. Germany is an open grave. The dead we are burying here are the tip of an iceberg. People are dying every day, and many more will die. This is not peace, this is merely the absence of war.

And if you can help these people resurrect their identities you will also be invoking a roll call of the dead. Are you sure you want to do this?"

"Yes," she said.

And Dekker thought that perhaps he was looking at the most determined, the most po-faced child he had ever met.

"Then perhaps in the end you may find all you can do is listen."

# §53

Of course, it did not work.

She began with her pipe-smoking acquaintance. The next time she saw him, he had moved fifty feet, was sitting in the sun and had traded his camp stripes for a brown woollen jacket that fitted loosely and grey flannel trousers that bagged around his bottom and thighs. He still squatted, but instead of dirty bare feet he balanced in a pair of shining brogues, confiscated from some bourgeois citizen of fastidious cleanliness. The dust of Belsen had not even had a chance to settle on them.

She squatted opposite him, a leaky fountain pen and a small stack of index cards in her hand. In the absence of a camera, she would sketch. She would put in a name, a date of birth, a place of birth, an occupation and a simple sketch. If possible she would add medical history. If further possible a date and place of arrest.

He raised his head. His pipe was lit. He did not ask for tobacco.

*"Dziewczyna z Berlina."*

The girl from Berlin.

*"Tak to ja. Czy mogłabym Cie prosić o Twoje imi?"*

Me again. Could I ask you your name?

*"Co tu robisz w tym brudzie?"*

What are you doing down here in the dirt?

*"Có . . . Co robisz w tym brudzie?"*

Well . . . what are you doing down here in the dirt?

*"Jestem psem . . . jestem gorzej ni psem . . . jestem niczym . . . jestem numerem."*

I am dog . . . I am less than dog . . . I am nothing . . . I am number.

He rolled up the left sleeve of his woollen jacket to reveal the number tattooed into his forearm.

*"Jestem Auschwitz."*

I am Auschwitz.

# §54

In the morning she passed him again. He was standing now. She'd never seen him stand before. He was over six feet tall. He was looking out through the wire.

She didn't wait for him to speak, and held out the tobacco before he could ask for it.

The eyes that had looked at nothing could see her clearly now. He took the tobacco, looked at it in the palm of his hand, looked down at her.

"Nowak," he said simply. "My name is Aurelius Nowak. I should have told you that when you asked me. I am sorry. It was rude of me. Hunger is madness. You must forgive me."

She took out her pack of cards.

She had two for him, all they showed was an inky sketch and the word "Krakau." She wrote in his name.

"Did you think I had forgotten my own name?"

"I thought it was possible . . . hunger is madness."

"I can forget nothing. I wish I could."

"Anything would help. The SS burnt everything. We have no records. Nothing. Can you tell me your date of birth?"

"I can but I won't. It's just another number. I am . . . through with numbers. I have been a number too long. Sit with me a while. Play the prisoner with me in the dirt again."

While they squatted Nowak lit up his pipe and in scarcely more than fragments gave her the bare facts of his life.

"I was professor of music in Kraków. They shot most of my colleagues in 1939. Perhaps I was not enough the intellectual to merit a bullet. I was merely expelled and found work in a bakery. They came for me only in the March of last year. My entire family was sent to Auschwitz. My son died on the train. I never saw my wife again after we arrived. In January this year, at least I think it was January, they marched us out of Auschwitz fifty kilometres to a railway yard and put me back on a train. This is where the train stopped. I fell from it alive. Many did not. The rest you know. I was, I have been, as you found me that day in the dog kennel . . . mad with hunger."

She tried to reduce his narrative to keywords, found herself crossing out and rephrasing. Ink leaking onto her fingers.

"Can I ask you about your medical history? Diseases and the like?"

"Ah . . . the British doctors. Everything in its place. Yes. And I shall answer. I had not a day's illness in my life until last year."

"And . . . then?"

"I caught an incurable disease."

"What's it called?"

"Germany."

# §55

Of course, it did not work.

As more and more inmates moved from the squalor of the camp to the relative order of the nearby Panzer Barracks, the British organised hospital wards. Nell followed, and as the British Red Cross nurses treated the results of prolonged malnutrition, she gently probed, filling in her cards, sketching faces, trying, as Nowak had told her, not to make it all sound like statistics. Statistics were no more than a hypodermic in the hands of a German nurse, and that no less than a Luger in the hands of a Wehrmacht soldier. Fear was everything. Once overcome, there was listlessness, aggression, and lethargy.

On one day, she estimated, she had made out over one hundred and fifty cards. She gave each individual a card and handed the duplicate set to Dekker. The next morning she found dozens of them, blowing with the dust or strewn across the ward floor. It was predictable. So many of the women on the wards had looked blankly at her as she had pressed the half-filled cards into their hands. She doubted that any had really forgotten their name, but a good number had seemed incapable of uttering it.

"Futility," Dekker said, "is the name of the game."

"Meaning?"

"Meaning you have to risk it; nothing ventured nothing gained. And when it all goes *Fuß über Kopf* you accept it as futile and start again."

She gathered up the cards. Sat in the nurses' lavatory, tearful, trying to interpret Dekker's homily on futility. It would have been hubristic ever to think that she could give anyone back their identity, and she had only ever thought that for a second. The best she could do was help someone, anyone, resurrect their own identity. Nowak, in his unsubtle way, had pointed out the gulf between identity and an identity card, but what other method was available to her? Was Dekker's "perhaps all you can do is listen" all there was to be done?

Two Red Cross nurses came in to scrub up.

"Ah," said one. "The little ink girl."

And she saw herself as some transparent, useless flake of a child in a Hans Andersen tale. No longer invisible, but futile. The Little Ink Girl.

Then the other one said, "Cheer yourself up, ducks. I always find a bit of makeup does me the world of good. That and a nice cup of char."

And she pressed something small, hard, and metallic into her hand.

Nell unfolded her fingers.

It was a tube of lipstick.

She had never worn lipstick.

She pulled off the little golden cylinder. It was searing red, and the imprint of the nurse's lower lip was sculpted in. A twist grip on the base propelled the lipstick upwards. It was a toy.

She looked at the bundle of cards, sifted

through them. Her sketches now looked to her to be all alike — the same hollow cheeks and new moon eyes, the same shining skull.

She clutched them in hand, pen, cards, and lipstick and returned to the ward. Most of the women were milling around in a susurrus of slow Polish talk, the effort of animation all but beyond them.

Alone on her bed sat a Belgian woman she knew only as Bruges — knees tucked up to her flattened chest, Nowak-style, Belsen-style, hands around her ankles, head down. Her card was on the top.

Nell sat on the edge of her bed and held it out to her.

She looked up and offered no reaction.

Nell set the rest of the cards on the bed — the pen rolled off the pile, she reached out for it. The lipstick rolled off the pile and another hand grabbed it.

What to Nell had been a toy was a magic wand to Bruges. She took the twist grip between finger and thumb and turned it as slowly as was possible, the fierce red tip peeping out like the tongue of a cat. And when she looked up she was smiling.

Nell looked around, almost desperate for a mirror. She tipped a few shreds of gauze out of a kidney dish and held the flat base up to her.

Bruges tipped her head from side to side, coping with the distortion, looked once at

Nell and then put the lipstick to her lips.

It occurred to Nell that there were few mirrors in the barracks and none in the camp — it could be the first time Bruges had looked at herself in an age. But Bruges was focussed, if she was shocked by her thin face and sparse hair, she did not show it. She applied the lipstick with artistry, arching her top lip, stretching her lower, pursing them together in a scarlet pucker, almost blowing a kiss to herself in the mirror.

She smiled at Nell, as Nell lowered the dish, and held the lipstick out to her. Nell did not take it — around her, all around her, gathered like silent shadows, every woman in the ward.

# §56

Later the same day, the afternoon brightening into April sunshine, Nell sat at a makeshift desk outside Dekker's office filing her cards alphabetically.

"Sabine Michel," Bruges had said at last. "I am twenty-six years old."

Nell had sat on the edge of the bed and listened, and then she had sat on the edge of every bed in the ward and listened as every pair of red lips told a tale.

She had just filed Katya Żebrowska when the quartermaster, Staff Sergeant Cox, appeared with a cardboard box under his arm.

"I hear you can use these," he said.

She looked at the stencilled label on the outside.

"Field Dressings × 40. RAMC type 101/7. Dec. 1944"

"Thank you Mr. Cox, but I think not."

"Not so fast, Inky Fingers."

He flipped the lid off. There were no field dressings, the box was full of lipstick, hundreds of tubes of lipstick, all marked "Max Factor," and "Made in the USA" — rose red, poppy red, flame red . . . every red that Max could factor.

"My God! Where did you get this?"

"You don't think I ordered them do you? Nah. Cock-up back at HQ. I was getting ready to send 'em back before some light-fingered bugger got his hands on 'em and sold the lot on the black market, but then I heard about you and yer tube of lipstick."

"You heard?"

"The whole bleedin' camp heard."

Nell sat on the edge of a bed, any bed, and listened to red lips talk. She would go on listening for over three months.

# §57

Of course it did not work.

Dekker had been right about futility, right about the pursuit of futility, but as soon as resources permitted he assigned Red Cross nurses to record keeping. And some of those who would not or could not talk to nurses would talk to Nell, and Nell would listen.

She would go on listening for over three months. She would go on listening for eternity.

# §58

Weeks passed. The Allies, in the form of the Supreme Headquarters Allied Expeditionary Force — a phrase that put Nell more in mind of an Antarctic trek than a total war — recognised the nature of the problem and found a bureaucratic solution. By the thousand printed, tick-in-the-box, Displaced Person cards arrived. Twenty questions poised upon a precipice. The card asked all the questions Nell had been asking and several she might not. It invited the contempt Dekker had so accurately predicted, and Nowak so acutely embodied with his "just another number."

So often the answers were all too predictable.

"Do have a husband?"

"Auschwitz."

"Do you have children?"

"Auschwitz."

"What was your last address?"

"Auschwitz."

"What is your religion?"

"I left that in Auschwitz too."

And sometimes not.

"You are a Displaced Person."

"No I'm not. I know exactly where I am."

What she had learnt fed into the system. And the cards fell in the dust, fluttered in the wind, blew out across the heath into a symbolic, anonymous confetti of freedom much as her first efforts had done. She had not learnt not to care, she had learnt not to mind.

Dekker could not resist a joke. Which was more prevalent the Displaced Person or the Displaced Card?

## §59

On May 20 no one died. The first day without a death, but by then they had buried over twelve thousand, and would bury more.

On the twenty-first the original Belsen camp was evacuated. The survivors were housed in the former Panzer Barracks, now renamed a Displaced Persons Camp.

The British burned Belsen to the ground and threw a party.

Nell went home to Klaus, as she did every night.

## §60

On a light evening in the middle of August she came home to find the house silent again.

A common occurrence. It seemed to her that Klaus had vanished into silence. Into silence and vegetables. As the days had lengthened he spent more and more time in the garden — planting out his cabbages, earthing up his potatoes. His evenings were spent behind his pipe and the gentle smoke screen he blew. If the radio or the gramophone went on it was because Nell put them on. Things that had interested him before, few though they were, seemed to have dropped away, petals, leaves and all, leaving the husk of the man. The British, who had rounded up and pressed into service — fetching, carrying, cleaning . . . burying — hundreds of the younger able-bodied, had left old Klaus alone.

It had been April, almost the end of April, when she had tuned in to the BBC and they had learnt of the death of Hitler. An occasion that might have been cause for rejoicing in a house such as theirs received only a muttered, "Well, that's that then" and a rhetorical "How many millions have died for him?" The news of Admiral Dönitz's unconditional surrender, *Stunde Null,* a matter of days later, drew forth a sigh of utter world-weariness and an equally rhetorical, "Was it all for nothing?"

The house was silent, the doors open front and back to let the breeze pass through.

She called out his name, and when there was no answer walked through the dining room towards the back door.

On the dining table an envelope was propped against a bottle of Cognac and an empty glass.

To my niece,
Christina Hélène von Raeder Burkhardt

It was closed and sealed with red wax, and the imprint of his signet ring, an interwoven KvR. The ring itself he had dropped into the empty glass.

The message was simple.

We all knew. Forgive me. KvR.

She knew he was dead. It was a simple matter to find the body.

Out in the garden he had dug one more trench and lain down in it. She had no idea how he had killed himself, but knew he had. A rational strand in her mind told her that he had spared her the task of cutting him down from a roof beam or mopping up the blood from a shot to the head. He had left her but one task, to bury him. He had left his garden spade in a mound of earth and he had pinned his two iron crosses onto the left breast of his jacket. He lay ramrod straight, his eyes closed and his arms folded like a Teutonic knight carved on a tombstone.

She was still looking at Klaus when she

became aware of someone looking at her.

Nowak was standing on the other side of the grave. She had not seen him in days, perhaps weeks. She heard he had volunteered as a porter and stayed on after many of the able-bodied had chosen to leave. He had put on weight, his hair had grown back. She could see now that he was a young man, probably well under forty, whereas before he had been both aged and ageless. He was clean, if dusty, and he was carrying a fawn knapsack much like her own.

"I came to find you. The door was open. I wasn't sure if you still lived here. I came to find you. I came to say goodbye. I am leaving."

She said nothing. He picked up the spade and said, "It's the least I can do. A thank-you for all the tobacco he gave me."

She watched as Nowak buried her uncle, thinking that the old man had outlived his time and that perhaps it was a rare gift to know when to die, and thinking that three months ago Nowak had scarcely had the strength to lift a pipe let alone a spade.

At last she said, "Leaving? Where will you go?"

"The Dutch have already gone back to Holland and the Belgians to Belgium. The Jews are lobbying to go to Palestine. The Czechs are on their way to Czechoslovakia. Few of the Poles want to go to Poland. You couldn't pay me to go back to Poland. So . . . I think perhaps I shall go to England. This displaced person is displacing himself once more."

"How?"

"I'll walk if I have to."

"And papers. Do you have papers?"

Nowak smoothed out the mound that covered Klaus and stuck the spade back into the earth. From his inside pocket he took a folded card and handed it to her. It was dog-eared and grubby now, but it was the same card she had given him as they sat in the dust together at the gates of Belsen. The inky sketch she had done of him now dated as he had gained both flesh and hair.

"That won't get you very far."

"On the contrary my dear, it will get me into heaven. And you, what now for you?"

"I am a Berliner," she said. "I belong in Berlin. I should be in Berlin. I have . . . perhaps had . . . family in Berlin. A mother and a father."

"And when did you last hear from them?"

"In January."

Two portentously vacant words, and they both knew the possibilities inherent.

"And how will you get there?"

She looked at Nowak, remembered how she had arrived with her little fawn knapsack with the red leather straps, and all that mattered to her stuffed inside.

"Oh, I'll walk if I have to."

§61

Dekker was sceptical.

"It's over two hundred kilometres."

"I should say closer to three hundred."

"And the green border . . ."

"The what?"

"The line between us and the Russians. It's hardly fifty kilometres from here. We drew back, gave them a chunk of Mecklenburg and some of Hanover. All agreed beforehand apparently. Wherever we stopped, wherever the Nazis surrendered we'd revert to the line agreed at some conference or other."

"And do they patrol this line?"

"It would be very unlike them not to."

She had placed her RAMC battledress on the desk between them.

Dekker removed the "I" (interpreter) armband and handed the jacket back to her.

"Keep it. I doubt it would fit anyone else, and, who knows, it might ward off a few bullets."

She was pleased. A gift. Something to make her think of Dekker in the days to come when she would know nothing of him. It did not suit the summer weather, but that was by the by.

"I am sorry," she said.

"About what?"

"That I was not of more help. I think perhaps I blundered in . . . the medical

227

records . . . just little scraps of card."

"Au contraire. My nurses think you broke the ice. Do you have any idea how many people traced their families as a result of the conversations you had, the notes you took — those little scraps of card?"

She hadn't, so he told her.

"One hundred and fifty-eight."

"Out of . . . ?"

"Forty thousand, give or take a few."

"That's . . . that's pathetic."

"No, Nell. It's marvellous. One hundred and fifty-eight people too frightened to talk to anyone else. One hundred and fifty-eight people who thought they were alone in the world now know they're not."

She wondered. Was she alone in the world? Was she a "Displaced Person"? Had her parents lived or died in Berlin?

It was as if he had read her mind.

"Do you really have to go to Berlin?"

"Yes. I'm a Berliner. It's still home. What's left of it."

Dekker walked with her as far as the gate, and she had taken but half a dozen steps eastward when he called after her, "How old are you really?"

She turned, looked at Dekker for the last time.

"Eighteen."

"And that's a lie isn't it?"

Nell said, "The only one I've ever told you."
But it was a lie she stuck to ever after.

# §62

She packed what she could but left most things.

Food would be a problem. She had money to buy food, but would there be food to buy?

It was summer, almost anything would rot before she could eat it, so she filled her knapsack with hardtack . . . with apples and nuts, with potatoes and carrots from the garden — with sweaty cheese and black bread from the larder.

Leaving, she thought what she might do with the key, and then she knew. She left it in the lock, for anyone to turn. It wasn't her house, it had never been hers. Let anyone who wanted have it.

It was warm, too warm for the RAMC battledress Dekker had given her, but she was determined to wear it — a badge of honour. She wore it open and loose, its belt tag dangling over her billowing green skirt, the sleeves rolled up to her elbows — and the strange insignia at the shoulder . . . a serpent coiled around a staff, peeping out between the straps of her woollen-sheathed British Army water flask. She had meant to ask Dekker what the insignia meant but had never remembered.

Celle was full of people. It seemed as though the whole of Germany was pouring into one town.

Celle was full of soldiers.

A sergeant wearing the armband and fiercely raked cap of a military policeman stopped her in the street. Gave her the once over, his eyes ranging down from the grips in her hair to the brittle leather walking boots on her feet.

"Now, where do you think you're off to dressed up like a dog's dinner?"

It was not a phrase that translated readily but she got his drift.

"Berlin," she said, and the man grinned.

"You'll be lucky."

"I am a Berliner. Berlin is my home."

"Papers," he said as abruptly as any German cop.

Hers were out of date. A wartime identity card and a ration book she had not used in weeks, not since the army had fed her.

But Dekker had taken the precaution of writing a letter for her in both English and German. It requested her safe passage. Wherever.

The sergeant read it, said, "I know Captain Dekker. I'm sure he means well . . . but you need a pass to cross zones."

"I have no pass."

"Well . . . you won't need it till you meet a Russian. If you was my girl I'd be telling you to turn back right now . . . most o' your lot are coming in the opposite direction. Look around you. We got Pomeranians, we got Sudetens, we got Silesians. We got half of East Prussia. Nobody wants to be in Berlin. Anyone who can outrun the Russkis is doing it. So many been through here these last few weeks, I reckon Berlin must be just about empty by now."

"I am a Berliner."

"So you say. Well . . . I'm not gonna be the one to stop you. But if I were you I'd travel very carefully. The countryside between here and the green border is full of DPs — Displaced Persons. Refugees, foreign workers, POWs . . . the lot. None of 'em partial to Germans. And then there's renegades, werewolves and what have you. And if there's one thing I know about a British battledress, it's that it don't stop no bullets."

# §63

*Cambridge:* November 1946

Mrs. Wissit slapped a bowl of Irish stew in front of him and said, "The colonel phoned for you. But you was out. I told him."

Wilderness looked at the unappetising mess — chunks of fatty mutton in transparent gruel — not waving but drowning.

"Important, was it?"

" 'Course. He don't pick up the blower for

nothin' now does he?"

"And?"

"And I wrote it down, din I?"

She fumbled in the pocket of her pinny, turfed out a handkerchief, a couple of hair-grips, a pair of scissors, and a note she had folded over so many times it was hardly bigger than a postage stamp.

"It says . . . Pack yer kit, clear out and report to me at . . . 'ang on can't read me own wotsit . . . somethin' somethin' Commission in Knightsbridge tamorra mornin' 8 a.m. sharp."

"Is that all?"

"Said thanks to me, and told me he'd be sending some other bloke to take your place."

"So, I'm off and you're all paid up?"

"Yeah, been grand ain't it."

# §64

He spent the night back in Sidney Street. The only sign of Merle was the snaking tendril of her scent. He heard her come in around two in the morning and thought better of a mid-nighttime encounter. When he got up at six a note on the kitchen table read simply, "Wotcher, Johnnie."

At the Control Commission for Germany HQ in Knightsbridge the staff sergeant on desk duty handed him another note, and Wilderness wondered if it might be the start of an album like stamps or autographs or fag cards.

Report RAF Wyton. 10 a.m. tomorrow morning. Travel light. Mind your manners. Try saluting once on a while. ABJ.

"He's not actually here, then?"

"Who?"

"Colonel Burne-Jones."

"Don't be daft, son. I can't answer questions like that. We're meant to be a secret service. How secret would we be if I answered everything some Tom, Dick, or Harry asks me?"

"Are the whereabouts of RAF Wyton a secret?"

"Nah. It's just outside Cambridge, everybody knows that."

"I've just come from bloody Cambridge!"

"So you'll have no difficulty finding it then."

# §65

The pattern repeated itself. Wilderness went to bed, Merle came in hours later. The only difference was that she left no note for him to read as he set off for King's Cross at seven in the morning. He left one for her.

Looks like I been posted. See when I see you. J x

But he didn't. He never saw Merle again.

# §66

Crossing Wyton field, kit bag perched on his left shoulder, it occurred to him that he was about to come face-to-face with a wartime legend. His first look at an Avro Lancaster heavy bomber.

There was no sign of Burne-Jones.

He dropped his kit by the crew hatch and circled the aircraft, awed by its size. It had seen better days. In the eighteen months or so since it last dropped a bomb this Lancaster had been stripped of its machine guns and had not seen a lick of paint. The gun turrets looked like the glassy eyes of some giant dead fish — the gunmetal grey of aluminium showed in streaks beneath the peeling black paint.

As Wilderness came full circle a man dropped feetfirst out of the hatch to the grass. A tatty-haired bloke wearing the Saturn rings of a squadron leader on his sleeve.

Wilderness saluted.

"Knock it off, old man. This is my last op. Tomorrow when this crate touches down back here I'll be in Civvy Street. And not a day too soon. Be fucked if I spent my last day returning salutes to erks like a bloody jack-in-the-box."

He stuck out his hand for Wilderness to take.

"Miller," he said. "Dusty Miller. You must be the kid Alec was telling me about."

"Yeah, that's me. Joe Holderness. Is the colonel . . ."

Wilderness hesitated. Was one "on board" or "inside" a plane? Was a plane more like a ship or a lorry?

Instead he pointed . . . "Up there?"

"No. Alec flew on ahead. He gave me these for you."

He handed Wilderness a small buff envelope and a square of pale blue serge with a propeller motif on it.

Wilderness must have looked more puzzled than he felt.

Miller said, "It's your promotion old man. You're a leading aircraftman now. An extra five bob a week in your pay packet. Don't forget to sew it on."

He grabbed hold of the fuselage above his head and in a neat, practised movement swung himself back into the plane.

Wilderness opened the letter.

Meet me in the main bar. Victory Club. 7:30 tonight. ABJ.

Victory Club? What Victory Club?

235

The Lancaster's engines turned over, catching Wilderness in a blast of cold air that whipped his cheese-cutter cap away into oblivion.

A head popped out of the hatch.

"Skipper says get on board or get left behind."

Wilderness tossed up his kit bag and grabbed two willing hands just as the plane began to move.

"Upsadaisy!"

He fell into the plane, heard the hatch slam shut behind him and found himself sitting next to a flight sergeant.

"Are you a rabbi?" he said.

Not the greeting Wilderness had expected, but the man probably had his reasons.

"No? Is it essential?"

"Nope, but last week we flew out three rabbis and a Catholic priest and I had to mind me p's and q's all the bleedin' way."

"Where are we going?"

"You mean you don't bloody know? Hamburg! You're on the milk run, mate."

Wilderness had some grasp of RAF slang. "Prang," "crate," and so forth. Doubtless if he had stayed in basic training he'd be fluent. "Milk run" meant easy, didn't it?

"Piece of cake?" he ventured.

The flight sergeant grinned.

"Oh that too, but I meant we're flying out condensed milk. You're sitting on five thousand cans of the stuff."

Wilderness looked down at the box he had perched himself upon, at the crude stencilling: "Milk. Con. Units 200. WD."

"And then you got yer flour. Two thousand pounds of grey British flour."

"Flour? But we've got bread rationing!"

"That's 'cos we ship bleedin' flour to bleedin' Germany innit. Then there's yer canned cheese. Don't matter whether it says cheddar or double Gloucester on the outside it all comes out lookin' like yeller rubber. And fags and matches and fag lighters and footballs and razor blades . . . two crates o' Bibles . . . two complete Shakespeares . . . and then there's blankets . . . and ex-army greatcoats and half a dozen sheepskin flying jackets. Speakin' o' which, best help yerself. No one'll miss it. Certainly not the RAF. It'll be bollock freezin' once we get airborne. We'll fly within sight of land, no goin' up to thirty thousand feet, but cold all the same. And when we get there, Hamburg's on the same latitude as Liverpool. But if you ask me it's more like Aberfuckindeen. Cold as a witch's tit."

The crew was as stripped as the plane. No guns, ergo no gunners. No navigator, just a pilot and a wireless operator.

Wilderness sat in the former navigator's seat as the Lancaster took off. An interesting surge, he thought. Not as traumatic as his imagination might have led him to believe, but a definite sensation in the lungs and stomach.

As the plane levelled off the flight sergeant said, "Front turret's empty. Lie down. Get some kip if yer like. It'll be more than two hours to Hamburg and nothin' to see till we cross the Dutch coast. Even then Holland's like my mum's Yorkshire puddin', flat as a pancake."

Wilderness lay down in the front turret in his RAF flying jacket feeling fraudulent, wondering who had lain here in the war aiming his machine guns at German fighters. Wondering to no particular point about the war that he had gratefully missed. He nodded off, the North Sea had little to captivate. He woke up somewhere over the Frisian Islands, a pleasing chain arcing out across the northern end of the Zuyder Zee.

About ten minutes out of Hamburg the pilot sent for him.

"Take the flight engineer's seat. I'll give you the Hamburg tour. You'll get a better handle on the place if you see it from above. Dunno what you've heard about the raids we made on Hamburg, but exaggeration is close to impossible."

"I'm a cockney," Wilderness said. "I was in the East End right through the Blitz. I've seen enough ruins to last a lifetime."

"Not like this you haven't."

And he hadn't.

Miller put the Lancaster into a slow curve and took the city at less than a thousand feet.

London, the East in particular, was dotted with ruined houses. Occasionally a whole terrace might have vanished. One side of the street reduced to rubble, the other still standing, albeit with every window blown in.

Hamburg looked as though it had been hollowed out with a spoon, like sinking a spoon into ice cream and just scooping out the middle till the sides were scraped clean. Every house was wrecked, every street was wrecked. The flesh had been seared off. All that remained were the bones, the teetering, improbably slender facades of houses and blocks of flats, gutted from attic to cellar, looking as though the first stiff breeze would fold them in like a tower built from playing cards. Nobody lived here. Surely nobody could live here?

"Did you do this?" Wilderness asked, wondering if Miller might take offence.

"No, no I didn't. But if you're ever in what's left of Cologne . . . well . . . I did three runs over Cologne. And I think the only thing that can be said for Cologne now is that it got off marginally lighter than Hamburg."

The arc Miller had steered took the plane across what appeared to be endless acres of brand new Nissen huts — an instant town, drawn to a line and a grid. It looked grim and heartless — a town, a real town, a town that had "growed," however ugly, could not look as forbidding as this. They'd sprung up like mushrooms, like the prefabricated houses back home. Bulldoze the ruins of London and build a home in a day.

They were approaching the edge of Fuhls-büttel, the base taken over by the RAF. They all but skimmed the roofs of what looked to Wilderness to be a shantytown that fringed the airfield — a mishmash of makeshift shacks and tents. Just when he was thinking there could be nothing worse than a sea of Nissen huts.

"Nobody could live here you said a minute or two back?" said Miller.

Wilderness thought he had only thought this and was surprised to find he had uttered it out loud.

"Quite right, old son. This is where they live. I reckon about a million Hamburgers fled what we did to them, and this is what's come back. Not many, but it seems like an awful lot sometimes."

"Why here? Why right next to a British base?"

"Because this is where the easy pickings are. Hamburg is rotten, like an overripe fruit. Ready to burst. I shan't be half glad to see the back of it. Civvy Street here I come."

Wilderness didn't understand the image, or the idea, but asked Miller what he had done in Civvy Street.

"I was a trader."

"Stocks and shares?"

"Yep. Not going back to that."

"I was a trader too. Off a barrow in the Whitechapel Road."

Miller hooted with laughter at this.

"Hang on to your seat son, we're going down."

# §67

An RAF corporal met him by the guardhouse at the Fuhlsbüttel perimeter. He drove a staff car, a commandeered French Citroën given a cursory lick of RAF blue paint, doubtless executed with half a working brain by some poor sod on jankers, and seemed none too pleased to see Wilderness. He stood to attention, scanned him fruitlessly for any sign of rank, and none being visible beneath the sheepskin jacket, looked appalled when Wilderness held up his corner of blue serge with the propeller on it.

The corporal scowled. Shoulders slackened, elbows and knees abandoned symmetry, the spit and polish on his shoes faded into history. All pretence of deference vanished in an instant. He thrust a small brown envelope at Wilderness.

Wilderness was getting used to this.

241

You're billeted at the Atlantic Hotel. Meet me. Breakfast 8 a.m. tomorrow. Sleep well. ABJ.

He might travel to the ends of the earth, to Samarkand or Boggley Wollah only to find Burne-Jones had departed minutes before and left him a small brown envelope and instructions to guide the course of the rest of his life, in Richard Burton's words — "Pay, pack, and follow."

Wilderness made the by now stock response.

"So the colonel's not here then?"

"The fuck should I know. All I know is I got dragged off a winning hand at Tuesday night poker and ordered back to the base double quick to pick up a VIP. And what do I find. I find you. An erk. So that's what I am now . . . a chauffeur for erks without so much a bit of scrambled egg to their caps. You ain't even got a cap. What's so fuckin' special about you you get a staff car all the fuckin' way in to fuckin' 'Amburg?"

"I've no idea," Wilderness replied. "But I'll carry my own bag if you like, Corporal."

"Fuck you, kid. Get in the car and keep yer gob shut."

They got to the Atlantic Hotel in the last of daylight. A blanket of grey falling upon the ash and rubble, not a hint of colour, the temperature plummeting towards freezing.

The gift of an RAF sheepskin flying jacket notwithstanding, Wilderness wondered if he might regret the decision to make room in his kit bag for his Welsh Guards outfit by ditching his winter woollies. The only words the corporal spoke to Wilderness as they crossed the Hamburg suburbs were, "Three kings, I had. Three kings and a fortnight's pay riding on 'em."

## §68

That the Atlantic Hotel had survived at all was a miracle. It towered over the Alster Lake, with all the hallmarks of a prime target. Its luminous white facade now dulled to a dirty grey, but all that needed was paint. It was battered, pockmarked but far from decrepit.

Another churlish corporal checked his papers at the door.

"This is supposed to be officers only."

Wilderness said nothing to this. Let the twat think he was Bomber Harris in disguise if he felt like it. Whatever string Burne-Jones had pulled to get him in here mattered more than the two stripes on this bugger's arm. He took back his papers, hoisted his kit bag with a silent "fuck you."

It was as grand as the Ritz — and the night of his cocktail in the Ritz with Merle had been the last, the only time he'd ever set foot in a hotel like this.

He was on the top floor, almost under the eaves, but the bed was as wide as the Thames and the bathroom not much smaller than Wembley Stadium. He slept the sleep of the just with ne'er a dream nor waking thought of corporals.

At breakfast he was shown with chilling disdain to the table at which Burne-Jones was already seated.

"Glad you could make it."

One of Burne-Jones's pointless pleasantries. The pretence he occasionally indulged in that rank was of no import. Of no import in a room full of brass. Wilderness sat down quickly, feeling that heads would start to turn soon if he didn't.

"Tell me," he said. "Am I the only erk billeted in this place?"

"Quite possibly. The others are all out at Fuhlsbüttel. But I need you here."

"Where you can keep an eye on me?"

Burne-Jones ignored this.

"Bacon, eggs, and coffee OK? Or are you still a cockney sweet tea man?"

"You and your little digs, eh? No, I'm a reborn sophisticate. Coffee will be fine. Black, no sugar."

Burne-Jones smiled, tucked into his breakfast, and between mouthfuls muttered, "How quickly they grow up."

Out in the street it was, as everyone had predicted to him, bollock freezing. He zipped up his flying jacket, and the look on Burne-Jones's face told him he had thought better of asking if it was nicked.

"Let's take a walk. I need to show you Hamburg."

"I got the aerial tour last night."

"I need you to see it at ground level. In fact I need you to see Germans."

They stepped around a child collecting fag ends in a tin mug.

The kid looked up, a bright smile on hollow cheeks, a dead light in his blue eyes.

"He's your first," Burne-Jones said. "They call them *Kippensammler.* Literally fag collector."

"Choc, Tommy? Fags, Tommy?"

Wilderness had half a Mars bar in the pocket of his blouse. He'd eaten the rest on the flight. He held it out to the kid and the kid snatched it out of his hand and ran.

Wilderness stared after him.

"You weren't expecting gratitude, surely?" said Burne-Jones.

"No," said Wilderness. "I wasn't. I was thinking there goes the master race. Blond hair, blue eyes, begging for half a bloody Mars bar."

"Jolly good. You're getting the idea nicely.

This will all be about Germans, and that's an awfully good place to start."

He led off into the ruined centre of Hamburg, across St. Georg in the direction of Borgfelde and Hammerbrook — districts that had been razed by the firestorm of 1943.

"The child, you see, collects fag ends. These he sells to some lucky bugger in possession of a rolling machine who can reassemble the bits our chaps throw away into the semblance of a whole, if not wholesome, fag. A good fag retails at seven or eight marks, but even a roll-up using bog paper will fetch three or four. It's the new currency. Money doesn't count in Germany any more."

"Like my stamp collection."

"Eh? What?"

"I used to collect stamps when I was a nipper. I had all those pre-Hitler stamps from the Weimar days — had a whole page of perforated *200 Millionen Mark* stamps. Wasn't worth the sheet of bog paper you say these blokes roll their fags in."

Burne-Jones wasn't paying much attention to their surroundings, concentrating on his argument, but it was clear from everything he'd said that he expected Wilderness to, that he expected him to combine what he heard from Burne-Jones with what he saw in the streets. Of course, it wasn't London, as Miller had said, so much worse. But in common, it seemed to Wilderness, was the extraordinary survival power of church spires. In streets that were but dust and rubble, every so often a church spire would loom up in desolate isolation. Just like St. George's-in-the-East back in Stepney or St. Anne's at the bottom end of Wardour Street.

"Let's go back a little further. 1919."

"The revolution?"

"Quite, because you won't understand the Germans if you don't understand that. They don't call it the revolution, of course — it wasn't after all — they call it the "stab-in-the-back" — Hitler's early speeches are littered with the phrase. It's what that begat that mattered. The Nazis weren't the only group to spring up, to cohere in the wake of 1919 — if anything they were rather slow off the mark — but there were dozens of other groups, right and left. Spartacists, Steel Helmets, Reichsbanner . . . Freikorps. If you were young and angry in the 1920s you could join a movement. Some of them petered out before the republic fell, some joined the Nazis and so on. I'd say there was a time between the wars when, if you joined, you almost joined a state within a state. The paramilitaries made the Oddfellows or the Freemasons look like a Thursday evening Ping-Pong club in Scunthorpe. If you wanted they provided everything . . . more like life insurance than politics . . . if you wanted you could be married and buried by the movement you joined.

It was . . . total. You could live in it."

"And?"

"And you have to ask yourself what it was in the German character that all this appealed to. Good-natured and malicious, Goethe called them. Or was it Nietzsche? No matter . . . it was something in the German soul, in the dungeons and corridors of the German soul. It wasn't just Nazism. It could have been any faction. The Nazis just came out on top."

"I'm not sure I believe in national character. It's like saying all Irish are piss-artists or all Frenchmen are terrific in bed but we aren't."

"Good point. But everything in its temporal context. Think what these people had been through at the end of the last war. Military defeat. The collapse of the state — something we've never experienced. And add to it what they've gone through since 1933. A fragile democracy snuffed out in a palace coup. Then twelve years of the Thousand-Year Reich. It's tempting to be too intellectual about this. To say that there is deracination of the mind if you like. But these people are made by their culture and twice made by the collapse of their culture."

"What are you trying to tell me? That Germans aren't like us?"

"Yes. Exactly that. Not all Germans and not all Germans forever, but the Germans of now. The post-1945 German isn't like you or me, and I don't want you to think he is. That would be a great mistake. Germany and the Germans . . . right now . . . they're a moral vacuum. And you're going to be working with them. Millions of them."

"What?"

Wilderness stopped in his tracks. It suited Burne-Jones that they should stop. Another of his illustrations. A chain gang of women — women of all ages from teenage girls to grandmothers — wrapped in rags against the cold, they were passing bricks from person to person. The first one picked a brick out of the rubble, the last, seven or eight pairs of hands later, stacked it on a pallet.

"*Trümmerfrauen,*" Burne-Jones said too simply. "Rubble women. They've been picking over the bones of Germany's cities practically since the day the Führer put a bullet through his brain. They get extra rations, and bit by bit we get the streets cleared. And one day Hamburg will get rebuilt. Wasn't much to look at in the first place, so who knows . . . perhaps they'll build a better Hamburg. Meanwhile you get an object lesson in the German character."

"Obedience?"

"Determination."

Wilderness wondered if Burne-Jones had chosen the turnaround point at which they headed back in the centre or whether it was due to time and chance.

They had ground to a halt — Burne-Jones had stopped talking, they had both stopped walking — in front of a blitzed terrace. It would not, with a slight shift of style, have looked out of place in London, in Stepney or in Deptford. The whole terrace was roofless and windowless, but as they reached the middle, any assumption that these houses were deserted was swept away. A door creaked open, miraculously still attached to its hinges, and a housewife swept dust and dirt out into the street. And when she had done that she reached behind her for a bucket, got to her knees and began to scrub the step. He'd seen this a thousand times in childhood. Houses that were damp, with flaking plaster and cracked windows, with buddleias sprouting from fractures in the brickwork, with leaking gutters, with . . . with scrubbed, whitened thresholds, the face presented to the world that boldly declared "this is not a slum, this is my home."

## §70

They'd crossed the Lombard Bridge between the two Alster Lakes, into Neustadt. Burne-Jones had talked all the way. His potted history of life and death amidst the ruins. Wilderness had listened. In between the spacious paragraphs of Burne-Jones's narrative he was listening out for the sound of the city.

London did not sound like Cambridge, Cambridge did not sound like London, although removed from both he could not have articulated the difference. Hamburg sounded like neither. Hamburg rattled. No, not precise enough. Hamburg clinked. Clinked to the sound or brick hitting brick, stone falling on stone, as the *Trummerfraüen* sifted the city. It was the ever-present sound, softer than bells, louder than trickling water. In a couple of hours Wilderness had come to regard it as a musical abstraction. Burne-Jones seemed not to hear it at all, but then Burne-Jones seemed not to see the writing on the walls.

After seeing it half a dozen times, Wilderness pointedly stopped by one painted inscription.

Nell. I'm alive! Where are you? Joe.

There'd been dozens, perhaps hundreds, adorning every wall they'd passed. A public noticeboard for the missing and the dead. The *Times* personal column for the homeless and desperate. There'd been plenty appealing to Nell — whoever she was.

"You are paying attention, aren't you Joe?"

"Of course. I can repeat your last sentence if you wish. But don't you wonder who Nell is?"

Burne-Jones stared at the message. Double-

Dutch not German as far as he was concerned.

"Now you come to mention it, no. I don't. Now . . . what was I saying?"

"You were telling me about Germany being in denial. Not a phrase I'd heard before. But while we're here. Eighty-eight."

"What?"

"The number 88. I see that more often than I see 'Where's Nell' or 'Find me Hilde.' "

"Oh. That's old. They were painting that on the walls about nine months ago. Once they realised that liberation didn't mean instant transformation into a land of milk and honey and that they might just have to clean up the mess themselves, they started wishing they had Adolf back. Eight is H, the eighth letter of the alphabet. Ergo . . . HH is Heil Hitler. But as I said, they've passed that. They now want to pretend he never existed. If you were to believe every German who claimed to have been part of the July 20 conspiracy, then you'd marvel the Reich made it to the twenty-first — the conspirators seem to have had more regiments than Joe Stalin, more divisions than the Pope."

They'd reached the Dammtor Bahnhof as big as any in London and suffering from the same glass and iron Paxton pretensions to being a cathedral. The war, the British, had somehow left it intact. Like the Atlantic, frayed and ragged, but intact.

Opposite was a clean, unmarked, vast, eight-storey building. Not a scratch on it. A sign curving around the front read, "Victory Club NAAFI — Other Ranks."

"I know what you're thinking," said Burne-Jones. "It didn't survive the raids. It wasn't there. We built this from scratch last year. Ballroom, gym, shop . . . you name it."

Wilderness stared.

"Ballroom? A bloody ballroom?"

The building all but shone. In a city where people shuffled around in rags, half-starved, picking over the contents of dustbins — a city in which that which was not grey with ash was yellow with vitamin deficiency — where people lived in holes in the ground . . . we had built this?

He said as much to Burne-Jones, and Burne-Jones replied, "*Siegerrecht.* To the victor the spoils."

# §71

In the middle of the day, the club was largely empty. They took deep bucket chairs and a low table in a bar that would not have looked out of place on the Queen Mary. In fact, everything about the Victory Club reminded Wilderness of an ocean liner. He'd never seen one, inside or out, but just the same . . .

Never one to rush anything, Burne-Jones continued his lecture while they were served coffee, but with the first sip said, "How many Germans were Nazis, would you say?"

"All of them," said Wilderness knowing that Burne-Jones was inviting the obviously wrong answer.

"We reckon about twelve million."

"Why so sure?"

"Because party records survived the war intact. They were at a paper mill in Munich waiting to be pulped when the Americans arrived."

"That's . . . incredible."

"Nonetheless it happened. So now almost every German has had to fill in one of these."

Burne-Jones slid a thin sheaf of papers across the table to him, four pages bound by red string with shiny metal tags through punched holes at the top left-hand corner.

Wilderness leafed through it. Four pages, two columns, questions in two languages.

"We call it the Personnel Questionnaire. The Germans just call it *Fragebogen* — 'Questions.' One hundred and thirty-one in all, and how they answer determines what category they get bunged into and whether they get one of these."

Another sheet of paper slid across the table. Small and yellowing, the sort of thing you'd fold up in your wallet next to your identity card, a smudged blue number stamped into one corner, an unreadable signature in another.

"This is an *Entlastungsschein*. They call it a *'Persilschein.'* "

"What, like the washing powder?"

"Exactly. It washes whiter than white. It's official exoneration. You have one of these and you can prove to any employer, any copper, or any nosy parker that you're not considered an enemy or a threat. I'd go so far as to say it's the most valuable document in Germany . . . until we find Adolf's will or Eva's love letters."

Wilderness flicked through the questions.

"Were you a member of the *Korps der Politischen Leiter*? Were you a *Jugendwalter*? What the fuck is a *Jugendwalter*?"

"Hitler youth leader. In all likelihood a teenager good at ordering smaller teenagers around."

"All sources of income since 1933? . . . and they answer this lot?"

"Indeed they do. They all want their *Persilschein*. As you might expect there's a fair trade in fake *Persilschein*, but that's not our problem. Our problem lies with the ones we've been asked to re-examine."

At last, the rat Wilderness had been sniffing since breakfast.

"That's why you got me here?"

"Yes."

"How many?"

"One million three hundred thousand, give

or take."

"You couldn't just send me back to square-bashing and jankers?"

"Very funny, Holderness. Stop sneering and let me put you in the not-so-pretty picture. In the first few weeks after the war, things got a bit gung ho. The French wanted vengeance. There were a few, shall I say, *incidents* that won't ever make the papers. The Americans, strangely, also seemed to hate the Germans more than we ever did. The result was chaotic . . . and answers to this form, matched against party records, led to a hell of a lot of minor Nazis — *Muss-Nazis* — being dismissed from public life, kicked out of their jobs, denied their *Persilschein.* Madness. After all we knew full well that some jobs under the Reich couldn't be held down without joining the damn party and every boy and every girl in Germany were, theoretically, enrolled in the various branches of Hitler Youth with neither consent nor responsibility. Interpreted too rigorously the *Fragebogen* became a rubber stamp for the joke you cracked a few minutes ago. Everyone, absolutely everyone, was a Nazi. I say again, chaos. To give you just one example: eighty per cent of all schoolteachers in the American Zone got the sack. Extrapolate that to public life as a whole and you can guess what happened, the civic structure just caved in. Nothing got organised because there was no one

256

there to organise it. Germans were starving, most lived off rations not much better than a prisoner got in Belsen. Now, odds are, Germany was going to starve anyway. But it's undeniable that the mess we created made it worse. So what happened next? Uncle Sam puts the machine into reverse. Revises its classification system and starts actively hiring ex-Nazis. But, there's more to it than that . . . for years, perhaps since the first doodlebug landed on London, they . . . I think I mean we . . . the Allies . . . have wanted to get our hands on the blokes who designed V-1s and V-2s. Mostly this was done in the American Zone at Peenemünde, Nordhausen, and Dora. And no one really gave a toss whether these blokes were Nazis or not. Personally, I think that's a mistake. If they weren't party members, they still had a lot to answer for. Dora was a concentration camp manned by slave labour, they worked people to death. But it was pretty obvious no one was going to ask Werner von Braun about dead slaves. We collared our share. Shipped a dozen boffins back to Cambridge. The Russians indulged in an unholy scramble that included kidnapping people off the streets . . . but above all the Americans wanted their rocket boys. They have most now, but not all."

Burne-Jones looked around for something, reached for a roneoed, smudgy menu off the next table — egg and chips, saveloy and

chips, peas and chips, chips with everything
— and turned it over. A rough map of Europe
sprang from the tip of his pencil. A shapeless
blob for Ireland, a blob with proboscises for
England, a square for Spain, a boot for Italy.

"We know that a lot of Nazis have escaped
Germany in the last eighteen months."

He scribbled arrows down through Italy,
across the South of France and into Spain
and Portugal.

"There are fairly obvious escape routes.
Most, we reckon went south. Most ended up
in Lisbon, a city where nobody asks too many
questions, and from there to Brazil or Argen-
tina. A five-bob postal order and a Mars bar
to the man who spots Martin Bormann or
Adolf Eichmann. But, supposing some clever
bastard went north?"

A long, thick black arrow was scribbled in,
like an imaginary, unswerving autobahn from
Stuttgart to Hamburg.

"You could lose yourself in the British
Zone, but getting a ship out to anywhere
would not be easy."

"So you think some of these boffins are hiding out in Hamburg."

"I don't know. But the Americans are
insistent that we look."

"How many?"

"I don't know."

"Who? Who are we looking for?"

"Don't know that either."

"So we're searching for people who might not exist, might not be here, and we don't know what they look like?"

"That about sums it up. But if they're here . . ." He picked up the *Fragebogen*. "They've filled in one of these, and they've lied. That's where you come in. Read them through, look for the loopholes that tell you they're lying."

"One million three hundred thousand!"

"Of course not. Just Hamburg, and just the ones we're sceptical about. A few hundred at most."

Wilderness scanned the pages again.

"Who interviews these people in the first place?"

"Straight to the heart as usual . . . yeeees, that's our problem really. Fluent German speakers, of course . . . many of them former refugees themselves . . . but few of them regular soldiers . . . in fact I've not yet met one who saw combat. They tend to be older men, men who were in Civvy Street much of the war."

"And?"

"And they can be next to useless. On the one hand all the pent-up hatred of chocolate soldiers, Blimps who watched the war from an insurance office in Guildford, on the other Mr. Chips, soft old prep-school Latin masters who think a smack on the wrist and forgive and forget will fix anything and anyone. Even

a Nazi. Not a lot in between in my experience.

"We're re-interviewing. You'll be working
with a Pioneer Corps chap, Captain Yateman."

The rat loomed larger.

"Twat, is he?"

"Don't spare the qualifiers, Holderness.
He's a fucking twat, to use your habitual
phrase."

"If he's so sodding useless, why don't you
replace him?"

"Because I didn't appoint him. I don't get
to appoint the denazification team. I get to
appoint the intelligence officer attached to
the denazification team. In this case, you."

"Me? Leading Aircraftman Holderness?"

"Yes."

"Then why not make me an officer? How
easy is it going to be if I have to contradict
an army captain with nothing but an LAC's
rank to stand on?"

"You'd hate it. You'd absolutely hate being
an officer. You've risen to LAC. Accept that
promotion and be content for the time being."

"Hate it? Give me a half a bloody chance.
I'd have been LAC nine months ago if I
hadn't gone to Cambridge."

"If you hadn't gone to Cambridge you'd be
in a military prison. Where were you when I
found you?"

Wilderness said nothing and stared at him. Anger was a waste of time.

"Where were you?"

"In the glasshouse."

"Quite. In the glasshouse on a charge sheet as long as your arm. Be grateful for small mercies, Joe. Being an LAC is a small mercy. Not being in prison is a big, fat, Technicolor mercy."

Wilderness said softly, "Sergeant would be good, even corporal, much as I hate corporals."

"And you'd hate them even more if you were one. Think how happy you'd be in the NCO's mess surrounded by them. Stick with this, Joe. We'll talk about promotion in a month or two."

Wilderness did not believe this. They might never discuss his promotion again.

"OK. Let's get back to the real question. If Yateman fucks up how do I overrule him with no pips and no scrambled egg?"

"Trust me. You'll have that authority. You can investigate anyone you think fit, whatever the good captain says. He might rant, he might have steam coming out of his ears and arsehole . . . you just refer him to me."

# §72

This called for a little privacy. Back at the Atlantic. Up in Burne-Jones's suite. They

261

awaited a man Burne-Jones referred to as the
armourer, whom he greeted as Major Weatherill. About Burne-Jones's age, and in the
same Guards regiment.

"Standard procedure. You're part of the occupying force. You have to carry a gun. King's
regs and all that. You're lucky. I can give you
a pistol. There are plenty of chaps nipping
out for a swift stein of lager lugging Bren
guns with them. Now, would you kindly
remove your blouse, LAC Holderness."

Wilderness obeyed silently. Somewhat awed
by the man's apparent indifference to his lack
of rank. He did not give orders; he made
requests. It was like being at the tailor's. A
gentleman was a gentleman — a bloke whose
cheques didn't bounce.

Wilderness held up his arms as Weatherill
fitted a shoulder holster under his left armpit.

"Comfortable?"

"Fine."

When did officers ever care about your
comfort?

"Good. Try this."

Weatherill upended his satchel and took out
three automatic pistols.

"The Colt .45."

It was big and felt like a log inside the
holster.

"It's won't be easy to get at under my
blouse."

"The point is to have it," said Burne-Jones.

"Not to get at it. Or did you see yourself having to outdraw Wyatt Earp? You can have a button-flap waist holster if you insist but you'll look like a military policeman."

"Hmm . . ." said Weatherill, ignoring Burne-Jones. "Perhaps not the Colt."

Wilderness could almost hear him saying "perhaps something in dark blue."

He handed the Colt back, wondering at what point he should speak up, and thinking now might not be the moment.

"Try this. Beretta .22."

It was like a toy, vanishing down the mouse-hole of his holster, all but weightless.

"No. Not that either. Never really cared for the .22. More of a lady's gun, alright in a handbag but . . . but . . . we still have the Sauer 38H. Point 32, takes standard 7.65mm ammunition, and God knows Germany is awash with that. We confiscated about twenty-five thousand of these off Jerry. Does the job. And the German coppers seem to like it."

Wilderness slipped it into the holster, decided he liked the feel of it, hefted the weight of it in his hand. Took a look at it. Small, smaller than his own hand, only about six inches long, black with an elaborate S stamped into the grip.

"Of course some of them have red swastikas inset. We tend not to give those out. Some chaps would simply sell them to souvenir hunters after all. Now, you happy with that?"

"Perfectly, sir. There is just one thing."

"Yeees?"

"I've never fired a gun in my life."

Burne-Jones looked up from the newspaper he'd been reading.

"What? What? It's part of basic training."

"Where was I when you found me? I hadn't got as far as weapons training when they bunged me in the glasshouse for the last time. The most I've done is swing a broom handle around and attempt to slope arms with it."

"Bugger," said Burne-Jones.

"Bugger indeed," said Weatherill. "It might be best if you didn't try and shoot anyone. At least not just yet."

## §73

After a month Wilderness had come to look forward to his meetings with Major Weatherill.

He spent his days in a clumsily refurbished office, seized from the Hamburg Port Authority, overlooking Planten un Blomen Park. They consisted of repetitive sessions with Captain Yateman.

The first session had not gone well.

"Intelligence Officer? You're an enlisted man!"

"The English language is prone to creating confusions, sir."

Burne-Jones had been emphatic about the

"sirs." And when talking to a short, stout, ruddy man who had spent most of the war behind a desk at the Hatfield branch of the Herts and Cambridge Allied Assurance Society, it was as well to P the ps and Q the qs. Yateman puffed up like a bantam cock, and stood on enough dignity to provide a solid footing for the Empire State Building. He sat behind a desk here too — complete with in-tray and out-tray, although there was never anything in either as Wilderness held the files, and Wilderness concluded that the captain could not bear to be parted from them, the symbols of his authority . . . his crook and mitre . . . his helmet and truncheon . . . his inkwell and quill. He'd probably brought them with him from England.

They interviewed Germans together. Tedious beyond belief, and on Burne-Jones's advice Wilderness intervened only when necessary and as yet necessity had not arisen.

Alle Ihre Dienstverhältnisse seit 1. Januar 1930 bis zum heutigen Tage sind anzugeben.

And once they had reached that at the top of page three, Wilderness would be listening for what seemed like hours to every job the bloke had ever had and every pfennig he'd ever pocketed.

Some of them were lying, perhaps more out

of fear of the tax man than the English man, but it struck Wilderness as trivial. Anyone who lied about their party membership was caught as easily as swatting a fly. They checked against party records. And most who tried that lie had been caught at the first examination not the second.

Yateman's failing, Wilderness concluded, was that he favoured the *Muss-Nazi* for no better reason than that they tended to be of the same class — searching for a word that bridged the two languages, he coined "burger." Roger Yateman was a "burger." The sort of man who was a Rotarian and a pillar of the Chamber of Commerce, who gave generously to selected charities and who despised the poor as feckless and lazy, and who despised the rich as feckless and lazy. The sort of man who had no politics, so he joined the Conservative Party — the sort of man who had no faith, so he joined the Church of England. A "burger." Most of the selfish, prim, morally vacuous sods arraigned before them were "burgers." Solid citizens of a bourgeois world that had dissolved around them. Men with no real conviction but enough savvy to have bent to the political wind, and not to have much troubled their consciences these last thirteen years. They too might have been insurance office managers in Hertfordshire. Wilderness agreed with Burne-Jones — the *Muss-Nazis* probably no longer mattered. Yateman no longer mattered, except in his capacity to fuck up.

A *von* or a *zu* affixed to a German surname could drive the man apoplectic. Nazi or anti-Nazi, they seemed to bring out in him a scarcely veiled counter-snobbery.

Again Wilderness did not intervene, any more than he did with the burgers, confining himself to "this way, follow me," "thank you," and "good luck." Whether he intervened or not would depend on what he did with his nights — reading through pile upon pile of *Fragebogen* looking for Burne-Jones's rocket scientists. And thus far not finding them. The rest, the underwhelming majority of the culpable, the innocent, and indifferent were of no concern. "In denial," Burne-Jones had said. Germany was a land of ostriches. And heads buried in the sand could bleedin' well stay in the sand.

But . . . two mornings a week he and Weatherill drove out to the far east of Hamburg, past fragile suburbs, to abandoned farms, and an empty silage pit lined with sandbags. There he learnt how to shoot.

"You know, LAC Holderness . . ."

He was never just Holderness or Joe.

"We have an advantage. Missing out on basic training leaves you nothing to *un*learn. No comparison between a close-quarters weapon like this and a rifle. You were quite right in your summary. Knowing how to swing a Lee Enfield .303 around on the parade ground with occasional cracks at a paper target isn't knowing how to shoot. After all the bloke with the Lee Enfield isn't there to shoot. He's there to die."

"Eh?"

"Do you know how many bullets from a Lee Enfield it took to kill a Jerry in the First War? I'll tell you. A quarter of a million. And all but one would miss the bugger. That's how useful the rifle and the bloke holding it are in the twentieth century. What mattered was that he died doing it. I'm not here to teach you to die, LAC Holderness. I'm sure you'll manage that very well without me."

"Then what are you here to teach me, Mr. Weatherill?"

"I'm here to teach you to kill."

Wilderness did a silent double take at this.

"Ah . . . such innocence. Tell me LAC Holderness, what kind of an organisation did you think you'd joined?"

Wilderness never answered this for fear Wetherill would put him right. He had few illusions, but he much preferred to hang on to them.

By week three, Major Weatherill was complimenting him on his accuracy. It brought a silent, he hoped, invisible pride to Wilderness's mind. The first thing he'd been really good at since Abner taught him to crack a safe. Russian and German were good things in their way, and his education at Rada's hands was worth three years in any university . . . but this . . . a Sauer 38H in his fist . . . six inners and two bulls . . . this was . . . physical.

# §74

The Atlantic Hotel was a refined version of hell. Wilderness did not fit in anywhere. There was no specific area for "other ranks," but all the same the white-coated German waiters, all under the supervision of class-and-rank-conscious English batmen, always managed to sequester him several tables apart from any officer by what amounted to a cordon sanitaire. This pattern only altered if Burne-Jones was in town. The officers of the Control Commission ignored him — which had one advantage. He did not have to salute at five-second intervals every time he passed one.

Most evenings he pored over the files Burne-Jones had dumped on him, and he had worked out that the reason — perhaps one of the reasons — he had been billeted here, the fish out of water, was that Burne-Jones wanted none of his files going astray. On the nights he took for himself he usually drifted over to the Victory Club — past the by-now familiar cries of "Fag, Tommy?", "Chocs, Tommy?", "Jig-jig, Tommy?" — at least the

269

Victory had "other ranks" in letters a foot high over the door.

One night, in the first week in December, he was in one of the bars at the Victory Club, drinking alone as he had made no friends among the NCOs either, and had turned down an offer to have his cock sucked for a packet of ten Player's Navy Cut. His "war" was at the opposite of most. He was zenith or nadir — it didn't matter which — starting his task as others were finishing theirs. Much of what they did and said was reminiscence, and he had no memories to trade. Every other night, perhaps even every night, the Victory Club played host to someone's demob party. The joy soon went out of them, and if a dozen blokes came in hell-bent on getting rat-arsed, burning their pay books in the ashtrays, showing each other their backsides and staging water battles with stirrup pumps and fire buckets, he'd usually drink up, go back to the Atlantic and his pile of paperwork. But it was frustrating. Hamburg was a city that lived by crime. The black market was the only market and it seemed to be ubiquitous and elusive at the same time.

On this occasion, a hand clapped onto his shoulder and a voice asked, "What'll you have, mate?"

It was the flight sergeant from the Lancaster that had flown him out. The hand moved into mid-air ready for Wilderness to shake.

"John Blackwall. Call me Johnnie."

"Joe Holderness. Call me Joe. I thought your time was up?"

"Nah, I got six months left. Skipper's time was up. After we dropped you off he nicked anything that wasn't nailed down, flew the old girl up to a little harbour near Kiel, put her down on the sands — hairiest landing of my life — and winched a yacht, sails and all, into the bomb bay."

"Don't the coppers and customs look out for that sort of thing back home? How do you sneak a yacht past the military police for Christ's sake?"

"We didn't. We dropped it into the Solent like it was one of Barnes Wallis's bouncing bombs. We tried it with a Merc last summer. Skipper made whopping great water skis for each wheel. Looked like the daftest flying boat in history. Sank like a stone, just off Ventnor. Then in September we dumped five hundred pounds of NAAFI coffee beans wrapped in tarpaulin. Floated long enough for his pals to get it ashore. We got it right this time too. The yacht's moored at Milford-on-Sea, just opposite the Isle of Wight, now. Expects me to crew for him next summer. I should cocoa."

This was ambitious. Impressive. A thief with nerve and imagination. Wilderness was looking for a good nick, but this was a nick far beyond him.

"So what's the crack, then?"

"Crack?"

"There must be something happening in Hamburg. Everybody nicks everything. Everybody has something to sell. Everybody lives by the black market."

"True, fags are better than pfennigs and a bag o' coffee's worth a quick fuck in an air raid shelter. And enough bags o' coffee'll buy you a Leica. You're getting nothin', then?"

"Not a sausage. Sorry . . . I mean not a *Wurst.*"

"I reckon I can tell you why. You based here?"

"Not exactly. I'm with the nobs at the Atlantic."

Blackwall sucked in breath sharply.

" 'Struth. Need someone to black their boots do they? Or is it regimental arse-wiping?"

"Security reasons, or so I'm told."

"O'course. The skipper said you was one o' the colonel's bright boys. But . . . it's the Atlantic that's stuffing you mate. All the action's out at the base. 'Cos that's where all the pickings are. There's fuck all here. You can't nick from the NAAFI, can you? I mean, look at those women they have behind the counter. They catch you light-fingered they'll crush you to death with one hand. They get you between their tits and you'll never see daylight again. Nah, you got to be out at

Fuhlsbüttel. A quick visit to stores, a bit of a bung to the quartermaster and bob's yer uncle. I always say, any posting, any town . . . you need to find the easy pickings."

"All I can do is flog off my own fags and chocs ration."

"Never get rich that way. So, you haven't dealt much with reichsmarks?"

"Hardly at all. All I see is Little England on the Baltic. Sterling rules. I take some reichsmarks if I sell me fag allowance. But mostly I give fags away. There are so many just begging for them."

"You give 'em away?"

"Chicken feed," Wilderness said.

Clearly, Blackwall did not agree. He unrolled a 5RM note onto the tabletop.

"Take a look. You see the little plus after the number? That means the Yanks printed it. If there's a minus, the Russkis. Try not to take minuses. Stupid bloody Yanks gave the Russians the plates, they print money the way we print 'Property of HM Forces' on bog paper. It could all end up worthless. Before the war, there was a tale that people in Berlin papered rooms with reichsmarks because it was cheaper than buying wallpaper. One day all this could be so much cheaper than bog paper we'll be wiping our arses on it. Here endeth the lesson."

Two pints of Flensburger arrived almost by osmosis. Blackwall gulped an inch off his and

273

said, "Easy pickings, kiddo, easy pickings."

It was a slogan to live by, the sort of thing Abner might have told him.

# §75

At last.

Peter Camenzind caught his attention. His *Fragebogen* was not one that had been singled out arbitrarily. He'd applied for a job with the state, the state being the Allied Control Commission for Germany, and that made a second look mandatory.

Thirty-four years old, a former teacher from Berlin. His *Fragebogen* was bland. He'd never been in anything, not the Nazi Party, not a trades union, he'd never done any kind of military service, and he'd never been abroad.

Before talking to Yateman, Wilderness put a phone call through to Berlin. The school Camenzind claimed to have taught in was rubble — the whole street was rubble. As was the Ministry of Education, in which any record of his scrupulously accounted employment might have been kept. All very plausible, all rather neat, and making further checks impossible.

It was not a day when Burne-Jones was in Hamburg. At the start of the day's work Wilderness set Camenzind's *Fragebogen* in front of Captain Yateman.

Surprisingly Yateman remembered him.

"So he's found a position. Jolly good luck to him. Should be a rubber stamp affair. In and out in two minutes."

"Position" not "job" was enough to show the extent to which the burger Yateman identified with the burger Camenzind. Certain people had careers, certain people had professions, certain people had positions, the rest had jobs.

"No," said Wilderness.

"No, LAC Holderness?"

"Since you do remember him, sir. Why did you not query his lack of military service? He was born in 1912. He'd have been called up for the invasion of Russia in 1941, if not before. If he was lame or ill, he'd have been in the Home Guard. At the very least, sick or fit, short of being in a wheelchair, if he could put one foot in front of the other, if he was anywhere near Berlin last year he'd have been in the Volkssturm, with the old men and the schoolboys. And he taught in a grammar school. Yet he lists no party or union membership."

Yateman was polishing his spectacles, avoiding eye contact with Wilderness.

"Perhaps he wasn't in either?"

"The National Socialist Teachers' League was pretty well compulsory, and the pressure to join the party itself would have been nigh irresistible. Like joining the Freemasons if you want to get on back home."

The wire loops of his spectacles hooked back around his ears with a dip of his head. And when at last he looked at Wilderness, the thin English lips were set like the slit in a pillar box, the little red moustache twitched independently in suppressed anger.

"An odious comparison, Holderness."

"If you say so, sir."

All the same, they sent for Camenzind.

There was a joke doing the rounds that had eventually reached Wilderness via Johnnie Blackwall one night at the bar in the Victory Club.

A bloke sweeping the street pauses for a breather to find another bloke looking at him from a street corner. The cleaner turns to the other bloke and says, kind of haughty like, "I was a senior clerk at City Hall before all this denazification nonsense — now I'm sweeping the fucking streets." And the second bloke says, "Before all this denazification nonsense *I* was sweeping the fucking streets."

And little fleas have lesser fleas and so ad infinitum. It was a world of fleas. They were meant to be finding little Hitlers not little fleas.

Peter Camenzind was a flea — a flea in so far as he looked no different from any one of a hundred other men who had sat in front to Wilderness and Yateman. His jacket was ragged at the elbows and cuffs, his shoes resembled burst sausages, he had no topcoat, he looked as though he shaved with a rusty can lid, and he stank. He had applied to resume his former profession of teacher of mathematics to children of secondary-school age. He expressed no resentment at having his *Fragebogen* flourished in front of him, merely a hint of boredom and a passivity that passed for cooperation in the flea world. Wilderness had rapidly concluded that this was the chief characteristic of the "new" Germany — passivity, a mental exhaustion, a level of sloth that would not whip up enough adrenaline to get out of the way of a rolling tank. Less death wish than lethargy. An indifference born in defeat.

But the scarecrow appearance did nothing to disguise the man. He spoke with a patrician Prussian accent, and nothing about facing a British army captain and his insignificant assistant dented his calm or his manners. He held himself well — the sort of boy who'd been beaten if he slouched, shouted at if he put his hands in his pockets.

His hands weren't in his pockets, they rested on his crossed legs, on the all but transparent fabric of his threadbare trousers, nails bitten down to blood, fingers stained to a deep ochre with nicotine.

"Would either of you gentlemen have a cigarette to spare?"

§76

He passed muster. Smoked his way through half of Wilderness's fags and told plausible lies.

Why had he not served with the armed forces?

Asthma.

Why had he not been called to the Volkssturm?

By 1944 he had been in Hamburg, but was registered in Berlin.

Why was he in Hamburg?

Berlin's schools were bombed out, its children evacuated. A friend had offered him a job in Hamburg. The friend died, and the job with him.

... "And since the war was lost — only an idiot or a fanatic would think it was not lost by the autumn of forty-four — was I to go home and await slaughter or capture by the Russians . . . or stay here and wait for the British?"

How had he lived?

"By my meagre savings and by the kindness of strangers."

He waved a lit cigarette in the air, smiling at Wilderness, a trail of smoke like a passing dragonfly in the air between them.

"Lately it has hardly been an issue. Money becomes irrelevant when there's nothing to buy."

# §77

Out in the corridor, Wilderness said, "He's too cocky by half."

"You don't believe him?"

"With all due respect, sir, the man is blatantly lying."

"You know LAC Holderness, I doubt you know the meaning of the word 'respect.' "

"Then just keep him here."

"What?

"Bugger respect. Just keep him here. Detain him, arrest him, play fuckin' tiddlywinks with him. I don't care. Just keep him out of my way while I turn over his gaff."

# §78

Camenzind lived in a converted air raid shelter. Conversion consisted of installing electricity (one bare bulb to a room), beds (straw-filled palliasses on rickety wooden frames), the odd scrap of furniture (a hat stand that could not have seemed more out of place than an antimacassar or an aspidistra table) and a gas ring that strove, in company with the kettle, to become a kitchen. The only running water was from a standpipe in the street. All but the top three feet of it was below ground level and it had no windows. It had ten rooms and was home to thirty-six men, half of whom were in residence when Wilderness called with an escort of military police and turfed them out into the winter cold where they shivered with only the merest of muttered complaints. A one-eyed man — a black patch over his left eye and a ragged red scar across the cheek beneath — wearing the remains of a haphazardly dyed Wehrmacht uniform — grey with black blotches, one breast pocket hanging loose like a waving handkerchief, the trousers baggy around his now-skinny frame — showed him where Camenzind slept, in a damp, dirty concrete room he shared with three other men.

"You are here to search the room?"

"Yes."

"What is there to search?"

He walked away and left Wilderness to it.

The man had a point. What Camenzind owned, and this seemed to apply to his roommates too, he was probably wearing.

A small cardboard suitcase beneath the bed yielded clean if tatty underwear and three pairs of socks in need of the darning needle.

Next to the bed was an upended crate that had once held oranges. Camenzind was using it as a bookcase. A couple of novels by German authors Wilderness had never come across, a volume of Schiller's poetry, a maths textbook full of quadratic equations and a slim, paperbound physics treatise. He shook each book in turn, hoping for something concealed, or simply something being used as a bookmark.

Strips of torn newspaper fell from the Schiller and were nothing more than bookmarks a couple of inches across and ripped from the page regardless of the meaning of what was on them.

From the physics treatise fell the one piece that had been clipped with scissors. A photograph captioned in a language he did not recognise. But he recognised the photograph. It had been in one of Rada's files — the one curtly, aptly labelled "Armageddon." Her copy had been cut from the *New York Times.*

He looked at the title page of the treatise, and all the fragmentary unease he had felt from the moment he had first read Camenzind's *Fragebogen* cohered, crystallised.

Über den Nachweis und das Verhalten der
bei der Bestrahlung des Urans mittels
Neutronen entstehenden Erdalkalimetalle
von
Dr. Peter-Jürgen von Hesse
Max Planck Institut
Berlin Dahlem
1939

Rada had sent him away with books as well as files — all part of the education she wanted him to have, and he was pretty certain Burne-Jones was insistent he had. Some he read with pleasure, some from duty, and some he abandoned as boring.

*Peter Camenzind* by the Swiss writer Hermann Hesse had been one of the latter — he'd given up in less than fifty pages. A turn of the century bildungsroman. Something about an angst-ridden Swiss teenager with a bit of a thing about St. Francis of Assisi.

But . . . if you were looking for a change of name . . . it was wise to hang on to your Christian name — as you'd never answer to another — and from Hesse to one of the other Hesse's literary figures? Well it saved stretching the mind too far. And what were the odds anyone had ever read the book?

So, he wasn't Peter Camenzind, he was Peter-Jürgen von Hesse of the Max Planck Institute in the Berlin suburb of Dahlem. A place with quite a reputation. Einstein had been its first director in 1917.

The language on the captioned photo he concluded was probably Danish, as it depicted a gathering of Europe's finest physicists in Copenhagen in 1937. Niels Bohr was in the middle, so readily recognisable. Lisa Meitner, not quite so recognisable, was on his right, a young woman he could not identify on his left, and standing, just behind her left shoulder, was the man posing as Peter Camenzind.

# §79

Another "Where are you Nell?" was in the process of creation on the outside of the shelter. The one-eyed former soldier, brush in hand, was signing his name — Joe.

Wilderness asked, "Why do you do this?"

"In hope. And if hope proves false, proves worthless, then it is an elegy. You take everything away from us, would you take away our elegies too?"

"No."

"Then leave me with hope. Hope that one day . . . Joe and Nell will find each other."

Wilderness held out the packet of cigarettes that he'd opened for Camenzind.

"You smoke?"

"Of course, who doesn't?"

"As a matter of fact, I don't."

Johannes — Joe the painter — laughed as he lit up, laughed out the flame on his match.

"God that's funny . . . the only currency left is tobacco, and it doesn't even matter to you. You English amaze me sometimes."

"Keep the packet," Wilderness replied. "It may well be the last I ever give away."

# §80

He waited for Burne-Jones at breakfast the following day. Burne-Jones was late. He read a three-day-old copy of the *Manchester Guardian* almost cover to cover.

Burne-Jones dashed in looking frazzled.

"Sorry, old man. Didn't get in till after two. The RAF aren't as reliable as the Great Western Railway I'm afraid. All getting a bit Heath Robinson these days."

He looked around for a waiter. Gestured at the one he found and then turned to Wilderness.

"Have you eaten?"

"Nah. I was waiting for you. The service is better if you're on the other side of the table flashing yer crown and pip. I've had three coffees though. I'm swimming in caffeine."

"And bursting to tell me something."

"That obvious, eh."

"Rather."

Wilderness placed the Danish photograph in front of him and pointed to Camenzind.

"Swedish?"

"Danish. A physicists' conference in 1937. I have this bloke in a cell right now."

"Good lord. Who is he? One of the rocket boys?"

"No. You got luckier than that. He calls himself Peter Camenzind, but he's really Peter-Jürgen von Hesse. He wrote this."

Wilderness slipped Camenzind's treatise across the table.

"Bloody hell. What does it mean?"

"Your German's better than mine."

"No, I mean, what does it mean *mean*?"

"It's about what happens when you fire neutrons at uranium. It's one of the immediate precursors to the theory of a chain reaction."

"You mean atoms and stuff?"

"I mean atoms, stuff, chain reactions, and bombs big enough to take out Hiroshima."

"Ah," said Burne-Jones. "The penny has finally dropped."

"He's not one of your rocket boys. He's a bigger fish by far. If, and you'll know better than me, Germany was trying to build atomic bombs this would be the bloke who made them."

Burne-Jones said nothing while scrambled eggs, crisp bacon, and white toast were set in front of them.

It bought him thinking time and Wilderness could readily see that he was wondering how much to tell him.

"We . . . that is the governments of both Britain and America . . . were always concerned that Germany might be building a bomb. Most of the boffins with the know-how were German after all, and while most them worked for us . . ." He tapped the treatise with his finger. "There were a fair few who stayed on. No real way during the war of knowing quite what they were up to, so we took out their heavy water plant in Norway just in case. In '44 the Americans set

285

up a special unit in London with one purpose, to travel with the Allied troops as they crossed France and Germany and find out just how far the Germans had got. Led by a chap named Boris Pash. Met him a couple of times. Tough cookie, as our cousins would say. First American into Paris. In fact, his unit tended to be the first anywhere. They didn't follow, they led. In April last year they took a small town way down south, Haigerloch, not far from Stuttgart, and only about fifty miles from Lake Constance. They captured a wagonload of boffins and Germany's nuclear thingie."

"Thingie?"

"Cycle something. Science was never my strong point. I was more a Latin and Greek man."

"Cyclotron."

"If you say so, although quite how you know this sort of thing baffles me."

"They don't have public libraries in your neck of the woods? I used to sit in Whitechapel Library and read *Nature* while my mates kicked a tin can around the streets."

"Quite an education."

"Yeah. That and Cambridge and Rada."

"Good old Rada. Where would we be without her? Now, have you talked to this chap."

"Oh yes, he's chatty."

"Not too chatty I hope. Yateman doesn't

have your clearance."

"I wasn't aware I had my clearance, but there's nothing to worry about. The good captain lost interest once Herr Doktor von Hesse revealed his *von*. Brought out the Pooter in Yateman. He hates toffs more than he hates me.

"I asked von Hesse why he was in hiding. He said he didn't really know, but was perfectly happy to be in jail instead. He can smoke for Germany, so I kept plying him with fags and let him rattle on. I think, based on what you just told me, that he's telling the truth. He was at Haigerloch. He maintains they were nowhere near building a successful bomb. And he lit out only a day or two ahead of your American pal getting there, headed north — on the assumption he'd be looked for heading south for Switzerland — and managed to lose himself in Hamburg. I think he knew he'd get caught one day, and decided we were preferable to the Americans. Once I'd asked him the first question the mask seemed to drop quite readily. As though I'd lifted a burden from him. He seemed to want to cross-examine himself. A lot of it was waffle. I got most of his life story, but in the end what it came down to was guilt by any other name. By that I mean he never used the word."

"Guilt about what? The war? The Jews?"

"Guilt about staying on. What he fears is

not arrest or imprisonment; after all, he's had three of the squarest meals of his last year in the twenty-four hours since I picked him up, all the fags I could have sold on the black market and me last bar of Cadbury's Bourneville — for which you owe me by the by — and the only charge he faces is lying on his damn *Fragebogen.* A smack on the wrist, a fine he can't pay? And he'll probably get to keep his *Persilschein.* What he fears is the judgement of fellow scientists. Einstein got out, Lise Meitner got out, Leo Szilard got out . . . he stayed."

"Not a Nazi?"

"Not anything, and I think that's what bothers him. He doesn't know who he is any more. He teased that out into a whole thesis last night . . . what is Germany, who are the Germans? *'Wer sind wir, was sind wir?'* He said, and this is illustrative of the way he thinks, he said, 'How can I listen to Schubert lieder, how can I write a love letter, how can I describe the splitting of an atom in the same language that told a million lies in propaganda, created euphemisms such as *Die Endlösung* to disguise mass murder, and ordered children into gas chambers. It would be an obscenity.' "

"Obscenity?"

"That's what he said, and he said it in English."

"Who are the Germans?" Burne-Jones

echoed. "Who are the Germans? I rather think we'll all be asking that for many years to come. We now have the German question . . . perhaps it'll replace the Jewish question? Although I was never wholly certain what that was."

The German question?

And Wilderness thought of the one-eyed soldier in his hand-dyed Wehrmacht motley asking his own German question for years to come, perhaps asking for ever

Nell. I'm alive! Where are you? Joe.

# §81

*Lower Saxony:* August 1945

Nell stuck to unpaved roads. To limestone tracks that snaked across heathland, wound their way in and out of woodland copses, past farmhouses and barns.

On the third day, making slower progress than she had imagined, close to dusk, she could see in the infinite distance what appeared to be an encampment at the side of the road. It was the way she had imagined pilgrimages would end. Approaching the city, it seems to recede, to be always visible and always out of reach, its plume of smoke curling skyward merely to tantalise.

It was a caravan — much in the gypsy style.

It had been off the road a while, grass and

bindweed in the wheels, the shafts tied up, pointing to heaven and the cart horse put out to graze.

By the side of the track a child of indeterminate gender was stirring an indeterminate stew over an open fire, with a Wehrmacht helmet serving as the cauldron.

The child's trousers — baggy like pantaloons — puzzled Nell. Who would dress a child in bright red out of choice? But who had a choice? Then she saw the black arm of a hakenkreuz peeping out at the seam. And the faint rattle she had been hearing for the last minute began to make sense. A sewing machine. Someone, someone close and out of sight, was sitting at a treadle sewing machine turning Nazi flags into children's clothes. The 1945 revision of "swords into ploughshares."

The child had noticed her.

"Mutti!"

Nell followed as the child ran around the end of the caravan.

An old woman was indeed paddling away at a sewing machine, her hair tucked up in a headscarf made from the same material, her hands feeding more of the red and the black under the needle.

"Hullo dearie. Come far have you?"

"From Celle."

"I don't know where that is. Are you hungry?"

"Yes, I suppose I am."

"Well . . . there's enough for three. There is only me and Gretchen now."

She pulled the redefined flag from the sewing machine, snipped the trailing threads and held it up — another pair of baggy pantaloons. The Third Reich rendered into the costume of a circus clown.

Then she eased herself up with her walking stick.

"Won't be long. Come and meet the kids."

Behind the caravan, the horse grazed on the sparse grass of heathland — half a dozen rabbits nibbled in a wire run — cabbages and carrots struggled in the sandy soil — and three wooden crosses stuck in the ground marked the lives of Mutti's children.

"My daughter Kattrin, my son Eilif."

"They died here?"

"No. They neither of them died here. They died in the wars. They died on the road. And we've been on the road since the day the Russians entered East Prussia. The graves are markers — tokens if you like. In a world where everything is ersatz, they are ersatz graves for the children I never got to bury."

"Why . . . why here?"

"Here? Because this is where the horse stopped. He would go no further. Folk there are who would have stuck old Pickles like a pig and feasted on horse meat, but he had been too loyal for me ever to do that. Hauled us all the way from Gumbinnen, where I bought him. Before that we pulled the wagon ourselves. He has been too good a horse to end up in the pot. A thousand kilometres and more between the shafts. Allenstein, Graudenz, Bromberg, Landsberg, Berlin. No, dearie. It's rabbit stew for us. Come, fill up the hole in your belly before you fill one under the ground."

They ate from tin plates. Nell was pleased. She had not been at all sure she could have eaten from a Wehrmacht helmet.

"Going far, dearie?"

"Berlin."

"Ah . . . I was there in . . . March I think it was. Far enough ahead not to hear the Soviet tanks grumbling at my arse."

"I have not seen Berlin since December. But it is home. I am a Berliner."

"You are a Berliner. I am a Gumbinner. And I will never see my home again. Forget Berlin, dearie. Berlin is gone."

In all the warnings she had received — Dekker, the British policeman in Celle — it had not occurred to Nell that Berlin might be "gone."

"Berlin cannot be gone," she said.

"Once Berlin was not. Then Berlin was. Now Berlin is not."

"I must get to Berlin."

"No, dearie. You must survive. *Sie müssen überstehen.*"

"How?"

Mutti appeared to be thinking, but Nell knew it was the pretence of thinking, and that what she would say next had been on the tip of her tongue.

"Never tell all you feel, or better still, feel very little. And always know the price of flour and sugar. Coffee too for that matter."

She liked the old woman. The old woman fed her, lent her blankets for the night and let her sleep under the wagon . . . but Nell knew she could not live that way if that was what it took to survive.

# §82

The map she held was ancient. The newest map of Germany to be found in Klaus's library dated from 1888, the year of the Kaiser's accession. On the fourth day she felt she must be somewhat north of Wolfsburg, and close to the green squiggle Dekker had drawn on the map to show her roughly where Russian rule began.

Another dusty limestone track was leading her to another elusive pilgrim shrine — the iron gates and stone gateposts of a schloss — the castle itself being just visible beyond the trees, its roof peppered with missing tiles, and its slender, spiral turret sporting a shell-shaped hole.

Someone was singing:

Oh the grand old Duke of York,
'E 'ad ten thousand men.
So they banged 'im up in Pentonville.
An' 'e won't do that again.

The singer was tuneless, and out of sight.
As Nell rounded the gatepost he finally came
into view. A small man, swinging a rifle about
and marching up and down somewhat in the
manner of Charlie Chaplin. His top half appeared to be a British Tommy of some sort.
The lower half beggared belief. Pants as
baggy as those Mutti was making out of flags,
and in so many colours . . . blacks, greens,
and reds . . . with stripes.

She was staring, and she knew it.

He lowered the rifle.

"Wot you looking at?"

"At you, of course."

"Wossamatter? Anyone would think you'd
never seen a corporal of the Seaforth Highlanders before."

"I haven't. In fact I've never seen anyone
dressed like you before."

"You can talk. I've never seen a battledress
worn with a flowery frock before. At least
mine's legitimate."

"So's mine. Issued to me by His Majesty's
Royal Army Medical Corps. And I've never
seen rainbow-coloured pants before."

"Pants! These ain't pants, these is trews
these is!"

"Shouldn't you be in uniform?"

"This is my bleedin' uniform!"

From behind the Tommy a second appeared, dressed in the same outfit, but this one was clearly an officer of some sort, knocking the heads off thistles with his swagger stick as he approached.

"Sharpe! I thought I told you no more! Keep the buggers out!"

Sharpe, if that was his name, turned around and gave as good as he got.

"Don't shout at me you stuck-up fucker! You're not on the fuckin' parade ground now. It's just one more Kraut an' a little one at that, no more'n a kid."

"We're up to our necks in fucking *Flüchtlings*. What is the point of you being on guard duty if you guard nothing?"

He drew level with them now and either proximity or the recognition of Nell as being young or female caused him to lower his voice and change his expression. He was not quite smiling, but not frowning either.

The battledress threw him. Nell thought he might even be waiting for her to salute. She stared him out.

"Bill Dobbin," he said at last. "Captain, 3rd Seaforth Highlanders. And my man, Beckwith Sharpe, corporal of the same. And you are?"

Before she could answer Sharpe said, "I ain't his bleedin' man. Batman, birdman . . .

all that malarkey . . . that all went out with the war. And the war's over. I don't answer to Sharpe no more. It's Mister Sharpe to 'im and Becks to you."

"And I," said Nell getting a word in between these bickering conquerors, "am Christina Hélène von Raeder Burkhardt."

"Wot a mouthful," said Sharpe.

"Au contraire," said a voice she had not heard before, "a very familiar name."

They all turned. An old man had come upon them silently, and was now leaning heavily on his walking stick, and he was smiling, really smiling as though pleased to see her.

"My dear," he took her hand and pressed his lips fleetingly to the back of her knuckles. "Graf Florizel von Tripps of *Schloss Verrücktschwein*. I have known Klaus von Raeder all my life. Your grandfather perhaps?"

"My great-uncle, sir. My grandmother's elder brother."

"Has he lived through it all?"

"I'm afraid not."

"Ach, so many dead, we must look to the living. Gentlemen, we have room for one more, another *Flüchtling* for our ark."

So saying he offered her his arm and led her through the maze of thistle and nettle into his lost domain.

"Another?" she heard Dobbin say. "Is he going to take in the whole of Germany?"

"Told yer," said Sharpe. "An' if he is there's no point whatsoever in bleedin' guard duty is there?"

"You mustn't mind the 'heroes.' They are both good men, they are merely frustrated," von Tripps said to Nell. "They spent most of the war as prisoners. When the British freed them they were assigned to me as guards."

"Guards against what?"

"Oh, Poles mostly. Some French as well. Liberated slave labourers. In the spring the countryside was full of them. Taking what they wanted. Destroying what they wanted. Killing who they wanted. And who could blame them? Then . . . then someone in the Allied command had the bright idea of sending in British POWs to guard us. The displaced, the former slaves were rounded up or began the long walk home. You look rather like one yourself — they all wore bits of uniform, any uniform. A ragbag army, a barmy army. Perhaps that was Hitler's ultimate achievement, to have abolished the status of "civilian" and to have put us all into uniform, any uniform . . . the pan-uniform of the Europe of 1945.

"And then, after the fall of Berlin, the Prussians came west by the thousand. Dobbin would have me turn them away. That I cannot do."

So saying he put his shoulder to a studded oak door and they entered the great hall of the schloss — a room designed to seat and entertain a hundred aristocratic guests and which now housed a hundred refugees — *Flüchtlings*, like her.

It reminded her too sharply of Belsen, a swelling sea of neglected humanity — an idea she fought at once. Many might be hungry, but none of these were starving, none of these were dying. Many waved or shouted greetings to von Tripps as they passed through, out of the far door and into the garden. More refugees, makeshift tents by the dozen, women cooking over open fires, children running naked, dogs lazing in the summer sun. What they had brought with them as they fled west amazed Nell. Fleeing for your life, you pack up a brass-ended double bed and a couple of long-armed bed-warming pans. Just a few kilometres ahead of the Russian horde, you load the portraits of your ancestors onto the cart.

"For myself, and for the 'heroes' too, I keep half a dozen rooms. My own bedroom and the old kitchen. My bedroom would house a few dozen more I know, but there are limits to altruism."

Even as he said it she knew it wasn't true. He didn't mean a word of it.

"Were you in the last war?"

"I was. Under von Kluck on the Western Front. I lost my leg at Soignies in August 1914. The war was scarcely three weeks old and it was over for me. There are no one-legged cavalry officers."

So saying, he struck his left leg with his walking stick and Nell heard the clunk of wood on metal.

"Sawn off above the knee."

# §83

Von Tripps cooked for them all.

Dobbin and Sharpe sat and bickered while he did so.

It was her second decent meal that week. Chicken stewed with onions, tarragon, and garlic. Enough garlic to make Sharpe pull a face. He ate it all the same. Three of the *Flüchtling*s joined them — three men as old as von Tripps himself, which Nell put at sixty-something, silent beneath their Hindenburg moustaches, enduring the pidgin German of Dobbin and Sharpe, eating everything that was set in front of them.

As Nell cleared away, neither of the Englishmen so much as moving to help her, Sharpe set out a deck of cards on the vast, scarred kitchen table.

"Wanna see a trick?" he said to the *Flüchtling*s.

Von Tripps translated.

They looked at each other. Faces breaking into grins as though nothing had amused them in recent memory.

"This is called 'Find the Lady.' "

He took only three cards from the deck — the eight of clubs, the three of diamonds and the queen of spades. Held up all three for everyone to see.

"Now yer see it, now yer don't."

Nell watched from the sink as his hands flew across the table, juggling the cards from left to right and back again.

*"Nun,"* said Sharpe. *"Wo ist die Dame?"*

The *Flüchtling*s looked at one another again, a few mutterings Nell could not quite hear, then the old man in the middle put his finger down on the card on the far right with a look of utter confidence on his face.

Sharpe flipped up the three of diamonds. The other two laughed out loud at the consternation of the first, slapped him on the back, revelling in his mistake.

*"Wieder,"* they said to Sharpe, *"Wieder."*

Nell sat next to von Tripps and watched the hand deceive the eye again.

The next *Flüchtling* duly picked out the eight of clubs, and the laughter spread around the table. One voice startled her — amid the English, horsey snorts of Dobbin, the restrained chuckle of von Tripps, and the uproarious satisfaction of the *Flüchtling*s, one voice stood out, high and clear and unknown to her. It was her own. And she realised she had not laughed . . . had not laughed since some time in the autumn of 1944.

300

This cheeky, pushy, careless young corporal of the Seaforth Highlanders had made her laugh.

He winked at her. One brown eye closing.

Two more rounds and no one found the lady.

"*Genug.* I am for my bed," von Tripps said.

"Me too," said Dobbin. And to Nell, "If you find yourself alone with Becks, young lady, don't play for money. He's a wide boy. Another bloody cockney wide boy."

With the *Flüchtling*s gone too, she did indeed find herself alone with Beckwith Sharpe.

"What is a wide boy?"

"I suppose Bill means that he thinks of me someone not quite honest, not quite straight-forward . . . a bit short of calling me a cheat or a crook. I don't mind. We're mates. At least mates while we're here. Once we get back to Blighty . . . well . . . normal service will be resumed."

"You may not see one another?"

"We sure as hell won't see one another. 'Cept maybe at a regimental reunion, but I don't plan on attending many of those."

"Do you cheat? Do you steal?"

"I cut corners. Corners I have to cut to get by. That's all. It's what I have to do to survive."

"Do you always know the price of coffee?"

This seemed to baffle Sharpe for a moment,

then he grinned and said, "That's the yard-stick is it? That's how you get the measure of a wide boy?"

"It's one way, so I'm told. And the three-card trick?"

"Harmless. Just a bit o'fun. Harmless. 'Ere. I'll show you how it's done."

Afterwards, ever afterwards, Nell would wonder at the charm, the spell this cockney "wide boy" had cast over her. Sharpe's tricks were inconsequential and silly. They made her laugh. So little in her life had ever been allowed to be silly. Almost nothing had been inconsequential. She moved in a world of consequences, of action and reaction. Of responsibility. Quite possibly of guilt.

Something as simple as making her laugh would always seem less than the whole, less than the truth. And at the time, she could not possibly have envisioned where this would lead.

# §84

She stayed three days, longer by far than she had meant to. Sharpe taught her every varia-tion on his card game — including playing it with shells or coffee cups — and how to shuffle a deck to deliver almost any hand you wanted.

The ripple as he split the deck and inte-grated it card by card at the speed of light never ceased to make her laugh. Then he would deal her a perfect straight flush or a full house. It was a game, it was all a game. Every night a game. It was, as Sharpe kept saying, "harmless."

In the days she walked the garden, picking her way through half the furniture of East Prussia, seeking out anyone from Berlin and finding no one. She craved news, she longed to know that 21 Pfefferstraße still stood, that her parents were alive and well.

And on the fourth day she told Graf von Tripps that it was time to go.

Von Tripps made her put down the knapsack and sit with him awhile, out between the greenhouse and the potting shed, between the Pomeranians and the Silesians.

"Can I not persuade you otherwise?" he asked.

"Why would you wish to?"

"Look around you. Everyone you see has fled from east of Berlin. Berlin is in Russian hands."

"The British tell me they have a sector, a part of Berlin that they control. My home was in Charlottenburg. Charlottenburg is part of that sector, I believe."

"They do, and so do the French and the Americans. But for how long?"

"It's what I have to do."

"Nell, who are you trying to save?"

"I don't understand. Why would I be trying

303

to save anyone?"

"You tell me, but in all your conversation I have sensed a desire to . . . to put things back together again."

It was almost the same phrase she had used to Dekker all those weeks ago — "put them back together again." Of course she was. It was just that the words would never pass her lips for fear of hubris.

"You could go to England with Dobbin and Sharpe. They'll be repatriated soon. They'd find a way. If it was left to Sharpe he'd pack you in his kit bag. England, Nell. England. You'd be safe for ever."

"I'm sure I would, but I'd never dare look in the mirror again."

Von Tripps prised himself up off an outsized, inverted flowerpot and opened the shed door.

"For you," he said. "It may cut a day or two off your journey."

And he presented her with a green Raleigh bicycle, complete with brass plate declaring "Made in England," its tyres pumped and plump, its chain and Sturmey-Archer three-speed gears oiled and glistening.

"It is — was — my son's. Nothing has been heard of him since Stalingrad. And what use does a one-legged man have for a bicycle?"

In the panniers were two bottles of schnapps.

"You will have to be very careful crossing

the green border. The Russians are thieves and rapists, but if we appeal directly to the former you may never meet the latter. If they stop you, make sure they find the schnapps."

"And while they drink it I make my escape?"

# §85

On a dusty, deserted road somewhere between Tülau and Kunrau, just beyond a village named she-knew-not-what, where east and west now met, stood a lone Russian soldier by his lone wooden hut. Of His Majesty's Forces there was ne'er a sign.

A skewed placard read, "You are now leaving the British Zone" in four languages, each looking as though scrawled in haste, and just below that, most certainly scrawled in haste, in English and in red chalk, "Watch yer arse!"

And just beyond that another placard read "You are now entering the Soviet Zone" in four languages, looking handcrafted by a skilled signwriter.

But the red-and-white-striped pole was cocked skyward and the lone guardian of the East looked tired and bored.

"Велосипед," he said simply, his hands gripping the bars as though he might shake her loose.

"Schnapps," Nell said, even more simply.

He sank half the first bottle in what seemed

to Nell to be a single gulp.

There was a pause, a prolonged stillness of several minutes as he drank, belched, blinked, and eventually sat down sharply on his backside.

Some sense of duty returning to his rapidly clouding brain, he said, "Удостоверение личности. *Papiere.*"

Nell said nothing.

He took another swig from the bottle, belched again. Swigged once more and the bottle was empty. She marvelled at the man's constitution. All the same, she handed him the second.

"Спасибо," he said, with unexpectedly good manners. Then he fumbled for what he should be saying, *"Pap . . . Pap . . . Papiere."*

Nell reached down and picked up his rifle from where it had fallen as he had grabbed the schnapps and with both hands on the barrel spun herself around like a discus thrower and flung it as far as she could into the next field. Then she got back on her bike and rode away.

The next challenge, she knew, would be crossing the Elbe. One lone idiot on a dusty road might be replaced by an entire squad at any of the Elbe bridges. So she pedalled south and east. Rather than take the bridge at Tangermünde — was it even still there? Either side could have seen fit to blow it up — she would gamble on the ferry at Rogätz

— gamble that it was still working, gamble that the Russians thought it less significant than any bridge.

Whole families seemed to be making the river crossing in both directions. The battle-dress hidden at the bottom of her knapsack, Nell tagged along with a family boarding the ferry — mother, father and three daughters, one of whom was also pushing a bicycle. Nell struck up a conversation with the girl, walked on with her side by side and the Russians scarcely looked at them.

That evening, a warm, light August evening, she entered the American Sector of Berlin from the Potsdam side, passing both Russians and Americans, none of whom seemed to care that she did so.

# §86

*Berlin:* August 1945

Berlin had been bad when she left. Now it was worse. What had been damaged was ruined. What had been ruined was obliterated. Buildings stood eyeless and hollow, ribs without flesh — skeletal, slender fingers of brick pointing meaninglessly to a heaven that had forsaken them. They looked less like buildings than trees, winter trees. And the trees themselves were leafless and blasted — late August and not a green leaf to be seen.

And everywhere people. Berliners drifting

as though blown by a wind none but they could feel. And the Allies, static, rooted to the street corners gazing around, hands in pockets, detached from the living scene, watching it all as though it were no more than sideshow entertainment . . . the hurdy-gurdy man at the corner of her childhood. The beggar at her childhood's end.

Crossing Adolf-Hitler-Platz a Russian grabbed her bike by the handlebars, just as the border guard had done. He had a better vocabulary.

To "Велосипед" he added *"Fahrrad"* and "Byike."

He wasn't alone. Only a few feet away his pals were standing around smoking. And in the other direction half a dozen Americans, smoking and flirting with every girl that passed. As the Russian tugged at her bike she could hear the constant refrain of "Frat? Frat? Fraulein?"

She let go of the bike, gave the Russian a momentary taste of victory then clouted him round the ear with the flat of her hand as hard as she could. He let go, clapped a hand to his stinging ear and Nell clouted him on the other.

"Waaaaaghhhh!!!!"

Every head turned. Nell took her bike by the handlebars and dared him to try again — not wholly sure now if she was fighting for her bike or her life.

Then it started, a deep rumble from the Russians that the Americans picked up. They were laughing, they were all laughing. Not at her . . . at him. She had thought "thigh-slapping" no more than a metaphor, but that is what Russians did, they all but doubled up and slapped their thighs. And she knew she'd got away with it when the man himself began to laugh.

She wheeled her bike forward, nodded politely at the Russian as he stepped aside and said, "Спасибо. Добро пожаловать в Берлин." Thank you. Welcome to Berlin.

One of the Americans chased after her.

"Fraulein, fraulein. Spreckenzy English?"

She wheeled on, with him close behind her and did not turn around until she felt clear of the Russians.

"Yes. Of course. What is it you want?"

"Er . . . I guess . . . y'know . . . Frat? I never seen anyone tackle a Russki like that. Lady, you got . . ."

He stopped short of an obscenity. But Nell no more wanted anything to do with him than with the Russian.

"Buy you drink, hon? Buy you a meal? I got zigs, I got shockylade. Maybe a little jig-jig, y'know fick-fick?"

"How kind. But you must excuse me. I have to find my home."

Along the Kaiserdamm every naked tree seemed to draw a crowd. As one thinned she could see the reason. Notes on card and paper, notes by the dozen, notes by the hundred pinned to the trunk. Men seeking wives, women seeking husbands. Pleas for the missing. Lost children, lost parents. Lost lives. Berlin was lost.

"Else, where are you? I am back."

"Matthias Bergman is alive and well and living at 71 Köpenicker Straße."

And one writ large that seemed almost aimed at her . . .

"Nell. I'm alive! Where are you? Joe."

Common as the name was, she'd never known anyone called Joe.

# §87

She found 21 Pfefferstraße. What was left of it. Nos. 21, 23, and 25 had collapsed into their own cellars. One wall of 27 stood. Most of 19 was intact, but had neither doors nor windows. Halfway up its wall she could make out the floral wallpaper of what had been her bedroom. The fireplace was intact, jutting out into space, defying gravity, and on the mantelpiece a rag doll she had won playing hoop-la at the *Weihnachtsmarkt* Christmas fair held in the Lustgarten in 1937. Berlin had blown away, swept up on a hurricane of high explosives — and her rag doll, light as a feather, still sat upon the mantelpiece.

A fence post had been stuck in the rubble of No. 21. Another note for Berlin lost nailed to it.

Marie Burkhardt now resides at No. 92.

So, her mother was alive. Other people "lived." Her mother "resided." She didn't doubt that Marie had written it herself.

No. 92 had fared only slightly better than No. 21. The top two storeys had vanished. They had not collapsed into the cellar, the cellar was occupied. A stout if improvised door half a dozen steps down from the street, a stovepipe sticking out of a peephole window at ground level. On top of the broken wall, just beyond the reach of a human hand, three galvanised buckets of earth, sprouting with parsley, thyme, and a solitary, dusty tomato plant.

Tacked to the door was a card.

Prof. Burkhardt — Teacher of Music

Städtisches Konservatorium, Berlin

Königlichen Konservatorium, Dresden

And below that.

Piano wanted. Cash paid.

So the piano had died in the war. Her

mother's precious Broadwood.

The door was padlocked. Nell sat on the steps and waited. Dusk could only be half an hour away. Was her mother out teaching some child the piano? Could anything so normal be taking place in this desert of rubble?

Very few people passed. Those that did looked at her without concern, more interested in the bicycle than the girl. Ten minutes passed, and an old woman was coming towards her pushing a pram, her head wrapped in a scarf, her body swathed in layers of ragged skirts, her hands in thick leather gloves. A coating of ashen dust from head to foot. She got within ten feet of Nell before Nell recognised her.

"Mama?"

Could this old woman, this tramp, possibly be her mother?

"Mama?"

Marie Burkhardt pulled off her headscarf in a shower of grit. Her face was brown and dry, her eyes dull, and her lips cracked.

"Oh God, Nell. Why have you come back?"

# §88

Marie yanked on a string and the light flickered on. A single, unshaded overhead bulb. Nell had been expecting squalor. A hovel. It wasn't. Her mother had turned some neighbour's cellar into a home. Nell found herself trying to remember which neighbour — Herr Obermann who'd vanished into *Nacht und Nebel* in 1942? Herr Schumann who'd been killed in an air raid in '43?

She recognised none of the furniture. At least none of it as being the furniture she had grown up with. She recognised all of it obliquely. The sofa looked like the one Frau Wagner had had at No. 35. The spiky plant in the brass pot looked like Frau Graz's and the table it stood on had surely been made by Herr Kaufmann for his wife's birthday in 1939. Then she realised. All lives had been rearranged. The pieces were the same, they just weren't in the same place on the board. And the lives that owned those pieces had been contained, discrete — now blown open, and blown apart. What lives had been spared salvaged what had been spared. One day perhaps, some enterprising child might procure a long stick and knock her rag doll off the mantelpiece and claim it as her own — and someone seeing this might wonder whatever happened to Frau Burkhardt's little girl.

But her eyes drew her inevitably from the trivia of memory to the one fact that mattered. It was a woman's home — no trace of a man anywhere.

Marie was sitting on the edge of the sofa, head down.

When she looked up she answered the

unasked question.

"Your father is dead. In all probability dead."

"How?"

"A Russian bullet most likely."

"Where?"

"Somewhere near the Reich Chancellery. The last report I ever had of him was somewhere on Wilhlemstraße on May Day. The Volkssturm fighting off Russian tanks with cutlery and broomhandles. All in the name of a Führer who was already dead."

"But . . ."

"No, Nell, there is no body. No one saw him die. But who could live through that?"

"And you?"

"It's like this. I do what I have to do to get by. I stole the pram. The first thing I have ever stolen in my life, but not the last. The potatoes the British tip in the street in a free-for-all. I find a woman can punch as hard as a man. I give more black eyes than I get . . ."

"And?"

"I get by."

"Then *we* shall get by."

"Oh God — the inexorable logic of being Nell Burkhardt."

And her head dropped again.

Nell knelt, wrapped her arms around her mother. Marie stayed rigid, flexed herself against the alienness of embrace, and as Nell squeezed the harder softened and relented, her arms around her daughter's shoulders, her tears running down her cheeks.

"When you were little," she said between sobs. "When you were no more than nine or ten, and you were beginning to understand what was happening to Germany, to us all, to us as a family, there were no tears, no self-pity, just your resolve. You said 'Mama, we will survive and we'll be safe, we'll be safe for ever.' Is this surviving? Is this safety? Is this for ever?"

And nothing would staunch her tears.

# §89

Two rooms in a cellar amounted to luxury.

Marie made up a bed for Nell on the sofa.

In the morning she dressed in her protective layers again, wrapped the headscarf around her hair, put on her rawhide gloves.

"I am a *Trümmerfrau*. I clear rubble. It gets me the highest ration the British will allow. The lowest ration Berliners call the death card. It is hard work, but . . ."

"I can do it too?"

"You won't have any choice. It's compulsory. But, I can get you on a gang with me. You'll need papers, you'll need to register with the British for your ration card. See your Uncle Erno. He hasn't moved. He's survived everything. He'll help you. I have no time now. I have cleared Kantstraße and Leib-

315

nizstraße . . . and Berlin runs out of philoso-
phers . . . so I'm on Bismarckstraße. But I
must go now."

After a cup of ersatz coffee — "always know
the price of coffee" echoing in her mind —
and a cold wash standing with her feet in a
bowl — Nell set off in search of Uncle Erno.

As she crossed sectors at Lietzenburger
Straße she could almost swear the sound of
the wolf whistles changed. On the north side
of the street it seemed to her that the Tommies whistled at least a semitone lower than
the Amis on the south side.

Erno was not a blood relative. He was an
old friend of her father's. Nor was Erno
Schreiber his real name. Long, long ago he
had hidden his real identity, his Jewish name
and ancestry and become a "ghost." The
Nazis had never found him.

He lived on Grünetümmlerstraße in Wilmersdorf in the American Sector, surrounded
by books, newspapers, and the tools of his
trade — forger.

Nell had no idea how old Erno was. He had
always looked sixty, but it was likely that he
was not much older than her father — who
was a child of the nineties and dead at fifty-
one.

On an August morning, the heat of the day
already rising, Erno had the windows closed
and a small fire going in the iron stove —
always something to be burnt, always some-

316

thing incriminating to be disposed of. Always a light on, in a room that was pools of light and pits of darkness.

He showed no surprise as he opened the door to her. Kissed her on the forehead, said, "I'd have known if you were dead. I should have felt it in my bones. I live, you live . . ."

A ginger tomcat wove its way between her legs.

"And no one ate Hegel," Erno added.

Over more acorn coffee Nell recounted the last nine months to Erno, and at the end reiterated, "I lied to the British about my age. It is a lie I wish to hold on to. It is a time to be a grown-up. Sixteen doesn't seem grown-up. Eighteen does. Besides, I'm tall for my age."

"Quite. But only a sixteen-year-old would say that. So . . . you want an identity card dating you to . . . when exactly?"

"January 14, 1927."

"Consider it done."

"Mama says you will tell me how to register with the British for my ration card?"

"Why bother. I can give you that as well. Will you be a *Trümmerfrau* too? Then a grade two card."

"Who gets grade one?"

"Would you believe the Russians reserved that for artists? They cannot feed us, they cannot house us, they cannot flush away our ordure . . . but they've already put on their first opera."

## §90

There was one trace of "man" in the cellar. Ferreting around she found her father's best suit, not the one he had worn to the office — she assumed he had gone into battle wearing that, that he had died wearing it.

On her first day as a *Trümmerfrau,* Nell rolled up the trouser legs and drew the belt tight into her waist. The symbolism was not lost on her mother.

"Deutschland, Deutschland — who wears the trousers now?"

The British had laid track down the centre of Bismarckstraße, a miniature railway, tilting steel wagons that could be loaded from either side and then pushed along the East–West Axis all the way into the Tiergarten, where Berlin was being tipped.

A morning of loading these and Nell was exhausted. Marie switched her to cleaning bricks, a job that could be done sitting down at the rate of twelve reichsmarks per thousand. Nell lost count within half an hour.

Arriving home, she craved sleep, which she would most certainly get, and hot water, which she most certainly wouldn't.

The electricity was off. A candlelit meal of boiled potatoes and cabbage — seasoned with fresh parsley — and tinned beef stew. Nell eating slowly, but not as slowly as her mother.

"Mama — the beef. About the beef. Do you buy on the black market?"

"I told you. I do what I have to do to get by."

"When I found the suit . . . well, there were six tins of beef."

Marie finished her meal in silence. Then . . .

"Do you remember how Goebbels would warn us all about the Russians, the Slav beast, the Mongol horde . . . all that nonsense?"

"On the radio? Yes. Of course."

"It wasn't nonsense. It was more of a self-fulfilling prophecy. The Russians took Berlin almost four months ago, the British did not arrive until six weeks ago. In between the Russians did as they wished. *'Uhri, Uhri, Uhri.'* "

"What? I don't understand."

"It was the first word any of them uttered. Quite possibly one word in a vocabulary of only three. They were obsessed with watches. I know no one who now owns a wristwatch. I saw one Ivan roll up his sleeves and show off a dozen or more on each arm to his comrades."

Nell could see what was coming.

"And the other two words?"

"They were *Frau* and *komm*."

"And . . ."

"And I did what I had to do to get by."

"Were . . ."

"Don't ask."

Marie shook her head as though dislodging an insect, held her head up, lowered it to meet her daughter eye to eye.

"One way, possibly the only way, to avoid being taken by force is to give yourself voluntarily. Yuri is my protector, Yuri is my carer, Yuri is my breadwinner, *Yuri ist . . . mein Mann.*"

"Yuri? Who's Yuri?"

# §91

The indeterminacy of his uniform was at odds with the brightness in his eyes. His eyes were deep sea blue. Was he green or was he brown? Nell decided he was green. A little green goblin of a man, with eyes that shone and laughter lines that could turn his face into a walnut, somewhere between a giggle and a guffaw.

It was Friday night. They had a weekend to themselves. He sat on the sofa next to Marie, took her hand in both of his. The gentleness of the gesture was striking. It occurred to Nell that her mother had taken up with this man within days of her father's death, but the obvious affection he had for her pushed the thought further back in her mind where it might linger without too much troubling her.

His German was good. Her Russian was better.

He told her he was a major in the NKVD and came from a small village just outside Gorky, the city on the Volga some three hundred kilometres east of Moscow — hometown of the author in whose honour the USSR had renamed the city from its original Nizhny Novgorod. And no, he'd never met Maxim Gorky. He rather thought he might have died.

"I love your mother. For my work I am often away, often in Moscow. But no Soviet soldier will touch her. No Soviet soldier will harm her or you."

From somewhere Yuri produced half a kilo of fresh loin of pork. It occurred to Nell to wonder what Prussian peasant might have been robbed of his pig to furnish this meal, but quite obviously it did not occur to her mother.

Over dinner Yuri told her of his childhood in Gorky, how his father had died when he was ten, how they had given up the farm and moved to the city, how he had been twelve at the time of the revolution and already a party member. How at nineteen, shortly after the death of Lenin, he had been summoned to Moscow, taught English and German and told to get ready for the next German war.

Limited as the conversation was, there was also an apparent rough charm to the man.

With the meal over, Yuri and her mother retired to the bedroom, and Nell made up her bed on the sofa and decided not to think about her father. Instead she dreamt of the old woman she had met on the road — Mutti at her sewing machine, turning Nazi flags into pantaloons. Doing what she had to do to get by.

Mutti drew the twin threads from under the silver foot of the machine, snipped them with her scissors, threw the pants into a wicker basket on top of a dozen others, and then held out her hand to Nell.

*"Gib mir Tabak,"* she said.

# §92

The war was over. Everybody told her so. And still people died in their tens of thousands. Cholera, typhus, vengeance . . . starvation.

The winter of 1945–1946 in Berlin became known as Starvation Winter.

Nell and Marie had cleared Bismarckstraße, had gone on to clear Kaiser-Friedrich-Straße and by December were on Brandenburgische Straße. Berlin would never run out of streets with high-sounding names, nor would it ever run out of rubble. Nell had heard one of the British officers say that it would take twelve or fifteen years to clear the streets and another twenty to rebuild. She had heard others say that Berlin would not be rebuilt, that Germany would be returned to a peasant economy without cities or industry. It did not strain the metaphor too much, brick after brick after brick, to say that Berlin had returned to the Stone Age.

It was neither stone nor starvation that killed Marie Burkhardt. It was wood.

They would pile up timber found among the brick and concrete to take home and feed into the stove at the end of the day. It was dark before five, and the *Trümmerfrauen* stopped work when the light went. Gathering up her pile in semidarkness a splinter pierced the grey muscle at the base of Marie's right thumb, between the glove and the wrist. It went deep, the tip emerging on the palm of her hand.

Being unable to pull it out, she snapped off all but half an inch.

"I'll be fine," she said to Nell. "I've had worse than this. We'll get home, find the tweezers and you can pull it out. Remember how you used to cry when I pulled thorns from your hand?"

Nell could not get it all out. The splinter had fragmented inside the wound.

In the morning Marie felt unwell, but insisted she would go to work.

By five in the evening she was weak and delirious.

Nell got her home, put her to bed, and ran

to Erno's.

He came back with every medicine he had and a thermometer.

"Thirty nine point nine. My dear, your mother is seriously ill. This is beyond aspirin. We need a doctor."

"Are there any left?"

"Köhler, in Pestalozzistraße. I'll get him."

Dr. Köhler seemed to Nell to have survived by being too old to have attracted any attention from either side. She thought he must be over eighty.

Marie felt nothing as he opened the wound, removed the fragments, and cleaned out the pus. Her brow ran with sweat, and her head rolled from side to side, and she felt nothing.

Köhler and Erno went into a huddle of whispers, which Nell would not allow.

"I'm not a child. You must tell me whatever it is."

Köhler took off his spectacles, made a show of wiping the lenses.

"Without treatment, your mother will die."

"What treatment?"

"There are new drugs. The British have them, the Amis too. Antibiotics. Fungal cultures that kill bacteria. Your mother has a bacterial infection. It must be stopped before it reaches her heart."

"All that . . . from a splinter?"

"Yes. The body does not discriminate between a splinter and a bullet, although a bullet might have been cleaner. I don't have such drugs, no German doctor has. They keep them for themselves. There's no point in even asking."

Her mother groaned loudly. Nell looked at her and had one thought.

"Do the Russians have these drugs too?"

"I don't know," Köhler replied. "I really don't."

And if they did? Nell had not seen Yuri for at least three days, and had no idea where to find him. She stayed home. Erno went in search of Yuri and could not find him. He asked every black market *Schieber* he knew, German, American, British, for the "miracle-drug penicillin" and found no sellers.

Thirty-six hours later, around six in the morning, Nell was woken from her sleep on the rug beside the bed by the sound of her mother's voice.

"Max."

Nell lit the candle.

Her mother was sitting on the edge of the bed, bolt upright, eyes wide.

"Max," she said again, stretched out her arm to Nell and died.

# §93

They buried her at the Luisenkirchhof, on the far side of Sophie-Charlotten-Straße — yet another street that Marie had cleared of

325

rubble. Rubble would be her only memorial.

Nell thought she had prepared for this. Death had never lost its mystery or its sting, but it had lost its novelty the first day she set foot in Belsen. And from that day until the day she had seen her mother wheeling her pram down Pfefferstraße she had been aware that she might never see either of her parents again. She had crossed Lower Saxony on foot and by bike, with no expectations beyond the unquenchable simplicity of hope.

Hope, she found, had died with her mother.

She lay on the sofa, inert. Nothing moved but the blinking of her eyes.

When at last he spoke she realised she had no idea how long she had lain like this or how long Erno had been in the room. Had he stepped into her dream or she into his?

"Nell. Let us go now."

"What?"

"Don't stay in this cellar. The room above me is now empty. One room, but a big room, on the top floor where there is light and air. Don't stay in this cellar."

Inertia ruled. She let Erno do as he wished. Let him grant her light and air. Far from the back of her mind she knew why he was moving her. If she stayed in the room where her mother had died then death would be forever clutching at her skirt. And hope would really die.

It was two weeks later, a week before Christmas, Nell installed on the top floor at Grünetümmlerstraße but scarcely settled, when Yuri reappeared in all his greenness. The goblin at her threshold. His blue eyes clear and sad.

He handed her the gift he had always brought her mother. A *pajok* — a food parcel.

She wondered if men had no visible emotions. She could not remember that she had ever seen one cry before Belsen.

Yuri wasn't crying. He stood, it seemed to her, respectfully — holding his hat in both hands.

"Erno has told me all," he said. "Прошу прощения. I am sorry. I was in Moscow."

Nell set the *pajok* down on the table, held her hands clasped in front of her. They were mirrors now. Two respectful strangers with no clear idea of where the boundary lay.

"I will not leave you. I will not see you go hungry. I will not leave you. I will bring you *pajok*s."

It was more than a statement — it was his manifesto. The terms of the relationship.

"You are kind, Yuri. But I am not my mother. I will not sleep with you for this."

"And I will not ask you to."

*Berlin:* 1947

It was love at first sight. He and Berlin were made for each other. He took to it like a rat to a sewer.

In the new year of 1947 Burne-Jones met him for breakfast in the Atlantic. Between the crisp bacon and the reconstituted scrambled egg Burne-Jones slid a military buff envelope and another strip of wool across the table to him — corporal's stripes — the mark of Beelzebub.

"You've earned them."

Wilderness thought he'd earned a damn sight more than that.

He tore open the envelope. A travel warrant to Berlin. The Silk Stocking Express.

"What's the job?"

"Well . . ."

"More fuckin' fragebogeys?"

"Inevitably so, but nothing like the pile you've just gone through. And this time you'll be number one. But you'll be doing a lot more interpreting . . . and some driving."

"I still haven't passed a test."

"Well . . . you managed not to prang my MG in Cambridge, didn't you? Mind you, a lot more gears on a Land Rover."

This was goading. They hadn't mentioned the MG in ages.

Wilderness decided not to take the bait and

said simply, "But that's not all."

"No, it's not. I'll be requiring your special talents from time to time. Not that you can or should regard everything else as a cover . . ."

" 'S'OK. I get the picture."

# §96

The Silk Stocking Express was crowded that Saturday afternoon. He almost wished he'd put on his Welsh Guards outfit and been able to demand a seat, but it was too precious, too useful to risk getting busted over a railway journey and a warrant and a uniform that did not match, so he sat on his kit bag in the corridor with a thousand other erks. If the train was heated he couldn't tell. He'd hung on to the flying jacket Johnnie Blackwall had given him on the flight out to Hamburg, slipped his arms inside it and shoved his hands into his armpits. With depressing regularity someone would fart or belch, the corridor would stink, and Wilderness began to wonder if he was the only person whose guts were in tune — but then, lavatories being frozen as well as everything else, once in a while a window would go down, the cold, clean air would knife in and a bag of shit got thrown out, proving that he wasn't. "First we bomb your cities flat, then we shower you in shit."

A stout, misleadingly miserable-looking lance bombardier of the Royal Artillery met him at the Charlottenburg station.

"Welcome to Bizonia," said Eddie.

"Marx Brothers, right? Groucho singing 'Hail Bizonia.' "

"That was Freedonia, Joe. This is Bizonia, as of last week. A fairy-tale kingdom. Look out for dwarves, unicorns, and a thousand tons of 'ooky fags. I'm your driver. Been sent to take you wherever you want to go, seeing as you are now a high and mighty corporal."

"What a turn up for the book. How long have you been in Berlin?"

"Since last August."

That was galling. Wilderness knew he'd drawn the short straw with Hamburg — but somehow Eddie got posted to Berlin. A city where you could smell money on the breeze.

This was not a breeze. This was a wind that cut to the bone. Suddenly the train seemed like warmth. It was far below freezing, all extremities tingled with cold and his breath hung in the air in billowing nimbus clouds.

"I got the canvas up, but the car's still like an iceberg on wheels. The sooner we get to our digs the better."

"Our digs?"

"Yeah, we're sharing till the next lucky sod gets posted home. We could walk from here, it's that close, but we'd be like abominable wotsits by the time we got there."

Eddie drove them along Kantstraße and into Fasanenstraße at the north end, under the railway bridge to a battered five-storey apartment block.

Wilderness had no reaction to the state of the city, except "you've seen one ruin, you've seen 'em all."

As they passed another gang of *Trümmer-frauen* Wilderness said, " 'If seven maids with seven mops swept it for half a year, do you suppose,' the Walrus said, 'that they could get it clear?' "

Eddie said, "My old dad used to read that to me at bedtime. And I think the answer's no. Come back in ten or twenty years' time, there'll still be gangs of women sweeping away bits of Berlin. I don't think there's a hole big enough to tip it all into. There are three words that sum up life in Berlin, and for all I know in the whole of soddin' Germany — *Trümmer, kaputt,* and *Ersatz.* Everything is either rubbish, broken, or fake."

The room they shared was on the top floor. As Wilderness gazed around, Eddie went on, "D'you know, they drink tea made from apple peel and coffee made from acorns. They call the coffee *Muckefuck.* It's the only German word I know of that needs no translation."

*"Muckefuck?"*

"And that also describes the taste pretty well. Fortunately . . ." Eddie picked a plain brown paper packet off the dresser. "Fortunately we have . . . best NAAFI dark roast, none of your instant and none of your acorns. I'll put the kettle on."

He disappeared behind the wooden partition that separated the two beds. Wilderness looked at the room. It was a jolt down from the Atlantic Hotel, but it was warm — a sputtering gas fire set into the chimney breast — and clean — anywhere Eddie lived would be, he lived by order, everything in its place — and light — tall, slender windows that stretched almost floor to ceiling.

Wilderness dropped his kit bag on the bed, sloughed off the sheepskin and his blouse.

Eddie was staring at the shoulder holster.

"Wossup?"

"Never seen one before. Standard issue, is it?"

"I got it from the armourer, so I suppose so. In Hamburg everyone carried a gun outside the base."

"Not here they don't. It's compulsory in theory, but the MPs don't give a toss about interpreters and medics. Just the combat blokes. I haven't carried a gun since November. Just as well. Too many opportunities to start World War Three."

"Good. I was never crazy about having it."

He pulled at the top drawer in the tallboy. It was empty.

"This one mine?"

"Yep."

He wrapped the straps around the holster and dumped the gun in the drawer.

Eddie said, "Makes you wonder what Burne-Jones has in mind for you doesn't it?"

It had and it did, but Wilderness was never going to say that.

"I suppose you're hungry?"

"Yeah. There was nothing on the train, and if there had been — no way of getting to it short of throwing blokes off the train."

"Pilchards on toast?"

"I don't want to pinch your ration, Ed."

"Ration. Bollocks. I don't do rationing."

He disappeared behind the partition once more and returned with a pot of aromatic black coffee and a sixteen ounce can of pilchards.

"Toast is doing. Won't be a mo'."

As Eddie sliced the lid off the pilchards, Wilderness said, "You got a source then?"

"Have I got a source?"

Then he let the short sentence rest as an enigma. Loaded pilchards onto toast, swilled coffee and looked like what he was inside — happy. The miserable exterior, Wilderness had long since concluded, was simply a way of repelling boarders.

Food was good, but Wilderness would never be able to find in it the consummate pleasure that Eddie did. He ate quickly, Eddie savoured.

"Coffee's good," he said, hoping to break Eddie's mealtime self-absorption.

"Yep."

"Used to sell for a bob or two back in Hamburg."

"Does here too. Get your hands on a few packets and you'll make . . . a packet."

"So, there's fiddles, then?"

"O'course. Didn't you have fiddles in Hamburg?"

"Nothing I could get at. All based out at the airfield, and I was in the city. Just like I am now."

Eddie was shaking his head. Wilderness could almost swear he was grinning.

"No, no, noooo. Sources? Do I have sources? Fiddles? Do I have fiddles. Just sit tight for a minute."

Again he ducked behind the partition, only to reappear wearing his army greatcoat and humming a daft tune.

"Da da daaa dah. Da da daaa dah."

And as much as a little fat bloke could this little fat bloke was dancing.

The greatcoat opened and closed on the beat, and Wilderness realised he was doing the Royal Artillery's version of a fan dance — Eddie's own *Folies Bergère.*

On the inside of his coat, from buttons to armpit, was a network of string and safety pins from which hung all manner of goodies.

Eddie pulled off a pair of frilly knickers,

334

tossed them over Wilderness's head and onto the bed.

"Da da daaa dah."

A matching bra.

"Da da daaa dah."

A small bottle of Chanel perfume.

"Da da daaa dah."

A bar of pink Cadum soap.

"Bump, da bump, da bump" — as he turned, stuck his arse out and lobbed half a pound of coffee beans onto the bed without even looking at his aim.

The music stopped, the grin was teetering on girlish giggles.

"Do I have fiddles? Do I have fiddles? My greatcoat is a box of earthly delights, Berlin is our paradise regained, the NAAFI our cornucopia. Joe, we're going to make a bob or two together."

Joe grinned back at him, and did not say what he was thinking.

A bob or two might be only the beginning. He and Berlin were made for each other.

# §97

Eddie took him to the Marrokkaner Club — a tiny entrance in a side-street cut between Savignyplatz and Uhlandstraße, that opened up into a vast, low-ceilinged cellar, too low ever to disperse the fug of tobacco and the lager-miasma that hung suspended above the tables.

"Tomorrow we'll go down the Tiergarten. The *Schwarzmarkt,* they call it now. Even the tram conductors call it that. They just yell *'Schwarzmarkt.'* "

"An open secret?"

"It's like Berlin, a secret without a roof and mostly without walls. All out in the open. In all weathers. You could sell gumboots in June, deckchairs in December if someone else thought they could sell 'em on at a profit."

But tonight, Eddie introduced him to his "partners."

Pie Face — so called because he had a big round moonface and a flat nose, as though he'd gone a few rounds with Freddie Mills. Pie Face was from southwest Essex, Hornchurch. Once Wilderness had ridden to Hornchurch, at the furthest reach of the District Line on London's Underground and thought it the edge of the world. It was a county corner that was all but indistinguishable from urban East London, and Pie Face had much the same accent as Wilderness. A corporal, and Royal Army Service Corps clerk, he was attached to the NAAFI/EFI stores on Adolf-Hitler-Platz.

Spud — so called because he looked like a King Edward, his face pockmarked with "eyes" — was from the top end of Essex, a farm boy from the Stour Valley, with a lyrical

East Anglian accent — a lance corporal, with the 62nd Transport and Movement Squadron, he worked in the Army's "garage" and kept countless jeeps running.

Eddie did not need to explain, but did. They were the perfect partners. Pie Face had access to all the stuff in the NAAFI — every fiddle and theft began with him, and Spud had the means to get them around Berlin.

Wilderness was wondering what Eddie's role might be in this wideboys' fraternity, and as if mind-reading Eddie said, "And I'm the brains of the outfit."

Wilderness smiled even as his heart sank. He liked Eddie, and it was no exaggeration to say that he was probably the best friend he'd ever had. He was a gentle man, bright as a button . . . but a criminal mastermind he wasn't.

"I do a lot of driving," Eddie said, with a fingertip tap to the side of his nose.

"I thought you were on Fragebogeys like me?"

"Burne-Jones said I was crap at it. Took me off it. So I drive brass around in me jeep, translate for them and report back to him."

"You mean you're a spy?"

Eddie began to grin, the grin became a giggle.

"It's all bollocks isn't it? I never hear a damn thing worth remembering let alone reporting. I drop posh blokes off at meetings, pick 'em up again an hour two later, and in the meantime . . ."

"You do yer fan dance."

"Absolutely. Go out with a full greatcoat, come back with an empty one and pocket full of kraut money."

"We all do," Spud chipped in.

"Always room for one more," said Pie Face.

And Eddie was smiling. And Wilderness realised he had just joined a club he hadn't even applied to.

# §98

Sunday morning in the Tiergarten rewrote Wilderness's idea of Germany. The Tiergarten in winter was bleak. On a day when an English family would be at home listening to a variety show on the radio or sleeping off Sunday lunch, Berliners were out en masse. It was insect-like, a swarm from the hive. The sky was grey, the buildings were grey, the world was grey. The people were . . . yellow . . . a poxy, wasted, vitamin-deficient yellow.

He and Eddie stood not fifty yards from the hollow shell of the Reichstag — in a sense they were at the heart of Germany, at the urban pulse of Berlin, stamping their feet against the cold where a million jackboots had goose-stepped . . . a patch of bare frozen ground that Berliners had now turned into an allotment to raise vegetables. Someone had planted gooseberry bushes. Goosestep to gooseberry in only twelve years. An imperial city to . . . a madman's folly. Wilderness wondered if Berlin would leave the Reichstag as it was — a permanent memorial to that folly.

The scale of the *Schwarzmarkt* was almost unbelievable, the number of *Schieber*s uncountable. Everyone sold, everyone bought or bartered, hence everyone was a *Schieber.*

The thing that most struck Wilderness was the number of prams and pushchairs. He reckoned about one in a hundred actually carried an infant — the rest were full of contraband. The odd copper moved among the crowd, but the sudden cessation of trade seemed to him be an act of caution and respect rather than convincing concealment — "let's not flaunt it, let's not fling it in his face."

Eddie said, "Of course most of it's barter. Kettle, toaster, portrait of Frederick the Great that's been in the family for a hundred years . . . all up for swapsies. All tradeable for anything you can eat or drink. I don't know what the German is for junk . . ."

*"Ramsch."*

"That'll do nicely. There is no such thing as *Ramsch* any more. Every piece of crap has a value. I met a bloke just before Christmas selling his mother's false teeth."

"Did you buy 'em?"

Eddie's point was being made in terms of tragedy not twenty feet away. A man held a violin in one hand and a cardboard and crayon sign in the other.

Once owned by Adolph Busch. Will trade for shoes.

Busch had been one of Rada's favourites. She had wound up the gramophone and put on Busch playing Brahms or Schubert and made him listen. Of course it could be a lie . . . he might as readily have written Josef Kreutzer, but the expression on his face and the state of his shoes said otherwise.

"The coppers don't care much about swapsies. In fact they don't care much about cash deals until someone back at the nick orders a *Razzia,* and then they'll round up every man woman, kid, and dog. A show of force, mostly amounts to nothing . . . until the next time."

"What's in demand?"

"Right now . . . spuds. Last year's stocks are running out about now."

"And we don't do spuds?"

"Nah . . . we're in a different league. Follow me."

Eddie picked his way through the crowd to a van that sold hot drinks and soups. The chalked-up menu announced a choice of potato, parsnip, or pea soup.

The proprietor nodded as he saw Eddie approach and moved to the back of the van.

When they got round the back, the door opened and Eddie said, *"Wie viele willst du heute, Fritzi?"*

And Fritzi replied, *"Zwölf."*

Eddie opened his greatcoat, like a bat spreading wings and Fritzi unhooked twelve bags of coffee from the cat's cradle. A fat envelope full of reichsmarks vanished into Eddie's pocket and they moved on.

"You don't count it?"

"Nope. Trust matters."

"So does money."

"Which is why we agree a price every Wednesday. Price o'coffee changes all the time. And it never gets any cheaper. We agree a price and we stick to it."

"How many do you have left?"

"Six. We'll get rid of them between here and home. Not a day to be bothering with frilly knickers and perfume."

"Is Fritzi your biggest buyer?"

"One of 'em. I've three or four blokes who buy big-time."

Big time was a troublesome phrase. Nothing about the Tiergarten *Schwarzmarkt* struck Wilderness as big time. He thought again of insects.

"I don't think I can do this, Ed."

"Why's that?"

"I don't have a greatcoat."

341

"What? You lost it?"

"No. I gave it away to a bloke in Hamburg looked like he was about to freeze to death. You'd have done the same."

A lie. Eddie, he knew, would have given away his shirt and trousers as well.

" 'S'OK. Pie Face can get you another out of stores."

So that was that, he was a *Schieber*. A nickel-and-dime, under-the-greatcoat *Schieber*. An insect.

# §99

On the Monday morning, Wilderness reported to 45 Schlüterstraße — with no real idea to whom he was reporting.

No. 45 was a few hundred yards from his digs, in a short stretch of Schlüterstraße, overlooking both the Kurfürstendamm and Lietzenburger Straße. It was a big, turn-of-the-century apartment building in the bourgeois style, five or six storeys high — a boastful, bulging frontage as though the building could not quite contain itself, and had blossomed into bay windows and roof dormers. It looked to have come through the war largely unscathed — a few chips and bullet scars on the columns either side of the row of steps leading up to the door, a street that had not been hard-fought.

In the lobby he was surprised to find an

ornate ceiling arcing overhead and a panelled staircase hinting at art nouveau origins. It was the most undamaged piece of Germany he'd yet encountered. Something the RAF had missed.

The office of Information Services Control was on the ground floor.

He knocked at the secretary's door and walked in.

A good-looking blonde in a severe charcoal grey two-piece was ripping paper from the roller of her typewriter. She paused with the pages mid-air, looked at him, then screwed them into a ball, carbon and all, and lobbed them over her shoulder.

"Butterfingers," she said.

"No, Holderness."

"Very witty. You must be the colonel's bright boy. We've been expecting you."

"Am I going to be Burne-Jones's bright boy wherever I go?"

"Dunno. There's not a lot of competition round here at the mo'. But you could always try *not* living up to it."

She picked up two pages and a carbon and fed them into the typewriter.

"You know I could have stayed at home, done the deb thing and married a Guards officer. I didn't have to learn to type, and on days like these when I wake up with ten thumbs I wish I hadn't. But, alas I didn't know all that many Guards officers. Back

343

down the corridor, second on the left. There's a desk for you, and a pile of Fraggywotser-names to be going on with. I'll finish the major's letters and be with you in about half an hour."

"The major?"

"Major Frampton. He's in charge. He'll want to see you at some point, but as you answer to Colonel Burne-Jones it's not all that urgent he sees you today. I can brief you. As I said, second on the left."

It was a large, light room — bigger than the room that housed him, Eddie and two cots. The desk was a monstrosity in carved oak, at least seven feet wide and three deep. Designed to intimidate. It intimidated him until he remembered, it was *his* desk. He wasn't sharing with anyone. Just as well, he did not share with easy grace.

A foolscap envelope was on the desk, addressed to him.

He shook it.

Two pamphlets slid out onto his desk.

Control Council Directive No.24: Concerning the Removal from Office and Positions of Responsibility of Nazis and People Hostile to Allied Purposes. January 1946.

And . . .

Allied Kommandatura Order No.10: The

Elimination of National Socialism and Militarism from Public and Economic Life. March 1946.

Wilderness almost sighed out loud. But, on the back of the latter Burne-Jones had scribbled.

Wouldn't bother reading these if I were you, but it might be as well if you left them lying around on your desk. Might intimidate the natives and fool our side into thinking you actually have read them. ABJ.

Then there was the pile of *Fragebogen,* forty or so — 131 × 40 = 5,240 soddin' questions, and 5,240 soddin' answers.

There was one consolation: it was bollock freezing outside, and he was indoors and a damn sight warmer than any German.

There were two consolations: the secretary was a looker, a bit of posh with, it seemed, no snooty ways about her.

He'd read a dozen *Fragebogen* by the time she reappeared.

"Are they all musicians? How many second violins did the Berlin Philharmonic have?"

"Not all . . . no . . . but the list will be skewed that way. In theory you have the right to pick up any Fraggey you wish and recall its author. In practice almost everything we do is geared to the archive the Nazis abandoned upstairs, the files of the Reichskulturkammer. Somehow, in the two months the Russians had this building they managed to miss it. Any artist who wanted to continue working under the Nazis filled in a German version of a Fraggey. Now they all want to work again, indeed we want them to work again, and it doesn't matter if they're Fred Schmidt or Wilhelm Furtwängler, they all have to be assessed. Hence we have in this building the Spruchkammer für Entnazifizierung, which is a kind of court that will exonerate, but only if we, in this case you, say so. That would amount to official denazification. Once whitewashed they are eligible for certain perks in the way of rationing. A leading actor may well qualify for a class-one card, the same as a chap doing heavy labour or a *Trümmerfrau* — by the by we didn't think this one up; the Russians did, we just sort of levelled it a bit — and the choice they make is between, say, the German equivalent of Sir Cedric Hardwicke and some music hall comic who's just had a walk-on in a Will Hay comedy. All a bit of a farce really.

"And of course we have a pretty wide brief. Class one is artists and scholars but also engineers and the like. Who, after all, is to say that an engineer is not an artist? So somewhere in that pile you may stumble across an architect or bloke who designed bridges. But the bottom line is this. It doesn't matter if a chap has traded in poetry for plumbing — if he filled in a Nazi *Fragebogen,* and they're the basis of the 250,000 files in the Reichskulturkammer upstairs, he fills in one of ours.

"But . . . we also have the Kulturbund zur demokratischen Erneuerung Deutschlands. And please don't ask me to repeat that. Dozens, no hundreds of chaps mill around here every day to get fixed up with cards by one lot and then the other tries to keep them gainfully employed in the propagation of non-Nazi art. And then it all turns into a rather thirdrate coffee-house-cum-arts-club and you summon the chucker out. It's all a communist front, of course, but there's nothing we can do about it. They're on the floor above. You're bound to come across them but there's no real reason to have much to do with them. You deal with the Spruchkammer, and they're pretty much at your mercy. No *Persilschein* from you, no privileges, no work. They're absolutely full of it of course, so try not to get stuck in a lift with any of them. And I'm Rose Blair, by the by, thank you for asking. And thank you for not flirting. I'm at least ten years older than you, and not interested. Now, any questions?"

Wilderness wanted to laugh. He could not tell from her expression whether she expected him to laugh.

"There wasn't a lot in the envelope Burne-Jones left me. Did he say anything specific to you?"

"Yeeees. He did rather. Work your way through the pile. There'll be more over the next couple of days. Your first interview isn't until Thursday, and you're only interviewing in the mornings. In the afternoons the colonel asked that you, and I quote, 'Get to know Berlin, you're —' "

" 'No use to me if you don't know Berlin.' "

"Exactly. His very words."

# §100

His days achieved a pattern of tolerable dullness. He read *Fragebogen,* he rubber-stamped Berliners back into gainful employment by issuing *Persilschein*s. He would have said he was attentive, but this long after the war, in a country where everyone and no one had been a Nazi, he could see little point in the job. Burne-Jones had warned him not to regard the job as a cover. So he tried to see it that way. Burne-Jones had had him issued a spy's gun, not a soldier's. Had him trained to use it. What was it Weatherill had said? "I'm sure you don't need me to teach you to die. I'm here to teach you to kill." He tried that on too. And when added up it all came to one question: "When will Burne-Jones reappear?"

In the afternoons he walked Berlin as Burne-Jones had requested, wondered at the ease with which he could cross from one sector to another unmolested, strolled the length of Unter den Linden, trying to reconstruct it in his imagination. To see it draped with Swastikas in black and red. To see it at the turn of the century, as it had been in the Kaiser's day. Late afternoon, in the twilight hours, he would meet Eddie in either Eddie's jeep or his own and they would unburden themselves of coffee, soap, perfume, tinned fish . . . whatever . . . on the eager citizens of Berlin. A people starving, on the ration or off it. The stick insects.

He could not deny it made money. He, Eddie, Spud, and Pie Face were no more short of money than they were short of food. They weren't starving.

But it was a diversion at best.

The real game was somewhere else.

It had to be.

# §101

It was the second week of February. Wilderness had just issued a *Persilschein* to a bloke with a badly damaged hand. Afterwards he could remember little about the man — they all tended to blur into one single importuning German — but he held a cigarette in a little black holder stuck between the stumps of the fingers on his right hand, and had old-fashioned good manners. Perhaps because he wasn't scared of Wilderness. It brought a reciprocal response. Against habit Wilderness had shown him to the door, chatted about so much nothing in the lobby, only to see a young woman fly down the stairs and hug the man — he in turn had embraced her with his good, left arm as she chattered away in faster German than Wilderness could keep up with.

He watched as she walked him to the front door. Small. Slim. Beautiful. Long black hair, piled up and pinned up for the office. A bottle-green dress that seemed far too summery for the time of year. She could be anything between sixteen and twenty.

"So, you've noticed?"

He turned. Rose Blair was standing in her office doorway.

"Noticed who?" he lied.

"Our Fraulein Burkhardt. Or rather, their Fraulein Burkhardt. Works for the Kulturbund upstairs. Gorgeous, isn't she? You don't stand a chance. All the actors try it on with her — at least all those that aren't queer. Come to think of it, maybe you do stand a chance."

Her door was about to close.

Wilderness said, "You know her? I don't suppose . . ."

"Burne-Jones pays me to keep an eye on

you Corporal Holderness, not to fix you up with dates. You want a *Schatzi,* find her yourself."

## §102

He did not find her.
  She found him.

## §103

Nell had known Werner Fugger all her life. His father was her godfather, and had worked for the city of Berlin alongside her own father, alongside Berlin's mayor-elect Ernst Reuter. Werner was two years younger, and playing with him when she was ten had seemed like an ordeal and required coercion. Not much had changed. Unlike her he'd been in the Hitler Youth — the natural scepticism of his father had not been enough to get him out of that — and while she'd been away, with Great-Uncle Klaus, with Nicolas Dekker, Werner had served with the Volkssturm, and at the age of fourteen had fought in the streets outside the bunker, had taken out a Russian tank with a crude but effective weapon known as a *Panzerfaust.* The Führer had surfaced from his bunker, perhaps for the last time, to pinch cheeks and pin medals on Werner and a dozen others. Only one of

351

them had been younger than Werner.

One of Werner's comrades-in-arms had slung his iron cross into the rubble when news of Hitler's death emerged, saying it would become a curse upon them. He urged Werner to throw his away too. Werner wouldn't.

Nell could respect Werner's experience, without respecting his opinions. Werner veered between denouncing Germany and denouncing the Allies, without ever denouncing the Reich. His mental footwork lacked skill as it lacked years. And he and Nell had the same argument over and over again in cafés and bars across the city centre.

"Auschwitz was Russian propaganda. The camp and its gas chambers hastily faked by the Russians in January 1945."

Nell would counter this by telling him what she had learnt firsthand talking to survivors of Auschwitz in Belsen.

Scarcely conceding her point with a "for the purposes of argument only, let us suppose you are right . . ." Werner would then argue strongly for Hitler having been surrounded by a "conspiracy of silence . . ."

"Surely you can see that if the Führer knew about such things, he would have put a stop to them at once."

"Why would he? It was everything he believed in, the summation of every policy he ever espoused, every speech he ever made.

Everything he did and said from the day he got out of the army was destined to end with Auschwitz."

If Werner insisted that the Führer had known nothing, sooner rather than later, he could kill an evening. Their mutual friends would drift off, exasperated and bored by him.

Nell regretted that she had asked him along this evening, but to leave him to his own devices only meant that he would fall in with more idiots who thought as he did — and God alone knew how many of those there were. Half Berlin was only too eager to wrap itself in the stars and stripes, and half would fly the hakenkreuz if only they had the nerve. Perhaps her choice of bar was a mistake — the Marrokkaner Club in Grolmanstraße? Perhaps any bar was a mistake when dealing with a war hero not yet seventeen?

Werner had moved on to the subject of the Nuremburg Trials. Two of their friends had left already, leaving only Nell and Franz, a thoughtful, near-silent young man of nineteen, an undecorated, unheroic, unbelieving veteran of the Volkssturm, to listen to Werner.

"The idea of collective guilt is nonsense . . . an entire country cannot be guilty . . ."

"Then," Nell said. "Perhaps guilt is the wrong word. Not *Schuld* but *Haftung* — responsibility."

"Are you saying we are all responsible,

responsible for things of which we knew nothing, for things you say were done by our parents' generation? We were children . . ."

"Some children fought and some of us won medals," Franz said softly without a hint of sarcasm. "Or is this where you tell me you and I were only following orders?"

"Yes. I followed orders, but . . ."

And where Werner was concerned clauses beginning with "but" could last all night.

From the other side of the partition she could hear the voices of the occupiers. Another reason not to bring Werner here. It was a favourite with the Allied troops — it was in the eastern end of the British Sector where Charlottenburg met the zoo and the Tiergarten, only walking distance from her work in Schlüterstraße, a short hop from the American Sector, which began only a few metres south of No. 45.

An English voice was holding forth. A little louder than conversation might permit. Not a lecture, not a raised voice . . . a game.

"Right gentleman . . . now yer sees it, now yer don't . . . all you have to do is find the lady."

Sharpe!

"The quickness of the 'and deceives the eye . . ."

Sharpe!

She stood up, in the middle of whatever rubbish Werner was uttering and walked around the partition to the other banquette.

Sharpe!

Three British soldiers were sitting around the table with half-drunk beers and scrappy piles of reichsmarks in front of them, poised as a fourth in the pale blue of the Royal Air Force worked his huckster's magic, hands flashing across the cards.

One of the soldiers was Swift Eddie Clark, who'd worked at Schlüterstraße from time to time. She didn't know the other two, and the man in RAF blue wasn't Beckwith Sharpe. Too young, too handsome, too tall. He simply sounded like Sharpe.

She was about to apologise for the interruption when he looked straight at her. Fair hair and light blue eyes. A beguiling rogue's smile. Were all cockneys charming rogues? Was Sharpe simply a blueprint for the London millions?

"May I?" she said.

Eddie pulled out a chair for her.

"You can't beat Joe, Miss Burkhardt. He's the gaffer at this."

Silently adding "gaffer" to her English vocabulary, she took the deck of cards the one called Joe was holding out to her, picked out the queen of hearts, a seven and a nine and held them up for all to see.

*"Nun, meine Herren. Mal sehen, wer die Dame finden kann."*

The Cockney spoke.

"In English, Miss. Eddie and I are OK, but Pie Face here hardly speaks English let alone German."

Nell concluded the one not laughing was Pie Face. Besides, he had a face like a pie. Flat and puffy at the same time.

"*Entschuldigung.* And that will be my last word in German."

She held the red queen and the seven in her left hand, the nine in her right, palms up. Palms down and her hands moved faster than a Paganini variation.

Pie Face said, "It's Toy Town money after all. Five doodads on . . ."

He put his folded note on the card nearest to him.

Eddie followed suit.

The third man said, "An' I'm Spud" as he put his note on the centre card. How aptly the English applied their nicknames. Spud, indeed. *Kartoffelgesicht* was clumsy by comparison.

That left the blue-eyed Cockney.

The blue eyes were fixed on her.

She had no wish to give him ideas, and looked in turn at all the others, waiting for him to place his bet.

At last, like a ball decelerating on the rim of a roulette wheel, her eyes came to meet his, the imaginary ball jumping from slot to slot, clicking like a ratchet until their eyes locked. He would get the wrong idea. She knew he would.

His hand poised over the cards, then dropped a 5RM note onto the centre card.

She flipped the outside card, heard Pie Face sigh in defeat as the seven showed. Stared back at Joe.

He moved first, flipped the centre card, nine up.

Eddie said, "Bloomin' 'eck. Joe, she beat you. I've never seen anyone beat you at three-card monte."

Nell flipped the queen and raked in her winnings.

Now, Joe was not looking at her, he was looking up and over her shoulder.

She turned.

Werner was standing behind her.

"We should go now."

"No, I want to stay. This is fun. You go if you want."

The she heard Joe say, "Or you could join us. Doesn't have to be three-card monte. Doesn't have to be for money. Just a game."

She didn't want this. She didn't want to be left alone with the Englishman, but she didn't want Werner as her chaperone either.

Werner spoke as though he'd been slapped in the face and challenged to a duel with sabres.

"I do not care to sit down with the Allies, Herr Corporal."

Nell had not even noticed Joe's rank. The

sneer as Werner said "corporal" was impossible to miss.

"Now, don't you go bashin' corporals. We may be a bunch of numskulls but some of us go on to run empires that last a thousand years."

Werner turned on his heel and was gone.

The three soldiers were giggling like schoolboys. Nell was not laughing, nor was Joe.

"Sorry, is he a friend?"

"Oh yes. We do not deny our friends, do we?"

"Probably not Miss Burkhardt, but I don't have any friends that deny Auschwitz."

Oh God, had Werner talked that loud?

"Nell," she said. "My name is Nell."

# §104

Nell. I'm alive! Where are you? Joe.

# §105

"Can I drive you home?"

"Thank you. But I live only walking distance from here. In the American Sector. In Wilmersdorf. Near the Ludwigskirche. On Grünetümmlerstraße."

Bit by bit there was too much detail for this to be a brush-off. Everything short of a zip code. Somewhere in there, amongst the longitude and latitude, he was certain, was an implicit invitation. Coupled to an equally distinct "not now."

"Then I could walk you home."

"And you, Joe. Where do you live?"

"Fasanenstraße."

"Near the synagogue?"

"Down the street from it, or from what's left of it. I think the RAF got there before me."

"I'm sure they did, but in this instance they bombed a ruin. Goebbels's SA sacked the synagogue on Kristallnacht in 1938. My father saw it burn. I went inside once. When I was a girl. It was beautiful."

He ought to say "good night" now. He knew it. But couldn't.

Then she said, "Why don't I walk *you* home. You can pick up your jeep later. I'd like to see the synagogue again, even as it is."

It was a variation on an old adage. Advice given to young ladies back in London. "It is easier to walk out of his place than to have to throw him out of yours."

The walk was not long enough. A matter of minutes. They stared at the gaping cavern that had been the synagogue. He felt nothing and had no idea what she was feeling.

He showed her the block he and Eddie, and fifty other erks, lived in.

She kissed him lightly on the cheek and

walked back down towards the Ku'damm
without another word.

# §106

"Eh?"

"I'm moving out."

"I got that bit. It's the moving in bit I can't
quite grasp."

"Admit it, Eddie. You'd love to have the
place to yourself."

"How long has this been going on?"

"You know, we try hard enough we could
have this whole conversation in song titles.
About six weeks. Since the night she took us
on at three-card monte in the Marrokkaner."

"And Fraulein Breakheart has asked you to
move in?"

"Yes. How many ways do you want me to
say it."

"I wouldn't have said she was the type."

"Is there a type?"

"Well . . . she's not like us, is she?"

"What do you think she is?"

"Honest."

Wilderness went on packing. Eddie
scratched his head with an invisible hand,
not moving a muscle.

"How old is she?"

"Twenty."

"Older'n you, then?"

"I lied about me age."

360

"Great start, Joe."

Wilderness hefted his kit bag under his right arm, wrapped his left around Eddie's shoulders.

"Eddie, we'll be fine. You, me, Nell — fine."

"It's for real is it, Joe?"

"It's very real, Ed."

# §107

Top floor. Tucked under the eaves. Flaking whitewash. Moonlight on broad elm floorboards. A brass bed held together with bent bits of wire that had creaked embarrassingly the first time they had made love and on every occasion since.

She lay curled in the crook of his arm. Mouse small.

"Why do they call you Joe?"

"It's me name."

"Not your real name."

"Never really been a John. Hated being called Wilf. Joe was the compromise. The English love nicknames."

"We like . . . diminutives."

"Like Hansel and Gretel."

"If you like."

"Like Nell?"

"Oh Nell. She is the grown-up. The little girl was Lenchen. To my father I was always Lenchen. Christina Hélène von Raeder Burkhardt is such a mouthful. So I am Nell."

"One woman called me Wilderness. I don't think she could quite pronounce my surname. So she called me Wilderness."

"Sounds . . . savage. You know . . . like Kaspar Hauser."

"Maybe. Wild child. But I doubt it. Eddie calls you Fraulein Breakheart when he's trying to make a point."

Up on one elbow now. Eye to eye. Almost nose to nose.

"Breakheart?"

"Yep."

"Is that who we are? Wilderness and Breakheart."

"Yeah . . . but we're nowhere near as bad as it makes us sound."

She slumped into the curve of his arm again. Fell asleep. Oblivious to all the things that kept him awake. Since he arrived in Berlin not a single night had passed without the sound of gunfire. And when he nodded off, the pungent smell of carbide lamps drifting up from the street could penetrate any depth of sleep.

She stirred. Up on one elbow once more. One eye opened, one eye closed. He touched the scar beneath her left eye with his fingertips.

"My . . . war wound."

"Tell me about it."

So she did.

# §108

Nell kept a journal. Fat, ochre-coloured with coarse onion-skin pages. It sat upon a writing slope, which in turn sat upon the small table that passed for her desk. It would not have occurred to Wilderness to look inside, curious or not. What intrigued him most was not the possibilities of content, but the pencils she used. Different colours worn to different lengths. When she had finished writing whatever it was she wrote, she would arrange the pencils on her desk in order of length. If he moved one, sooner or later he would find she had moved it back. A creature of some disorder himself, he could admire order — he admired Eddie's sense of order, a man who matched up socks and rolled them into balls; an act for which Wilderness thought life too short — but Nell's order prompted questions, questions without form or language. An elusive sense of belonging and not belonging, of wondering where he fitted into this woman's life.

He thought of all the women in his life — the few. His drunken, feckless mother, who had died with a gin and lime in her hand, who had scarcely seemed to know he was alive. Mercurial, beautiful, utterly amoral Merle — a woman without a care in the world because she cared for no one and nothing, who had seduced him on a whim. Rada

— a demanding, generous mind, the biggest influence in his life — trapped in her own memories even as she narrated them to him, nurturing an inconsolable, unarticulated grief that had killed her. Nell — charming, severe, funny, humourless, driven . . . above all else driven — the weight of the world on her shoulders. Standing straight, standing tall in a city which lay in pieces at her feet. A one-woman moral storm.

He came to realise that her distinction between guilt and responsibility was vital. The apartment was one room — cooker and sink at one end, bath at the other, bed and all else in the middle. It was too big for one woman by the standards of Berlin in 1947. As he learnt on their second "date," Nell had no living relatives — a condition Wilderness thought much of Berlin might be in — and felt that to live alone, in a room of one's own was wrong. However desirable, wrong. But for this he doubted she would have let him move in after so short a courtship.

The nearest thing she had to a relative, she told him, was the man who lived on the floor below. Erno Schreiber, and old friend of her parents. A man in his late fifties, or there-abouts. A Jew.

"How did he survive?"

"Hid his identity. Changed his name. Forged all his papers. And forged them for others. I should think there are over two hundred Jews in Berlin who owe their lives to Erno's skill as a forger. His masterpiece was the *Bombenschein*. Rather like your *Persilschein*. It was a catch-all document stating that all other papers had been lost in an air raid."

This intrigued him. This was his territory, far more than it was hers.

Arriving home ahead of her one day, the door to Erno Schreiber's room was ajar. He knocked, the door swung inward on its own weight and Wilderness found himself looking at a small, white-haired man in an unravelling cardigan, hunched over a desk, writing by the light of a twenty-five watt lamp, surrounded by junk — piles of newspapers, overburdened bookshelves, the paraphernalia of the practised hoarder. Nowhere to sit, no way to move. Walkways through the junk, like looking down on the pattern of a maze.

The ginger tomcat perched on the highest shelf looked down at Wilderness. Erno did not look up.

Just said, "Ah, the boyfriend. I had wondered when you might call."

"Yes," Wilderness said. "And you're the forger."

Now he looked up. His glasses unhooked from the right ear to dangle by their brass loop from the left.

"And you're the *Schieber*."

"She told you?"

"My dear *Schieber*. We're talking about a woman whose honesty may well be her only vice."

"Well, we're all *Schieber*s of one sort or another aren't we?"

"Indeed, it is the norm. I cannot think of any other reason why Nell would tolerate one let alone . . . admit one. She is so earnest, so adamant about sharing in the common fate."

"Not so long ago, thinking like that would have got you killed."

"Quite, so easy to die of obedience or conformity. Now, what can I do for you Herr Schieber?"

"An identity card."

"What kind of identity card?"

"A pay book. British army regiment. Welsh Guards."

He picked up a pencil now, ready to take notes.

"Date of birth and name?"

Thinking on his toes. If he made his doppelgänger older, what was his war record?

"August 3 . . . 1926 . . . Rupert . . ."

Most officers were Ruperts or Tobys.

"Rupert Charles . . ."

Most officers had three Christian names. You weren't a proper toff without three initials. Most officers had a posh surname hyphenated with a common one. Burne-Jones sprang to mind to be readily dismissed.

"Rupert Charles Montgomery Tatten-

Brown."

"Montgomery. Hmm. How patriotic. And the rank?"

"Second Lieutenant. No . . . make that first lieutenant."

"You want pips with that?"

"You got pips?"

On the wall above Erno's desk was a cabinet of fifty tiny drawers, something out of an apothecary's shop — the chemical symbols in gold leaf that had faded into near-nothingness.

"Welsh Guards . . . Welsh Guards . . . let me see."

A few seconds rummaging in CuSO4 and two shoulder pips were placed on the desk in front of Wilderness.

"You got pips for everything?"

"More or less. You want to pass for a tram inspector or an SS Standartenführer, I'm your man, although the tram inspector will cost you more. And if you really were an SS Standartenführer wanting to pass for a tram inspector you can double any figure you might be thinking of. And I'd still call the police. Now, you want the tree to put on your cap?"

"Tree?"

Erno held out a Welsh Guards cap badge.

"That's not a tree, it's a leek. And I already got the cap and badge."

"What's a leek?"

"Sort of like an onion."

"How quaint . . . no swords or daggers . . . just vegetables. Food is so much more important, you will agree. Were you thinking of paying me in food, Herr Schieber?"

"If you like. What do you want? Chocolate? Tinned stuff?"

"Coffee."

"Consider it done."

"Coffee is the one thing Yuri never puts in a *pajok*. Far too precious."

"Yuri? Who's Yuri?"

# §109

"Who's Yuri?"

They were seated at opposite sides of the little table in the portion of Nell's room that passed as "dining." A close parody of the prim and proper. Once in a while this seemed to be what Nell wanted. And the rest of the time she was content to sit on the floor or sprawl on the bed.

He had brought fresh eggs. Nell had scrambled them and served them with tinned broad beans she had been saving. She stirred the egg on her plate slowly and looked up at him.

"Yuri was . . . is . . . my mother's protector. An NKVD major."

"Was? Is? You mean he's your protector?"

"I think he is, although he does not visit as

regularly as he used to and the *pajoks* are fewer."

"*Pajok?*"

"Food parcel. You bring *pajoks*. You just didn't know the word."

"Protector?"

"A man who took you on board in '45, who brought you *pajoks* and told every other Russian that you were his was a protector. If he did none of those things he was a rapist. My mother avoided rape by accepting his patronage, his sexual exclusivity . . . and his *pajoks*."

"Yet still he brings you *pajoks*."

"For which he receives nothing but my lasting gratitude. He hasn't been here in weeks. It is his habit just to vanish from time to time."

# §110

Yuri showed up the next day.

When Wilderness returned late in the afternoon a small man in a nondescript uniform was sitting with Erno, drinking the coffee he had given Erno yesterday.

He did not know how to read Russians in uniform. He'd passed them in the street every day. One or two even came to the Marrokkaner. Laughing loudly, never breaking their circle, wanting to know no one. But, then, he'd never tried. And if those who spoke Russian never tried talking to Russians who would?

They were raggy men in baggy pants and jackboots. Some of them were even raggy women. Collar flashes could be blue, could be yellow, but, as with Yuri, were mostly dirt-coloured. The only thing that broke up the muddiness of his battledress was a row of medal ribbons in all the spectrum of the rainbow, the single gold star of a major on each shoulder, and the shiny brass button on the flap holster that held his seven-shot Nagant revolver.

He'd lost track of the initials too. The Soviet Union and the Third Reich had this in common — they'd invent a new organisation and a new acronym on the spot to cope with contingencies. Nell had said he was NKVD in 1945. It was easiest to go on thinking of him that way.

Yuri hoisted his cup of coffee, by way of toast, by way of greeting.

"Good good," he said. "Is yours?"

Yuri swirled the coffee in his cup and downed it in a single gulp. Erno poured a cup for Wilderness, muttered an apology about the lack of milk. Yuri cradled the empty cup in hands that seemed huge, out of all proportion to his body, with fat fingers, broad flat thumbs and tiny slivers of fingernails — brown hands peeking out of brown sleeves, hands that had been calloused and scarred and tanned. And in the sunburnt, Asiatic face, nut-brown and wrinkled like a walnut, when his deep blue eyes opened from their narrow slits, they twinkled with mischief. He held out the cup for more.

"Good good," he said again, and Wilderness realised he had not answered.

"Yes," he said. "Part payment. Erno is doing a little job for me."

This was one way of flushing the fox out. Major Myshkin would hardly be sitting there if he too were not "one of us" — a *Schieber* of one kind or another.

The cup was laid gently down on one of the piles of old newspapers that seemed to serve Erno as furniture. The right hand slid across his midriff to flip the button on his holster.

Wilderness's gun was in a drawer in Fasanenstraße. He wasn't even sure which drawer.

Yuri withdrew his hand and Wilderness found himself looking down the barrel of a saxophone-shaped Hungarian pipe, as Yuri gestured with it.

"Perhaps you can do a little job for me?"

The left hand rummaged in his jacket pocket, pulled out a worn, square tin of Ogden's Walnut Plug.

"That might be possible," Wilderness said. "How much would you like?"

The tamping and the lighting up, the sucking and the puffing slowed the conversation to a tortoise crawl.

"Fifty pounds. I can use fifty pounds."

"I can get your brand of tobacco too, if you like. It's English."

"Da, so. My own private *pajok.*"

Suck, puff, breathe out a cloud of smoke, suck puff, puff puff. Wilderness had never found this unpleasant — it had been Abner's choice of brand too — but he had concluded in childhood that men smoked pipes only to make other men wait.

"From Leeverrpol, da?"

"Da," said Wilderness.

"But . . . you must bring to me."

"What? In the East?"

"Da. I cannot always come West. And I can hardly stand in Tiergarten like a Berlin *Hausfrau.*"

"Where in the East?"

"That should be a moveable feast. We'll move around. Points east, east of Pariser Platz."

"A hundred."

"Is that your price?"

"No. The quantity. It has to be worthwhile if you want me to shift stuff over the line, and run the risk of your cops as well as ours . . ."

"My people will leave you well alone, believe me."

"And ours are at their nosiest at the line . . . a hundred pounds of coffee and I'll deliver to you in the East."

Suck, puff, cloud.

"Okeydokey, Englishman. A hundred pounds a time. Now, can we talk money or had you forgotten that?"

Wilderness had not forgotten the money any more than a dog forgets to eat, but he was worrying about something just as vital — where could he get a hundred pounds of coffee?

# §111

Later that night, in the Marrokkaner.

"You said what?"

"A hundred pounds of coffee."

"Jesus wept," Pie Face said. "You silly sod."

"All the same, my character not withstanding . . . you can get a hundred pounds?"

"Possible. Risky. Someone might notice."

"What's the most you've ever got out at one time?"

"Sixty. Week before last."

"So you'll try?"

"Yeah. I'll try."

It was Eddie's habit to hear everyone out before speaking. He spoke now.

"How are we going to shift it? I can't manage twenty pounds under me greatcoat, let alone a hundred, and we're almost out of greatcoat weather. Any minute now the MPs'll be able to nick the black-marketeers by pulling in anyone daft enough to be wearing an army greatcoat in the sunshine."

Wilderness said, "We motorise. We have three staff jeeps at our disposal. Mine, Eddie's, and Spud's. And once we cross the line we're free of our blokes — they've always been the real threat, not the Russians. We've always had more to fear from our own lot just selling by the bag on the street."

"Vehicles get pulled just like blokes on foot," Spud said. "An' that's a fact."

"We won't have it on display."

"MPs know the hiding places. And they got mirrors to look under the car."

"Jerry cans," Wilderness said. "How many jerry cans does a staff jeep carry?"

"Four," said Spud. "But there's fixings for six."

"Capacity?"

"Twenty litres each."

"Can we pack a hundred pounds of coffee into that space?"

"Just. Only just. But it would mean no spare petrol."

"And when have you ever run out of petrol driving around Berlin?"

Spud smiled the smile of acceptance.

"Brilliant, Joe. Bloody brilliant."

Wilderness nodded and waited. Watched Spud improvise.

"I slices the bottoms off the cans in me workshop, bit o' spot welding, fit 'em back with an inner sleeve, and bob's yer uncle — six giant coffee cans undetectable to the nosy copper."

Eddie was smiling too.

"Might work," he said. "You never know."

Walking back to Fasanenstraße, Eddie said, "And the money? You never mentioned it and they never ask. They're like a pair of schoolboys. They care more about the lark than the profit."

"He'll pay over the odds, and I insisted on Western marks. No minus money. For all I know he prints his own."

"How can coffee, how can anything be worth more in East Berlin than it is in the West? We're getting four hundred reichsmarks a pound as it is."

" 'Cos it don't stay in East Berlin. Leastways that's my feeling. Yuri is big time. Party apparatchik. Commissar during the early part of the war. I reckon anything we sell him will go to the arselickers and the comrades back in Moscow."

"Ruins yer faith in humanity, doesn't it?"

"Yep. I'll never vote Commie again."

"Big time? This Yuri is . . . big time?"

"Like I said."

"Are we big time now, Joe? Bulk orders? A hundred pounds at a time?"

"There's sod all profit and sod all pleasure in selling half a dozen bags at a time to the stick insects."

"Or do we just not know what we're getting into?"

"Y'know I'd go right off you if you ever turned into an optimist, Ed."

# §112

The first time, they met in *Das Eierkuhlhaus* — the egg-cooling house — in Osthafen. This part of the city, on the north bank of the Spree, had been Wehrmacht property. A prime target, with one of Berlin's largest goods stations — the *Ost-Güterbahnhof* — smack in the middle of it. The RAF had pasted it, and somehow managed to miss a warehouse with 75,000,000 eggs and the opportunity to create the biggest omelette in history.

Yuri delighted in telling him this.

It surprised Wilderness not half as much as the fact that the Russians — having shipped anything that wasn't nailed down, to say nothing of much of what was nailed down, back to the Soviet Union — were once again using the egg house for its intended purpose and storing eggs.

Two silent Slavs unloaded one hundred pounds of coffee, looking slightly baffled by the whole process of concealment.

Yuri counted out fifty thousand reichsmarks.

Wilderness flipped through them looking

for plus signs.

"You don't trust me? That's OK. I wouldn't trust me either. Here, a present for Nell."

He handed Wilderness a dozen eggs.

"Two hundred and fifty marks in the Tiergarten. Now, perhaps you will trust me a little?"

"Two hundred and seventy five. And we'll take trust one day at a time, shall we? Like giving up fags or booze."

Yuri laughed out loud at this.

"Da, da. The Alkononics Anonomy. We are a pair of junkies! Addicted to the deal."

Yuri slapped him on the back. A lot of force for such a little man.

Wilderness said, "We could speed things up a bit, you know."

"How?"

"Get hold of six more jerry cans — they're everywhere in Germany, it's why they're called jerry cans after all — and fix them up the same as mine. Then, instead of waiting while your blokes empty them out, we just swap cans. Dammit, we could park side by side on Unter den Linden and be away in thirty seconds."

"Risky. I prefer some cover."

"Just a figure of speech."

"And I would have to trust you about what was really in the cans."

"You'd be free to open any one of them at any time."

"Okeydokey. Good good. I get one of my 'blokes,' as you call them, to do the job. Next time, eh? One day at a time."

Wilderness drove back across the Brommy Bridge, into the American Sector. Fifty thousand reichsmarks was a small fortune if exchangeable into dollars or sterling, but it wasn't. The trick, if such, was not be caught holding the parcel when the music stopped. And it would surely stop one day?

# §113

Wilderness did the next run himself too. It took Pie Face a fortnight to get one hundred pounds of coffee.

He grumbled endlessly.

Yuri grumbled endlessly. So much so, Wilderness bought time by insisting Yuri meet the team at the Marrokkaner.

The rough and wrinkled peasant had all the diplomatic skills of a candidate for the US presidency. If there had been babies he would have kissed them.

Wilderness was well aware that few people Spud and Pie Face had ever met could represent the "unknown" as fully as Yuri. Leaving the square mile of their birth had been a major step, going overseas a life milestone, setting foot in a French brothel a total violation of their upbringing . . . something to be remembered, relished, and never spoken of again.

Eddie was different. Eddie was an imaginative man in a dull exterior. It was a brilliant defence. Who would ever suspect the little fat bloke who exuded dullness and misery? He had always reminded Wilderness of a bumblebee — unlikely, one of nature's freaks . . . but when the creature chose to fly . . . ?

Besides, Eddie had been through the same course of Cambridge indoctrination that he had himself — and he spoke better Russian. Spud might be charmed as Yuri bought him beer after beer and they compared notes on childhoods spent on farms in East Anglia and rural Russia, Pie Face might be bemused by it all, but little would dent Eddie's cynicism.

As ever, he saved his critique until they were alone.

"You think he's dodgy, don't you?" Wilderness said.

"Dodgy? More like downright bloody dangerous."

"He's in the same game we are, Ed — that's all."

"Before I was in this 'game' I was a driver and interpreter and you flogged china on a market stall in Whitechapel. Spud's a farmboy-cum-mechanic, as happy chewing straw as smuggling coffee. Pie Face is part of the great East End diaspora, living on the Thames estuary, living off memories of Limehouse or Wapping and less than happy with anything else. Wogs begin in Kent as far he's concerned. But what about our new pal? What did Yuri do in the war? For that matter what did Yuri do before the war? He's twenty years older than us. He's an apparatchik, an NKVD officer, a former military commissar for fuck's sake. He doesn't deal in coffee he deals in death. In either capacity, commissar or NKVD . . . how many deaths is he responsible for? You don't know and neither do I."

"Yet, he took care of Nell and her mother in '45."

"Doesn't make him St. Francis."

So, Wilderness made Eddie do the run with him. Just to set his mind at ease.

The venue was another industrial relic, the *Eisfabrik* on Köpenicker Straße, again just spitting distance from the American line. It reminded Wilderness of nothing quite so much as the illustrated pages of his School Cert history book — Chapter 7, the Industrial Revolution. It was like the interior of a Lancashire cotton mill — although the pages of his history book were the closest he'd ever been to one — an iron jungle of boilers and flywheels and overhead cams. Pleasing, it its way. Languishing, under a few years of dust. It probably hadn't turned out a block of ice since the war turned against the Reich in 1943. One day it might make ice again — until then it seemed to be Yuri's warehouse. One of many.

Yuri's bloke — Yuri offered no introduction, and the man never spoke — set six jerry cans in front of them. Identical to the ones they'd brought in with them, even down to the British Army stencilling on the side and the little red and green flashes, copied from memory without comprehension.

"Good good," said Yuri.

Wilderness handed him a tin of Ogden's Walnut Plug.

"On the house," he said, and as Yuri looked both pleased and baffled by phrase and gesture, added, "A present, from us to you."

"Good good. So . . . kind. New tin. So pretty. Mine is so worn. So pretty pretty. And I . . . have present for Eddie."

Yuri summoned one of the silent men, and with a bold hint of ceremony a bottle of "*Pugachev* перцовка" vodka was handed from him to Yuri to Eddie.

It was bright red, a fact readily explained by the sketch of a cluster of red peppers on the label. But not as red as Eddie. Eddie was blushing, as though he'd blundered into the Olympic arena after a casual stroll in the park only to break the tape ahead of the marathon winner. An unexpected honour.

"Bottled in 1932," said Yuri.

"Thank you."

"One hundred twenty proof."

"I'm touched."

"Made from capitalists' blood."

381

The slap on the back that followed almost made Eddie drop the bottle.

Wilderness laughed, which brought a nervous smile to Eddie's lips, but Yuri was roaring hysterically at his own joke. He drew breath long enough to translate for his blokes and then half a dozen of them were laughing together.

"Next time?" Wilderness said to bring them back to earth.

"Next time, zoap."

"What kind of soap?"

"Lady zoap. Pink and smelly. As much as you can get."

Driving home, clutching the bottle between his knees, Eddie said, "He's a bundle of bloody laughs isn't he?"

"I rather think that was the price you paid for your all-too-obvious suspicion."

"So now we need a mountain of soddin' *zoap*?"

"We can get a mountain of *zoap*. Might not be pink but it'll be smelly. Whatever the NAAFI has in stock. In fact from now on it's open orders . . . we sell him whatever we can. And we split the driving. You, me, and Spud. Different faces, different jeeps, different locations . . . all lowers the risk."

"And our regulars?"

"Regulars?"

"The blokes at the back doors of all the caffs we supply, the blokes in the Tiergarten."

"Small change, Ed."

"They're still *our* regulars."

"There'll be enough to go round, trust me, there'll be enough."

"You're driving Pie Face potty, you know that don't you?"

"Then maybe we need another source."

# §114

Eddie got home to Fasanenstraße after a day of chauffeuring, interpreting, and dealing to find Wilderness in shirt and underpants. Wilderness was pressing his Welsh Guards outfit. Adding a second pip to the shoulders.

"High time I got promoted."

"Oh bugger. You're going out in it."

"Damn right I am."

"Joe this isn't London. This place is crawling with MPs."

"So?"

"If you go down the Marlborough Club . . . suppose someone recognises you? It's officers only. You'd be had up for impersonation. You want a night out, what's wrong with the Winston Club. It's only two streets away. We could both go."

"Eddie, you're worrying about nothing. I just want to see how the other half lives. I'm not going down the Winston — all those pompous NCOs would make my blood boil."

"Mine too but . . ."

383

"And I'm not going down the Marlborough. The other half I want to see is American. I'm off to Harnack-Haus."

Harnack-Haus was out in the suburb of Dahlem, at the southern end of the American Sector. It had been commandeered as a social club for US forces in 1945. At some point during the war, according to Peter-Jürgen von Hesse in one of his interminably rambling confessions, Germany's nuclear physicists had met here with a view to building an atomic bomb. They had been indecisive. Now, the most lethal thing mixed here was a green St. Patrick's Day cocktail, relying heavily on chartreuse and lager.

Wilderness paid off the cab opposite Harnack-Haus — remembering that officers tipped. Patted the pocket, where Erno's fake ID nestled. It was immaculate. The work of a master craftsman. He just might be Lt Rupert Tatten-Brown.

Harnack-Haus was a monstrosity, worse by far than the Victory Club in Hamburg — a Prussian bludgeon of a building — but on the same vast ocean-liner scale. A bar the size of a ballroom — and packed, Friday night revellers, in spick-and-span uniforms, on pleasure bent. It was not, and this surprised him, "Officers Only" — America being a democracy, by the people for the people of the people, its distinction was not between classes but colours.

He wasn't at all sure why he'd come. He stood at the bar, ordered a Krombacher Pils and began to think he'd made a mistake. He'd not been sure what he wanted — a taste of the high life, a sense of being at the centre rather than the edge. But that was the British condition post-war — to be on the periphery. Groups of Americans, mostly airmen out of Tempelhof, looked like closed societies, sealed units. It would have been quite impossible to intrude with a "hello chaps" and a handshake, impossible to penetrate that level of laughter and inclusive fellow-feeling. His childhood had set him up. He wanted to mingle with Americans for no better reason than that they were the people who'd appeared on-screen at the Troxy cinema in the Commercial Road. He was looking at servicemen in olive green, when really what he wanted was Carole Lombard or Melvyn Douglas — better still, he wanted a glimpse of Myrna Loy and William Powell, seated at a round table swirling cocktails, swapping gags, the dog at their feet just waiting to nip your ankles.

He'd have another beer and call it quits.

He'd just raised a hand to signal the barman, when a voice on his right said, "Let me get this."

This was a big one. An American army captain as tall as he was himself, but bulking up at twice his size, barrel chest, a jaw like

Desperate Dan.

"Krombacher, right?"

"Thanks, old man. Awfully good of you."

Even as he spoke them the words sounded fake. The whole venture sounded fake. He could kick himself. Having opened his mouth as a toff he'd have no choice now but to keep it up.

With two glasses of Pils set in front of them, the American hoisted his with, "Mud in your eye."

Wilderness could think of nothing more English than "Cheers."

"Haven't I seen you somewhere before?"

Oh shit.

"Don't think so, old man. Tatten-Brown. Welsh Guards."

"Sure. At the . . . oh hell . . . my German is complete crap . . . Kult . . . Kult . . . *Kulturkammer* . . . nah, *Kulturbund,* that was it . . . what a mouthful . . . the place on Schlüter-straße. The DeNaz place. Where the Krauts come to get their *Persilschein*s."

Shit, shit, shit.

Wilderness looked back at the greeny-brown eyes. The half-wry smile on his lips. He didn't look hostile. Perhaps he wasn't hostile.

"Just a game, mate," he said. "Just a bit of fun. Seeing how the other half lives. A dressing-up game. No harm in it."

"Sure. I mean. Why not? Tell you what.

Let's see if we can find a quiet table to ourselves."

Wilderness decided that if this bloke was going to shop him, he'd have done it by now, and most certainly would not have said, "Run a tab" as they picked their beers and made their way to the far corner of the room.

As they drew back chairs, a huge, soft hand shook his.

"Frank Spoleto, Captain, US Army Intelligence. Been here since '45. Came in with the 82nd Airborne."

"Joe Holderness, Corporal, Royal Air Force Intelligence. Came here on the Silk Stocking express this winter."

"Yeah, I guess you are just a kid at that. Ever see combat?"

"No. I got drafted . . . after."

"Tough. But . . . but . . . just a kid is as maybe. I hear you're the man."

*The* man?

"Why not just spit it out, Captain?"

"Nah, it's tale to be told not a fleck of phlegm to be coughed up. I got here with the first American troops in July '45, when the Russkis drew back to the line. You think Berlin's badly off now, but that's nothing compared to '45."

"Why are you telling me this?"

"Stick with me, kid. In '45 everything was up for grabs. Everything was up for sale. Stuff we took for granted back home was priceless here.

"Cigarettes, cigarettes were obvious. I mean. They had a whole army of kids picking butts off the ground, begging them off you before you could even flip them onto the sidewalk. Rolling up fresh ones from the dregs was a cottage industry. Even a gasper finished off with toilet paper was worth five reichsmarks back then when the real thing was worth twice that. The places that made them weren't factories . . ."

"I know all this. I've had this lecture."

"Hear me out . . . they weren't factories . . . they were the Bank of England, they were the Federal Reserve, they were Fort Knox, because cigarettes were currency. I gave up smoking. I ask you, would you set fire to money and stick it in your mouth? But what really wised me up was a date with a German girl I was sweet on. I'd taken her out a couple of times. Third or fourth date I was hoping to improve my score, maybe get to third base if not a home run. Gave her a box of Fairy soap. Nothing special. Just ordinary soap, some white, some green. She fucked me stupid and sold the box for three hundred marks. I knew then. The guy with the key to the PX was Rockefeller, Carnegie, Pierpont Morgan. Goddammit, he's Errol fuckin' Flynn."

Wilderness said again, "Why are you telling

me this? I know all this."

"Because we could do business."

"We could?"

"I'm the man with the key to Fort Knox. And from what I hear, you're the man. The man with a tame Russki in his pocket. The last couple of years have been sweet, but it can get sweeter. In '45 you could exchange marks for dollars and wire them home. More'n ten million bucks went home that way. Then that got capped, and then stopped altogether. Since then . . . the smart money ain't been in money at all. It's been in commodities. Hard stuff. The stuff you and I deal in."

Wilderness wondered how much he knew, and concluded he probably knew everything. How was another matter.

"I still don't see where you're heading with this."

"Aw, c'mon. You have a network, I know you have a network. Most guys in this room are selling cigarettes and nylons, one to one. Dodging the MPs in the Tiergarten or Alexanderplatz. Penny-ante stuff. You're not selling on the streets to desperate Krauts, you're selling in bulk to the Russians. You got the network. I got the supply. I got the PX at Tempelhof sewn up."

"And I've got the NAAFI stores on Adolf-Hitler-Platz sewn up. Why would I need you?"

"What can you steal from the NAAFI? A

389

hundred pounds of coffee at a time."

Remarkably, this was disturbingly accurate.

"Last week one transport alone, just one, flew in fifteen hundred pounds. And I can make half of it vanish just like that."

A snap of his finger in the air to make his point.

"How?"

"I pay off the guy who processes the paperwork. They ship fifteen hundred, but who counts, all that matters is the paperwork, and on paper the manifest says seven-fifty so only seven hundred and fifty arrives. The rest . . . well."

"That must cost."

"He ain't greedy."

"Perhaps I am."

"We're businessmen. We'll come to an arrangement. There'll be enough for everybody."

"I have partners."

"Sure. Three of 'em. We'll cut 'em in."

This bloke knew too much. Safer by far to have him on the inside pissing out than on the outside pissing in.

# §115

Nell and Wilderness made a point of not arriving at Schlüterstraße at the same time. Undoubtedly Rose Blair, the woman on the ground floor ("matron," as Wilderness called her behind her back), knew, but Nell was confident no one else did. The one disadvantage of pretending not to know each other was that it eased Wilderness's disappearing act — some days he would be gone after breakfast and not reappear until past midnight. Knowing about his rackets was a finite fact — it was the sum total of what she wished to know. Detail would not help. He was a *Schieber* — the common condition of life in Berlin in 1947. That much she knew, that much she accepted. If she could accept *pajoks* from Yuri Myshkin, she could accept Wilderness and all he got up to. Detail did not matter.

But, today, she had not seen him for two nights, and presumed he had slept back at Fasanenstraße. It was not that she worried — he had all the qualities of a survivor — but she missed him. She missed his jokes. She missed his deftness with words and hands. She missed his unguarded affection.

When she got home a teapot was on the landing outside Erno's door. An agreed sign. He was at home and was inviting her to take tea with him.

"Eh, Lenchen?"

As ever he was at his desk. Conjuring up one of his magical pieces of card and paper, the forger's origami that put space and freedom between the unfortunate individual and the powers of Occupation. Her "two hundred" souls saved by Erno's forgeries once the deportation of the Jews had begun was, in all probability, an understatement. Her own papers were Erno fakes. Having added two years to her age to bluff Nicolas Dekker, she had kept them — otherwise she might not even have the job she had.

"You know, lately I have seen more of Herr Schieber than I have of you, my dear."

She sat by the iron stove, flicked open the door — an orange glow upon her, as far as the hem of her skirt — her legs as disembodied as Erno's hands under his spotlight.

"His name's Joe. I call him Wilderness. But . . . read nothing into that. It's just a rhyme in English. He calls me Breakheart."

"Ah. And I shall read nothing into that either."

He wanted to talk. That was why the teapot was there. But he seemed to be saying nothing. The hands moving slowly and delicately across a page she could not see, his face and eyes hidden. They were legs talking to hands. And suddenly it seemed easier that way, a memory of a lapsed Catholic girlhood, of the very few times she had ever confessed to anything . . . or nothing.

Child. Have you sinned?

No. Not this week.

But everyone sins!

Not me. Not this week.

To the hands she said, "He disappears. Just

like Yuri, but never for as long."

"The racket?"

"The racket. But . . . we're all in a racket. That is Hitler's legacy. But . . . he says it's the 'only game in town' . . . an English phrase that seems clear enough . . . But . . . there are times I think the game matters more than the end result . . . and that it matters more than me. Then I start to wonder, and so I suppose it all comes down to one question. Why am I with this man?"

The hands did not stop moving, the angle of the head did not shift.

"What was it your mother used to call you?"

"I was her 'po-faced little angel.' "

"As true today as it was in 1936. Lenchen, yours is a structured life. It was ever thus. At the age of four you would put everything in your doll's house back in place before you went to bed. Your doll's house is now your mind, as ordered as your desktop.

"Do you know the old Greek tale of the Hedgehog and the Fox? The hedgehog knows one big thing. The fox knows many smaller things. 'Πόλλ' οἶδ' ἀλώπηξ, ἀλλ' ἐχῖνος ἓν μέγα.' You are the hedgehog, Joe is the fox. In your structured life he is the random element your unconscious craves. He is the unpredictability you will not quite surrender. Remember, you told me how you met him? What was he doing?"

"Cardsharping."

"Exactly. A game of chance."

"At which I beat him."

"All the same he personified the random element. It was why you sat down with him in the first place. It was what . . . drew you."

"In . . . in this tale of yours. Are the hedgehog and the fox always opposed? Do they fight? Does someone lose and someone win? Is there any chance of a happy ending?"

"Ach. To tell you the truth I cannot remember. Let us not make too much of a simple analogy."

# §116

He introduced Frank to Eddie, Spud, and Pie Face in the Marrokkaner.

Frank said, "This is a dive. Let's go somewhere better."

He drove a 1942 Plymouth painted up in drab, a white star on each of the rear doors.

They followed him as far as Gänsefettstraße, in the American Sector, a couple of blocks from the Soviet line.

Eddie said, "Why don't we make cars with roofs?"

Spud said, "Because the army wants you to freeze yer bollocks off in a jeep."

Frank had parked opposite a nightclub — Paradies Verlassen. There wasn't much left of the upper storeys. It didn't matter, the midnight blue staircase wound down and

394

down. By the time they stopped in front of a pair of quilted and buttoned, pitted and gashed, scarlet velvet doors that looked as though they'd withstood an attack by the SA, Wilderness estimated they were three floors below ground level.

It was deceptive. He knew it would be bigger and better than the Marrokkaner — he would not contend Frank's assertion that the Marrokkaner was a dive — but he'd anticipated nothing so wide, so high, so . . . well preserved — this place had survived the SA, the RAF, and the Russian infantry. It wasn't a low-ceilinged smoky room, crammed with tables. It was spacious, galleried, with a dance floor that would allow a hundred couples to take to the floor if they so desired. It was a slice of Weimar-era Berlin in aspic.

A waiter greeted Frank like an old friend and showed them to a table two steps up from the dance floor. Frank stuck money in his hand and ordered beers all round.

Eddie was almost spinning on his heels, with his eyes turned up to the star-painted ceiling. Spud gazed around and uttered a simple truth, "Fuck me. The Dog and Duck it ain't."

There was a telephone in the centre of the table, and a serpentine network of tubes wound overhead to end in an art nouveau snake's head, its jaws gaping over a small black net, rather like the ones on the side of a billiard table.

Wilderness picked up the phone, but it was dead.

Frank said, "Before the war they all worked. You could dial anyone at any table. Or if you preferred you could write a message, stick it in the snake's head, yank on the handle and the pneumatic tube would whisk it up to the top gallery and they'd redirect it to the right table."

He pointed up to a swirl in the tubing a few feet above their heads, from which dangled an enamelled plate with their table number inscribed on it — a stylised 21 in a familiar, arty font dating back to the 1890s.

"The tubes still work."

"So . . . it was a . . . pick-up joint?"

"Still is . . . you just can't whisper your sweet nothings any more. You got to write 'em down."

"So . . . a single woman at another table . . . ?"

"Not decadent enough, Joe. *Any* woman at *any* table."

The room was filling up. The noise level was rising.

"Cabaret's about to start. We'll talk after."

A faux maître d' walked to the front of the stage, a young woman with slicked back hair and a greasepaint moustache applied some-what more delicately than Groucho Marx's, clicked her heels in the Prussian style and announced in heavily accented English, clearly knowing only too well who her audience were, "Und now. A liddle diddy entitled 'I Sold My Heart for a Peanut Budder Cubcake.' "

The song was not great lyrically or musically — what it was was daring. Whoever wrote for these girls had avoided the strictures on not poking fun at the Allies, by holding up a mirror to Germans themselves — and inevitably Britain and America were reflected in it too.

A dozen scantily clad *Tanzgirls* slipped in and out of the lights, striking angular poses, thrusting pelvises, dangling arms, chanting in a sinister whisper:

*Folgers . . . Hershey . . . Hellman's . . . Heinz.*
*Folgers . . . Hershey . . . Hellman's . . . Heinz.*

Just when Wilderness was beginning to think it was a form of hypnotism, two lead singers took centre stage and alternated couplets in English.

*In '43 we won the war,*
*In '45 we lost it.*
*We've no more room for Lebensraum.*
*What we want is Spam.*
*Hershey bars and Camel fags,*
*We'll trade for blow jobs and for shags.*
*The Millennial Reich for coffee beans,*
*This is all our empire means.*
*We'll sell you Prussia if you like*

For fifty packs of Lucky Strike.
You can have the spires of Worms and
    Mainz
For 57 brands of Heinz.
And thank you for the Marshall Plan,
But we'd rather live in Michigan."
And again . . .
"Folgers . . . Hershey . . . Hellman's . . .
    Heinz.

Hissed out like snakes, the breathy h's and sibilant s's making it seem like a witch's curse from some updated version of *Macbeth.*

Frank said, "If they'd seen Michigan . . . they wouldn't want to live there."

"I don't think anything else rhymed with plan," said Eddie.

"I guess not. But . . . if that's their shopping list who are we not to give it to 'em?"

Wilderness said, "It's as if they knew we were coming."

"Kinda brings us to the point, doesn't it?"

Wilderness could feel Eddie bristling with discontent. Pie Face and Spud simply slurped beer and waited for fate to take its course.

"To put it in a nutshell . . . you guys need me. I could be so good for you."

Spud spoke first, "Joe told us. Just one thing. You're an officer."

Frank grinned the grin of startled innocence.

"So?"

"We're not. We don't like officers."

"You mean you don't trust 'em."

"Yeah. That too."

Frank turned to Wilderness.

"You have this problem too?"

"No . . . no, I don't. Listen up all of you. Frank's an officer, but he's an American officer. Not the same thing at all. There'll be no tugging on the forelock. I mean, look at him. Does he even look like any officer we've ever jumped for? Time to think big, lads. Time to think bigger."

Frank was grinning now, chock-full of bonhomie.

But so was Spud.

He pushed his empty glass across the table to Frank.

"So, Frank, you're one o' the boys now. Get 'em in, why don't you?"

Frank's grin erupted into a hoot of laughter. He wheeled around in his chair, hand raised for the waiter's attention.

Several beers and one lewd, suspender-belted, braless cabaret act later, Spud and Pie Face had headed for the Gents, Eddie was staring at the murals trying to separate one writhing female body from another, and Wilderness found himself the sole object of Frank's gaze.

"Next time bring the Russian."

Yuri raised not a murmur.

"Why not?" was all he said.

Paradies Verlassen had its fair share of all the occupying powers. One more little Russian was hardly out of place, hardly remarkable.

Spud and Pie Face had copped out, leaving Eddie to speak for their interests. Frank had spent like a sailor and persuaded the club to raid its cellars for a Duhart-Milon Rothschild '34. Not that he even knew the name, he'd just asked for "a bottle of the good stuff." The waiter had held it up to him and in stage whisper informed him that it had been "liberated" from the cellars of the Adlon Hotel in 1945 and sold on to them by a Russian infantryman.

"Yeah, whatever," was all this elicited from Frank. And to Wilderness, "The kind of guy who'd try and sell me Boadicea's knickers on London Bridge."

All the same, Frank never even asked the price. Generosity was a powerful weapon in his armoury. The soft sell in the hard shell. He'd had no difficulty winning over Spud and Pie Face. Wilderness had no doubts he'd click with Yuri either. Clicking seemed to be what Frank did.

He stood and shook Yuri by the hand.

Said, "What can we get you, Major?"

Yuri looked at the bottle, turned the label towards himself.

"Good good," he said, as he always seemed to.

"Red's OK with you?"

"Of course, red's OK with me; 1934 was verrrry good year for claret."

"Better red than dead, eh?"

If there'd been ice to break this shattered it into a thousand pieces. Frank was grinning, pleased at his own joke. Yuri was laughing his croaky laugh and gave Frank one of the spine-cracking slaps on the back that Wilderness reckoned to be his stamp of approval.

Frank poured. Yuri did the entire routine of sniff, taste, swirl, and swallow.

"Good good."

Then.

"Better than your Coca-Cola. Рвотная масса в бутылыке."

Frank's smile dropped a degree. He looked to Wilderness.

Wilderness said, "He says Coke is bottled vomit. And he's right."

The smile winched itself back into place.

"Am I gonna start World War Three over Coca-Cola? Am I fuck!"

And then they were laughing again, like old friends.

It would have been a relief to leave them to it. The negotiation was simple. The negotiation was non-existent. They merely had to see each other for what they were. Not trust each other — that would be asking too much — but to recognise the common interest. As Frank would have said, "just two businessmen." As Wilderness did say, "two more buggers on the make." But Yuri's English faltered too often, and Frank's Russian got no further than *Da, Niet, and Nemnozhko*. To leave it all to Eddie did not seem quite fair.

They'd reached a point where he could just duck out. Yuri had heard Frank's pitch and had placed his shopping list — what was hot, what was not. Frank had enough savvy not to ask where half the contents of the PX eventually ended up.

Now they were on to the third bottle. And on to Joe Stalin. Wilderness was not entirely sure how they'd got to him, but they were all three of them, Frank, Eddie, and Yuri, the worse for the booze.

"In Russia we have saying. Lenin wore soft shoes, Stalin wears high boots."

Eddie said, "Like jackboots?"

"Quite so, little fatty. Jackboots."

Frank said, "You mean Lenin kinda soft-shoe shuffled his way through things — and Joe Stalin just tramples on everything?"

Wilderness said, "Stride, Frank. Stride would be a better word than trample."

"Sure. Seven league boots — you can stride over everything. Like in the Brothers Grimm."

"Enough with fuckin' Krauts," Yuri said. "We were talking Russia."

Frank could not resist a joke, a little dig.

"I hear Joe Stalin smokes Edgeworth. How about a few tins of Edgeworth for the next time you see him?"

Yuri smiled, not enough for pleasure.

"Edgeworth is foul. Like smoking dried shit. I like Walnut Plug. Get me more Walnut Plug and let Stalin find his own tobacco."

Wilderness was startled by what sounded like a rush of air above his head and looked up to see a brass cylinder land in the net of the *Rohrpoststation*. Frank reached up and got the cylinder. Inside was a folded sheet of paper.

"It's for you."

Wilderness looked at the scrawl on the page, "Table 21. RAF."

He unfolded it, puzzled.

"I'm across the way at table 13. Buy a girl a drink. LT."

He looked out across the deserted dance floor. The girl at table 13 wasn't a girl. She was a woman in her thirties wearing the uniform of an NKVD major. Neater than Yuri's. Looking as though she had it cleaned and pressed once in a while, but the same gold star upon the shoulders. Two NKVD majors in one night seemed like one too many. Pickup or setup? All the same, he made his excuses, leaving Eddie to interpret, all sense of fairness evaporating rapidly, and walked across the floor to her table.

She had her nose stuck in a book. Her eyes left the book and her hands closed it with pleasing thump when he was about six paces away.

With her right foot she pushed a chair out for him.

Wilderness sat down, glanced back at Frank and Yuri who scarcely seemed to notice he'd gone. Eddie glared at him.

He looked at the major. A good-looking blonde with big, brown eyes and a perpetual pout to her lips.

"Why are you sitting here on your own? You could join us."

The big eyes opened wider.

"Why am I sitting here?"

An accent like Frank's when he was expecting one like Yuri's.

"Why am I sitting here? Because I don't want to know what Yuri's up to. He hardly ever comes West. Not since his *Schatzi* died. And I've certainly never seen him in here before. Yuri's a nice guy, but he's . . . how to put this . . . bound by the limitations of his origins, and I say that regardless of how far he's come."

"Meaning?"

"He's still a peasant. He knows what he knows and so far, and while he has imagination, it leads to a pretty low horizon. He

404

distrusts what he doesn't know. Makes him a good intelligence officer. Everyone's an enemy. He still has peasant barter as his model for any exchange. He's just switched from chickens and beets to cigarettes and whisky. Makes him good at whatever racket it is you guys are running."

"Why are you so sure it's a racket?"

" 'Cos you're sitting over there with Frank Spoleto, that's why."

"And Frank's a wrong 'un?"

"Of course he is. A charming, beguiling rogue. Mr. Personality. Another New York smart-ass."

"You know New York?"

"You think I picked up this accent at Berlitz? Gimme a break, kid. New York, London . . ."

"London? Then you probably have a take on me too."

"Indeed I do."

"I'm all ears."

"Well . . . your Russian's not bad, but the accent's atrocious, so I figure you've been trained up by the British. A crash course in Russian and German, and you speak both with the accent of a cockney wide boy. You should work on that, by the way."

"Funny. I had prided myself on being a good mimic."

"Oh, so you can do London posh, can you? The arf arfs and the tally-hos? You just

405

haven't mastered the Russian version? Look, when it comes down to it you're not that different from Yuri. Bound by your origins. But you're a city kid. Gives you an edge. Gives you more imagination and more chances. You have a bigger horizon. Yuri will always be a peasant. You may not always be an East End gutter rat. But, whatever they promised, whatever the British told you, you're still a low-grade NCO. Intelligence hasn't made you Bulldog Drummond. You interpret, you eavesdrop and that's about it. And you're bored. And when you're bored you look for a new game. And the black market is the only game in town."

Wilderness aimed for motionlessness. Not a muscular flicker to tell her how well she'd hit home. How the hell did she know all this?

"I'm impressed. Brains and beauty."

"Stop trying to flirt with me. I'm thirty-six years old and an officer. You're a corporal and you're what twenty-two, twenty-three?"

"Nineteen. Twenty next month."

"Sheeeit. Green as cabbage. Kid, stop flirting and start looking out. Guys like Frank and Yuri land on their feet. An' speaking of feet. You ever notice the size of their hands?"

"Yes, I had as it happens. Frank's are in proportion . . . Yuri's . . ."

"Portion shmortion. They both have hands like shovels. All the better to grab with. They land on their feet with their hands full. Guys

like you . . . touch and go. But guys like Swift
Eddie. They fall on their faces. They're life's
victims. Don't make him one. Don't put a
guy who's worth two of you and a dozen of
Frank or Yuri at risk."

"Ah, you know Eddie?"

"Everybody in Berlin knows Swift Eddie.
And right now he's out of his depth. He just
doesn't know it. Tell me, kid. Did you just
introduce Yuri to Frank?"

"Yes."

"Dynamite, match . . . match, dynamite."

Wilderness let this sink in, wanting to give
her the impression that he understood regardless of whether he agreed with her or not.

"Can I buy you that drink now?"

"Jesus. Is your flirt-mode on automatic?"

"Yes."

"Fine. Buy me a martini."

In all his masquerading as an officer in the
restaurants of London, Wilderness had played
safe, stuck with scotch without ever acquiring
a taste for it. It was what "me" drank. He'd
never ordered another cocktail since the day
he downed a sickly Tom Collins in the Ritz
bar to please Merle. It must have shown.

"What's the matter? Out of your depth
already?"

"Yes. And I think you knew I would be."

"No big deal. You ask the waiter for what
you want. Doesn't matter that you haven't a
clue what you're saying."

As if by magic a waiter appeared at their table.

She had him wait a moment as she pitched questions at Wilderness.

"You can have a martini with vodka or gin. Needless to say I prefer vodka. The only other ingredients are vermouth, ice, and a twist of lemon. So what's it to be?"

"No sugar?"

"Jeez! Who in hell would want to put sugar in a martini?"

"Then make it vodka . . . can I drink with a Russian and not have vodka?"

"No, you can't. Now, shaken or stirred?"

"Er . . ."

"It doesn't need any thought. Nobody shakes a martini. Martinis are stirred. Only a complete *shmo* would shake a martini."

"I'm in your hands, Major."

"Damn right."

She turned to the waiter.

*"Zwei Wodka Martinis, bitte. Gerührt nicht ge-schüttelt. Wenig Eis."*

*"Es tut mir leid, gnädige Frau. Wir haben kein Eis."*

"You hear that? No ice. Berlin in summer."

"Would you adam and eve it?"

There was a pause as the meaning of the phrase surfaced for her, then she started to giggle, and the giggle became an outright laugh. Wilderness saw Frank and Yuri look over for a second to see what the joke was

408

and turn back to business abruptly. Eddie still glared.

She was tiny, she was funny, she had deepest-brown eyes like a pair of conkers, a laugh like Ethel Merman, a bosom like Jane Russell. She was gorgeous, she was Russian, and she was unobtainable. And that was fine with him. Flirtation was one thing, and Nell was all the others.

"Maybe we should introduce ourselves. John Wilfrid Holderness. Corporal, Royal Air Force. Known as Joe."

She caught her breath as the laughter subsided.

"Nice to meet you, Joe. I'm Larissa Fyodorovna Toskevich. Major, NKVD. Known as Tosca."

# §118

As Nell had predicted, from time to time Yuri would simply vanish. Eddie was content supplying their regulars. Once in a while Wilderness would work the Tiergarten with him, watching as another sadistic winter got Berlin in its fist, watching as the calorie count in the ration dropped as quickly as the mercury in the thermometer and the stick insects got brittler and brittler. And it seemed blacker — was there an overcoat in Berlin that wasn't black? Had an entire age been reshot in monochrome? Had all the colour been looted and shipped back to Moscow?

Wilderness concluded that it was during absences like this that Yuri went back to Moscow. All the stuff he was piling up in the *Eisfabrik* at last went to meet orders. An apparatchik having a Christmas party at his state-owned dacha in the woods outside Moscow might be in need of fifty tins of Californian bluefin tuna, twelve bags of Jamaican Blue Mountain Coffee . . . a couple of thousand Pall Mall cigarettes. And the party favours . . . for the Representatives of the People, a dozen bottles of Laphroaig whisky . . . and for the wives, a few dozen bars of Cadum soap. All of which Wilderness had sold to Yuri over the weeks.

They spent a quiet Christmas.

Nell had no more belief than Wilderness but loved the traditions of a German Christmas. Erno remarked that he had "sampled" most religions in his time and thought Hinduism appealing — what other faith encouraged you to take off all your clothes and jump in a river? Wilderness remarked that the Spree was frozen over, but that he was welcome to try.

The Christmas Eve tradition of eating carp was honoured.

In the absence of carp, or anything resembling carp, Nell shaped a fish out of mashed potato and onion, cut slices of carrots for the glassy eyes, baked it in the oven and added the last sprigs of dill from her window box to make a tail and fins.

Erno laughed out loud when he saw it, and duly ate his share.

On Christmas Day Wilderness waved his magic *Schieber*'s wand and produced a fresh chicken — for which he had bartered twelve bars of Palmolive and three hundred cigarettes.

On Boxing Day Nell insisted they walk somewhere, anywhere. Along the snow-covered path of the Landwehr Canal, across the far corner of the Tiergarten and through the Brandenburg Gate, where the Soviet Sector began, to Pariser Platz at the western end of Unter den Linden.

A hurdy-gurdy man had taken to the streets once more. Wilderness had not seen one in all his months in Berlin. He thought that perhaps this was why Nell had come here. For this glimpse of her childhood. For this cranked-out, barely recognisable tune and the colours — the rich colours, the deep reds and the vivid golds of the music box in a city of blacks and whites. Like everyone else in Berlin, the hurdy-gurdy man's mode of transport was a pram, in which the hurdy-gurdy sat askew, like a cinema organ in miniature. A balding toy monkey perched on top, paw outstretched with a tin cup. Nell opened her purse and dropped coins into his cup.

Something like a column of soldiers was advancing down Unter den Linden. Like, in that it was a slow, unrhythmical march, more of a dead-foot shuffle, a column without discipline or dogged by exhaustion.

A couple of GAZ jeeps swung into Pariser Platz and half a dozen Russian soldiers, rifles at chest height, gesturing wildly with the butt end, cleared a space in front of the remains of the US embassy with what was probably one of only half a dozen words in their German vocabulary — " *'Raus, 'raus.*" It went with *Uhri* and *Frau*.

The hurdy-gurdy man stopped turning his handle. Syncopated Strauss running down like a watch spring.

"Let's go," Wilderness said. "If these silly sods are up to something I don't need to see it. They're unpredictable at the best of times, and this looks like a stunt they mean to stage. We don't have to be their audience."

Nell was staring down the street, past the broken stumps of the linden trees at the shuffling group of men and their bored, impatient escorts.

"No. Wait."

"Wait for what?"

She looked up at him, anxiety in her eyes.

"I don't know. Just a feeling. An awful feeling."

"They put on shows like this just to scare us . . ."

"Not this time . . . this is . . ."

He did not press her to finish.

More jeeps drove down the sides of the column, more infantrymen got out, marking out a defended square between the embassy and the Adlon Hotel.

After an age that seemed to pass in frosted silence fifty or sixty dishevelled, gaunt men reached the square. A voice behind them boomed out, "Halt!"

They stood, not even looking around. Men in rags that had once been Wehrmacht uniforms — flashes of colour, flashes of rank peeping out from the universal mud hue they had acquired — waiting upon the next order.

The next order never came, with balletic speed and coordination the Soviet troops got back in their jeeps, circled the square they had made, and with engines roaring shot off back down Unter den Linden. Several of the men simply fell to earth, into the filthy slush of trampled snow. The crowd that had stood back began to drift forwards staring in disbelief. The eyes of the prisoners did not look back. It seemed to Wilderness that they had been beaten lifeless while still living — when all responses were met with blows it was best to have no responses.

"Nell, let's go."

A hand upon her arm. She wrenched free, ran down the column, around the back to meet Wilderness coming the other way. Six feet from him she stopped. Her hand to her mouth suppressing whatever cry was bursting from her lips.

Right in front of her one of the skeletal men sank to his knees, sat back buttock to heel, still staring out at nothing. His hair a dirty, white unkempt haystack. His clothes, the wreckage of a pinstripe suit. A tin cup on a string around his neck his only possession — all worldly wealth in a dozen cigarette butts. The monkey was richer by far.

Nell put a hand on his shoulder.

The man looked at her, as it seemed to Wilderness, without seeing her.

Now she knelt, grabbed Wilderness's hand and pulled him down next to her.

"Daddy, Daddy. Don't you know me? It is Lenchen — your Lenchen."

# §119

Max Burkhardt looked about five ten. Wilderness reckoned he weighed less than eight stone. He'd got him naked on the bed and could count his ribs.

Nell had the gas burner roaring and every ring on the hob boiling pans of water.

In the absence of any doctor Erno looked him up and down.

"No open wounds, no rashes . . . his feet are a mess of sores and blisters. God only knows how far he walked. With his club foot, without the offset shoe, they might have crippled him for life."

Nell said, "Why doesn't he speak?"

"Perhaps he doesn't want to."

"Why doesn't he look at me?"

Erno shrugged.

"I can see his body. Battered but intact. I cannot see his mind. Let us just say that too is battered."

Erno and Wilderness lowered him into the bath. The warmth of the water seemed to seep into him. For a moment his eyes focussed, flashed with recognition at the sight of his daughter. Then they closed.

The next time Max Burkhardt opened his eyes, they had him in bed, in between the sheets, blankets piled deep.

"Clean," he said.

Then nothing.

Erno nodded.

"Clean is good," he said. "Clean can be ecstasy. Up there with food and orgasm."

# §120

Nell and Wilderness slept on the floor.

Her father made hardly a sound. His breath no more than a distant sigh. The beat of a moth's wing on air.

"I thought he was dead."

"I know."

"Why do they do this?"

"The Russians?"

"Yes. Keep men so long. The war is over. What is my father to them? A man they found on the street defending Berlin with a pitchfork and a potato peeler?"

"There are millions. The speed at which they let the POWs go, there'll still be men in Soviet camps in 1967."

"Why him? Why now?"

"I don't know," he lied.

# §121

On the twenty-ninth, Max sat up in bed. On the thirtieth, he sat at the table for breakfast.

Wilderness made porridge.

He liked porridge the Scottish way, with salt. Max needed calories. He spooned a hefty tablespoon of Tiptree raspberry jam — a NAAFI perk reserved for officers — into Max's bowl.

Max finished it slowly.

Stared down into the bowl, then looked intently at Nell and Wilderness.

"*Und wenn du lange in einen Abgrund blickst, blickt der Abgrund auch in dich hinein,*" he said.

Later Wilderness quoted Max's words to Erno.

"It's that arse Nietzsche again," he said. "You gaze into the abyss and the abyss gazes back. Who knows what he meant? Abyss,

416

shmabyss. It was Germany, it was Russia? Ach."

"It was just a bowl of porridge."

# §122

On New Year's Eve, the small, darkest hours of January 1, Wilderness awoke to a blast of freezing air that was coiling itself around him.

The window was open. And the bed was empty.

He pulled on his shirt and trousers and climbed out into night and cold and winter.

The building next door had a flat roof. At the far side a figure sat, wrapped in a blanket, gathering a coat of snow.

When he touched Max, he knew he was dead. The life had leeched out of him a couple of hours ago. He was in the first stage of rigor. Ice in his hair. Ice on his eyelashes.

# §123

"This has happened before. In 1945. My great-uncle. I still don't know how he died. Only that he did it himself. He dug his grave. He lay down and he died. It seems odd that people can just choose to die. But he did and so did my father."

"My father killed himself."

"Oh my God. Why did you never tell me?

How . . . how did he die?"

"He died much as Max died and for much the same reason. He took off his clothes and walked out into the North Sea one day in 1946. If he hadn't drowned, the cold would have killed him in minutes."

"The reason?"

"He had been in the war from start to finish. He survived everything. Everything but what he saw in himself."

"Is that the abyss? Our selves?"

"I don't know. You've heard me speak of Rada? Rada Lyubova? She killed herself the same year. I know of no one who looked deeper into herself than Rada. Two world wars and a revolution had not driven her to suicide. But something did. Some accumulation of grief, some final straw."

"And yet you did not tell me."

"Everything takes time. It takes years for people to get to know one another. I know your body far better than I know your mind."

"Have we got years, Wilderness?"

# §124

*January 1948*

A cremation without service in Wilmersdorf — in the American Sector. Secular to the point of silence. Nell did not even ask to receive and scatter the ashes.

Yuri turned up in full dress uniform. Bright

blue against the snowbound cemetery. Nell hugged him. Wilderness stood with Erno a respectful distance away. Watched one of the huge hands gently patting her on the back.

Then she came over to Erno. Hugged him. Then Wilderness. Stood back looking up into his eyes. He'd never seen her cry and this occasion would be no different.

"Nothing has changed," she said. "This changes nothing. *Wer sind wir? Was sind wir?* We are what we were. We are as we were. A man who was dead came briefly back to life and now is dead again."

"Is Yuri waiting?"

"Yes. He waits for one of us."

"Then let me be the one."

She nodded.

"Go home with Erno. I won't be long."

Yuri was sitting at the wheel of a huge prewar Krasny, painted up in field green, a Red Army star on each door, a plume of white smoke trailing from the exhaust.

Wilderness got in beside him.

"Can you drop me back at Grünetümmlerstraße?"

"Конечно, of course."

The car moved off, passing Erno and Nell. She did not look at them.

"You did this, didn't you?"

"Yes."

"And you told Nell to be in Pariser Platz on the twenty-sixth?"

419

"Yes."

"But you didn't tell her why?"

"No. Suppose it had all gone wrong? Supposing Max Burkhardt had not been among those set free for Christmas?"

"Suppose he had died on the march? He must have walked two hundred miles."

"Over that I had no control. Joe, do not overestimate my power. I did what I could. I got Max bumped to the top of a list of prisoners of war who could be released. I could not commandeer a jeep or a railway train."

"Or a decent pair of shoes?"

"Or even a decent pair of shoes. I had no contact with Max. I rearranged names and dates on pieces of paper back in Moscow. Once they had set off I knew what would happen. My people would escort them as far as the Gate and then abandon them. And, believe me Joe, they were the lucky ones."

"How long?"

"Чтокак доыго"

"How long have you been setting this up? How long were you planning this?"

"Since May 1945. Since the day Marie told me her husband had vanished in the Battle of Berlin. Of course, he could have died in that battle. And if he didn't, a Volkssturm member is twice as hard to find as a Wehrmacht soldier — no uniform, no rank, no number . . . no papers. When Marie died I did not stop looking. Only from then on I was doing it for Nell."

"For Nell?"

"Yes, Joe . . . for Nell. You and I have this in common. We do for Nell."

All for Nell? Wilderness could not bring himself to believe this for a single second. It just added to the complicated mixture that was Yuri. "Who is Yuri?" had run through his thoughts a thousand times this last year. He came back to Nell's phrase, the same one Peter-Jürgen von Hesse had used back in Hamburg — turned it over in his mind.

*Wer sind wir? Was sind wir?*

# §125

That night Nell said, "He never asked about my mother."

Wilderness said nothing.

She curled up in the curve of his arm.

"What do you want of life, Wilderness?"

"I want . . . to watch sunset all day . . . to see forty-four sunsets in a single day."

"That's nice. You make that up?"

"No. I wish I had."

"There are times I think my life has scarcely begun . . . and then I think of all that is gone and gone for ever . . . and then with a twist of my mind I am back at the beginning . . . I am Max Burkhardt's little Lenchen again . . . back at the jumping-off point . . . and my feet have never left the ground."

421

Jumping-off point. That was the phrase Rada had used. What is a place of birth but a jumping-off point?

"You came back to your jumping-off point."

"Where else could I go?"

"Anywhere."

"Anywhere on a map of geography. We are talking maps of the heart."

"I know . . . you told me, you are a Berliner."

"Don't make me sound corny, Joe."

"I wasn't. But loyalty to a city is like loyalty to anything else. It may exact a price. Loyalty can be like a ball and chain. People can be like a ball and chain. They can drag you down into the grave with them."

"Are we talking about my father?"

"No, we're talking . . . in the abstract."

"Are you telling me neither people nor place matter to you?"

"No. But what matters most are ideas."

"Am I an idea?"

"You're every idea I've ever had. Or shall ever have."

"That sounds so sweet, so romantic . . . but it's bullshit isn't it?"

Wilderness said nothing.

A plane turned in the sky above them, and the roaring heart of piston engines smothered the sound of the beating heart of the woman lying next to him.

# §126

Nell insisted they return to work the next day.

"Grief is pointless. Grief kills. Grief is what drags you down into the grave."

He awoke to find her fully dressed, even to her topcoat. A pot of coffee cooling on the gas ring.

She stood by his bed, nimble fingers doing up her buttons, and said again, "Nothing has changed."

He grabbed a cup of coffee and took it back to bed with him. She'd want at least a quarter of an hour between her arrival at Schlüterstraße and his. He fell asleep and when he woke up again it was half past nine.

Wilderness got to Schlüterstraße late. Another fragment of a morning Fraggy-bashing, punctuated by the refined sarcasm and acid disdain of Rose Blair. It was gone ten and some. In time to find her cobbling together her tenses or elevenses, toasting bread and making coffee on the tiny paraffin stove she kept on top of a steel filing cabinet. She did not, ever, offer to share her coffee with him. He might well have declined anyway — the smell of NAAFI coffee had become like body odour over the last year. It clung to Spud and Pie Face. He wondered if it clung to him. The olfactory stigmata of the *Schieber.*

"You're late," he heard as he passed her door.

"Late for what?"

"You have a visitor," Rose Blair replied with heightened emphasis on the "or."

He opened the door to his office.

Burne-Jones was in the visitor chair — which showed some respect — with his feet up on the desk, which didn't.

It had been a year, almost to the day it had been a year.

"Just in from Blighty, are we?"

Burne-Jones swung his long legs to the floor and stood.

"By all means, let's not stand on formality. No salutes. No hint of recognition that we might both be in His Majesty's service."

"I get all the sarcasm I need from the bird in the next office. In fact she exceeds my ration. And you didn't come to Berlin to swap salutes and handshakes."

"Have I called at a bad time?"

"You know damn well you have, or Miss Blair isn't doing her job."

"Y'know, Joe. I think becoming a corporal might have gone to your head."

"Then make me a sergeant and see if it goes to me feet."

"Glasshouse, Joe. Never forget where I found you."

A pause that might be deemed respectful on Burne-Jones's part.

424

"I had heard about your girlfriend's father as it happens. Sounds dreadful. As though the war never ended for him."

"Him and thousands like him. If the Russians get you they can string that war out into infinity."

"Quite."

Burne-Jones rummaged in his briefcase and slapped a folder on the desk. Game over.

"Why don't we both sit down? There are things you need to know."

Wilderness pulled the file towards him.

Inside were three typed sheets and a mug shot.

"Jean-François de Villefranche. Civilian attached to the French Military Government. What we have on him is all in there."

Wilderness flipped through the pages.

"And the problem is?"

"We think he might be one of them."

"Queer?"

"Commie."

"Working for the Russians or just sympathetic?"

"The former."

"Do the French know?"

"No. And if they did they'd handle it with all the delicacy of a man trying to make tea while wearing boxing gloves. Broken china all over the place."

"And you want?"

"To know. To be certain."

"And then?"

"Not for you to know. We turn him, we turn him in. Entirely down to circumstances. His address is in there. Apartment in the French Sector. Turn him *over*. Tell me what you find."

For minute Wilderness read on in silence. Then said, "There'll be a shopping list."

"Fire away. I'll take notes."

"Two sets of lockpicks. Half a dozen screwdrivers in all sizes. A penknife with a carbon steel blade. Black trousers. Black shirt. Pea jacket. One of those peaked caps every other German bloke seems to wear. Rubber-soled shoes, size ten. A canvas bag. A blanket. Scissors to slice it up. A couple of rolls of sticky tape. Pigskin gloves, as thin as they come. A jar of concentrated nitric acid and an eyedropper . . ."

"Bloody hell . . . slow down. What's the acid for?"

"You surely don't want me to use gelignite?"

"Joe, I don't want you to leave any trace!"

"It may be necessary. Why don't we get it just in case?"

"If you can't crack a safe the way you did Rada's then don't try. No one must ever know you've been there."

"OK. All the clothing should be secondhand and looking like it, except the gloves. Get them new."

"Sounds like I'm kitting you out as a cat burglar."

"*Fassadenkletterer.* That's what Berliners call them. But the English has more poetry."

"And a camera."

"If you say so."

"And take your gun."

"What?"

"Rose tells me you never carry it. Take it when you do this job, and any other job that comes up."

Wilderness nodded, wondering how much dust it might have gathered after twelve months in a drawer.

"And a vehicle? You can hardly do this using a jeep."

"Public transport."

"What?"

"You've seen too many Scotland Yard films. Thieves escaping in a fast car. It's bollocks. Easiest way to lose any tail is on foot and on an underground train. He lives in Blaumontagstraße. There's a U-bahn station quite close. And if it restores your faith in the traditions of the Yard . . . throw in a magnifying glass."

"My, you really have got to know Berlin, haven't you?"

"It's what you asked for."

"OK. You'll have all this by tomorrow morning. You do the job tomorrow night."

"No. I do the job tomorrow afternoon."

"What in broad daylight?"

"I'd do it in narrow daylight if I knew what it was. You just tell me what I'm supposed to be looking for and leave it to me."

# §127

Wilderness had not pulled a job since Cambridge. Just putting on the gloves was pure delight. Picking the lock was too easy. Not leaving a mess took more time than robbery. He photographed every document in the apartment, and he searched for anything hidden. Few people had imagination when it came to hiding anything. Under the mattress, under the bath, in the cistern, behind the gas fire. Villefranche had papers from the Allied Kommandatura at the back of his shoe rack. Wilderness photographed them and then put them all back.

Burne-Jones smiled as he took the film from Wilderness. He did not tell him what it was he'd found.

He never did.

Wilderness burgled a dozen apartments over the next few weeks in every sector except the Russian.

"I'd love turn over one of the bastards. But what's the point? We know who they work for."

"I was thinking more of Germans living in the East."

"Too risky. You get picked up on the far side of the line . . . you'd be gone for good. Not a damn thing I could do about it. You said it yourself . . . 'if the Russians get you . . .' As things are you get picked up this side of the line, I'd still find myself disowning you."

# §128

*March 1948*

"Not a moment too soon," Rose Blair said.

"For what?"

"Burne-Jones phoned. I rather think he expected to find you here. Instead —"

The telephone rang. She picked it up.

Wilderness heard her say, "Yes. He's here now."

Then she thrust the phone at him without a word and went back to making toast.

Burne-Jones said, "Get over to Elssholzstraße. You're interpreting for General Robertson. My sources tell me Sokolovsky is up to something. You don't just translate. You take mental notes. I want to know everything."

Then Wilderness heard the click as Burne-Jones rang off. No goodbye, nothing.

"What's at Elssholzstraße?"

Rose Blair had a mouthful of toast and gulped it down to answer.

"Allied Control Council. Or did you think

429

Germany ran itself?"

"I'm their interpreter, it seems."

"Then you'd better get over there. They start at half past two."

"Surely Eddie Clark's their English–Russian interpreter?"

"Of course, I stood him down not half an hour ago. Burne-Jones wants *you* there. After all, you're supposed to be some sort of spy aren't you? So, try spying for a while — at least you won't be needing your kid gloves and your rubber-soled shoes. And they probably won't want to buy any coffee either. I imagine Eddie's sold them a lifetime's supply by now. It'll be a change for you on both counts I should think."

Elssholzstraße lay in Schöneberg, in the American Sector — a little over a mile away — in a Prussian palace that had been the Central Court before the war, the Kammergericht.

When Wilderness got there General Clay's Cadillac, its Stars and Stripes fluttering in the March breeze, was already parked in front of the palace. So was General Robertson's Rolls-Royce — a happy little fat man leaning on the bonnet, nose-deep in a volume of Penguin *New Writing*.

Eddie smiled when he saw Wilderness.

"Sent for you have they? Must be serious."

It was.

"How often you done this?"

430

"Done what?"

"Interpreted for Robertson."

"Lots. Every time I drive the general, I do the chatting too. Not much to it. Stenographers take down everything in three languages after all. Anything Sokky says in Russian, you pass on to the general in English. You never translate what he says into Russian. Leave that to the other side. Stick to that and you can't go wrong. Personally, I think Sokky speaks English, and for that matter probably French too, but he'll not utter a word except in Russian. And afterwards they throw a nosh-up that makes us look like beggars. Caviar, cream cheese . . . you name it. Other ranks included. And they get narky if you don't eat. I quite fancy an afternoon off, as long as you bring me out some grub. I'd miss the grub."

Wilderness saluted and introduced himself to Robertson. He was seated just to the right and just behind the general. He rather thought he might be the only man in the room without a row of ribbons on his chest.

And then Marshal Sokolovsky walked in — "Hero of the Soviet Union" with five Orders of Lenin to his name, and to his chest. Forty or more medals, not as symbolic ribbons but real medals, pinned to his tunic. Marshal Sokolovsky reminded him of nothing quite so much as a Christmas tree. Or a walking scrapyard. Wilderness wondered how the man breathed. Wilderness felt . . . naked.

Ten minutes later Marshal Sokolovsky rattled out. No caviar, no cream cheese.

# §129

Eddie was still leaning on the Rolls, still reading.

Wilderness came up running.

"Look sharp, Ed. Robertson'll be out in a second and in a stinker of a mood."

"What happened?"

"Sokolovsky just bunked off."

"So . . . he's Russian. That's what they do."

"It had all the hallmarks of permanence. A great fuck-you, 'Хуй тебе.' Meet me at Paradies at six. I have to report to Burne-Jones, and I have to find Frank."

# §130

"Just like that?"

"He let General Clay get as far as currency reform before he walked out."

"What do you mean by 'let'?"

"He was bristling. From the moment he walked in he was never not going to do this. He wasn't listening to Clay or Robertson or the French bloke. He was playing with them. He'd no intention of staying. Whatever the plan is it's in place. And I took a gander at the reception room as I was leaving. Normally they lay on a feast. There was nothing. They'd no expectations of entertaining anyone. No more free lunch."

The line went quiet, so quiet Wilderness wondered if they'd been cut off.

Then Burne-Jones said, "That's it then. It's over. Nobody's kidding anybody any more. As you so aptly put it, no more free lunch."

# §131

"What did he mean by 'over'?" Frank asked.

"Quadripartite rule of Berlin is over."

"Quadri what?"

"Four sectors, four military governments trying to act as one. That's over."

"Oh is that all? Well . . . fukkit . . . I thought you meant the peace was over."

"It is."

"I don't hear any tanks rolling."

"Frank . . . try rolling with this. The Russians have given up. The temperature has changed . . . it may not be a raging hot war . . . but it might be, to paraphrase Harry Truman, a bollock-freezing cold one."

"And that affects business how exactly?"

"I don't know. Depends on what the Russians do next. They've got us surrounded after all."

"You think they'd cut us off?"

Spud and Pie Face had sat silent throughout, as had Eddie — but it was Eddie's turn.

"They can cut us off Frank, and they will."

"Nah . . . they wouldn't dare . . ."

But Wilderness was nodding.

"Aw shit, kid . . . just when life was getting so fucking sweet."

*"Geld schmeckt süß,"* said Eddie.

"Yeah, whatever," said Frank.

# §132

On April 1 Russian troops stopped every American train on the Frankfurt–Berlin line at Marienborn on the Eastern Zone border, citing "technical problems" and introducing new "temporary regulations." Despite the date it was not a joke.

On April 2 General Clay ordered USAF C-47s to begin airlifting supplies into Tempelhof. He wasn't joking either.

That evening the *Schieber*s gathered at Paradies Verlassen.

Spud was last to arrive. He put a plain, off-white packet in front of them, like a cardsharp letting the punters see the full deck before he shuffled.

"Wossat?" Pie Face asked.

Spud tipped out two cigarettes.

"Try one."

Pie Face stuck one in his mouth and lit up. Frank picked one up with a muttered, "Why not? First in two years."

Spud was poised and smiling now.

Pie Face exploded, red-faced and coughing.

"Fuck me! What is this?"

Frank coughed once and stubbed the cigarette out in the ashtray.

"Jesus H. Christ!"

Spud said, "They're called Droogs, the tobacco's Bulgarian, and they're everywhere."

Pie Face took another drag.

"I suppose you could get used to 'em but . . ."

"But it tastes like dried shit?" Wilderness said.

"Yeah. It does. Dried dog shit to be exact. Where d'you say you got'em, Spud?"

"Tiergarten, where else?"

"How much?"

"Twenty-four reichsmarks a pack. But . . ."

"But what?"

"The bloke selling 'em will tell you the price in marks but only takes dollars."

Wilderness admired the way Spud had strung this out.

"Any chance you recognised the bloke?"

"Dunno his name, but he was one of Yuri's 'Silents.' "

Frank said, "So the bastard's undercutting us? In our own briar patch?"

"Hardly the point, is it?" Wilderness replied.

"OK Corporal Smart-ass, what would be the point?"

"The point is . . . he's taking only dollars . . . but he's paying us in reichsmarks."

"So," Frank mused. "He's building up a stash for something."

"I'd guess he has no intention of getting stuck with any reichsmarks when the big day dawns — our marks or their marks."

"Weeeell . . . fuckim."

"I think we need a word with Major Myshkin."

They thinned out at the cabaret — little of it was to the taste of Spud or Pie Face. ("Wot's the point of strippers who never get their bleedin' togs off?")

"What's the plan kid?"

"What Spud said just confirms what I've been thinking. We need to change tack."

"I been thinking the same."

"Me too," said Eddie.

"Now . . ." Frank went on. "I've said all along that we should be in commodities. I was right, and that was then. But right now, I'd say we need to be in cash."

"Why?"

Eddie answered, "It's perfectly clear to me, Joe. Currency reform's definite. It's going to happen. It changes the game. They mean to control inflation, get rid of rationing, get rid of the black market — above all else, get rid of the black market. What it all adds up to is an end to barter of any kind. The economy normalises . . . nothing is scarce . . . nothing

436

is hooky . . . and those of us who take easy pickings off it all are out of business."

It had sounded to Wilderness like the opening of one of Eddie's not infrequent "Workers' Educational" lectures. The result of reading Penguin books and the *Manchester Guardian*.

"Ed's right," Frank said. "We're better off out of goods and into cash. Means we take a loss at conversion, but we'll ride it out."

Wilderness made them pause. Sat silent while Frank got more drinks in.

"Spit it out, kid. I feel like we've just suggested skinning your grandmother and tanning her hide."

"No," said Wilderness. "It's not going to happen that way."

"Sez you. Currency reform's just a matter of time. Goddammit, we flew the bills in by the million as long ago as January."

"I don't believe in coincidence. Everything happens for a reason. Yesterday, the Russians cut us off . . . today they flood the West with cheap, dodgy fags."

"Yeah . . . and tomorrow they'll plug us back in. It's just a stunt."

"No it's not. It's a teaser. It's a foretaste of what they'll really do come reform. They'll turn this place into a fortress. West Berliners will get their deutschmarks . . . they'll revel in having real money for a day or two . . . the shops will fill up with all the stuff that's been hoarded for months till the price was right . . . then the gates of hell will slam shut again . . . West Berlin will become an island in a Soviet Sea and stuff will become as scarce as it was in 1945. So . . . I say we stay in goods."

"Jesus H. Christ. Ed, pass the bottle. The kid is frying my brain."

Eddie, pushed the bottle towards Frank, looking at Wilderness.

"So, what do we do?"

"First, we stop taking reichsmarks altogether."

"That cuts our market."

"And we spend what we have. Start offloading reichsmarks now. Buy anything and everything you think we can sell. And when we sell we take only dollars. Pay over the odds if it gets rid of reichsmarks. Let's have nothing left to convert when conversion comes . . . because we're going to be in no position to convert . . . that's when all the questions will be asked and we'll find ourselves nicked. From now on we're a dollar economy."

"Just like Yuri, huh kid?"

"As I said, we need to talk to Major Myshkin."

# §133

"Bastards. Fokkin' bastards!"

"Yuri, you're raking in every dollar West Berlin has with your crap fag racket. You don't want to get stuck with worthless currency, and nor do we. From now on it's dollars. You pay us in dollars."

"Or what?"

"It's not a threat. It's just terms of business. We supply you with very good stuff. For your dollars you get Pall Mall and Lucky Strike. For their dollars West Berlin gets Droogs. Think about it. We're not a flea market . . . Fortnum & Mason."

Yuri was sitting on a case of Jack Daniel's. The *Eishaus* was stacked with booty. They'd brought the whiskey in by padding their jerry cans. Forty-eight bottles a trip — trips beyond counting.

Frank grinned.

"Look under your own ass, Yuri. You're sitting on twelve bottles of the best."

Yuri didn't look as angry as he sounded, and it seemed to Wilderness to be merely tactical to be angry with them.

"OK, bastards. But there is a scratchy-my-back here."

"What kind of scratchy your back?"

"Penicillin."

"Penicillin?"

"Sure . . . we got clap running riot in Red Army. Everybody pissing razor blades. Hadn't you heard?"

They'd never dealt in drugs or medicines of any kind.

Wilderness turned to Frank.

"Can we get penicillin?"

"I guess so. Turns out we're stockpiling everything against the day these guys cut off the West . . . you and the top brass seem to think alike on that score . . . so it stands to reason we're stockpiling Band-Aids and aspirin . . . and probably penicillin."

"Good good."

"And you guys do mean to cut us off don't you, Yuri?"

"Da, da . . . but the English have a phrase for it."

"They do?"

"Business as usual."

# §134

Driving back Wilderness said, "You'd better act as banker from now on."

"What?"

"I need to rake in every reichsmark we have. It'll all be easier if you take everything, spend it, stockpile . . . and collect the dollars off Yuri."

"Jeez . . . you think our guys will go for that?"

"They'll do what I tell 'em. Besides, the pickings will be too good to resist."

"Still thinking big, huh?"

"Is there any point in thinking small?"

"How long do you think this Russian stunt will last?"

"Dunno. But maybe you're right, maybe it's a stunt — I prefer to call it a dummy run. Could last a week, could last a month. They're testing us. But when currency reform comes in it'll be real."

# §135

The little blockade fizzled out in ten days.

Two months later, on June 18, the deutschmark was introduced by the Western zones of Germany. It was to be valid in all the sectors of Berlin, but the Russians refused to accept its validity. Something resembling panic preceded this, as Berliners went on a forty-eight hour spending spree — paid every bill, bought any object to unload the potentially worthless reichsmark. By then, Frank had divested the *Schieber*s of most of their reichsmarks, and had sheds out at Tempelhof filled to the rafters with what he called "the solid stuff," as opposed to "the folding stuff."

On June 24 the Russians blockaded Berlin for real. No stunt. No dummy run. Road and rail links to the Western sectors closed and only the air lanes remained open.

On June 26 the airlift began. The British and the Americans flew in everything. From coal to candy. RAF Yorks and USAF Dakotas buzzed by Russian fighters in the biggest game of "chicken" since the end of the war.

The sound of planes landing and taking off

replaced the sound of gunfire as the ambient noise beneath Berlin skies, and the black market rose from the dead and exploded like an atomic bomb.

# §136

Nell had none of this and dutifully accepted her free allocation of deutschmarks and exchanged her reichsmarks at the set rate. It exasperated Wilderness. He had grown accustomed to her po-face, it was part and parcel of her unshakable virtue, but he could not understand the lack of self-interest.

"Gypping yourself is just stupid."

Nell did not understand the word.

"Gyp . . . from Gyppo . . . you know, Gypsy? Swindling yourself."

"How quaint. Does English use other races as derogatory verbs?"

"Well . . . yeah . . . Jew means much the same thing."

Nell was appalled.

"So . . . I Gyp and Jew myself. So fucking what?"

He'd never heard her swear in English before.

The same day, round about seven in the evening he got home to find a meal prepared from civilian rations. Meagre and unsustaining, but corresponding roughly to what Berliners now had to live off. Less than they had before the blockade. All the canned food Wilderness had brought her was piled up on the dresser.

"From now on," she said. "We live like Berliners. We eat like Berliners. We are Berliners."

"Every Berliner buys hooky stuff on the black market. You don't eat hooky food and buy hooky clobber, you're not a Berliner. Everybody has a *pajok*. Everybody!"

The word hit home. It was tempting to ask her what she'd do if Yuri turned up with a *pajok* of Russian goodies off-ration, but he didn't.

Nell said, "Very well. You may bring me eggs."

So po-faced, so patrician, even as her virtue admitted a vice.

"Eggs? Bleedin' eggs, is that all?"

"Yes."

That night as she slept and he didn't, he could smell the scent he had given her — L'Aimant by Coty. When she stopped wearing that he'd believe her.

In the morning he woke to find thin ersatz coffee, *Blumenkaffee,* a confection of roast acorns and who-knows-what, bubbling gently on the hob.

He tipped it away and made Java.

# §137

It was late July. Almost a month into the new game with the new Russian rules. Demand was high. They could have sold anything and everything twice over in the West, and still the demand from the East to be satisfied. The taps ran dry, the coal ran out and the electricity came and went like the man in the weather house. Still, they made money.

It was hard not to feel complacent.

Drinking alone was a strange pleasure. Wilderness hardly ever chose it — it arose if others were late and if no one in Paradies pinged him through the pneumatic tubes. That, after all, is what they were there for, and more often than not used not person to group or group to group but solitary individual to solitary individual. He had come to think of it as civilised. When the social code, the sexual code, dwindled to a tongue-tied mess, this was clear and direct. He'd even heard of men receiving notes as simple as *"Möchten Sie ficken?"* Fancy a fuck?

He heard a cylinder land and reached up for it.

Still creaming it, kid? You have to admit your Uncle Joe is good for business. The business of the USSR is business . . . ah. No that was some other guy, some other country. LT.

The club was half-empty, he could see clearly to Major Tosca's table, her face buried in a book. She must have known he'd got the message by now, but didn't so much as glance back, so he concluded she'd said what she had to say. If she wanted him to come over, she'd look up, smile, blow him a phony kiss. She didn't.

Frank arrived. He was getting fatter. Sweating through that beautifully tailored uniform in the summer heat. Perhaps Frank's pleasure was strictly food and drink. After that first girl he'd bought with soap, there'd never been so much as a mention of a woman, and if you couldn't get picked up in Paradies, you couldn't get picked up anywhere. He made tough-guy, "we're all men of the world," almost backslapping crude jokes about Wilderness and Breakheart, as he insisted on calling Nell — as though somehow the sexuality, the scent of their relationship had spread to him and those around him, like the undisguisable, acrid smell of a lubricated condom — but that stance just masked his celibacy. Wilderness figured Frank was one for hookers. Since everything was a commodity to Frank, he probably preferred to buy his women. It was neat and business-like. He would enjoy haggling. And no messy emotions to contend with. Eddie? Eddie was a different case. Women would just clutter up his ordered life. There were times Wilderness thought that he and Frank might well be the worst things that had ever happened to Eddie. They'd taken his little fiddle and . . . and Eddie had been quite happy with the scale on which he'd fiddled.

Frank summoned a waiter. Beer and wurst. Pile on the pounds.

"You're not eating?"

"Too hot to eat."

"What's that you're drinking?"

"White wine. An Orvieto from Italy."

"Where in Italy?"

"I thought you were an Italian-American?"

"Every American's a hyphenated American. Don't mean diddly. So happens Spoleto used to be Spoletowski or some such gobbledy-gook. Who gives a fuck? I'm a damn Yankee. Let me taste."

"Pity. I was about to tell you this was made only twenty-five miles from Spoleto."

"Showing off your Reader's Digest *Book of Facts* again, eh kid?"

"Nah. I'm educated I am."

Wilderness pushed the glass across the table. Frank sipped at it and pulled face.

"How can you drink this piss? Tinted water. Goes to show . . . if they don't make it in Milwaukee."

"Ah . . . but you're not a social climber, Frank."

Frank missed or ignored the irony, just as Eddie sauntered in. A smile upon his face, glee withheld, a surprise in the offing.

Frank got the waiter's attention and held up two fingers, doubling his beer order.

"What's got you?" Wilderness said.

"What day is it today?"

"I dunno, twenty-fifth or twenty-sixth."

"No . . . today is the day we all enter cloud cuckoo land . . . the dwarves and unicorns have finally landed."

He held up a 5RM note. Something white stuck to it. No bigger than a postage stamp.

"This is the new Russki Mark. Новая валюта. *Novaya Valyuta.*"

"You're kidding?"

"Issued today. Already got a nickname . . . *Tapetenmark.*"

Through his first mouthful of bread and wurst, Frank said, "What?"

"Wallpaper, Frank."

Eddie was grinning like a Cheshire cat as the punchline hove in sight. He waved the note in front of them — a mother's hankie shaken in the direction of a departing train and child. The white sticker fell off and floated down onto the table.

First Wilderness and then Frank, swallowing hastily to avoid choking but still showering them with crumbs, burst out laughing.

Eddie grinned from ear to ear.

"They just took the crappy old ostmark and stuck a coupon on it. You know what they make the glue from?"

Wilderness could not speak for giggles. Frank was spraying out crumbs and wurst faster than a Maxim gun.

"Taters," Eddie concluded.

He took another dozen notes from his pockets and waved them in the air and a shower of confetti covered the table.

Tosca looked up from her book. The stern librarian annoyed by a whisper.

Wilderness snatched a note out of the air.

"I don't believe it. I don't bloody believe it. It's pure Mickey Mouse. What a bunch of clowns. Potato paste. I don't bloody believe it. I used to make that to stick pictures in my scrapbook when I was a nipper. They all fell off too."

Then, the merest shift of gear, a moment of high seriousness.

"Frank, we're not accepting this crap are we?"

"Are you kidding. Dollars only. You think I don't listen to you? Dollars only, you said. On the nail. Yuri wouldn't dare offer us shit like this."

# §138

Nell had known Ernst Reuter as long as she could remember. He and her father had worked alongside each other at City Hall. Since she returned to Berlin she had not seen him, but then, who had she seen? He had been elected mayor, but the Russians had refused to acknowledge this. He was de facto mayor of West Berlin — a place that didn't quite exist. The Russians could obstruct and divide — they could in all probability assassinate him or simply kidnap him off the streets as they did with hundreds of others, but they didn't . . . and short of that they could not shut him up.

That summer, the summer of the roaring planes and the power cuts, Reuter addressed Berlin in the open air half a dozen times. Each time the crowd was bigger. In a crowd it is impossible to tell whether you are one of three thousand or thirty thousand. Later on newspapers will tell you — and none of them will agree.

Late in August, Nell stood at the eastern end of the Tiergarten in front of the Reichstag. She had learnt of this meeting from one of the American RIAS vans that toured the British and American sectors, using loudspeakers to create street-corner radio.

Reuter was not wearing his beret — his trademark as recognisable as Churchill's cigar and FDR's cigarette holder. Today he looked less like a bohemian and more like a leader, even to the carnation in his buttonhole.

"People of this world, people in America, in England, in France, in Italy! Look at this city and recognise that you must not give up this city, you must not give up its people . . .

449

Berliners don't want to be an object of exchange . . . we can't be traded in, we can't be negotiated and no one can sell us . . . In this city a bulwark, an outpost of freedom has been erected, which nobody can give up with impunity. Anyone who would give up this city and its people would give up a whole world and even more he would give up himself . . . People of the world! You also should do your duty and help us through the times that lie ahead of us, not just with the roar of your planes . . . but with the steadfast and indestructible guarantee of the common ideals that can secure our future and secure yours. People of the world, look at Berlin! And people of Berlin, be assured we will win this fight."

*"Völker der Welt, schaut auf Berlin! Und Volk von Berlin, sei dessen gewiß, diesen Kampf, den wollen, diesen Kampf, den werden wir gewinnen!"*

The crowd did not simply drift away. Inspired by what they read between the lines, they surged towards the Brandenburg Gate, through the arches and into Pariser Platz, just as a routine Russian patrol was heading the other way.

The Russian GAZ jeep was surrounded.

At first the four soldiers sat still as though waiting for the tide to pass.

"Stalin *'raus,* Stalin *'raus*" — a cry soon taken up by hundreds of voices.

Nell followed and found herself edged aside as British soldiers forced their way in from the Western side.

And then the Red Flag of the Soviet Union floated down from the top of the arch — someone had climbed up the internal staircase and cut it loose from the quadriga. As symbolic a gesture as the day in May 1945 when the first Russians to reach the Brandenburg Gate had put it there.

What Red Army soldier worth his ration could sit by and watch? All four got out of the jeep and tried to retrieve the flag — using the butts of their rifles they forced protesters aside only to find they had waded into jelly, an amorphous, amoebic mass that parted around them only to flow on and enclose them once more. And still they were no nearer the flag — and the flag was ripped to shreds and a cloud of red confetti blew past their heads in shards of fury.

No one would ever know who fired the first shot.

A stone thrown into a pond.

The crowd spreading out in ripples.

And at the epicentre was not one jeep but two.

The second jeep was British, and the driver lay slumped facedown over the wheel with blood gushing from the wound in his side.

# §139

They were talking only of something and nothing. Passing the time at Paradies Verlassen. Chewing the fat as Frank put it in a tasteless image.

Eddie was doing a crossword — in German. Frank was on his fourth or fifth beer and holding forth or fifth on baseball — as with any sport Frank launched into, Wilderness tuned out and nodded at regular intervals.

"God didn't mean anyone to be left-handed. Ain't natural. I mean, you look at the number of home runs Bill Dickey scored in the 1940 season compared to DiMaggio . . ."

Pie Face burst in. Saved Wilderness from throttling Frank.

"We got trouble!"

"What?"

"Some argy-bargy in Pariser Platz. Spud blundered into it and got himself shot."

Frank said, "Cool it, kid. Just sit down and just tell us what happened. Who shot Spud?"

But Pie Face was not in any mood to be cooled. It seemed to Wilderness that his rage was hungry and needed to be fed, and was better fed standing, looming over them.

"Dunno. There was plenty of Russkis about, but our blokes were there too."

"And Americans?"

"Nah, Frank. You was late again, just like

1914 and 1939. Never there when you're fuckin' needed."

Wilderness felt Frank stir and kicked him under the table. Frank said nothing.

"Is he OK?"

"Dunno. He ain't dead. Our blokes got an ambulance."

"Who got the jeep?"

"Fuckin' Ada, Joe. Is that really the next question? Who got the jeep? The Russians got the jeep, din't they? It was in the Russian fuckin' Sector wasn't it? But you needn't worry. Spud had delivered. All they'll find are empty jerry cans. He was on his way back."

"Frank, can you find out which hospital?"

"Sure. A couple of phone calls."

A stony silence. No one spoke and Pie Face did not sit. Turned around like a slowly spinning top, as though searching for words that eluded the tip of his tongue.

Wilderness said, "You need a drink, mate."

"Maybe I do, Joe. But not with you lot. You blokes are playing too fast and loose for us both. Joe, Joe . . . the way you're going on you're going to get us all killed. We've been lucky till today . . . but if you think about it for half a minute we could have been busted any time. It's a bleedin' miracle the MPs have never turned us over. We just sailed by right under their noses. There's blokes been banged up in the glasshouse for a fraction of what we've done. We've got away with everything short of bloody murder. But it ain't searches now . . . it ain't even some copper too stupid to do a proper search or who'll turn a blind eye for a bung. It's guns and bullets. And it's poor bastards getting shot. And it's over. It's all over. So, sorry an' all that, but include me out."

Wilderness spoke to get in ahead of anything stupid Frank might say.

"That's OK. I understand. We'll divvy up and you'll get your share."

"Nah, mate. You keep it. I don't want it. I won't touch it. It feels like dirty money all of a sudden."

# §140

When Pie Face had gone, Frank said, "Did he just tell us to go fuck ourselves?"

"Yes, but there was another point to what he said."

"I'm all ears."

"We need another way."

"We do?"

"One day they'll stop us going into the Soviet Sector altogether. One day quite soon. Our MPs have already stopped going in."

"They can't do that. It's not part of the deal. Yalta or Potsdam or Timbuktu, whatever. They come over here whenever they like. We get to do the same. OK, so there's more checks and more barbed wire. We've always passed checks. No one was wise to us. Even Pie Face admits that. It's not as if they're going to rip a British jeep apart is it?"

It occurred to Wilderness that "they" might be doing that right now, but he let Frank finish.

"They'll frisk all the civilians they want. I'd be amazed if they bother with us."

"I meant our own people will stop us. It's beginning to look dangerous. They won't want to provoke incidents. Spud getting shot is already an incident."

"So what are we looking for? A flying carpet?"

"No," Wilderness said. "A tunnel."

# §141

"What I need is . . . a tunnel."

"God I hate irony."

"Where's the irony?"

"We cremated a man who could have shown you every tunnel under Berlin last January."

"Your father?"

"Berlin City Engineer. Until the Volkssturm that is. He knew Berlin belowground better than he knew the streets above."

Nell turned over to sleep.

Wilderness said, "But . . . Berlin can't do without a city engineer. So . . . who has your father's job now?"

She turned back to him, tired or exasperated or both.

"It hardly matters, does it?"

"Of course it matters."

"Drop it, Wilderness. Just let this one go."

"You won't help me?"

"Why should I help you with your . . . rackets?"

"You've always known what I did. And . . ."

"And?"

"It's only money. We don't hurt anyone."

Nell lay back on the pillow.

"As I said. I hate irony. The current city engineer is my father's old deputy. Andreas von Jeltsch-Fugger."

"You're kidding?"

"It's no sillier than your Smythe-Brownes or your Bentinck-Cavendishes. He's the father of Werner Fugger, the boy you so annoyed the night we met and on every occasion since, unless I'm very much mistaken."

"Not much irony in that. He's a prick."

Up on one elbow now, flicking tiredness away with a jerk of her head and an errant lock of her hair.

"No, Wilderness. That's not the irony. The irony is that after the war, the British being so suspicious of men with aristocratic names, all those *von*s and *zu*s, made the assumption that they were all Nazis and for nearly two years Andreas could not work, until he got his *Persilschein* — got his *Persilschein* from you! Because, after all, you're not a snob are you?"

The sarcasm and the irony fought to the death in his mind in less than a second, and he said, "Can you get him to meet me?"

"I want nothing to do with your rackets. I told you."

"And I told you. We're harmless. Honestly."

"Harmless?"

She squirmed nearer to him, nudged his left arm with her head until he wrapped it around her.

"Hold me, stupid."

"Why?"

"Do I need a reason?"

"Of course not. But you have one all the same."

"I saw a man shot today. A Tommie. Just like you. Harmless, just like you."

# §142

He was surprised the name had not stuck in his mind. But the man had. He'd been one of the first he'd interviewed at Schlüterstraße, in the first or second week of February in 1947. The face was the face of an aristocrat, the sort to drive the Pooters and Yatemans of England to seething, silent fury — the long, aquiline nose, not unlike the late SS Obergruppenführer Heydrich, the domed forehead, the fuller top lip, the pale blue eyes.

457

And the middle two fingers and the top joint of his thumb on the right hand were missing — a war wound from the Russian front in the First World War. The arm rose weakly, hand to his lips, every so often as he dragged on a cigarette from a small black holder wedged between the stumps of the missing fingers.

"It had its upside," he had told Wilderness. "I cannot hold a rifle, cannot pull a trigger or shoulder a *Panzerfaust*. Hence I was of no use to Hitler, even when he rounded up the old men and boys in '45."

He'd been a member of the party, for the token reasons any employee of the city would give and had hung Hitler's portrait on his office wall as instructed. At the time, Wilderness had not sought to enquire further and had certainly never logged the precise nature of the man's occupation.

With no Yateman-Pooter to stand over him and argue the toss, Wilderness had granted him his *Persilschein* and wished him well. He had warmed to the man — it was, perhaps, his asking him if he liked Berlin that tipped the balance — as though he'd been talking to a welcome visitor of his own age and interests, not an interrogator half his age with the power to lock him up.

And then, a ludicrous sense of courtesy had led Wilderness to show Andreas von Jeltsch-Fugger out, and he had caught his first glimpse of Nell. As Jeltsch-Fugger reached the staircase, Nell had dashed down from the next floor, pecked him on the cheek and he had embraced her with his good arm.

It flashed by him now like a silent film upon a dusty scrim.

Nell had been the memory. A memory so strong she had erased the context, just like the old Dick Powell song from before the war, "I Only Have Eyes for You," and for a year or more Jeltsch-Fugger had been just one more German, a German he had happened to be seeing out when the vision that was Nell first hit him. Were the stars out tonight?

"How pleasant to see you again, Herr Holderness," Jeltsch-Fugger was saying.

Wilderness gently freed himself from the starless daydream. And the Nell of memory merged with the Nell who was in the room with them.

The room was a small, empty café in a side street off Potsdamer Platz where three of the four Allied sectors met — three not four, but who bothered much about the French? Once, a year or two ago, there'd been a painted boundary criss-crossing the cobbles and the tram lines of Potsdamer Platz, demarcating the sectors, British, Russian, American. They had been scuffed out of existence by a million feet, and no one had bothered to repaint them. Wilderness was not wholly certain which sector the café sat in, the British or the

American. Ambiguous. And anonymous —
but for the name, Der Kater Murr.

Wilderness had thought better of inviting
Frank and Eddie. If this worked they'd find
out then. If it didn't, they'd never know.

Nell was effusive. Her reservations were not
overcome, but Wilderness knew she'd never
be less than demonstrative. Things — no,
people — mattered too much to her. Jeltsch-
Fugger was, after Erno and her father, only
the third person he'd met who'd known her
as a child — or, as she put it herself, "before,"
and before what need never be stated.

She hugged him to embarrassment, both
arms around his chest — Jeltsch-Fugger smiling politely at Wilderness over the top of her
head.

Breaking loose she said, "This is my godfather. One of nature's gentlemen. And this
is my lover. One of nature's rogues."

"Au contraire, Hélène. The last time we met
Herr Holderness was courtesy itself."

And the broken right hand was extended
for Wilderness to shake.

They sat at a corner table. A round of small
talk as the waiter set coffee in front of them.
The smell alone was telling, best NAAFI dark
roast. Eddie had sold it to the proprietor
personally.

"How can I help you, Herr Holderness?"

"I'm trying to . . . to ease the tension
between East and West . . ."

"He's a smuggler, Andreas," Nell chipped in.

"Difficult times, Hélène. The man who finds you half a pound of butter today may go down in history as well regarded as any man who fought at Austerlitz or Waterloo. I say again, how may I help you, Herr Holderness?"

"I need a tunnel under Berlin. There are things I need to get from West to East without interference."

"Things?"

Wilderness tapped the side of his cup gently with a teaspoon.

"Ah . . . I see . . . baccy for the parson, brandy for the clerk, and coffee for the commissar?"

Who would have thought a German aristocrat knew Kipling? All the same it saved Wilderness precious words.

"Nell tells me you know the tunnels better than anyone."

Jeltsch-Fugger tilted his head slightly, the merest nod, a sip of coffee.

"The Nazis flooded Berlin's tunnels as the Russians advanced in '45. Breached the Spree and let the river in. I assume you knew this? So, we are looking at something deeper. Something below the swamp on which my ancestors built Berlin, below the impermeable clay. I believe there is such a tunnel. I was with Max Burkhardt the last time he

461

inspected it in 1939. I didn't make the descent, but I was there. I cannot vouch for the state of the tunnel after . . . after . . ."

"After what the RAF did to Berlin?"

"Quite. But I know the two entrances."

"And it crosses the line?"

"Runs under the Spree at the island, from Monbijou Park to the zoo, just by the flak tower. I'd say it crosses the line pretty well under Pariser Platz. About a hundred and fifty feet under Pariser Platz."

"That's as deep as the Piccadilly Line."

"It is indeed. I had the pleasure of inspecting your London Underground in 1932. But this was built without boring shields or machines of any kind. Neither I nor Max were able to find out precisely when it was built. But that in itself made the subject all the more fascinating. One can weave fantasies around such a structure. We think it was built most likely in the reign of Frederick Wilhelm II, which would be the last decade of the 1700s. Certainly no later than 1805. That's the year Monbijou Palace ceased to be a royal residence for spurned wives and ageing dowagers. After that I cannot think why anyone would have bothered to build it . . . and only royals would have had the money. In fact, even allowing for the folly of kings it's both amusing and impossible to imagine why it was built. It goes nowhere."

"I thought you just said it went to the zoo?"

"In 1800 that was nowhere. Just an obscure corner of the Tiergarten. The zoo has been there scarcely a hundred years. It would have made more sense if the tunnel ended at Bellevue. The construction of palace and tunnel would have been undertaken at roughly the same time. An escape route for queens and princes? But who knows? An error in navigation? Unlikely. But there it is, ending nowhere. And since the RAF all but flattened Monbijou in '43, beginning nowhere."

"But you can find it?"

"Yes."

A pause, the kind that might be called pregnant.

"You were kindness itself the last time we met, Herr Holderness, and it pains me to have to ask something of you in return. But — the devil drives."

Ask away, thought Wilderness. Coffee, butter, sardines in tins. Whatever.

"Ask away," he said.

"You can still issue *Persilschein*? I need a *Persilschein* for my son."

"No problem. I've met your son. We don't bother much with people that young."

"No, Herr Holderness. My other son."

Nell might have been stung. She swung around to face Jeltsch-Fugger in an instant.

"Andreas! No!"

Jeltsch-Fugger smiled his smile of well-bred tolerance and said to Wilderness, "Might you give us a moment alone?"

"No," Nell said. "You give us a moment alone. Joe, outside!"

Wilderness said nothing as they scraped back their chairs. Jeltsch-Fugger signalled the waiter for another coffee, unperturbed.

On the pavement, anger made Nell seem suddenly bigger than she was.

"I won't let you do this, Wilderness."

"I —"

"Andreas had three sons. Kurt died over England flying for the Luftwaffe. Werner you know. It is Otto he's talking about now."

"So . . . we don't take it out on kids. There's even a category called youthful indiscretion or some such. God knows, even Hitler's secretary got off scot-free under that one."

"Otto isn't a kid. He's the eldest. He served throughout the war."

It was obvious where this was headed.

"So tell me the worst."

"Andreas wants you to issue a *Persilschein* in the name of SS Obersturmbannführer Otto von Jeltsch-Fugger."

"Oh shit."

"He worked for Heydrich in the SD. It's a miracle he isn't on trial or in prison already, but he isn't. And if you give him a *Persilschein,* he'll get away with everything!"

"Get away with what exactly?"

"I don't know. Do I need to know? We all know what the SD did. Wilderness I cannot,

I will not let you do this."

Wilderness's "no" was accepted graciously. They finished their coffee discussing books and music, Wilderness's fondness for Brahms, Jeltsch-Fugger's love of English metaphysical poetry. As they parted on the pavement, Jeltsch-Fugger deemed the meeting most enjoyable, hoped they would all have the opportunity to get together under different circumstances soon, and handed Wilderness his card.

He looked at the sky, remarked that it "might come on to rain later," doffed his hat to Nell and walked away.

"It might come on to rain? How bloody English can a German get?"

"I told you, Wilderness. He's the most civilised man alive."

She kissed him.

"Thank you. Thank you, thank you, thank you. I know what it cost you. Joe Holderness resists temptation. I should get that chipped in stone."

# §143

That night, in bed, Wilderness said, "If his big brother was in the Gestapo . . . how can Werner go on saying what he says? Talking the kind of bollocks he talks. How can he go on denying what happened?"

"You said it yourself. He's just a kid."

"So were you during the war."

"But I saw Belsen with my own eyes. Werner fought the Russians when he was fourteen in the Volkssturm. He too believes what he saw. That the Russians were a savage enemy. It's a short hop from that to wanting to believe they faked Auschwitz. Though I flatter myself I've knocked that one out of him, he still wrestles with the same question they all do. *Wer sind wir? Was sind wir?* If you were French or Dutch, the Nazis occupied your country. If you were German they occupied your mind. Try to think of Werner that way."

"So . . . all the same, he's just a kid?"

"Yep. He's harmless, as you say of yourself. Only difference is I really believe he is."

"And you don't believe I am?"

"Of course not."

She turned over to sleep, squirmed her backside against his hip.

*"Wer sind wir? Was sind Wir?"*

A whisper and a mantra.

Nell. I'm alive! Where are you? Joe.

A scrawl upon a thousand walls.

# §144

He called Jeltsch-Fugger from the office in Schlüterstraße. Arranged to pick him up in the staff jeep by the Adlon Hotel, opposite the gigantic picture of Josef Stalin, in benign, paternal pose and festooned with medals. The Russian welcome to the Soviet Sector.

It was pouring with rain, the wettest summer in thirty years, battering down on the canvas roof of the jeep, and rivulets that coursed down Stalin's face — the tears he'd never shed.

"You have the *Persilschein?*"

"You have the map?"

"Indeed. I shall show you the eastern end, Monbijou. I doubt you need me to direct you to the zoo, after all."

"Just one thing. Nell is never to know."

"Of course. We are criminals bound together by a dark and dirty secret. Over the Schloss Bridge and left on Burgstraße."

The S-bahn overground metropolitan railway was no respecter of history or architecture. It sliced the "heart" of Berlin in two at Alexanderplatz, and it clipped the corner of Monbijou Park en route from the Börse station to Friedrichsstraße Station, passing close enough to have detracted from what had been a fairy-tale palace at the time the S-bahn had been built just after the Great War. After the new war it wasn't quite a ruin, but Wilderness could not think of a single word to describe the state it was in. Once it had fronted the river, much as the Naval College at Greenwich had done, with a garden of topiaried pine trees leading down to a shining white balustrade at the water's edge. It was an easy leap of imagination to see gilded barges moored at the steps, waiting upon the pleasure of queens and princesses.

At some point during the war, the Germans had bricked up its high windows. At some point during the war the British had caved in much of its roof.

He parked the jeep under the S-bahn between the stilts that propped up the elevated track. It was dark under the S-bahn, illuminated only in flashes — sunlight through the latticework, sparks from the electric line running overhead. It was like looking at an old-fashioned magic lantern show. And what he saw by the light of the lantern was an ornate cast-iron kiosk, rather like a Parisian pissoir — bigger, more elaborate and capped by a small spire that resembled nothing quite so much as the spike on a pickelhaube.

"How did that survive?"

"I would imagine," Jeltsch-Fugger replied. "That the railway line provided cover. Otherwise it might be in the same state as the palace."

"You're a Berliner?"

"Through and through. Apart from summers spent reliving the last shreds of the ancestral-country-house-life to please my parents, I've never lived anywhere else."

"Then you must be appalled by what has happened to the city."

"I'm an engineer not an architect or an historian. You are asking me to mourn Monbijou? Fine, catch me one night with half a bottle of schnapps inside me and I might. Indeed if the palace appeals to your taste for the rococo, take a good look. The Russians mean to demolish it — the Kaiser's schloss too. If they stay here ten years I predict they will flatten every structural symbol of imperial Berlin. But what is a flattened city to an engineer but a chance to build? And if you want my professional opinion, the survival of this absurd piece of cast iron under the S-bahn throughout six years of war is less surprising than it making it through the previous hundred and fifty years in one piece."

"You'd almost think no one had noticed it was there."

"That's more true than you could know. I think you'll find curiosity is not second nature to Germans. Once its purpose had been forgotten it probably never occurred to anyone to ask. It was there. That would be enough for most. What *is* is."

"Why didn't they knock it down when the S-bahn was built?"

"They didn't have 'permission' would be my guess — if they had they would have done — permission from God knows who, and in the absence of a god they left things as they found them . . . and as I just said, what is is.

Curiosity has no part in it."

Jeltsch-Fugger produced a ring of oversized keys, some of them six to eight inches long. They approached the kiosk.

"One of these should fit."

The third key turned the lock. The door swung open, groaning for oil.

"Remarkable," Jeltsch-Fugger said. "No one has opened this for the best part of ten years. Until Max and I came here just before the war, I doubt anyone had opened it in more than a century. Even then it opened without effort."

Wilderness looked inside. A wide spiral staircase, winding around a central void.

"A hundred and fifty feet you said?"

"Give or take."

Jeltsch-Fugger lobbed a pebble down the shaft. It seemed an age before Wilderness heard the clunk.

"Point taken."

Will you be going down?"

"No. I want to see both ends first."

Jeltsch-Fugger handed the ring of keys to him.

"You might let me have it back, when you have finished."

They spread a map across the bonnet of the jeep.

Berlin as it had been in 1938. Five years into The Thousand-Year Reich. A monument in the making.

A few drops of rain spotted the grey-white paper. Jeltsch-Fugger glanced up at the tracks above and held out a hand. Nothing more fell.

"You will appreciate, the original map on which Max found the tunnel is in a state not unlike confetti, and far too precious to bring out in a storm."

He took a red crayon and traced the course of the tunnel on the pre-war map.

It followed the route of the S-bahn under the Spree and the island as far as Friedrichsstraße, then curved south directly under Pariser Platz, and then ran parallel to the Charlottenburger Chaussee as it sliced under the avenues that radiated out from the central circle like the strands on a spider's web to end just north and slightly west of the Zoo Flak Tower.

Wilderness said, "It passes under an awful lot of lakes in the Tiergarten."

"All of them artificial and quite shallow. Max walked the length of the tunnel in '39. Nothing would stop him — not even his club foot. It was as though he had been given the key to Pandora's box. And he assured me it was dry. But, of course the flak tower didn't go up until '41. If anything was likely to affect the tunnel it's the tower. I've no idea how deep it goes. I've never been in it. When your people blew it up this summer all they blew up only was what was visible. The damn

471

thing could be like an iceberg. For all I know it goes down all the way to hell. But . . . I am alarming you unnecessarily. The tunnel and the tower are at least a hundred metres apart and the tunnel, as you can see, curves in from the north."

"Can I keep the map?"

"Can I keep the *Persilschein*?"

"Why are you doing this?"

The abrupt change of subject did not dent von Jelscht-Fugger's sangfroid.

"Do you think I can write off a son, Herr Holderness?"

"I think many a German has written off the family Nazi."

"The family Nazi. Like the idiot son sent into the church, or the importuning uncle hourly expecting a cheque in the post? The skeletons in all our dynastic cupboards. And I cannot. I cannot write off my family Nazi. Why I accept my son — note I do not say forgive — is none of your concern. Let us merely agree that I do. You should concentrate on what does concern you."

"And that is?"

"Nell Burkhardt, Herr Holderness. She should concern you more than the internal strife of my family. Give no more thought to my sons. Think of Nell. You are all she has."

# §145

The Zoo Flak Tower was formidable — at a height of one hundred and twenty feet, and with walls thirty feet thick, quite possibly the densest concrete structure on earth. With its own internal reservoir and diesel generators, it had resisted a Russian siege in the April of 1945 somewhat in the manner of a Norman keep, and had been taken only by a negotiated surrender.

Built to prevent the RAF from dominating the skies over Berlin, it had become a hospital, a repository for Berlin's art treasures and the looted gold of Troy, and finally a shelter. It was thought that up to thirty thousand people had taken refuge there in the last weeks of the war. Meanwhile, the antiaircraft guns mounted on the upper storeys lowered their sights and continued to harass the Soviet forces as far away as the Reichstag.

It was too significant to leave standing, visible above the treetops for miles around. The smaller tower to the north had succumbed to dynamite in the June of 1947. Later that summer attempts to blow up the main tower had failed. At last, at the end of July 1948, after drilling and packing more than thirty tons of dynamite the British had managed to blow it up. And down.

It could not be worse, thought Wilderness, but he did not say it.

Eddie did.

"Oh, bloody Norah. How the effin' ell are we going to shift that lot."

Wilderness looked at the detritus of the flak tower. Countless tons of shapeless concrete and twisted steel. A small mountain of rubble bulldozed up at the spot von Jeltsch-Fugger had indicated for the tunnel entrance, a far corner of the Tiergarten, tucked away between the Landwehr canal and the S-bahn, mud-caked and rain-spattered. Another hundred yards and his tunnel would have achieved perfect symmetry with both ends under the elevated railway tracks.

Frank said, "Do you think Jelly-Fucker got it wrong?"

Wilderness looked at the map, at the small red x that marked the spot like pirate treasure, looked from the map to the small army of British sappers clearing, carting off the remains of this vast symbol of Hitler's power, dumping it here there and everywhere.

"No. I don't think he did. I think the entrance is under there and I think he didn't know all this had been dumped. He hasn't been back to look. He just knew we'd finally blown up the flak tower. And how many times have we tried to blow it up and failed?"

He led off in the direction of the tower, across ridged tracks of mud that sucked at his shoes, through a sparse, balding forest of blasted, leafless trees — everything the

474

Berliners had not fed into their stoves last winter, but would chop down at the next turn in the seasons.

Frank keeping up, Eddie slouching behind.

"You got a plan, kid?"

"Frank, when do I not have a plan?"

The tower lay on its side, looking to Wilderness like a ship run aground, tilted on its keel — or a giant top hat that had been sat upon, its five storeys of solid concrete concertinaed and crumpled as though made of something far less substantial.

As they reached the site, a Royal Engineers sergeant had his back to them, barking orders at the unfortunate bunch of erks who'd drawn this particular short straw.

"Sergeant?"

The man turned. A little, red-faced bloke, his gut straining his belt, his arms bulging with muscle, all but bursting out of the leather, sleeveless jacket that, it seemed, only the sappers got to wear.

He looked at Wilderness with irritation, and just about saluted when he recognised rank on Frank.

"Sir," he said, without a hint of deference. "An international delegation, p'raps?"

"Nope," said Frank. "We're what you might call private enterprise."

"His kind of enterprise?"

He was pointing past them. They turned. Eddie had caught up.

"Hello, Stanley."

"Eddie. These blokes with you?"

"Yes, Stanley. My business partners."

"I don't need any coffee today, mate."

"It's not about coffee," Wilderness said, hoping to get them to the point before they started on news from home or the price of sausages. "We want you to tip your rubble somewhere else, and clear a way through that lot for us."

"Mind telling me why?"

"Yes. I do mind. We'll make it worth your while. You can be sure of that."

"Like I said. I don't need no coffee."

"Then tell me what you want."

"To open up that lot?"

"To clear a way to the middle. You can leave a circle of rubble for cover. Somewhere in the middle is a . . ."

For a moment Wilderness could not think what to call it. The last word he wanted to utter was tunnel. And pissoir might be meaningless to the man.

"Hole. We need access to a hole."

"Nole? You gotta nole?"

"How much?"

Stanley feigned thought, then said far too readily, "Soap. I wants a hundred bars of Lux, the good stuff with a nice niff to it, and twenty apiece for my three lads wot drives the diggers and dumpers. Take it or leave it."

Stanley, clearly, saw himself as a wheeler-dealer. Wilderness hoped he was not smiling. The man had named an astonishingly low price. He asked for a minute, stepped back with Frank and pretended to confer.

"The man's a clown."

"Sure. What we do now just mumble till it looks kosher? Like we've actually discussed it?"

They went back, Stanley and Eddie were indeed discussing news from home and the price of sausages.

Frank said, "Soap's OK. I can get soap. S-O-D."

"S-O-D?"

"Soap on delivery. I need to know you guys can do what you promise."

"Do what we fuckin' promise? We're British sappers not some nancy American outfit in pressed trousers and shiny shoes! We're muck and boots we are. We built Pentonville nick. We built the Albert fuckin' Hall! An' if yer believe Rudyard Kipling, Noah used our blueprints for his fuckin' ark!"

"So you can do it?"

" 'Course we can fuckin' do it!"

# §146

It took less than a day. The following morning Wilderness, Frank, and Eddie stood in a ten-foot-high circle of rubble, Hitler's Stonehenge, staring at their "hole." Once there'd been a cast-iron kiosk on top, just like the one still standing in Monbijou. There were fragments of it scattered everywhere. The pickelhaube aslant in the mud as poignant as the feet of Ozymandias.

"Bloody rotten luck," Eddie said. "We should have got here six weeks ago."

"Six weeks ago we didn't need it," Wilderness replied. "Spilt milk, Eddie."

He looked down the shaft. The spiral staircase seemed to be intact, but really, there was only one way to find out. He flicked on his torch.

"OK, follow me."

They both shook their heads.

"Nah," said Frank. "Not me. This isn't me."

"What do you mean, it isn't you?"

Eddie said, "Small dark spaces. Never could abide them. Like being locked in the cupboard under the stairs. Me grandad used to do that to me when I'd been naughty."

"Sure," said Frank. "Small dark spaces. Give me the creeps. Hell, I don't even ride the New York subway."

"You mean you're leaving it all to me? I'm on me tod? You pair of bastards."

All the same he set off.

"It's going to take me about two hours to get to the other end and back. I reckon it's about two miles each way. If you aren't coming then you're on guard duty. You watch my

478

arse, right? You don't leave this spot till I get back."

" 'S'OK," Eddie said. "I brought sand-wiches and a thermos."

It was surprisingly dry. Everything about it was a tribute to German engineering, a hundred or more years before the phrase was famous. He could stand up in it at the cen-tre, right between what seemed to be the stone version of railway lines cut into the floor. The tunnel was pretty well the same shape as the tunnels on the London Under-ground, but smaller, and arched in dressed stone rather than steel panels. It was easy to imagine that whatever the original purpose of this tunnel, some sort of wagon or carriage had run along here, hauled by donkeys or pit ponies — if, that is, it had ever been used. It was old, but it was pristine, no signs of wear. As von Jeltsch-Fugger had said, who knows who or what it was meant to convey and where? Ending at the zoo looked like error or abandonment.

The tunnel curved without any sharp bends. Nothing had collapsed, despite every-thing the RAF had dropped on the city above, despite the Nazis last-ditch attempts at scorched and flooded earth. The worst he had to contend with was the occasional puddle, lots of dust and countless cobwebs. He felt much the same about rats as Eddie did about the cupboard under the stairs, but he saw no rats. The spiders had the place to themselves.

It took about forty-five minutes to reach the other end, to stand a hundred and fifty feet below the kiosk von Jeltsch-Fugger had shown him. The ascent was tiring, and the reward was the light cutting through the iron mosaic of the kiosk, the dappling pattern it made on his uniform and the smooth click of satisfaction as the key von Jeltsch-Fugger had given him turned in the lock.

This was going to work. The adrenaline surge of certainty carried him back to the zoo end in half an hour, to catch Frank and Eddie each trying to fleece Stanley at pontoon.

"Find what you was after?" Stanley said.

"More or less," Wilderness equivocated. "I need one more favour."

"It'll cost yer."

"You don't know what it is yet."

"It'll cost yer whatever it is."

"Can you rig up a pulley, something like a block and tackle down the shaft, and another one at the far end?"

"Dunno. Where is the far end?"

"Monbijou."

"Russian sector?"

"Yes."

"Russkis is extra. It'll cost you another fifty bars."

Frank slapped down his hand of cards and

feigned exasperation.

"Jeez, do you think I'm made of soap?"

Wilderness said, "If that's your price. But I want a trolley, something like a small railway maintenance wagon. You can throw that in for the price."

"Wot? Like a push-me-pull-you? Suppose I can. What gauge? Did you measure it?"

"I did. Nought point seven of a metre."

"Nought point bleedin' seven of a soddin' metre? That's wot I hate about *Le fuckin' Continent.* Everything's fuckin' metric. What's wrong with an honest-to-God gauge like four foot eight and a half?"

There being nothing to say to this, Wilderness said nothing.

He took a pencil from his pocket, scrounged an old envelope off Eddie, and drew what he wanted.

"Flat bed, optional sides, right? Something that can be left off if needs be. Between the wheels, so the centre of gravity stays low, I want a motorbike battery. Light enough to haul up the shaft for recharging. Big enough to do the job. At either end I want a pair of brackets on the uprights, I want headlamps on the brackets that can be swapped over front to back for the return journey. Across the uprights at both ends I want a bar at this height."

He held a hand at nipple height to make his point.

"I don't want to have to bend all the time.
Wrap these bars in something soft, like
leather. OK?"

"Pullman class?"

"Whatever."

"S-O-D again?" Stanley concluded.

"Damn right," said Frank.

# §147

In Paradies Verlassen that night Frank said,
"What is the plan, kid? Pulleys? Railways?
Are we the Union Pacific now?"

"I think you'll find they went West, Frank.
We're going East. But, yes, we are indeed a
railroad. An underground railroad. Think of
it as a literal underground railroad. This time
it's soap, coffee and scent not runaway
slaves."

Frank understood him.

"We could . . . we could move more shit
than we ever did on the surface. There was I
thinking we're fucked, and . . . and
y'know . . . we just moved into the big
league."

"Yep. The tunnel's dead flat. A wagon well
oiled should roll at a touch. We could move a
thousand pounds of coffee as easily as a
packet of fags."

Eddie emerged from his *Bierstein* sniggering and blowing bubbles of lager.

"If we could get a thousand pounds of coffee!"

"Oh, you leave that one with me," Frank said. "Things are hotting up, things are really hotting up nicely."

It was almost magical timing. At that point Larissa Tosca walked by, smiled at Joe and Eddie, stuck her tongue out at Frank. Wilderness hadn't even noticed she'd been sitting there, and he relied on the constant buzz of Paradies to render any conversation private. But where had she been sitting. How close? At her usual table or closer?

Half an hour and two beers later Yuri joined them.

Wilderness brought him up to scratch.

"Good," he said. "Good good."

"I'll need a bloke or two at the other end, whenever we send something through. Pick a couple of big buggers, they'll have to haul the load up the shaft."

"Good good," said Yuri, and Wilderness began to think it might be all he would ever say.

Then he said, "Sugar. As much as you can carry."

Frank looked perplexed, "Sugar? Just like that?"

"Sugar I can shift. Sugar I can sell. Either you have sugar or you haven't. If not I go elsewhere."

Wilderness stepped in, "No, Yuri, you can't.

483

No one else will sell to you in the quantity we can. Anybody else will be taking the risk of passing the checkpoints, and if your blokes find sugar they'll just confiscate it in Joe Stalin's name, sell it back to West Berliners and you won't get so much as a shufty."

"Shufty? What is shufty?"

Frank said, "What Joe is trying to tell you is that we're a partnership, Yuri. You, me, Joe, Eddie. We're in this together. Why would you even think of looking elsewhere?"

Yuri croaked out a sour little laugh. "Partnership? All you dogs want is my dollars."

Then he swilled beer, wiped his lips, and as his hand passed over them he began to smile.

"The old team, eh? OK, comrades. How soon can you get my sugar?"

Frank and Joe exchanged glances. Wilderness took a punt.

"Friday. We can do this Friday."

When Yuri and Eddie had left Frank said, "I can get him two hundred and fifty pounds by Friday, but will Stanley have us up and running by then?"

# §148

In the absence of Spud and Pie Face it occurred to Wilderness that there were risks and gains in recruiting afresh, and that the risks outweighed the gains. The gain would have been labour — helping hands, to shift the equivalent of one fat man in sugar across Charlottenburg, into the zoo park, onto the pulley and down the shaft. Instead, Frank declining to dirty his hands with manual labour, it was left to a wheezing, sweating Eddie to lower the sugar down the shaft to Wilderness.

Fat Stanley had knocked up a Heath Robinson masterpiece. A solid oak deck, greased bearings, steel wheels. A flick of a switch and the tunnel was filled with light. A touch of the leather-bound bar and the trolley rolled. But Wilderness had not allowed for heat. Pushing was not like walking. After a mile of pushing the "one fat man" on the trolley, Wilderness stripped down to his underwear. Hotter, but also slower. He'd allowed forty-five minutes for a journey that took ninety. What would happen if Yuri ever asked for 250 pounds of butter? It would be close to rancid mush by the time he got to the other end.

When he flashed his torch up the Monbijou shaft Yuri's voice echoed down in anger.

"Черт возьми, где ты был?" Where the hell have you been?

He got quicker.

The next Sunday it was back to basics — coffee again. An all-embracing smell that seemed to fill the tunnel. And a lighter load. He got the trolley to Monbijou in just under an hour, his back and thighs aching like a galley slave's.

It occurred to him that he had grasped the shit end of the stick.

He said so to them both in Paradies.

"Can't be helped," Frank said. I ain't fakin'. Nor is Ed. Small, dark places, kid. Small, dark places."

He pushed a vodka martini across the table to him.

"A little of what you fancy. You earned it."

This, Wilderness thought, was condescending crap. Eddie could not, would not lie about claustrophobia, but Frank?

"Just tell me it's worth it Frank and stop soft-soaping me."

Frank leaned back smiling hugely, the paterfamilias, all-but-hugging in his bonhomie and so full of . . .

"Greenbacks, Joe. On the nail every time. Yuri pays up. Good as his word. We're creaming it. Gotta hand it to you, when Uncle Joe started his blockade I thought we were screwed."

His voice dropped to a stage whisper.

"But we're richer than ever. If this blockade lasts all winter, we can retire to the Ba-fuckin-hamas."

The grin was infectious. Wilderness sipped at his vodka, and couldn't help smiling back at the gleaming, white, all-American teeth Frank was flashing at him. That was the awful seduction of the con man — you wanted him to be real, you wanted to like him and him to like you.

"Bahamas," he repeated to himself, swirling the martini, looking back at Frank.

"Bahamas?" said Eddie. "I think I'd prefer Skegness."

# §149

Wilderness knew better than to boast or say "I told you so," but one day towards the end of August, as he and Frank were trying in vain to get to Der Kater Murr, a surge of schadenfreude proved almost irresistible.

The scuffed and faded line that had marked the meeting of sectors at Potsdamer Platz had become a fortress of barbed wire and steel posts. Some poor bugger was on his knees sloppily painting the white line back where it had been and being barked at by a British corporal. As for the MPs, there were more than he could count.

Frank said for him, "Well kid, you were right. It's our side cutting us off. I think you found your tunnel just in time. Sure as fuck . . . no more jeeps."

# §150

Smuggling became like adultery. A secret that would never trouble the conscience, but which required a strategy to avoid detection.

Wilderness kept a complete change of uniform, "bought" from RAF stores at the cost of three bottles of Courvoisier, at the bottom of the zoo shaft, but hardly ever had recourse to it in full. He pushed the trolley wearing only his underpants and took to bathing back at Fasanenstraße, with the same brand of soap that Nell favoured in the bathroom at her flat — an unadorned Palmolive green, with, luckily, no particular scent to it. It was soap that smelt of soap. A household rather than a boudoir item. The trick was to meet Nell of an evening exuding the right combination of cleanliness and grime. Never with wet hair, the biggest giveaway of all. Never soaked in the stinking sweat of hard labour . . . the merest glow of manly aroma that might have been acquired in a dishonest day's graft.

Tinned food was the worst, it bulked small but weighed heavy. Frank would dump five hundred tins of tuna at the top of the shaft and somehow imagine that this would be moved as readily as five hundred bags of ground coffee whilst weighing more than four times as much. Tinned food worked up a sweat, tinned food knackered him. Booze slowed them all down. Bottles of scotch needed careful handling. If Eddie dropped a case of tuna, they just dented. When he dropped a case of Lagavulin all twelve bottles shattered at the bottom of the shaft and

showered Wilderness in single malt whisky —
a smell that took three baths to get off him
and lingered in the tunnel for the best part of
a month.

The oddest load of all was caviar.

Wilderness hefted a tin in his hand before
Eddie dropped two hundred more down the
shaft.

"Have you read the label?" he asked Frank.

Frank was ever nonchalant, hand in pockets
as if to demonstrate that nothing would make
him get them dirty, standing around while
others toiled.

"Nah," he said. "You know I don't read
Russian."

Wilderness counted to ten waiting for
Frank's brain to kick in.

"Shit! I get it! This fish paste came from
Russia in the first place."

"Fish *eggs,* Frank. Sturgeon roe from the
Black Sea."

Frank picked up a tin as though knowing
what it really was had somehow improved his
grasp of a foreign language.

"Well, whaddya know? What's that phrase
you guys have? Coals to Newgate."

"Newcastle, you fucking idiot."

"French soap, Scotch whisky, Californian
tuna . . . Russian caviar. There are times I
reckon we could sell ice to Eskimos."

Most days had a run along the tunnel. He
would count it a bad day if he made the run

twice, and would feel like bollocking Frank, but that necessity never arose. Eddie would always get his two penn'orth in first.

Frank would say, "So? I do all the driving. I take the biggest risk of all. I drive a car from Tempelhof to the zoo, loaded down with stolen crap, past my guys, past your guys and past the Kraut cops. You two have a concrete wall ten foot high around you and Fat Stanley and his guys watching your ass. I take all the risks!"

Eventually, a month or so into their new venture, Wilderness replied with, "And you collect all the money."

Frank leaned in closer for confidentiality, "And he's still paying on the pop. We might have to open a bank account or something kosher. My mattress is bulging with mazuma. Bahamas here we come."

With consummate timing a message cylinder clunked down from the celestial network of overhead tubes.

"For Joe. Table 21."

Inside was a note. "I still say he's a rogue. LT."

Wilderness looked across the room. She was sitting at the table where he had first met her, sipping another martini, smiling but not beckoning. All it would take was a wave.

# §151

It might have been said that Ernest Bevin was a surprise appointment as Britain's Foreign Secretary in 1945. He had been Minister for Labour throughout the war, a post for which, as a former trades union leader, he would seem to have been eminently qualified. But Foreign Secretary? To understand Mr. Attlee's choice would require recourse to terms such as "rough diamond" and "autodidact" — although Mr. Bevin's didact was probably auto enough for him not to grasp the meaning.

He was a man who would call a spade a spade, and deem it so in an unwavering West Country accent. Part of the shock to the national, if not international, system, was that he followed in office Anthony Eden, a sophisticated, if neurotic old Etonian, former army officer and trusted lieutenant of the recently rejected prime minister Winston Churchill. A man who spoke fluent French, German, and Russian — to say nothing of Arabic and Farsi. Those there were who said that Bevin was not even fluent in English. Eden was the kind of figure of a man who'd grace a Noël Coward comedy on the West End stage with a gin and it in hand, not the saloon bar of the Dog and Duck with a pint of mild.

But . . . there might be another reason, another model of the statesman to which

Ernest Bevin conformed — Vyacheslav Molotov, the USSR's Commissar for Foreign Affairs since Russia entered the war in 1941, the hammer in Stalin's right hand.

They were two of a kind. No one in the British cabinet looked more like a Russian than Ernie Bevin. Indeed, swap Molotov's pince-nez for Bevin's horn-rims, draw a moustache on Bevin . . . and they might have been separated at birth — the rough bruisers of the diplomatic boxing ring. Although to be fair to Molotov he had kept better control of his waistline.

They hated each other.

Berlin had been the dominant issue of Bevin's time in office. Nothing loomed larger, and with the onset of the Russian blockade it became inevitable that he would turn up in Berlin. He had flown into Gatow for a brief appearance only days into the blockade, had been chauffeured to meetings with the democratic politicians of the Western sectors, visited the other airfields gearing up for the airlift and flown out again. It was understood, under no circumstances would Mr. Bevin travel into the Soviet Sector, meet any representative of the Soviet Union or its puppet Berlin Communist Party, and as for Comrade Molotov, " 'E can go an' shag 'isself." No one understood this better than Bevin's chauffeur — Lance Bombardier Edwin Clark RA.

For such as the Foreign Secretary, for visiting royalty (not that royalty ever did), and for the Military Governor of the British Zone of Occupied Germany — General Sir Brian Robertson — the usual rough and ready staff car (often just an open top jeep) was replaced by a black and grey 1935 Rolls-Royce Phantom II, complete with a tiny flagpole and tiny Union Jack.

Eddie counted driving the car as a treat. It was worth polishing the damn thing just to be able to sit behind the outsize steering wheel on a calfskin seat, facing a rosewood dashboard and burl-walnut door panels. And when no one else was around he could sit in the back, open the cocktail cabinet, put his legs up on the pull-out footrest and dream of the life of Riley.

The July visit had been hectic, but tolerable. To call it "fun" would be a word too far. Bevin had been civil to him, only a touch shy of friendly, and had warmed a fraction of a degree when Eddie had found a moment to tell him that his dad had belonged to Bevin's trades union. He was pleased at the prospect of Bevin's unscheduled visit at the end of November, even though he'd been given only twenty-four hours' notice. He polished the car again, told Frank and Wilderness that, for once, duty called and he would be unavailable until Bevin left. Telling Frank and Wilderness was a mistake.

# §152

It was six o'clock of a November night, a month away from the longest night. Berlin felt sharp and cold. The kind of night when the warmth of the tunnel might seem almost welcome. The kind of night when Berliners retreated to their beds and piled on every layer of bedding and clothing they possessed — and then got up at three in the morning to iron or cook as the stop-go supply of electricity permitted. Wilderness had suggested to Nell that they move into Fasanenstraße — since the whole building was occupied by British soldiers the electricity was more reliable — but Nell saw this as betrayal. Solidarity with Berliners demanded they feel the cold.

"Besides," she had said. "They'll cut us all off sooner or later. Occupiers and occupied. And here we have the advantage of an iron stove. We can burn anything we can find. Anything we can bear to part with."

On the coldest nights — twenty degrees of frost — they would drag their bedding down to Erno's apartment and sleep in front of his stove. Erno always had something to burn. An archive to feed into the iron stove. A tightly bound pile of *Völkischer Beobachter* from the 1930s would smoulder a whole night long. Words into smoke. Fiery rhetoric into heat and light.

Frank and Wilderness had hit Paradies early. The waiters were still clearing up from last night, rearranging chairs and wiping tables. They all but had the place to themselves. One of the singers was at the piano going over the verses to a new song with her piano player, again and again and again.

Something was on Frank's mind.

"Yuri came looking for us at lunchtime."

"In uniform?"

"Nah. Anonymous. Civvies and a dirty old rain slicker. He'd come over on the U-bahn. Didn't seem to have any problem with our guys. Even seemed to enjoy the sneaking in and out. I'd never take him for a Kraut with a face like that, but . . ."

"Aha."

"Found me. Seemed pissed off not to find you."

"Anything that won't keep?"

"Yeah — that's kind of his beef. He wants to up his order tonight."

" 'S'OK. I can handle a few pounds more."

"Thing is. He wants to more than double it. In fact, I did the math . . . he wants to sextuple it."

"What?"

"He has this big deal going down back in Moscow in a couple of days. He wants a thousand pounds of coffee. Tonight."

"You didn't tell him we'd do it?"

"Sure."

"Frank, even if we had a thousand pounds of coffee . . ."

"We have. Took some doing but I rounded up another three hundred pounds this afternoon . . ."

"I couldn't shift it. The biggest load we've ever done in a single run was that first load of sugar, and it was crippling. That was only two hundred and fifty pounds. Mostly I push about a hundred and eighty pounds."

"Jeez, I was sitting right here when you said it . . . we could move a thousand pounds just like . . ."

"Figure of speech, Frank. A thousand pounds is a half a ton! Even if we could get a thousand pounds of coffee down the shaft, you're looking at five or six runs. I'd be down there all night. Eight to ten hours. And loading all that onto the trolley would give Eddie a heart attack."

"Somebody call?"

Eddie appeared, spick-and-span in his cleaned and pressed Royal Artillery uniform, fresh from his stint as a chauffeur.

"I thought you were driving Ernie Bevin?"

"I was. But he's buggered off back to Blighty. If there's one thing our Ernie hates more than Russians, I reckon it's Germans. I did the usual rounds with him, we'd two more calls to make and he gets on the speaker tube and says, "Sod this for lark, tek me to Gatow." Next thing I know he's on a plane home and I'm sat there with an empty Roller. It's parked outside now. We can all go out for a spin a bit later. Motor Pool aren't expecting it back till midnight."

Wilderness was staring at him now.

"Wossup? What'd I say?"

"Outside now?"

"O' course. Who's gonna have the nerve to nick a Rolls-Royce the size of the *Queen Mary* with a Union Jack flying off the roof?"

Wilderness switched his gaze to Frank.

"Ever seen a Phantom II, Frank? The boot is the size of the Albert Hall, the footwell in the back is longer than even my long legs will stretch."

"I'm with you, kid."

"I'm not," Eddie said. "What the hell are you on about?"

"Rolls-Royce made armoured cars during the last war, the back axle's as tough as any tank."

"Just flippin' tell me!"

"Frank's brought us a big deal, too big to pass up. The grand slam. We have to get a thousand pounds of coffee to Yuri tonight."

"So? What's that got to do with me and me Roller?"

"We can't shift a thousand pounds of anything by hand, but we could pack it all into the Rolls. In the boot, in the back, in the front footwell. We fill up every spare corner, and I reckon we'll get it in."

"Oh, bloody Norah. No. No. No. It's too risky."

Frank said, "Where's the risk? You said yourself no one's dumb enough to steal the car. On the same principle no one would be dumb enough to pull it over for a search with Ernie Bevin sitting in the back and the flag flying."

"But Ernie Bevin won't be sitting in the back. He's gone. Flown. Buggered off. Scarpered."

Then the penny dropped. As Wilderness continued to stare him down, the bad penny rattled around in his skull.

"But I don't look anything like him."

"Sorry Ed, but you do."

"I'm forty years younger!"

"It's dark. All anyone will see is a short, fat bloke in a homburg."

"If I dress up as Ernie, we've no driver!"

"How do you fancy being driven to the other side by a lieutenant of the Welsh Guards?"

"Oh my God. Oh my God. Joe, you complete and utter bastard. You've got it all figured out haven't you?"

"Yes. No one will dare stop us on our side and sure as eggs are eggs none of Yuri's blokes will. We drive across the river, we go to Monbijou as usual, unload, drive back and the car gets returned to the pool by midnight. Pumpkin time. After all, who knows Bevin left early? Half a dozen people? Certainly none of the Russians know. They might be gobsmacked to see him, but stop him? It'd be like asking to start World War III. They simply wouldn't do it."

Across the room at table 13 Wilderness caught sight of Tosca. No one had been sitting there fifteen minutes ago. He hadn't seen her come in. But she had her head down in a book. Almost her habitual manner when there was no company. He'd seen it once or twice. A big battered hardback, but he'd never seen the title. She stuffed it in her bag as soon as he approached. One day he'd ask her what it was.

# §153

It might have been a mistake, to go to Schlüterstraße that day. He never wanted Rose Blair to think he was out of touch. And if Rose Blair thought he was in touch, so did Burne-Jones. If he didn't log in with her in the morning, he'd find five minutes in the afternoon. Enough to let her know he was not the loose cannon she might think he was. Rarely had it been this late, gone seven, when he appeared at her door. The grubby, inky, once-transparent cover was on the typewriter. Her kid gloves were out on the desk. Her Liberty headscarf was tied. She was buttoning up her overcoat.

"God, you cut it fine. He's been calling all afternoon. You're on tonight with your tomcat act."

"I can't be."

"You are."

She tore the top page off her notepad.

"I suggest you call him."

It was a Berlin number.

"He's in town?"

"Yes."

"What did you tell him?"

"That you'd done a couple of hours' paperwork this morning and I was expecting you back any minute. I don't think he realises that you haven't so much as looked at a fucking Fraggy in months."

He hadn't. Once the Russians had stormed out they'd stopped reviewing *Fragebogen,* so his doing so was close to pointless. He'd rubber-stamped everything without reading a word, and his office hours could be measured in minutes.

"Thanks, Rose."

"Miss Blair to you. I lied for you Corporal Holderness. First and last time."

Wilderness pocketed the page from her notepad. He did not call Burne-Jones.

He'd think of something.

He always did.

# §154

They loaded the car by the flak tower, hidden behind the giant molehills that Fat Stanley seemed to delight in making. Wilderness had scrounged a homburg, a black overcoat and a pair of bleary glasses off Erno. Eddie strained the front of the coat, the button-shanks taut as tightrope, but the hat fitted perfectly.

As Frank packed coffee into the last available corner, Wilderness donned his Guards uniform.

"You look the business," Eddie said. "I just feel a prat. A fat prat in a daft hat."

"Ed, you'll be fine."

"And . . . I get superstitious."

"Of what?"

"That damn uniform. It's a jinx."

"Name me a single thing that's gone wrong when I've been wearing it."

Eddie whispered, "First time you wore it here, you came back with 'im!"

Wilderness said, "Stow it, Eddie. I'm not listening."

Frank liked the sound of the boot closing so much he did it twice.

"Hear that. British perfection. Not a clunk or a click, more like a kiss. Listen. Swish . . . pop . . . kiss. One day soon I'm gonna own a Rolls."

Wilderness heard a sotto voce "Bloody

Norah," from Eddie and said, "Are we ready, Frank?"

"Rolling," said Frank. "Rolling."

Wilderness followed the route he'd taken with Andreas von Jeltsch-Fugger. Direct and prominent. The route a car that flew the Union Jack might be expected to take, if anyone ever expected such. Along the Nazi fantasy that was the east–west highway called Charlottenburger Chausee to the Brandenburg Gate. Police and troops from both sides — British and Russian — were clustered around the Gate. Wilderness slowed down, assuming that any diplomatic driver would, hoping that he'd not have to stop entirely. The British stood to attention, saluted, pulled back a makeshift wire barrier without a word and let him cruise through at less than ten mph. The Russians just stood back and stared.

Halfway along Unter den Linden a raspy whistle, a dusty raspberry, sounded by his right ear. The speaking tube.

"Can yo' smell coffee?"

"Of course I can smell coffee, what's your point, Ed?"

"My point is it's fuckin' amazing *they* couldn't smell coffee!"

Wilderness glanced in the mirror and smiled. But what he saw was a perturbed face not smiling back. This was not a happy little fat man.

502

On the Schloss Bridge the tube rasped again.

"Pull over, Joe."

"Eh?"

"Pull over!"

"Not on the bridge, Eddie. Give me ten seconds."

He stopped the car in the square in front of the remains of the Kaiser's palace. Eddie was out before he'd even yanked on the handbrake, stuffing the overcoat and the homburg through the window to him.

"I can't do this, Joe. I'm sorry. I really can't do this. Impersonating an officer's one thing. I'm impersonating a bloody cabinet minister. You'll get me sent to the Tower!"

Wilderness got out. Looked around. A couple uniformed coppers on the far edge of the square, stamping their feet and hugging themselves in the cold. No matter. The damage was done now. But he was almost there, and unless the coppers came over and started shooting it was not enough to stop him.

Eddie just kept saying he was sorry. Wilderness saw the coppers touch heads to light up cigarettes and knew they didn't give a toss. The night and the cold and the inherent coplaziness weighed more than duty or curiosity.

"Take the coat, Ed. Or you'll freeze to death."

He shook the overcoat and helped Eddie into it.

"Meet me at Paradies in an hour. Get a couple of drinks inside you and calm your nerves. I'll slip my RAF uniform back on in the gents', and take the car back. You won't have to do a thing."

"I'm sorry, Joe."

"It doesn't matter."

"Our biggest score."

"It really doesn't matter."

He watched Eddie head back towards the bridge, telling himself that no harm could possibly come to a little fat man in an ill-fitting overcoat between here and Paradies Verlassen. He'd just be waved through at the Gate. At most asked to present his ID. And if they knew him, they'd ask about the going rate for a bag of coffee or ladies' lacy underwear.

As he passed the two coppers, they hid their cigarettes behind their backsides, cupped in the palm of the hand, just like a British Tommy would do, and made a sloppy effort at standing up straight. Wilderness raised a hand to his forehead in semblance of a salute and drove on.

He parked under the S-bahn. Facing out, back to the iron kiosk on top of the shaft. He was only about fifty yards from it, but there was no sign of Yuri, no sign of any other vehicle.

He followed the S-bahn down to the kiosk. A train screeched overhead. Loud enough to drown out Armageddon. The iron door was locked. It made no sense at all for Yuri to be inside, let alone to lock himself in, so Wilderness concluded he was simply late.

As he walked back to the car another train passed, a shower of dust and rust falling, an immersion in noise that felt like drowning.

Then he saw them, slipping out from the cover of the columns that supported the steel lattice of the elevated railway. Half a dozen of them. Young men with guns. Young men with wartime Lugers. And the one aiming straight at him was Werner Fugger.

He still looked sixteen. About as scary as Minnie Mouse armed with a feather duster. But at fourteen this kid had hoisted a *Panzerfaust,* taken out a Russian tank, and had a medal pinned on him by Hitler in person. Wilderness did not so much raise his hands as merely spread them, enough to show he had no gun.

"Open the trunk, Holderness."

He did as he was told. The waft of coffee was more a blast as the boot door swung down. Kiss . . . pop . . . swish.

The teenagers spread out behind Werner in a semicircle. None of them seemed quite comfortable with their guns. They looked at each other, when they should have been looking at him. Their hands wavered, the guns aimed nowhere. Werner kept his aimed at Wilderness's midriff. If any of them had it in

505

mind to shoot him it would be Werner — and then the rest would scatter like chaff to the wind.

Werner's left hand motioned a tall, spotty kid forward. The kid laid his gun on the open boot door, took out a penknife and slit a packet of coffee. The smell of roasted coffee beans even stronger as he held out the packet to Werner.

Werner sniffed and smiled.

"We'll be taking the car too. You'll get it back sooner or later."

But Wilderness was looking past Werner, past the dilatory half-moon of half-attentive kids, to the iron kiosk. The door was open and a ragged *Trümmerfrau* had appeared, her head wrapped in a scarf, her skirt trailing in the mud, moving in and out of the moonlight shadows of the S-bahn, cutting a curious path towards them, clutching a piece of trash she had found — a wooden crutch, or a broken chair leg — almost as though she was circling them but somehow getting closer with every twist and turn.

Then he saw the broken chair leg for what it was. The familiar stunted T shape. A Mark V British Army Sten gun.

The first burst of fire took down five of the kids and Wilderness. The second killed the one kid who had managed to run. Shot in the back before he'd gone a dozen paces.

Wilderness fell against the boot, a bullet in

506

his side. A slow, wet wave, seeping towards his legs. Werner's dead eyes staring up at him. The spotty kid's gun lay where he had put it, flat on the boot door, only inches away.

As he reached for it, a hand picked it up.

"Eh, Joe," Yuri said. "You won't need that."

He pulled off the tatty grey wig, tore the ragbag blue dress off his chest, smiled his nicotine smile at Wilderness as Wilderness slid to the ground.

"Does it hurt?"

Such a strange question. But it didn't.

"It will," Yuri said. "Here. Take this. For the pain."

He took the spotty kid's penknife. Held up a packet of coffee. Showed Wilderness the bottom, with a red sticker slapped across it. Then he slit the packet. No fresh waft of coffee beans. A talcum-trickle of white powder. A hefty pinch of it perched on the end of the knife. He shoved the knife at Wilderness's mouth. Wilderness opened up and swallowed. A vile, bitter taste.

"Morphine. A little morphine for the pain. Sweet dreams, Joe. Sweet dreams."

# §155

Wilderness was staring at the ceiling. They didn't want him to move. He asked if he could sit up. They said "tomorrow." He asked for a book. Any book. They said they'd bring one. They didn't.

He wondered if there was a guard on the door. He wondered where he was. German nurses who spoke to him in good English. A prefabricated building. The not-too-close, not-so-far sound of planes taking off and landing. A hospital in the British or American zone. One of those they threw together in the summer of '45. All plywood and tarred felt. Looking shabby now. Out towards Gatow or Tempelhof. At least they hadn't left him to die in East Berlin.

He closed his eyes. He'd counted every crack in the sagging ceiling.

When he opened them Frank was standing by the bed. Wrapped for winter. Or travel or both. A bulky, lined, green army mackintosh, a Gladstone bag in his gloved hand. A bigger, bursting suitcase at his feet.

"I don't have long," he said.

"If I could get out of the fuckin' bed you wouldn't have five seconds."

"I didn't know, Joe. Honestly."

"Which bit didn't you know? That I was smuggling drugs as well as coffee?"

"Well . . . of course I knew that."

"But you didn't bother to tell me?"

"Would you have done the job if I had?"

"When exactly did we become dope dealers Frank?"

"In April. You told me not to convert to the new marks and to put everything into commodities. I bought all the coffee I could, and when that ran out I bought morphine. You didn't want to know. All you cared about was not getting stuck with old marks by the time currency reform came around. I tried telling you. We had US depots all across the sector packed out with penicillin, vaccines, morphine — you name it — Band-Aids, Q-tips, and suppositories to shove up your ass. We'd been stockpiling ever since the day Sokolovsky walked out. And once I'd got Yuri his penicillin, it was a piece of cake to get morphine. All it took was a little paperwork. I tried telling you. You just weren't listening."

"And last night?"

"It was three nights ago. You been out for a while. Docs reckon you took enough dope to knock out a Percheron. Yuri said he wanted it all now. I told you that. You know how impulsive he can be. He had a buyer. It was sell it or lose it according to him. The risk seemed low. Bury the dope in the coffee, and then you came up with the idea of using the Rolls. Brilliant. What could go wrong? Except I didn't figure Yuri for a rat."

"You'd no idea?"

"Of course I'd no idea. You think I'd of sent you and Eddie into a trap? We none of us knew."

Frank set the Gladstone bag on the bed.

"I have to be at Tempelhof in less than an hour. Uncle Sam wants me out of here. This is a third of everything we had left. Your cut. I gave Eddie his. It was like I scalded him."

"Everything?"

"We have slightly less than seventeen thousand dollars. In April you told me to spend all the marks and take only dollars from then on. Seventeen grand is the balance of what we took in dollars since April. The marks are gone with the coffee and the dope. Some of the dollars too. I had to spend to make up the last load. Yuri didn't pay up front. Yuri didn't pay at all. Winners keepers. *Siegerrecht,* as the Krauts say."

Good grief, Frank actually knew a word in German.

"How much did we lose?"

"Thousands. About eighty grand."

"Shit."

"You still got five and a half. Close to six. That's two thousand of your quids."

Wilderness had no idea if Frank was lying. The idea that Frank did exactly what he told him was a novelty. "I was only obeying orders" with a new, comical twist. But . . . he could have kept the eighty grand for himself. And it wasn't scalding either of them.

"Joe. I gotta fly. Literally. I'm on a flight back to London."

"Sure. Leave the money and fuck off why don't you?"

"Joe. Believe me, kid. I didn't know."

His head turned as the door opened. Burne-

Jones standing in the doorway. Not smiling.

Frank saluted. Burne-Jones returned it without a flicker of expression.

"I was just leaving."

Frank turned to Wilderness.

"So long, Joe."

Wilderness hoped it would be long. Right now he didn't care if he never saw Frank again. And then he was gone.

Burne-Jones lifted the Gladstone bag to the floor, Wilderness praying he did not open it . . . but he showed no curiosity. Just pulled up a chair and faced him.

"Repeat after me . . . I am a total fucking twat."

"I am a total fucking twat."

"Good. Glad we got that established. You make a twat of yourself if you want to. But you will not make a twat out of operations run by me and above all you will not make a twat out of me."

"Can't be helped now."

"It'll have to be. Now . . . what was in the Rolls?"

"Coffee, maybe a thousand pounds of it. And morphine. I don't know how much."

"The Russian got it all?"

"Is the car empty?"

"Russians found it about a mile away. Came back to us spotless."

"Then he got the lot."

"Any witnesses?"

"They were all dead when I looked. I was only conscious for a few minutes."

"And him?"

"Who?"

"Captain Spoleto."

"What are you asking?"

"I'm asking you what he knows."

"Can't tell you that."

"Good. Perhaps you'd care to stick to that line. There are some of Spoleto's colleagues who'd love to court-martial him. But they've no witnesses. Except you that is."

"Do you want me to testify against Frank?"

"No. I want to save what can be saved."

"How do we do that?'

"First, I think you know nothing of anyone else's involvement . . ."

Wilderness thought of Eddie, not Frank.

"Of course, I acted alone."

"Good . . . good. And you acted under orders."

"If you say so. What were those orders?"

"No one needs to know. Spoleto's being posted to England. Your Russian chum has vanished . . . we just need to cook up a cover story . . . you can leave that to me."

"Why?

"I repeat. You will not make a twat out of me. And to avoid that I have to exonerate you. Right now I'd prefer to lock you in the glasshouse and throw away the key. But that would not be expedient. I need you as spotless as that car."

"What . . . I get me own *Persilschein*?"

"How aptly you put it, Holderness. Yes . . . in this case a promotion. Don't even think you've earned it. It's for show. A show we put on to save my arse not yours. And, Joe, there are no second chances. Fuck up again and I'll let them have you."

Burne-Jones pushed back the chair, ready to leave.

"Promotion? Lieutenant? Second lieutenant?"

"No, I can't and won't make you an officer. I told you a while back that you'd be no use to me as an altruist — you'd be even less use to me as an officer. I need you as you are."

"You mean as you found me?"

"I was rather hoping for an improved version. I'll settle for a live one."

"Eh?"

"Start living in the real world, *Sergeant*. You almost made it into the next one. If it hadn't been for that woman you'd have bled to death under the S-bahn."

That woman? What woman? Nell?

# §156

Another night and most of a day passed. It was dark by four now. He'd realised that Burne-Jones's scheme required that there be no guard outside his door — he could leave whenever he liked, except that he couldn't walk. On the other hand he'd forgotten what day it was . . . for that matter, what month it was.

A woman appeared at his bedside at last. He'd been waiting for the woman. It just wasn't the right woman.

"Another fine mess you've gotten me into, Stanley."

For more than a moment he did not recognise her. The uniform was wrong. An American WAC. A sergeant.

"Is that . . . is that . . . a disguise, Major Tosca?"

"Sure. Like they'd let me swan in here in full Moscow spook outfit. It's mine. Had it for years. If I can get into it when needs must then I figure the years aren't being too unkind to my ass. Which kinda brings me to the point. I saved your ass."

"How? Thank you, but how?"

" 'S'OK. I didn't come here for thanks. I came to give you the explanation you're asking for. Yuri was up to something big that day. Cat that got the cream. Suppressed glee just oozing out of the little bastard. I set one of my guys to follow him. No interference, no action. Just follow and report. He saw Yuri gun down those kids, take your car. Make off with your stash. Then he came and got me. Another five minutes you'd have bled to death. We staunched the wound, drove you here and dumped you on the doorstep."

"I say again, thank you."

"*De nada.* So long as you get it and you do get it don't you?"

"Yuri left me to die?"

"Yep? And Frank?"

"Frank wasn't there."

"My point to a T. When the shit hits, when the bullets start flying is Frank ever there?"

Wilderness said nothing to this. He was in for a lecture and accepted it. God knows if one more person showed up with a moral or a caveat it could be a Toynbee Hall series for the improvement of the workingman.

"Kid, you got mixed up with a couple of bastards. Your one spark of redemption is that Eddie Clark wasn't there too."

"Have you seen Eddie?"

"No, but I can if you want."

"Tell him nothing's going to get out. We're clean as Persil. It'll all be covered up. I'm even getting promoted to sergeant to make it look kosher. He's nothing to worry about. He should just . . . carry on regardless. Ask him to come and see me."

"I'll tell him, but if he asks me my opinion, which is not unknown, I may have to tell him he needs you like he needs an extra belly button. And you . . . you don't need Yuri . . . you don't need Frank. You never did need 'em. You probably never will see Yuri again. The big score was brought on by him being posted east. He was cleaning up and clearing out with his pockets lined. Hell, he's probably a full colonel with a desk in Dzerzhinsky Square by now. But if you see Frank again, consider yourself unlucky."

After she'd gone, he squirmed a little, a spasm in his left arm — felt it come up against something solid. He reached his hand out of the sheets and picked it up. A book. Her book. He tilted the spine and tried to focus bleary eyes upon it: *Huckleberry Finn*. He knew the tale. Read it when he was twelve. He got the joke.

# §157

Nell came.

Two days later.

In all the misleading ambiguity of grey, crepuscular light.

Stiff little legs and her po-face.

A stellar constant in the gloom.

Said nothing.

Just held out her hand.

He knew what she wanted and pointed at the slim tower of utility drawers next to the bed.

"Top one," he said.

She took back the keys to her apartment and left.

He wasn't even sure she'd looked at him.

He thought that perhaps it was the strongest

sense of certainty he'd ever known. He'd never been quite so certain of anything in his entire life.

It was over.

It was over.

# §158

It was almost Christmas.

Eddie was leaning against the staff jeep out at Gatow Field. He had another volume of Penguin *New Writing,* an anthology that he could dip in and out of, half a dozen pages at a time without ever losing track, but his eyes had drifted off the text to an inner focus.

He'd joked with Joe — "You'll be the death of me." But he knew it wasn't a joke. Part of him, a large part of him, was relieved that Joe was banged up in hospital. He could interpret the promotion, as Joe surely could. Part reward, part punishment in that it meant Burne-Jones had him by the balls and his magnanimity was merely a demonstration of this. Whatever it was Burne-Jones had in mind, Eddie hoped it would take Joe far away from Berlin, as far away as possible. He liked Joe. Joe had been fun, but the fun was over. Joe was pure trouble. He had to be free of Joe. He wasn't sure how they might remain friends. And he didn't give a toss if he never saw Frank or Yuri again.

He could be happy again, just flogging coffee and nylons from under his greatcoat. The simple life and the safe. And no more London wide boys.

Yet, here he was, his greatcoat lined with ladies' underwear meeting a London copper off a plane. What was worse — that he was a copper or that he was from London?

Eddie looked up. There was a lost-looking geezer. No bigger than he was himself, too short to be a copper, almost an elf. He was trailing an RAF flying jacket. This had to be the bloke.

Eddie approached him. Gave him the instant once-over as he did so. This was no Joe, this was no East End wide boy. The overcoat was Regent Street or Savile Row, the shoes and the gloves were handmade . . . and he could hear the accent before the bloke even spoke . . . latent, immanent . . . it was going to be King's English, pure bloody toff.

"Excuse me, sir. I think I might be your driver."

The little chap turned jet-black eyes on him, stuck out his hand.

"Troy," he said. "Frederick Troy, Scotland Yard."

Eddie's heart sank at the sound of the public-school vowels. The presumptuous, world-is-my-oyster-so-fuck-you RP of the English upper class. This bloke smacked of trouble too. It could no more work out than had life with Joe. But at least it would only be for a couple of days. Then he'd be free of this prick as well.

# §159

*London:* Summer 1955
*The offices of Drax & Kornfeld, Maiden Lane WC2*
Arthur Kornfeld was used to letters like this. A thin brown paper envelope with HM Prison stamped in the corner. There would not be much inside, the briefest, the most courteous of notes — a request or a thank you. He slit the top edge with a paper knife and watched the flake of another's life fall onto his desk.

As a publisher he received up to a hundred letters a day. The other ninety-nine could wait.

HM Open Prison
East Blathering
Essex
June 11, 1955

My dear Arthur,
I hope you will have time to visit in the next month or so. I am in receipt of full remission and expect to be released in about six weeks. I have to make plans, but, alas, I have put off making plans. I would find it all so much easier if I could

talk things through with you beforehand.

Your loving friend,

Karel Szabo

convict no. 11197523

Kornfeld flipped open his desk diary. Friday the twenty-fourth was largely blank — if he could just shuffle off a couple of meetings with those tedious creatures . . . authors . . .

He stuck his head through the open doorway of the adjoining office, where his junior partner, and senior music and biography editor, sat working far harder than he ever did himself.

"Aurie?"

Nowak looked up.

"Last chance to see the inside of an English prison next week."

Aurelius Nowak had long ceased to find this funny. Arthur, a Viennese, had seen the inside of several English prisons as an interned enemy alien during the war. He spoke of it often. It had not been wholly without pleasure. Nowak, a Pole, had been "interned" too, in Auschwitz and in Belsen. He scarcely mentioned either. They had been wholly without pleasure.

Nowak returned his eyes to the manuscript he was marking up, pencil in hand, darting down the margin in a sequence of squiggles that for some reason always proved a source of delight to him.

"You will understand, Arthur, if I say that I shall pass on that wonderful opportunity and hope I do not live to regret it."

"OK. Would you mind taking a couple of meetings for me next Friday?"

"Of course not . . . am I to understand Dr. Szabo is about to be released?"

"Yes. He's in a bit of a funk about it all. I really ought to nip down to Essex."

How English these phrases sounded to Polish ears — "bit of a funk," "nip down." The art of understatement.

"Seven years is a long time. You and I did not serve that long between us. And think how difficult the readjustment was."

It had taken Kornfeld less than five minutes to adjust to freedom. As far as the bar in the nearest railway waiting room, in fact. Nowak, he knew, would never adjust. It showed in the way he reacted to meeting strangers, to sudden intrusions into his office, to any encounter with a man in uniform. From the postman to the beat bobby. If he lived to be a hundred Nowak would never ask a policeman the time, whatever the old song said.

Part of Arthur had wanted the company. Down by train as far as Chelmsford, and then a long cab ride out into the flat Essex countryside past villages with names that ended in Bumpstead and D'Arcy, thereby summing up what Arthur thought of the county, via West Blathering and Much Blathering to

Little Blathering and Blathering-next-Dyke to arrive at last at Her Majesty's Open Prison, East Blathering — home for most of his sentence to Karel Szabo, spy.

A little ringing round among those few friends that had found space in heart or mind to forgive and Arthur soon had the company of fellow physicist Marte Mayerling. Personally, in the time Arthur had worked with Marte before the war, when physics had been their mutual passion, he had found her passionless about anything else and pretty well humourless. That said, the one soft spot in that heart of pure maths seemed to be for Szabo. She had dismissed his treason with, "Frontiers, nations . . . are for smaller minds than ours . . . we are citizens of the world." A world they had damn near blown up. At the end of the war Arthur had not wanted to work in physics any longer. He was happy as a publisher — who ever heard of a physicist with luncheon expenses — how many mathematical geniuses took breakfast at Simpson's-in-the-Strand and charged it to the firm?

Marte had flown far nearer the sun than he and had worked at Berkeley on the bomb that destroyed Nagasaki. She had stayed with physics, resumed her place at Imperial College, London, and declined ever after to work on weapons of any kind.

A train ride with Marte, and she had

travelled down to Essex with him many times, always left Arthur feeling that he had been brought up to date in his former interest. She saved him having to read the *New Scientist*. Anything of import in it was at the tip of her tongue waiting to be imparted. Occasionally he wished she had learnt the knack of talking about the weather, but you can't have everything, and more often than not he relished her intensity and the glut of knowledge that threatened to overwhelm him, and, had East Blathering been closer to Colchester than Chelmsford, would most certainly have done so. An English summer's afternoon, a hip flask, a half-bottle of Chassagne-Montrachet '48, a little French bread and foie gras in his briefcase, the company of one of the smartest women on the planet . . . what was not to like?

"I do wish you'd learn to drive, Arthur."

"Stop being a sourpuss, Marte. You're so much more beautiful when you smile."

Indeed she was. He doubted she was much over forty, and still a bit of a looker. But she was immune to flattery.

"It's so tiresome. All the changes. Tube, train, cab, and back again."

She had learnt "tiresome" early on in their time as adopted English. It alternated with "ghastly" as one of her habitual upper-class moan words.

"Look at it from Karel's point of view. What

do you think he prefers, Blathering or Pentonville?"

"At least I can get to Pentonville just by flagging a cab."

"But such a ghastly place."

She knew he was taking the mickey, and changed the subject.

"Does he have plans?"

"Dunno. That's rather why we're here."

"Does he have . . . options?"

"You tell me. Would any British university have him back?"

"Of course not."

"Then he must find something else to do."

"Surely he must leave England?"

"He may not have to. He's still a citizen after all. Technically Karel is a traitor not a spy. They never took citizenship away from him."

"Good God, why on earth not? There are times I think we have landed down among lunatics. After what he did?"

"Perhaps they just forgot."

"He gave the atom bomb to the USSR. That, surely, is unforgettable?"

"I'm sure it is. But it won't be a matter of what the English forget but what they'll forgive."

Marte pondered this. Looked out at the passing countryside without seeing any of it.

Then she said, "He should leave. In fact, he must leave."

Her certainties, once uttered, were as fixed as Aristotle's Laws. He knew she'd say it to Szabo as readily as she had just said it to him, and she did.

Szabo looked sad. In all the years Arthur had visited him, he had never wanted to discuss the old country — any of them, not Hungary, not Germany, not Austria — and seemed to have most affection for the country he had betrayed. In part, Arthur thought, because he could not see the betrayal for what it was.

"Leave England? Where would I go?"

"There will be people, the muckraking journalists, the die-hard Tories who will expect you to go to Russia," Arthur said.

"But I've never been to Russia. I don't speak a word of Russian beyond 'das vidanye' and 'spasibo' and I only learnt those to be polite to Russians in the camps."

"What would you like to do?"

"I don't know."

"Would you like to work for me?"

"I don't know. I mean . . . that's very kind of you . . . but do you even know if you'd be allowed to employ me?"

"If you stay, the authorities cannot stop me. It is, as they tell you at every turn, a free country."

"If I stay?"

"Karel, they're not going to throw you out. I have this on some . . . authority. There that word again."

"What authority?"

"I talked to Rod Troy. He's shadow Home Secretary now. I've known him for years. We were interned together. He had a private word with the Home Secretary. They're not going to throw you out."

Marte had not spoken for several minutes. Arthur had been conscious of the grinding of the millwheels of her mind — or to do her more justice, the scattering of her alpha particles.

"Arthur. Would you be so kind as to give me a moment alone with Karel?"

Kornfeld looked at the impassive prison warder. Back against the wall by the door, hands clasped behind him, eyes focussed on nothing, deaf to the room, and realised that they could as well be alone and that whatever she wished to say in private might just remain that way. After all, all they had to do was switch to German.

"Of course. I'll be just outside."

# §160

Karel Szabo was released on August 27.

On September 3 — the anniversary of the war that had made refugees of both of them — he and Marte Mayerling caught the Dover to Calais ferry, and from Calais a train for Paris, Gare du Nord.

On arrival in Paris they vanished.

Four months later, in January 1956, they were reported seen in Dresden, now part of the German Democratic Republic — commonly referred to as East Germany.

# §161

*London Summer 1955: Campden Hill Square W8*
*The home of Lt Colonel and Lady Margaret Burne-Jones*

Wilderness had been to Burne-Jones's home many times. He was almost certain it was against all military protocol to mix socially with other ranks, but if protocol had mattered much to Burne-Jones he would have fired Wilderness in 1948, and for that matter in 1950, 1951, and 1954.

It had been 1949 the first time. They were both back in England. Wilderness had recovered from the bullet Yuri put in him at a BAOR hospital in München Gladbach. He had been there, he thought, long after his health required it and had concluded it was Burne-Jones's way of locking him up without the need of a key. It was January '49 before they granted him a clean bill of health and a travel warrant back to London. He landed back in Blighty in civvies, silently adamant that he'd "never wear a fuckin' uniform again."

Wilderness got off the bus in the Commercial Road and walked the length of Sidney Street. Much of it lay in ruins, much as it had when he had left in 1946. The bombed-out, roofless houses and the gutted factories. A gang of rowdy boys came haring out of a ruin and stopped just short of colliding with him, frozen with guilt about nothing worse than being boys. Another boy stared silently down at him from the first floor window, his face framed in jagged glass. Wilderness caught a glimpse of the boy he used to be — but this was a dog-eat-dog world, every boy for himself. He bid them "good morning" and walked on. Twenty paces on, the jeering and catcalling resumed to the sound of breaking glass.

Near the south end of the street a funfair was being dismantled — there was something visually startling about multicoloured wooden horses and scarlet and orange bunting in the grey, washed-out, scorched landscape. Nothing else had colour. Everything was ash.

He passed familiar landmarks that had survived the Blitz — the lemonade factory, with its towers of bottles, the brewery and the haze of hops and horseshit that seemed to emanate from it, the newsagents that sold rationed fags, rationed sweets, and under-the-counter pornography . . . the monumental masons, creating the only record most East Enders ever got, a tombstone.

He stopped at the railings and peered through, as fascinated by dates and death as he had been at the age of fourteen. Novellas written in solid stone . . . wife of . . . and also . . . of the above . . . aged six weeks . . . aged eighty-seven years.

It was their sole marketing ploy to stick a row of stones in a dozen different styles where they could be read from the street. He'd often wondered if they made up the names or if they simply made advertisements out of the stones no one had ever come to collect. Now he knew — the second from the right read far too tersely:

Abner Riley

1884–1944

What was Merle playing at? Why had she left him here? Why hadn't this been put up at the head of his grave in St. George's churchyard months — no years — ago?

He arrived on Merle's doorstep to find his key did not fit the lock. A woman he vaguely recognised opened the door to him.

"Young Joe is it? My, you've filled out."

Wilderness stared.

"You don't know me do you? Molly. Molly Riley. Married to your grandad's second cousin Paddy? Anyway, don't stand there freezing to death. Come on in."

It was cleaner by far than it had ever been under Merle's care. Some of the furniture was the same — the old, clumpy Victorian stuff that had belonged to Abner, and before that to Abner's father. Some of it was new — the lightweight, make-do-and-plywood look that was known as "Utility" — the Morrison shelter had gone, and in its place stood a folding Utility table as substantial as an orange-box. The most familiar object in the room was Abner's armchair next to the range. It had lost much of its stuffing even in 1941 — and judging from the array of safety pins holding the rest in, it was something Molly meant to survive. He could almost see Abner sitting there, easing off his boots, complaining about his corns, saying, "Make us a cuppa, Merle."

Merle. Where the fuck was Merle?

"Where's Merle?"

"Oh my God, don't tell me you didn't get her letter? She's married again. Paddy and I took over the lease from her at the end of the summer."

Not for one moment did Wilderness believe Merle had written to him. No more than she'd bothered to collect Abner's stone.

"Do you have a forwarding address?"

"Well," said Molly. "I did. But the last couple of weeks things have started coming back to me as 'not known at this address.' All the same you can have it if you want."

She picked up an envelope from the table and with a stub of a pencil scribbled down an address in Devonshire Place.

"Near Regent's Park?" Wilderness asked.

"Oh yes. Posh. She married a bit o' posh. Alistair or Angus or something. And one of them double-barrelled names."

"And my . . . things?"

"Your things?"

"Books mostly. I left a lot of books. In my room, that is the attic room."

"Oh, yeah, I'm with you now. Well. We got four kids — you got four little cousins now, three girls and a boy — all at school right now or else they'd be here asking you a million questions — so we, like we needed the space. It's young Doris's room."

"That's fine, Molly. I don't want the room. It's your house now. I just wanted the books, well some of them."

"Like I was saying. Merle took all your stuff and left it with that pal o' hers over in White Horse Lane."

Wilderness could not think who.

"You know. That blonde woman there used to be all the gossip about. Bit of a looker. Married to that grumpy old Jew who runs the tailor's opposite the Underground."

"Judy Jacks?"

"That's 'er. Anyway, she's got all your stuff safe and sound."

As he stood on the doorstep, under a January sky, breath freezing in the winter air, knowing he was standing on this threshold for the last time in his life, deciding to avoid ascribing any meaning to it, Molly said, "We could put you up on the sofa, just for a couple of nights, if you like."

And meaning took him regardless. "I'll be fine Molly. What's gone is gone. What's done is done."

He walked over to White Horse Lane, following much the same route he had walked with Abner eight years ago when the old man had collected him after the air raid that had killed his mother — across the top of Jubilee Street, down Redman's Road — thinking Stepney looked worse than Berlin — did no one clear up after a war? — and hoping Billy Jacks was not at home.

He wasn't. Judy Jacks answered the door. A flimsy, flowery summer dress as though they were not in the depths of winter. A Maginot Line of goose pimples running up her arms. He'd had the hots for Judy when he was a priapic sixteen. He didn't know a Stepney lad that hadn't. Blue eyes, blonde hair, hourglass curves . . . never seemed to age. Rumour had it that Billy had caught her and a young copper in flagrante across the kitchen table, but he'd never believe that. Billy Jacks would have killed both of them if that really had happened.

She was looking at him now, waiting for

him to snap out of it.

"Joe? You gonna speak or what?"

She was gorgeous, he thought, coming up to fifty and still fit to turn a teenager's head.

"Mrs. Jacks."

"I think you're old enough to call me Judy. I suppose you've come for your stuff?"

She walked back into the house, a silent invitation to follow hanging in the air between them.

In the living room, a meagre coal fire. You could count the lumps in the grate. On the mantelpiece an array of photographs, some framed, some merely postcard-sized, wedged into the frame of something bigger by one corner. In one of the frames, a man in the uniform of the Great War, a Tommy Atkins, he recognised as a younger version of one of the old men of his childhood. Mr. Jacks Sr. The man in the postcard, in the uniform of the Second World War, a REME corporal, he knew well — Danny Jacks, son and heir of the irascible Billy Jacks, tailor of Stepney Green. He was six or seven years older than Wilderness himself. One of the wide boys of the Green. He doubted Danny wanted to be heir to a tailor's shop. Then it dawned on him. He'd no idea if Danny had survived the war or not. The last year he was in England — the year of the great demob — had been such a roller coaster he'd never thought to ask about what people didn't volunteer to tell.

"He's a schoolteacher in Leytonstone now."

Judy was standing in the kitchen doorway, a kettle hissing in the room behind her. Wilderness found he was holding the photo of Danny, and gently wedged it back in the frame with the boy's grandfather.

"Who'd have believed it? My Danny a schoolteacher."

"And Billy. What did Billy have to say about that?"

"A big fat yes was what Bill had to say. Almost smiled. War changed him, you know. Changed everyone I shouldn't wonder. He's a local councillor now, solid Labour. Got himself a safe seat for Westminster next time around. Imagine, Billy Jacks MP. And you, young Joe. Has it all changed you? You were such a strange one, always with your nose in a book, always takin' the piss when you thought no one could hear you."

"It was the books I came about."

"Yeah, but there's no hurry. Have a cuppa and catch up. You been gone a while."

"Two and a half years. Long enough for Merle to do a bunk."

"Well . . . I can tell you about that. If you let me."

He did.

He sat and sipped at tea. Let her top him up. And heard how Merle had married a toff

— the whore's equivalent of a stage-door johnnie. How they had lived in Devonshire Place until Christmas, when he had inherited a castle in Scotland. Judy wasn't sure where, but Merle was bound to surface sooner or later.

And all Wilderness could think of was the money — he and Abner had stashed hundreds, possibly thousands, between 1941 and the old man's death, and Merle had trousered the lot. He and Frank had made a packet in Berlin, and Yuri had trousered the lion's share. Would he never get lucky?

She showed him up to the top floor, the room that had been Danny's. His books, his wooden model of a Lancaster, the remains of his Meccano kit, his striped belt with the snake-S buckle, his penknife, his Eveready torch missing bulb and batteries, his wristwatch missing the winding wheel, his dog-eared copy of *Health and Efficiency* from March 1938 . . . Rada's clipping files . . . all his worldly possessions were in three wooden orange-boxes under the bed.

Judy flopped onto the bed, watching as he sifted through his childhood. She picked up *Health and Efficiency.*

"You cheeky devil. I used to confiscate these off Danny."

"As I recall it was Danny gave it to me. Or, more precisely, he sold it to me."

"How much?"

"A bob."

She held the cover out to him — an arty black-and-white nude, eyes averted, head back, stretching her tits flat against her ribs. A marked resemblance to Merle's Hollywood namesake, Miss Oberon.

"You were robbed. She's not all that much to look at. Mine are better than hers."

He didn't doubt it. His adolescent fantasies had encompassed that. He rummaged through his Mark Twains and his R.M. Ballantynes, found his copy of Belloc's *Cautionary Verses,* his *Diary of a Nobody,* heard the swish as her dress hit the floor, saw it puddle next to him.

He looked up; she was unhooking her bra.

"See. Bloody good they are."

The weight of one in each hand, as though she were buying fruit down the market. Then she put her thumbs in her knickers and pushed them down to her knees.

"Where's Billy?" he said.

"Catford dogs. Won't be back for hours."

# §162

She ran her fingers over his belly. Found the scar, a softer, clearer skin.

"What's that?"

"Bullet wound."

"I thought you missed the war. I thought you got called up after."

536

"I did. And it's a long story. And I'd hate to be here when Billy gets back."

It was pitch dark on the doorstep. The shimmering gas lamp on the other side of the street did nothing to light them up. She looked both ways then kissed him a real smackeroo.

"You take good care of yourself John Holderness. No more bullets!"

Sometimes he did get lucky.

He rang Burne-Jones at home.

"What chance you could rustle up a chit for a billet?"

"Sorry, Joe. Don't quite follow you there."

"You know, some sort of order that'll get me a bunk in barracks somewhere in London. Just for a couple of nights. I find myself suddenly homeless."

There was a whispering on the other end. A soft discussion with Mrs. Burne-Jones no doubt.

"Where are you?"

"In a phone box on Stepney Green."

"Look, why don't you come here. Campden Hill Square. We're marginally nearer Holland Park than Notting Hill Gate. Just hop on the tube at Mile End, you'll be here in half an hour."

And so it began — a shift in Wilderness's geography from East to West. Holland Park was not "up West," it was beyond the up and was just West.

# §163

Mrs. Burne-Jones turned out to be Lady Margaret Burne-Jones, daughter of some toff or other. She stuck him in another attic. The bedroom of her eldest daughter, Judith. Judith was away at Cambridge, Newnham College, her first year studying for a degree in English Literature. The other three daughters, ranging from seven to fourteen, were in residence.

Burne-Jones led him up a seemingly endless, tortuous staircase to the top of the house.

"We're very proud of Judy," he said. "Of course Madge went to Newnham too, but one can never take anything for granted."

"I went to Cambridge," Wilderness said. "Are you proud of me?"

"You know Joe, you can always sleep in the dog kennel if you'd rather."

A plain, British ration-book dinner after which Wilderness pleaded the travails of the day and excused himself for an early night.

He lay back on Judy Burne-Jones's bed and inhaled . . . Judy Burne-Jones . . . breathed in the trail of scent she had left behind. He knew what it was. He just couldn't name it. Vanilla, more than a hint of vanilla. It hung in the air as though she'd been in the room minutes not days before. It was a girl's room — not in the sense of frills and fluffs, pinks and pincushions, it was if anything a simple room — but you'd no more mistake it for a man's room than a woman daft enough to walk into the gents' lavatory in a London bus station by mistake would ever think that that was other than what it was.

The scents entwined.

The new perfume of Judy wrapped itself around the . . . ah, two Judys in one day . . . the new perfume of Judy Burne-Jones wrapped itself around the sweat of Judy Jacks, mingled with the sharpness of his own semen, and the memory of Merle.

He might sleep well so ensconced in scents, as soon as the unresolved woman invoked by this olfactory assault let him go. With two Judys in his senses, Merle in his memory, he thought of . . . Nell Burkhardt.

He told her to go. She wouldn't.

He breathed in Judys. Still Nell persisted, her lips on his, her hair tumbling over his face . . . enveloping him in scent. That was it . . . the trail Judy Burne-Jones had left was the same scent Nell wore . . . L'Aimant — the magnet — by Coty. Orchids and vanilla. A cheap one, as scents go. Frank had knocked them off, and he and Eddie had shifted bottles by the hundred in 1947.

Taxonomy was a good game, but an obsessive one that tended to induce insomnia. But it was Coty, and now he knew it was Coty he would probably sleep. If he could name the word, he could dismiss the woman. Idea would always beat feeling as surely as scissors cut paper and paper wrapped stone . . . and stone blunted scissors.

# §164

At breakfast he met the other three daughters — Eliza, Olivia, and Dorothea.

"This is Sergeant Holderness," Burne-Jones said.

"Call me Joe," Wilderness said to thc girls.

And to Burne-Jones, "Official then, is it? I'm a sergeant now."

"Yes. And as I keep telling you . . ."

"Rank doesn't matter."

And the youngest girl said, "People are always finishing Daddy's sentences. He's so slow."

After porridge and a cup of coffee that reminded him there were many things he'd miss about Germany — and that while morphine had its moments he'd rather start the day with a good cup of Java — he said, "I'll look for a room today. I was thinking of Notting Hill. Cheap enough, after all."

"I think you mean shabby. And I wouldn't bother just yet. I need you in Vienna at the end of the week."

# §165

Vienna led to Paris, Paris led to Lisbon.

It was 1952 before he felt need of a home

of his own.

He and Burne-Jones arrived in Campden Hill Square late one warm Monday evening in May. Madge had left beer and sandwiches on the kitchen table.

Wilderness said, as he had said before, "I'll look for a room in the morning."

And for once Burne-Jones did not contradict him by mentioning a posting he had previously forgotten to mention.

"Why not?" he said. "Meanwhile I gather Judy made up her bed for you personally, before she went back to Cambridge this morning. Nice to know she's learnt something as a result of a very expensive education. I seem to see bugger all else by way of benefit."

Burne-Jones was picking up chutney jars and peering through his half-moon reading glasses at the labels, looking for something that might go with beef. A letter propped between a proprietary Bengal Spicy and a homemade 1950 plum and bramley fell over.

"It's for you."

"Eh?"

"Forwarded from your cousins in Stepney. Postmarked last Tuesday."

Wilderness opened it. Rarely, if ever, did he get letters, and almost never on headed notepaper.

"It's from a firm of solicitors in Chancery Lane. Etherington, Graham, and Yooll. Would

I be so kind as to contact them at their office, 'where you may hear something to your advantage.' What the fuck does that mean?"

"It means something very dear to your heart, Joe. Money."

Money, even more than taxonomy, could cost him dear sleep. But as he rearranged the pillows a second letter addressed to him fell to the floor.

Joe Holderness! Did you ever see *Sunset Boulevard*? Gorgeous, yummy William Holden plays a scriptwriter, and the script he never gets to finish before Gloria Swanson shoots him depicts two people who share a room — I think they even share a bed — and they never get to meet as one works days and the other nights. Isn't that us? Don't you think that's us? Three years now, and we've never met.

I graduate next month. I'll be around a lot more. That's a hint. You know how to take a hint, don't you Joe? You know how to whistle, don't you Joe? You just put your lips together and . . .

Judy

# §166

He found Etherington, Graham, and Yooll in Chancery Lane. Mr. Etherington (junior) saw him. An impossibly tall man of seventy or so, which begged silent questions as to the age of Mr. Etherington Sr., with a shining brown pate and a halo of stiff white hair.

"Concerning the will of the late Mrs. Alistair Carnegie-Little . . ."

"Who?"

"I believe her maiden name was Mary-Ann Evans."

Ah! Merle! So she was dead.

"Mr. and Mrs. Carnegie-Little died as a result of an incident involving Mr. Carnegie-Little's Bentley and a Scots pine on the banks of Loch Lomond in the small hours of New Year's Day."

"Drunk, eh?"

"That would . . . er . . . appear to be the case. Mr. Carnegie-Little died instantly. Mrs. Carnegie-Little lingered a week or so . . . long enough to have a new will drawn up. As Mr. Carnegie-Little predeceased her, she was, of course, the beneficiary of his not insubstantial estate, and while Mrs. Carnegie-Little saw fit to pass on the bulk of that estate to her stepson, she made a provision for you, Sergeant Holderness. The not inconsiderable sum of five thousand pounds."

Wilderness wondered at the man's pointlessly complicated use of double negatives, but said simply, "Five grand?"

"I believe that is the vernacular, yes."

Wilderness's thoughts rapidly cycled through "fuck me," "so she's spent all she nicked and bungs me few grand from her toff husband," "fuck me" (again), and "five grand? That's a fortune!"

"If you'll just sign here, I can make out the cheque forthwith."

It was a presumption. RAF NCOs didn't have bank accounts. Working blokes didn't have bank accounts. Wilderness did. Burne-Jones had made him open one years ago. He banked with the armed forces' bank, Glyn Mills. Their main branch was in Lombard Street. He could walk there in a matter of minutes and deposit the cheque. Five grand. A sum so big he did not think cockney slang even had a euphemistic term for it. He'd have to invent one. Five grand — a load of sand? Five grand. Fuck me. And fuck Rotting Notting Hill. He'd buy in . . . Hampstead. Hampstead, lovely Hampstead, where he had begun his career as a thief.

# §167

It was more than he wanted to spend. It was all he had inherited and more. It swallowed the last of the Berlin stash, although spending the stash was a way of burying it for good, of legitimising the last of his ill-gotten gains — sardines and soap, coffee and morphine . . . turned into bricks and mortar.

Perrin's Walk was an unpaved track, a hundred yards downhill from the Everyman

Theatre. The house looked as though it might have been mews for one of the far larger houses in Church Row at some point in its life. Three floors of narrow, neglected rooms stacked over a garage. He didn't need the garage. He'd find another use for it. If it had been mews then the chauffeur had never come back from the war. On first scent the house smelt of mice and emptiness — emptiness at a time when London was desperately short of housing, at a time when the new were not getting built and the old and bombed were scarcely patched up.

His no chain, cash offer was accepted at once.

He spent six weeks in a boardinghouse in Camden Town and moved in the day the paperwork was completed. He retrieved his boxes from Judy Jacks, emptied them out and they, with the one item abandoned in the mews — a striped deck chair — became his first items of furniture.

He'd never had this much space in his life. He'd never felt particularly exposed. For all that he had been, and nominally still was, a serving member of Her Majesty's Armed Forces, the only time he'd ever spent in barracks was his abortive basic training out in Essex. He'd had his own room in Cambridge, and in Hamburg . . . he'd shared with Swift Eddie for a while in Berlin . . . and after that it had been beyond question, no one had ever suggested he share a room again — sergeants did not share, spies did not share — but no room had ever been his in any sense that mattered. He was always passing through. He might be in one city, in one room for a year or more, but he was always passing through. That was part of the devil's pact he had signed with Burne-Jones.

This was his.

Every square inch.

About noon the same day there was a banging on the door, down on the ground floor.

Burne-Jones stood in the lane, clutching a magnum of Veuve Clicquot.

"Got to launch the ship in style, you will agree?"

Next to him, a small, beautiful blonde, hair in a ponytail, no makeup, slacks and a sloppy sweater, flat heels — what he thought of as woman's mufti.

"I don't have any glasses," Wilderness said.

The girl held up a brown paper bag, shook it gently so that he could hear the chink of glass on glass.

"House-warming present," she said.

Burne-Jones didn't wait to be invited in and set off up the stairs with "You know Judy of course" tossed over his shoulder, and Wilderness found himself face-to-face with Judy Burne-Jones for the first time.

"Known her for years," he said to Burne-Jones's ascending rump — and to her, "I've

546

read all your books. Almost the same as knowing you."

"Really? Which was your favourite?"

"*Vanity Fair.* I found I could really identify with the heroine."

"Ah . . . but it's a novel without a hero. You may not have noticed, but I have better manners than my father. Do invite me in, Sergeant Holderness."

"Do come inside, Miss Burne-Jones."

She kissed him on the cheek and ran up the stairs after her father.

# §168

Burne-Jones gave him a year in London. Wilderness did not think of it as a favour. He had enough work to do to prove that was not the case, and much of it was mundane observation work.

As rationing fizzled away to nothing and Britain began to recognise that it wasn't really broke after all, Wilderness acquired furniture — including a double bed all to himself. It was another symbolic freedom — to stretch out his long legs and feel the bed go on for ever.

Burne-Jones had made him get a phone, indeed had expedited his getting a phone by pulling strings to get around the GPO waiting list. Nor did he have to a endure a party line — "Can't have every bugger in London listening in, now can we? National security has to mean something."

About once every six weeks an invitation to eat at Campden Hill Square would arrive. The phone would ring, at home or in the office — occasionally Burne-Jones would appear in person, with the habitual phrase, "Feel like taking pot luck with me and Madge tonight?" He never got more notice than that. And he never said no. Odds on Judy would be there, and on the nights when Judy cooked, good food replaced Madge's rather perfunctory pots of luck.

Judy was a devotee of the work of Elizabeth David, and smiled like arrayed artillery when her father greeted a *navarin printanier* with "Mutton stew again," or *beignets de sardines avec pommes anna* as "Fish and chips."

Wilderness ate everything she put in front of him.

He learnt to like olives.

He learnt to like garlic — that it was not something you rubbed around the inside of a salad bowl to impart the ghost of flavour — it was something you mashed with the flat side of the knife and threw in by the handful.

He learnt to like Judy.

He was aware of the line. However much Burne-Jones rubbed at it and blurred it, and he had been doing that since 1945, it was still there.

It seemed to him that he could blow everything if he made a play for Judy Jones. So he didn't.

He was preparing for a posting to Helsinki . . . ("Finland? Why are we spying on the Finns? What did the fucking Finns ever do to us?" "Think of their next-door neighbours, Joe, think of one of the most heavily defended boundaries in the world.") when Judy rang him in Hampstead, about a week after the coronation of the new queen.

"Joe, I finish my BBC traineeship next month."

"Congratulations."

"No, I mean . . . I'll have a proper job and a proper salary."

"I say again congratulations."

"Do try and get the point, Joe! I mean . . . I don't have to go on living with Ma and Pa."

"Great, but I don't want your old room back."

"No, but I want yours."

"What?"

"Pa tells me you're being posted abroad by the not-so-secret service. Joe, rent me your house. I'll be Madge and Alec's little girl for ever if I stay with them."

"But that's what they want you to do. Stay."

"I can't."

"And I can't rent you the house. If your father has told you anything about what we do, then the uncertainty of it all must be apparent. I don't know when I'll be back. I never know."

"Then just rent me one room. The box room if you like. The big bedroom can stay as it is, and you can turn up whenever you like."

He did not return to London for over eight months. One night in the spring of 1954, he paid off a cab at midnight, let himself in to find the house empty, fell into bed, fell asleep and woke around seven to find Judy Jones sleeping next to him — her clothes scattered across his all over the floor, as though they had embraced instead of the flesh within.

He made coffee. Brought the tray back to bed and nudged her into waking.

"Have you been sleeping in my bed all the time I've been gone?"

"Yep. Tit for tat. You slept in mine for however many years."

"Are you going to make a habit of this?"

" 'Fraid so. Been a long time coming hasn't it?"

"Yep."

"Talk about hard to get. You were almost impossible to get. I left books for you, I left billets-doux, I cooked for you, I got you playing blindman's buff at the old 'uns Christmas party just so I could get you to feel me up . . . short of just taking off all my clothes and making a complete fool of myself I did everything I could to get your attention, Joe."

Wilderness looked over the top of his coffee cup at the bra that had landed on top of his shirt, at the stockings trailing across the carpet, the suspender belt clinging like cobweb to the doorknob.

"But . . . you did take all your clothes off."

"I suppose I did."

"Then call me Wilderness. Every woman in my life has."

# §169

The next night, still without her clothes, wrapped around him in postcoital sloth, Judy said, "What exactly is it you do for my dad?"

"I'm sure if he wanted you to know he'd tell you."

"But, sweetest, it's you I'm asking. You're no more an RAF sergeant than my dad's still a Guards officer . . ."

" 'Cept when it comes to pay. Your father's motto is 'rank doesn't matter' and mine is 'pay does matter.' But . . . since you ask. I'm MI6's resident cat burglar."

She hit him, laughed and hit him with a pillow.

It was an old one but a good one. Tell the truth and defy belief.

# §170

And so, on this day in the early August of 1955 Wilderness was to be found making his way from Notting Hill Gate Underground station to Campden Hill Square to test the line to destruction. It might resist like concrete and tungsten, it might vanish in a puff of smoke, when he asked Lt Colonel Burne-Jones for the hand of his eldest daughter in marriage.

Burne-Jones said, "What kept you?" as soon as Wilderness had asked.

Madge said, "I think I'll leave the two of you to it" and headed for the kitchen.

Wilderness had not thought that it would be otherwise.

A quarter of an hour later with a couple of shots of Burne-Jones's 1939 Laphroaig single malt inside him he went in search of Madge and found her indulging in one of her bad habits — smoking a king-size cigarette and knocking the ash off into the saucer of a half-drunk cup of tea.

"Well, Joe."

"Well, Madge."

"I don't know whether to read respect for tradition or a bit of a mickey-take into your rather old-fashioned way of doing things, but I can guess at Alec's response. He met you word for word, tit for tat, and asked if you could 'keep Judy in the manner to which she is accustomed,' didn't he?"

"Yes."

"And what did you say?'

"I told him that what I was paid was known

to him to the last farthing, as it was set by him. I'm on a sergeant's pay, plus some. But I'm unencumbered by debt, everything is paid for, and he knows that because he's been privy to my house buying since the day I first saw Perrin's Walk. I was slightly better off when Judy paid me rent, almost needless to say. But what's mine is hers."

"And what is yours, Joe? Quite the question to be asking a professional thief you will agree. But I don't think the answer matters all that much.

"Joe, if I were to say to you that you were not what I wanted for my daughter it would be because one never ceases to want, to yearn, to dream on behalf of one's children. One learns early on that it is impossible not to make plans but also to bend when they don't work out. Not to bend is to invite frustration.

"And if you were to ask me what it was I did want for Judy, I doubt I could answer you. My mother did what her parents asked of her, expected of her. Married well. Married into the aristocracy. Married an absolute shit. And the fact that my father was a shit became a family shibboleth. It was never mentioned. But if I'd brought home a prospective who was an habitual drunk and far too free with his fists, I think Ma would have shot him dead. I was not to do as she had done.

"Perhaps all I want for my daughter is for her not to marry a shit. I didn't marry a shit. And I know you're not a shit. But I also know what you do for England. What you do for England is legitimised by the fact that you do it for England — but tell me, what else do you do that might not be for England?"

He'd expected this, not perhaps expected it to be phrased so well, for the private and public lives to be intertwined so neatly, but sooner or later she would be the one to ask the questions Burne-Jones couldn't be arsed with.

"I haven't pulled a private job in years. Not since Cambridge in fact, and even then it was matter of vengeance rather than profit. My rather peculiar talents are, for the time being, at the service of Alec and Her Majesty. Many things are tempting. I still size up opportunities, I mentally 'case the joint' rather a lot. It's almost impossible not to walk into a room and look for the safe or tot up the value of the silverware. But that's just a hobby, keeping my mind sharp. And of course it's all temptation, but I'm not Oscar Wilde. I can resist temptation."

Madge smiled at this.

"Can you resist temptation, Joe, can you really? And why do you say 'for the time being'?"

"I won't be doing this for ever. Sooner or later Secret England will be through with me or I with it."

"And then, what will you do then?"

"I don't know. That's the risk I take, and the risk Judy shares."

"And Berlin, Joe. What was Berlin all about?"

At last.

"Oh . . . that wasn't thieving . . . that was . . . that was like watching a horse race and knowing it wouldn't be interesting without a bet on the side . . . Alec had left me on my own for a year . . . it was simply the only game in town."

"A game that ended with you getting a bullet in your belly."

"Don't worry about that, Madge. No one will ever get the drop on me again. From now on I shoot first and ask questions later."

"Hmm," she said. "Is that Roy Rogers or Hopalong Cassidy you're quoting?"

At that they both burst out laughing.

Madge stood up.

"Joe, give your new mother-in-law a hug."

And not once had she asked about his "people."

# §171

He bought a ring from a Piggy-wig — they took it away and were married next day by the Turkey who lives on the hill. That was the way it seemed to Wilderness — they had set

sail for unknown shores, young lovers in a
pea-green boat, and landed as Mr. and Mrs.
Holderness. It was all dreamlike, too dreamlike to be quite believable as real.

# §172

The honeymoon was brief. A single weekend.

On the morning of Monday September 5,
the telephone at the side of the bed, installed
at Burne-Jones's insistence, rang until Judy
picked it up and shoved it at Wilderness with
a muttered "Pa," and sank back beneath the
sheets.

"Get out to Heathrow, you're booked on
the eleven o'clock to Orly."

"What's up?"

"Karel Szabo got out of prison last week.
He got on a ferry to Calais on Saturday. No
problem with that. Full remission after all.
From there he caught a train to Paris. French
lost him at the Gare du Nord. Silly sods at
the Deuxième were looking out for a single
man — and he's travelling with a woman."

"What woman?"

"All in the file. There'll be a courier on your
doorstep in five minutes. Chop-chop, old
man."

Wilderness leaned over Judy and dropped
the phone back into its cradle. Whispered in
what he thought might be her ear, hidden by
the sheets.

"I think we might really be married after all. He just called me 'old man.' "

"Well," said in an irate if muffled voice. "Perhaps one old man ought to give a bit of a break to another old man and leave him alone on his fucking honeymoon!"

"There's worse. He's sending me to Paris."

He headed for the bathroom, just as she threw back the sheets and yelled, "Well, fuck you . . . old man!"

He read the file in the back of a cab, on the way to Heathrow.

He knew a lot about Szabo. Thanks to Rada. He, and the other creators of "the bomb" — Fermi, Szilard, Oppenheimer, Teller, Borg, et al — had fascinated Rada. They had, she said, made the world anew in unleashing the power to unmake it. Their lives and deeds had formed the bulk of the fattest file she had given him: the one marked "Armageddon."

Marte Mayerling was less known to him. Hardly even a name. Just the hint of a memory and the appeal of coincidence. Her file, like Szabo's, had several photographs, group and solo. Marte in middle age, a blurry photograph from a shaky surveillance camera told him next to nothing, but Marte in her twenties . . .

He called Judy from the airport. A security risk he thought, but a small one.

"Would you go into my study —"

"That pit you laughably call a study."

"And dig out one of my old folders. One of those Rada Lyubova gave me."

"Now. There's a name we haven't heard in a while. You used to talk about her so much I almost felt I'd met her. Which file?"

"Armageddon."

"OK. Might take a couple of minutes. Just hang on?"

She took more than five.

"Really Wilderness, you must learn to be tidy, just a bit more ordered."

"But you found it?"

"Yes. What is it in particular?"

"A photograph Rada clipped from the *New York Times*. 1937. The Bohr Institute Particle Physics Conference. There should be an identical photograph I added myself. But the text on that will be in Danish."

"OK. Got 'em."

"Front row centre. Niels Bohr, seated. Am I right?"

"That's what it says on the card, so to speak."

"And Bohr being a bit of a gent, he has the only two women in the photo seated either side of him?"

"Yep. Old-fashioned manners. The blokes stand and the ladies get to sit. And no one gets to put their foot on the tiger's head."

"On his right . . . a woman of about sixty. Lise Meitner?"

"Nothing wrong with your memory so far."

"And the woman on his left? Much younger, about twenty-five or so? Seated in front of a skinny young man called Peter-Jürgen von Hesse. What's her name?"

A long pause he found all but intolerable.

"It's really rather worn. Folded, faded . . . you know . . . but it looks like Mayerling. Let me check on the Danish one. Yes. Marte Mayerling. Name rings a bell. Does it do that for you too?"

"Oh yes, the whole Nine Tailors clanging in my ears."

"Jolly good. Now, how am I?"

"Eh?"

"Just ask me, Wilderness. Go on, try!"

"But I saw you not three hours ago."

She put the phone down on him.

# §173

It meant nothing. It was coincidence. He was flattered that his memory had been good enough to spot her, annoyed that he had never quite bothered to learn her name.

Nothing in her file told him why she had set off for who-knows-where with Szabo. Like him she was a naturalised British citizen and Wilderness could not see the necessity to flee or the profit in it.

Burne-Jones had said, "It's just a tail. Follow. Observe. Make no approach. You're not out to arrest them. We have no power to arrest. For all we know they're off to Monte Carlo for the roulette or Klosters for the skiing. Just stop the French from making more hash of it than they usually do. Oh, and take your gun."

He'd packed his .25 Baby Browning — a gun Burne-Jones told him wouldn't stop a dopey rabbit — successor to his Sauer 38H. The Browning tucked neatly beneath his jacket, more so than the Sauer. A generous cut by his tailor and you'd never know he was wearing a shoulder holster with the Browning in it. And then . . . he'd never had to fire it. He kept in practice — service regulations demanded that — but he'd never had to shoot a dopey rabbit or anything more vicious than a cardboard target.

The flic who met him at Orly in an old black Citroën had good news.

"They're in a small hotel in the Marais. Rue du Temple. Third arrondissement. Mr. and Mrs. Schmidt, would you believe?"

What was it Groucho Marx had said? Smythe is just Smith with a Y and fooled nobody? Surely the same applied to Schmidt? But if they had seen fit to bluff their names, then it was indicative — they were running away, not sauntering on. And if they had fake passports . . . then someone was assisting.

He spent a dull Monday afternoon watching Szabo and Mayerling play at being tourists. Sat outside Le Mistral bookshop for an hour while they browsed. Made himself inconspicuous behind a copy of *Paris Match,* half a dozen tables away in a barn-sized restaurant in Montparnasse.

By the time he had gumshoed them back to their hotel, the flic was waiting for him in the black Citroën. He'd been inside and questioned the proprietor.

"They're only collecting bags. They're booked on this evening's Orient Express to Venice. They'll probably just get a cab to the Gare de Lyon."

"What time?"

"Leaves at ten thirty. They're in compartment twelve, coach four."

"I'll get a cab there now. You follow them."

"Way ahead of you."

He handed Wilderness an envelope with a Wagon-Lits reservation in his name. Held up a receipt for him to sign.

"Who do I bill?"

"I don't care," Wilderness replied. "So long as it's not me."

"I need a name for the chit."

"Winston Churchill."

"Ah . . . that will annoy everyone very nicely. Sign here, Winston."

"Were you followed today?'

"No. And you?"

"Not that I could tell. But if they are travelling as Smith or Smythe, or whoever next, sooner or later someone, the someone who provided the passports and made the bookings, is bound to show up. Watching his investment after all."

"Perhaps he will put in an appearance in Venice?"

"Perhaps. But I doubt very much whether Venice is their final destination."

Observation work had always bored Wilderness. So often it led nowhere. Too often it meant a dusty, disused flat, a tape recorder and a pair of binoculars. First-class sleeper on the Orient Express was at least a step up. Just a touch of Graham Greene or Agatha Christie . . . "and ze murderer is . . . all of you!"

Long before they reached Milan he was bored stiff.

Szabo and Mayerling were all but unfathomable. As fleeing spies they seemed not to know how to play the game. They had neither caution nor suspicion. Noddy and Big Ears could have trailed Szabo and Mayerling. As runaway lovers they seemed not to know the game was even afoot — they neither canoodled nor did they smooch. Not so much as a stolen kiss or a peck on the cheek. Paris was made for lovers, arguably so was the Orient Express. Instead they talked intensely in German, and they talked shop — physics, physics, mathematics, mathematics, physics. He longed for Charles Boyer or Margaret

Lockwood to enter stage left and put a cat among the pigeons, strike love to spark among the particles.

In Venice they boarded a vaporetto, heading clockwise along the top curve of the Grand Canal's lazy S. It was slow enough for him to follow on foot, but the Grand Canal was hardly the Seine with a walkable bank — yet the vaporetto was big enough for him to board the same vessel and lose himself at the back.

The boat stopped within sight of the Accademia Bridge and suddenly he knew where they were heading, it made sense and nonsense. He'd heard that the old Russian embassy had been turned into a hotel — he'd not set eyes on it since his one visit towards the end of 1949. Another fleeting, inconsequential Burne-Jones mission. But as the vaporetto glided past he knew the building at once. A beautiful piece of faded glory. Too nice to be an embassy, and far too nice to be a Russian embassy. An iron-fenced canal frontage and a leafy courtyard of climbing vines that simply cried out for little round café tables and a beaker full of the warm south. Someone in the KGB had a sense of humour.

To follow them into the hotel would be a gamble. He found a café and thought through his options over a couple of shots of espresso — would there be anyone watching at this stage, what chance that whoever it was would spot him for what he was, and who should he be? He riffled through his collection of passports. Concluded his best fake was to be a colonial. No hammy accent, just a bit of plum in his voice and a South African passport. He phoned the hotel and booked a room. Assuming they were still playing the tourist, he'd give them an hour or so to clean up and get out into the warmth of a Venetian summer evening.

The signature above his in the book as he signed in read "Prof. Heinrich Behrmann & wife," and gave Dresden as a home address. He handed over his South African passport. As the desk clerk looked through it, Wilderness scanned the pigeonholes looking for the blue cover and yellowy-gold lettering of a DDR passport, paler than a British one, as flimsy-looking as an American. There it was. Room number 4. The paper trail had been set up rather well. A new identity with every change of hotel, and the latest told him where they were going next. He'd no idea why such a roundabout route had been chosen, when there were trains that went direct — perhaps for no better reason than pleasure, after all Szabo had spent seven years in prison — but without doubt, tomorrow or the day after Professor and Mrs. Behrmann would be on a train for Vienna, via Villach and Graz, and he'd put his money on them crossing the Iron

Curtain at Bratislava. Bratislava was spook paradise. Austria and Czechoslovakia met there, a bridge across the Danube — Hungary was a short drive away — it was a jumping-off point for the Soviet bloc.

A quick search of their room confirmed most of this — two tickets for Vienna the day after tomorrow and a reservation at the Imperial. Time to fade into the background. He'd leave a day ahead, follow from the front, call Burne-Jones from the embassy in Vienna and be at the Imperial by the time they arrived. Anyone looking out for him in Vienna, and he was fairly certain that that was where their man would show up, would not be expecting him to arrive first. He'd spend just the one night in Venice and keep as far away from them as possible. A night off in Venice would scarcely be a hardship. All he had to do was lose Szabo and Mayerling for a few hours.

He crossed over to Cannaregio, to the old Jewish ghetto. It was the last place anyone seeking the sights would ever go. It no more got tourists than the Mile End Road, and with any luck the food would be much the same. Kosher food wasn't a mystery — he'd eaten at Blooms in the East End of London countless times. You could keep your champagne and caviar, he was happy with chopped liver and matzoh ball soup.

Over the menu pasted to the window of a small restaurant, past the knishes and the pastrami, he caught sight of them, seated at a table along the back wall. All he had to do was lose them for a night.

Wrong, wrong, wrong.

He lingered a fraction too long, long enough to be intrigued by the fact that Mayerling's habitually sour puss was approaching something that resembled a smile. For a moment they were looking straight at one another. Then her head turned away, one hand reached out and covered Szabo's, and he realised that he might have misread them all along, might have mistaken the nature of their tangible intensity, that logic, argument, and discourse whilst lost on him might in themselves be expressive of feeling — the romance of formulae — and that rather than defecting they might simply be eloping.

He walked back in the direction of Dorsoduro and settled for *menu turistico* — rubbery pasta and half a bottle of overpriced Chianti.

# §174

Vienna, like the rest of Austria, had about a month to go before its independence was finally re-established. After the Anschluss, conquest, occupation . . . reparation . . . aid . . . treaties . . . any day now, the zones — American, British, French, and Russian — which had lasted more than ten years would be abolished, the forces of occupation, down to less than a hundred thousand, would withdraw and Austria would become the odd man of Europe . . . neutral by common consent, outside any sphere of influence . . . the ambivalence of aggressor/victim finally shuffled off into history.

Gus Fforde was a rogue. Wilderness spotted him as a rogue at first sight. Gus Fforde was also First Secretary at the embassy in Vienna. His office was chaos, a warren of packing cases and cardboard boxes.

"Please excuse the mess. I only got here a few days ago myself. We're going legit," he said. "No more delegations or military commissions . . . a full-blown embassy . . . diplomatic bags, cocked hats and sashes . . . the whole caboodle. It'll just take a little time."

Wilderness produced his warrant, said he needed to see the duty Intelligence Officer.

"Well," said Fforde. "Until one actually gets here I rather think that might be me. What can I do for you?"

"A secure line to London, perhaps?"

"Ah . . . you may find us not exactly up to scratch on the cloak-and-dagger stuff yet. I can get you on the scrambler but it would be as well if anyone you refer to is called Smith . . . in fact . . . if you could talk in riddles . . ."

Wilderness was put through to Burne-Jones

in his office.

"Vienna? Via Venice?" Burne-Jones sounded mildly incredulous.

"Just what I was thinking," Wilderness said. "They might just be two lovers running away. But for one thing . . . someone's laid out a good paper trail for them, and someone's paying for all this."

"What do you propose?"

"That I stick with them until I know who. If I'm right they'll get on a train across to Bratislava in a day or two. And their banker will make contact before they do."

"I agree. But that's where it ends. If they get on a train to Bratislava don't follow. Only if they don't get on a train or they get a train to somewhere else do you follow. And if their man surfaces, you make no contact with him. Understand me, Joe. No contact."

# §175

Fforde said, "Let me buy you dinner. You may be wholly unexpected, but you are my first diplomatic guest. Besides, it's all the same bloody pot isn't it? I put in a chit or you put in a chit. Six of one half a dozen of the other."

They went to Café Landtmann. A traditional Viennese dinner of boiled beef, over which Wilderness filled him in.

"Of course I remember Szabo. Who could

ever forget him? Did us no end of harm with the Americans. I thought they'd never shut up about him."

"Yet," said Wilderness. "Wherever he goes no one seems to recognise him."

"Mind you. Can't say I remember her at all. What did you say her name was?"

"Marte Mayerling."

"Nope. Not so much as a tinkle in the old brain box. Now, what exactly are we supposed to do with this pair?"

"Just watch. It's all I've done since they left Paris. They have every right to travel."

"On false passports?"

"Hardly our problem. We're watching for the simplest of reasons. Everything Szabo knows he told the Russians just after the war. Almost everything Mayerling knows is academic and can probably be accessed in any one of half a dozen journals that have published her work. They can't teach the Russians anything they don't already know."

"Then why are we even watching?"

"The Russians can have them, that's a given. It's any third party that bothers London. Burne-Jones has sent me to see who's paying for the joyride, that's all he wants to know. If it's Russia he'll just say fine . . . and if it's not . . ."

Wilderness shrugged away the end of his sentence.

"But who?"

"Gus, name me a country that doesn't want the atom bomb."

"Iceland, San Marino, Andorra . . . the Vatican."

"No Gus, a real country, not a provincial town masquerading as a country . . . and I think the Vatican probably does want the bomb."

"So what are we talking about? The Arab bomb? The Chinese bomb? Or just the highest bidder?"

"I've no idea and I couldn't give a damn. But the highest bidder? No. Money doesn't interest this pair. They act on principle."

"So what you're saying is that your job is to see them safely into the hands or our enemy."

"Yes. That sums it up nicely."

And Fforde said, "Supposing the Russians don't get that?"

# §176

On the way back to the Imperial, Fforde said, "I could get you into the Sacher. They're just about up and running again. We've had it since the end of the war. Of course, the Russians had the Imperial. They've not been gone more than a matter of weeks, and it stands to reason they'll have packed the place with bugs."

"Then I'll be wary of that. But, no thanks. I need to be where I can see them. This is a snark hunt. It'll be over in a day or two. I'll hang up my gun and we'll prop up a bar together. Meanwhile . . . I might need a camera."

Three mornings, three breakfasts later Szabo and Mayerling checked out of the Imperial. Wilderness anticipated and bagged a cab to the Nordbahnhof ahead of them. No one, as far as he had seen, had yet made contact, and turning over their room had yielded nothing new — who after all would bother to book for the thirty-minute train ride to the border? It could only go wrong if he had guessed wrong.

He hadn't. Ten minutes after he had arrived, Szabo and Mayerling got out of a cab at the station to be met by a short, stout, Slavic-looking man. At last.

It seemed to Wilderness that Russia made its KBG-niks on a production line. This bloke was just a younger version of Yuri Myshkin — the same peasant sturdiness, the same look of joy in cunning and mistrust. Smiling as he stripped the rings off your fingers. Another apparatchik thug.

There was a formal handshake — Wilderness didn't think they'd ever met him before — then they were briskly escorted through the barrier to the 11:40 morning train for Bratislava.

He kept back, and with the little pre-war Leica II he'd borrowed from Fforde got half

571

a dozen clear shots of the man in profile as he put Szabo and Mayerling on the train. As he clicked for the last time, the man turned full-face, and for a second Wilderness thought he had seen him. But he turned back to Szabo. Shook hands a second time. Waited as the train pulled out of the station. A fond uncle packing the kids off home after a month in the country. It was nothing. He'd seen nothing. Wilderness flagged a cab and went back to the embassy. If Burne-Jones's team back in London couldn't find a match in their records, so what? He'd no doubts. The bloke was KGB. Written all over him. He should know. He'd never forget that pudgy little face, with its almond eyes and ruptured blood vessels, looming over him — the impish grin, the bitter taste of morphine.

The job was over. All that knowledge, all that destructive, subatomic power safely delivered into the hands of an enemy who had no further use for it. Priceless and worthless.

# §177

Fforde gave every impression of being bored. A new job, a new country and he seemed to crave company.

Wilderness handed over the Leica, said, "Let's get it developed and the prints off to London in the bag."

Fforde dropped it into the middle drawer of his desk and said, "I'm famished. Let's nip out for lunch."

They had lunch.

After lunch he said, "Do you fancy dinner at Landtmann's again? Bags of stuff on the menu I haven't tried yet."

He was like a kid in a sweetshop the day toffee came off the ration.

Wilderness went back to the hotel. Stripped off his jacket. Caught sight of himself in the wardrobe mirror. Shoulder holsters looked absurd, a cross between a straitjacket and a bra. The job was over. He slung the holster into his suitcase. He couldn't do that with the gun. It was a Burne-Jones rule. If you're not carrying it, it's still your responsibility. You do not lose it, you do not let it get stolen or otherwise mislaid.

In the bathroom was a mirror-fronted medicine cabinet, set flush with the wall. Neat enough for him not to have realised it was a cabinet until his second night there. Inside were the first-aid basics — aspirin, cotton wool and Elastoplast.

He tore off two long strips of Elastoplast and taped his Baby Browning to the back of the mirror. The maid would not be back until after he checked out in the morning, and if he couldn't spot that there was a cupboard, why would anyone else? He wiped his own fingerprints off the mirror with bog roll.

# §178

Over fish soup and grilled venison, Fforde missed England.

"But you've only been here a fortnight."

"Not the point, old man. It's a matter of how long I've spent in England. Welsh Guards during the war. A spell in Washington, two years in Lisbon, a year in Ankara . . . there are times I feel I've lost touch with the country I'm supposed to represent."

"I've not been there too much myself the last few years, but I was there most of '52 to '53."

"Lucky bugger! You were there for the coronation?"

"Yes . . . but if you let me finish. You've missed nothing. England's . . . stuck."

"Stuck?"

"Moribund."

"Yeeees . . . awfully good word, 'moribund.' I had rather come to the same conclusion."

"They're still fighting a war that ended ten years ago . . . in their minds at least . . . and on the cinema screen . . . and when they win that war, the war inside the head, they expect to find England just as it was in '39."

This set Fforde off. A thesis on an unlamented, lost England. Against all appearances Fforde was a bit of a radical and had used his serviceman's vote in 1945 to vote Labour, to vote against class and tradition, for the

New Britain whose birth seemed to require a gestation longer than an elephant's.

Wilderness listened. It wasn't boring. It reminded him of the conversations he had with Burne-Jones, but once he'd shot his bolt with "moribund" it was not an argument to which he felt he could contribute much.

Over the course of the meal, they moved from red wine to white, to Tokay, to brandy.

Outside the embassy, Fforde suggested they breakfasted together. Wilderness wondered if he could cope with the intensity of another Fforde meal and Fforde thesis, but he liked Gus so he said yes and walked on to the Imperial.

I am not drunk, he told himself, with a drunk's acute sense of euphemism, I am tipsy.

Perhaps it was the booze. Perhaps it was the innate connection between being off duty and off guard. The first blow to the belly doubled him up, and the second to the face sent him to the floor scarcely conscious. He'd just about taken in the fact of the attack when he found himself dragged by his shirt collar to the bathroom. His eyes returned to focussing in time to see the bath full of water before his head was plunged in.

When he thought he was dying, hands yanked him back up, he sucked in air and as his head went down again a voice uttered one of the few words that was common to most European languages, "Idiot."

After the third ducking, the hands let him go, and he fell against the side of the bath wheezing.

He looked up. The little Russian was sitting on the painted wicker chair by the bathroom door — a semiautomatic in his right hand.

"Идиот," he said again. "You treat me like an idiot."

Wilderness got to his feet. Stripped off his sodden jacket. He felt blood on his face and in his mouth. He leaned over the basin, spitting. The gun stayed on him.

"At the Gare du Nord, you are out in the open as though you think you are invisible. On the Orient Express you linger over your meals and gaze out of the window as though you have nothing better to do."

Wilderness stuck two fingers in his mouth and wiggled a loose tooth. Then he cupped water in his palm and rinsed a pink trail into the basin. He looked in the mirror. This bloke wasn't wearing gloves, and there were no prints on the mirror. He'd been very careful in his search and wiped it down — or he hadn't looked.

"In Venice you . . . you English have a bird word for it . . . you *swan* around like a tourist . . ."

"Bamdid," Wilderness said.

"Что?"

"Band-Aid."

The Russian just waved the gun.

Wilderness opened the cupboard. His Browning was still taped to the back of the mirror. The Russian could have found it. He could have emptied the magazine. He could have stuck the gun back up. But, then, the point of taping it up had been that any movement of the tape would probably show. It looked to be as he had left it, but there was really only one way to find out. He'd know by the weight as soon as he had it in his hand.

He took out the roll of Elastoplast and closed the door.

The Russian set down his gun in his lap and lit up a cigarette. Cocky, casual, but he could grab the gun in a split second.

"And in the Nordbahnhof this morning, you practically waved a camera in my face. And still you think I do not notice you. English, you treat me like an idiot."

Wilderness tore off a strip, slapped it on the cut on his right cheek.

The discourse rattled on. "Idiot, amateur, dilettante, бабочка." Accomplished bore finds captive audience. Indeed, it occurred to Wilderness that the bugger might have gone to the trouble of sandbagging him simply to be able to give him a piece of his mind.

He opened the cupboard door, put the roll of Elastoplast back, pulled the Browning free and aimed.

The Russian just grinned — cigarette in his left hand, fingertips of his right resting on his gun. He took another long drag on his cigarette, exhaled a plume of utterly contemptuous smoke.

"You're doing it again. Treating me like an idiot. I know you English. You're all just amateurs. Play the game chaps, play the game. Sticky wicket, googly, a maiden over. You think of Agincourt and cannot begin to imagine Stalingrad. What an absurd nation you English are. I know all about you. Gentlemen and players. Professionalism is vulgar, practice is cheating. Gentlemen and players? Ha! You won't shoot. Your kind never does."

Wrong, wrong, wrong.

■ ■ ■ ■

# III
## THEN WE
## TAKE BERLIN

■ ■ ■ ■

So we beat on, boats against the current,
borne back ceaselessly into the past.
F. Scott Fitzgerald: *The Great Gatsby*
1925

# §179

*New York:* May 1963
*The Gramercy*

Frank had drifted in early, as though there were more on his mind than he was admitting and he admitted nothing.

Wilderness was still shaving, half a mask of white foam across his cheeks. Frank lay on the bed, leafing through a copy of *Life* magazine and singing not quite tunelessly to himself.

"You're doing swell, you'll go to hell, you can be sure of Shell."

Over and over again.

"Frank?" Wilderness called from the bathroom.

"Hear you loud and clear kid."

"Steve's wife's aunt. Hannah Schneider, right?"

"Right."

"A Jew?"

"Is the bear Catholic, does a pope shit in the woods? Of course she's a Jew. You think a guy like Steve would marry outside the tribe? Hasn't seen the inside of a synagogue in thirty years, but he'd never marry a shicksa. Personally I don't get it. Who talks religion in the sack? Even if you fuck on Sunday."

Wilderness ignored this. Frank at his crudest. If the USA ever permitted the advertising of condoms, Frank was their man.

"Steve's been here how long?"

"Born here. Round about 1900 or 1901. His old man came over from Ruritania or somewhere in the nineties. One o' them pogrom things I guess. Changed the family name during the First War."

"And his wife. That is, Debbie's family?"

"About the same time I reckon. I heard her life story ten times over. Damn woman never shuts up."

"Aha . . . but the aunt got left behind . . . somehow."

"Yep."

"Where?"

Wilderness heard the magazine rustling stop. As though he had Frank's attention for the first time.

"Whaddya mean where?"

"Germany?"

"Germany? Sure."

"Berlin?"

"I guess so."

"And she survived?"

"Obviously."

"In Berlin, during the war? Frank, how many Jews do you think survived in Berlin during the war?"

"None. I guess."

"Actually, a couple of thousand survived. Against the odds but they did."

"You don't say?"

"Yep. I met some of them. When I was living with Nell."

"There's a blast from the past. Nell Breakheart. Old flames never die, eh Joe? 'You're doing swell, you're fucking Nell . . .' Well . . . you may be right, but I never met any Jews in Berlin."

The magazine was rustling again. When Wilderness stepped out of the bathroom, Frank was angling the magazine sideways to take in an advert.

It was hard to tell. Frank was indifferent to so many things it was often impossible to be certain whether or not he'd just given you the brush-off.

# §180

They took breakfast downstairs in the Gramercy. They had it almost to themselves. Frank let his guard down, an old, familiar air of who-gives-a-damn.

Between coffees Frank slid a passport and a driving licence across the table to him.

Wilderness picked them up.

"James Johnson?"

"Easy to remember."

"From Hoboken?"

"New York without being New York. It's across the river in New Jersey. Sinatra's home town. You used to do a good impression of Sinatra. Ought to be an easy accent if you ever need it."

Wilderness leafed through the passport.

"It's fake?"

"Of course it's fake. But it's a good one. Guys at Checkpoint Charlie will never spot it, ours or theirs."

"Then why do you need me?"

"Excuse me?"

"If you can get hold of fake passports this good, why not just get one to the old woman and have her walk across? Why bother with the tunnel?"

"No can do. She speaks no English, so it would have to be a West German passport. And she'd never stand up to questions. Retired schoolteacher. Toughest ordeal of her life was probably facing the PTA."

"That and living through the Allied bombing of Berlin and a secret life as a Jew in Nazi Germany."

"Whatever. You guys have a phrase for it . . . 'Wouldn't say boo to a gander'? Something like that. Anyway, there are Kraut fakes around, maybe even good ones, but even if I could get my hands on one the Ivans are wise to them. Getting East Berliners out has become something of a sport — maybe that's understating it . . . maybe it's a badge of honour among the new generation of Germans. Kids for whom the war is a distant memory, if that. Bunches of 'em have been trying to get Easterners out ever since the wall went up. The fake passport scam worked for a while, but it's over. It's become a one-way ticket to a labour camp. I couldn't risk that. Besides . . ."

He slid a brown envelope across to Wilderness. Wilderness opened it — a postcard-size photograph of an unsmiling young man of about twenty.

"Manfred Oppitz. Student of Political Science, and leader of half a dozen idealistic kids who have been tunnelling. You need to meet with him."

"Tunnelling?"

"Yep. Got twenty-nine out before the Russians shut 'em down. Twenty-fuckin-nine, Joe! And now . . . every sewer gate and manhole between East and West is welded shut."

"I don't need tunnellers, I have a tunnel."

"I was coming to that. You do need this kid. The tunnel may well be intact, after all . . . has anyone been down it since you? I doubt it. But the Tiergarten end has been built on."

"You could have told me this yesterday."

"It's not that bad. It's just a car park for

the zoo. Since you and I stomped around there the zoo's got a lot bigger."

"Just a car park?"

"Sure. It's not as if they built the fuckin' elephant house on it. A sheet of blacktop. That's all. Last time you shifted tons of rubble — the remains of the goddam flak tower."

"Last time I had Fat Stanley, the Sappers Corps, and a couple of bulldozers."

"Fat Stanley? Whaddya know? Jeez. I had totally forgotten him. But, no matter. Don't worry. This ought to be what you call a doddle and I call a cinch. You set it up. The kids do the digging. You get ten grand. They get another old Kraut, another feather in their caps."

"In a municipal car park? With traffic cops and Joe Public to contend with?"

"You'll think of a way. You always did. A few deutschmarks scattered around, grease a few palms, a few more fake documents, knock out another batch of inky smudges. Come on Joe, earn your ten grand."

"And where will you be?"

"Good point. Goooood point. No real reason I should be in Berlin is there? At least not until Fraulein Schneider is out. London, I'll be in London. At the Connaught. Call me when it's over."

It was an inept choice of phrase, almost custom-made to remind Wilderness of the relationship that he and Frank used to have, "Call me when it's over." He could almost see him picking flecks of dust off his trouser turnups.

"Yeah. I'll do that. Although I'd hate to drag you away from dinner at the Ivy."

Frank was stuffing his face with ham and eggs, oblivious to sarcasm.

" 'S'OK. Just leave a message."

# §181

*West Berlin:* June 1963

Frank's arrangements did not skimp. Wilderness might have chosen somewhere quieter, somewhere off the main drag, but he could not argue with Frank's generosity in picking the Kempinski Hotel. It was big and bold and shiny. Its name in huge letters along the curving roofline. It was a part of the new Berlin that was coming into being. Berlin never arrived. Berlin was always in the process of arriving, always giving birth, and by now Wilderness had concluded it would be that way for ever. A process rather than a place.

In 1948 the Kempinski had been the ruin at the end of their street, bombed into oblivion by the RAF.

Wilderness had checked in, had a martini in the bar, and after a second martini in the bar had felt nostalgic enough to want to wander down Fasanenstraße and look at the old apartment block he and Eddie Clark had lived in. He'd not done this on the last trip or the one before or the one before that. It had gone, and in its place something new was rising up behind the sheeting and the scaffolding and the labour pains. The RAF and the Luftwaffe had seemed lethal at the time, yet were as nothing compared to the post-war municipal wrecking ball. But . . . the synagogue had risen again. Very little of the original remained, but somehow the portico arch had been incorporated into a new building — it was now called the *Jüdisches Gemeindehaus* — in a modern style Wilderness could only think of as "chunky." That was the thing about the new Berlin, it was "chunky." Modernist slabs of flat concrete and plate glass that could leave the observer craving the ragged beauty of ruins — but Albert Speer had planned for ruins, had imagined all his grandiose designs in a state of decay many years hence and, if ruins were what one craved, Berlin still had enough of those to go round.

He drifted on, southwards. At the far end of the street he stood on the corner of Lietzenburger Straße, once the non-line between the American Sector and the British, in front of the old Imperial Hotel. A Berlin summer evening, a time to stand and stare. The perfect post-martini, pre-Copernican moment — to be standing on a street comer and feel the world revolve around you.

What surprised him now had surprised him on every visit since he had left in '48. Trees. He'd never get used to trees in the Berlin streets. Living trees. Trees with leaves. Trees in bustin' June blossom. Trees not waiting to be chopped up for fuel. Unter den Linden still hadn't restored its lime trees — perhaps the DDR never would — but West Berlin had trees, a waving, rustling sea of green.

On the other side of the street a short, stout-ish man — overdressed for the time of year, buttoned up to his chin in a dark green overcoat, a Tyrolean-style hat on his head — was staring back at him. Wilderness was about to cross when a pale yellow tram shot between them and blocked his view. When the tram had passed, the man had gone. What lingered was that the man had looked like Yuri Myshkin.

# §182

At Checkpoint Charlie first the Americans and then the Russians had turned over every page in his passport scrutinised his visa and waved him through without requiring a word from him. He might never get to try out his American accent.

He'd driven his rented Opel Rekord out to Pankow. The car was grey, relieved by a taste-less streak of blood red along each side. And

591

he'd parked in front of this eight-storey slab of people's apartments.

It was just another plain block of flats in the Soviet style that had made East Germany a byword for grey and boring. Both words were too often invoked to describe not just its architecture but also its food, its people, and its culture. Wilderness had nothing against any of these. The flats seemed at least as practical as the tower blocks now dotted around East London and rising up like triffids all the way out to Dagenham — the people looked little different from the way they'd looked at the end of the war — fatter perhaps, but still fed on spuds and cabbage, a literally "grey" diet lacking protein and vitamins that dulled the skin and took the shine out of their eyes. Culture? Well, in the post-war carve-up they got Brecht. We got . . . God knows, he loathed the "university" wit of Kingsley Amis, he loathed that sodding professional Yorkshireman John Braine . . . perhaps the hope of England rested on this new bloke Alan Sillitoe. He had read a couple of his books and thought they had bite. None of 'em were Brecht, but did Brecht make up for spuds and cabbage?

He was daydreaming. Found himself staring up at the windows. He knew why. It was the name. It was the sort of thing only new, revolutionary, or self-inventing countries ever bothered with. They named streets after heroes. Even literary heroes. England seemed not to want to acknowledge its heroes and settled for naming everything after monarchs or battles — Victoria, Waterloo . . . one day some innocent tourist might enquire who King Euston was or where the Battle of Euston had taken place. This was Arnold-Zweig-Straße, named for the novelist of the Great War who'd gone on to be something big in East Germany's arts, president of this, chairman of that. Somewhere in the East Zweig might still be alive. He'd be eighty-ish. He might even be living on Arnold-Zweig-Straße. Or if not then he'd probably be quite at home on Ibsenstraße or Zolastraße. Kingsley-Amistraße? God forbid.

Apartment 606 was not on the sixth floor, it was on the fifth. Wilderness stopped dreaming, stopped guessing and rang the bell. A slow grinding followed as the clockwork mechanism ran down with no sound much resembling a bell — but it was enough to bring Hannah Schneider to her door.

She looked at him across the chain that might keep out another old lady but wouldn't last two seconds against a jackboot.

"Herr Johnson?"

"Schubert," Wilderness said — the password he and Frank had agreed on.

Hannah Schneider just looked baffled, then a look of enlightenment flickered in the nut-brown eyes.

"Oh do forgive me . . . I am so unused to this sort of thing . . . *Der Erlkönig.* That is the reply?"

And the chain slid off, the door swung open.

*"Bitte."*

Every entrance was a world. Whether he'd been politely admitted by the front door or scrambled over the rooftops and in through a skylight, every entrance was a world, an invitation to a world made by someone else. A peeping tom's delight. A gallery of symbols and signs, a carousel of slides waiting on him to be deciphered and rearranged into meaning — the world in a room, a life in a dozen objects.

He turned around in the tiny sitting room, coming to face her.

The room told him next to nothing. It looked like a stage set. Like am dram at the Hornchurch Players. Furnished from a props cupboard. It was pared down to blankness. It was beyond the minimalist habits of people accustomed to living in small spaces — even then there were a hundred variations on a theme, from those who kept nothing that didn't serve a purpose, to those who hoarded everything, stacked everything and moved around in orderly piles of junk and clutter all but oblivious to it. This flat was spotless. Not a speck of dust. Not a cobweb. Not a smell of polish or disinfectant to mask emptiness or newness. As though it was uninhabited and had been vacuumed from top to bottom only hours before. The show flat in a sales brochure.

She was looking at him now. Leaning on a walking stick — a prop in both senses. Not quite smiling, as though it were too much effort. Waiting for him to speak. She spoke first.

"Can I get you a cup of coffee?"

It was the opposite of a Rada moment. Meeting Rada had become a benchmark in his life. Meeting any older woman automatically brought her and rather unfavourable comparisons to mind. No one ever measured up. Fraulein Schneider was a good-looking woman, who looked as though she had put on her makeup in the dark. The wig was silly. A grey bird's nest with darker hair peeping out beneath it. At least when Merle had worn wigs the disguise was effective. Fraulein Schneider's disguise simply drew attention to itself. The loose, flowery dress looked like something she'd never choose. The ratty cardigan with its woolly bobbles and holes at the elbows was a neat touch though.

"Yes," he said. "That would be nice."

"Please, be seated. I won't be long."

She leaned her walking stick against a chair, and switched from putting weight on it to walking unaided, without a limp or any hint of pain. He watched her through the arch that separated the living bit from the kitchen

595

bit. She lit a gas ring, stuck on a kettle and then opened a cupboard, then another and then a third and finally set out two mugs and a jar of instant coffee.

There was a picture of Steve and a woman he took to be Debbie on the sideboard. He'd seen an identical photograph in Steve's office. There were books on a shelf next to the gas fire, set in the wall. The selection seemed random. A battered hardback of one of Fontane's historical epics, a translation of Irwin Shaw's *The Young Lions,* Goethe's *Elective Affinities* — and a dozen more, all looking as though they had been bought by the yardage on a market stall. Visual ballast. The only thing that rang remotely true was there that there was a novel by Arnold Zweig — *Der Streit um den Sergeanten Grischa.* And how many copies of that had been printed East or West in the last forty years?

It was tempting to open the cupboards and peek inside drawers, but he knew that he'd find nothing. They'd all be empty.

She down opposite him. Set a small tray in front of him. Milk jug. Sugar bowl, teaspoons, and two mugs. They all looked new. He could see where she'd scraped the price tag off the jug with her thumbnail. No one was trying too hard. She sat in a room that reflected nothing of her. The invisible threads that might have connected her to her surroundings were not there. She touched, there was no other word for it . . . she touched nothing. She brought her own space with her, a translucent, almost visible pocket that surrounded her like a vacuum. She held herself too tightly, as though stitched and buttoned against an unwelcome reality. If he asked her now how she had survived in Berlin what would she say? Would there be a prepared story of being hidden by Aryans and dodging *Greifers,* or of false identity papers or submitting to a tribunal and convincing them she wasn't Jewish. There was not a single item in the room to say she was. And in his East End childhood, where every other neighbour was a Jew, Wilderness didn't think he'd ever met one, however godless, of whom that could be said.

"May I say right now, at the beginning, that I am very grateful to you. To you, to Steven, and to his friend."

"Frank? You mean Frank Spoleto?"

"Yes, of course. Herr Spoleto. Such a kind man."

"But you've never met him."

"No . . . I never met him, but he has . . . arranged all this."

It seemed to Wilderness that she had barely withheld the gesture of an open hand sweeping the room. She was allowing him to think that she was referring to the operation. That Frank had brokered the deal. And Freud had led her almost to the edge of truth. That Frank had arranged all this in the most literal and immediate sense. Her "never met him" was a lie. Frank's implied "never met her" was just another unspoken lie.

"Will I have to wait long?"

"No," he said. "Not long. It may take a few days. Perhaps ten at the most. From the end of next week, be ready to travel. Pack a bag and leave it packed."

"A tunnel, I believe. Will I have to crawl? Will I get wet or dirty? I only ask as it might help to know what to wear."

"I can't tell you about dirt or damp at the moment. I need to check one or two things first. But, no you won't have to crawl."

He answered all her questions. Not once did she ask about Steve or Debbie, although he made it obvious he'd seen Steve recently. Not once did she show anticipation about America, about arriving in New York. Not once did she express any emotion about things or people she might leave behind. Her questions were precise and practical. He told her it would all run smoothly, and left it at that.

As he was leaving, on the threshold, she said, far too casually, "I suppose you will have much to do in the next few days?"

"Quite a lot," he replied and then added in English. "Wish me luck."

"Of course," she replied.

# §183

He was furious with Frank. Frank was shaft-
ing him again and was too damn lazy even to
do it well.

# §184

He went in search of Erno Schreiber. Erno
had not moved. Erno would never move. He
was still in the same building in Grünetümmlerstraße he was living in when Wilderness
first met him in 1947. He was lucky Berlin
had not demolished it around him.

"How long has it been, Joe?"

"Only a couple of years Erno. Your memory
must be playing up if it seems longer than
that."

"So, so . . . I am getting old. Rub it in, why
don't you."

He led Wilderness to the back of the room,
down corridors of newspapers. As big a tip as
ever. Wilderness could almost swear the pile
of magazines teetering on the tabletop was
the same one he'd seen in '61, '58, or '47.
Erno hadn't added to it. He'd probably taken
nothing off it. He hadn't even dusted.

Only the cat was new. Hegel had gone to
the great linen basket in the sky. This one
was tabby.

Erno put a match to a gas ring, set a kettle
to boil.

"What can I do for you, Joe?"

"Same old thing, Erno."

He handed him the American passport in the name of James Johnson.

"You want me to copy it?"

"No. I want to know who faked it."

Erno flicked on an anglepoise lamp. It shed its hoop of light onto his worktop, the only spotless point in the room, a fresh sheet of blotting paper every day — and yesterday's burnt.

Erno took several minutes to go through the passport. Every page under scrutiny.

"You go East on this?"

"Just once, so far."

He took a magnifying glass to the personal details page. After a minute or so more, he swapped this for a jeweller's eyepiece, and when he took that out he turned to Wilderness and said, "Fake? What fake? This is real."

"Real American? Made in America?"

"Pure Uncle Sam. Where did you get it?"

Wilderness paused. But Erno had never let him down.

"From Frank," he said.

Erno chuckled.

"Oh my God. You and Frank together again? Joe, Joe, Joe . . . he'll steal your trousers while you take a crap. He told you this was a fake? Now why would he want you to think that?"

"That's what I'm trying to figure out.

But . . . while I do, can you kit me out with another?"

"Of course. Another American?"

"No. Not American. I won't be using Checkpoint Charlie again. I'd rather use one of the others. Make me German."

"What would you rather be, West German or West Berliner?"

"West Berliner. I'll play safe. Better not to trust to my vanity over getting accents right. Make me from Berlin. I can still do a pretty good Berlin. I'll use . . . Bornholmer Straße . . . yes, Bornholmer Straße."

"The bridge? No problem. Now . . . age?"

"My age will do. Thirty-five."

"My, my. Joe. Almost the grown-up. Make tea while I find the Leica."

Erno pushed the curtain aside. Wilderness could hear him rummaging around in the next room as he poured boiling water onto tea leaves, an act he could never perform without thinking of rationing.

"Erno, while I'm running up a bill. There's one more thing."

"Ask."

"A gun. Automatic. Nine mill. Could you arrange that?"

"Cash?"

"Of course cash."

The curtain moved. Erno reappeared blowing the dust off his camera.

"If you'll settle for a 7.65 I have a Walther

601

PPK I could let you have. Unless of course you're trying to kill a grizzly bear."

"I'm not trying to kill anyone."

"Then you can have it later today."

"Make it the day after tomorrow, will you. A spare clip and a holster, if that's possible."

"Day after tomorrow. For sure. Going somewhere are you?"

# §185

On the landing, outside Erno's apartment, Wilderness glanced up the stairs.

"It's empty," said Erno, reading his mind. "Nell left in 1951. Since then a succession of young women. But right now it's empty. Take a look if memory has you in its grip. I am out of matches and must dash to the *Tabak* on the corner."

He ran down the stairs, lightly for a man of his age, and left Wilderness to make up his mind.

The door opened to a touch, swung inwards on emptiness, an emptiness he could fill to bursting.

There were four dents in the floorboards where their bed had stood. There was a line on the wall where Nell had hung a picture. No one had ever redecorated, but ten years and more of other people's occupancy had left no more trace of Nell than this thin line of dirt along the stained plaster. He could smell scent, the faint lingering odour of some woman's perfume. But that wasn't Nell. He couldn't remember the name of Nell's perfume any more, such was time and erasure, but this wasn't it.

He stood with his back to the window, his mind reconstructing the room his eye could not see. Here stood her desk, there her dressing table, and there the plaster statue on which she draped her scarves and hung her hats. Then he turned to the window — the window box in which Nell had grown straggly thyme and parsley, and in the summer of '48 three heads of lettuce, was still there, empty of soil, its boards splitting. He looked across into the window on the other side of the street, a room he had glanced into so many times without ever meaning to — it had been an old lady's apartment, trapped in the deep, dark colours and bloated fashions of the Empire, now completely stripped and redecorated in a garish yellow. And down into the street, a fantasy that he might see her returning home.

There was a small man on the opposite pavement. The same ridiculous goblin-green overcoat, but no Tyrolean hat. He ran for the stairs took them three at a time and hit the ground floor just as Erno was coming in the doorway.

"Did you see him?"

"Did I see who?"

He looked down the street. No man in a green coat. He looked down the nearest alley. Walked back to a perplexed Erno, hovering on the threshold.

"You didn't pass a little man, all in green."

Erno shrugged.

"I wasn't looking. Unless he was a horned goblin I doubt I would have noticed. All in green? Did I miss Rumpelstiltskin?"

# §186

He called Frank at the Connaught. But he'd take no risks with Frank.

"Stop what you're doing. We need to meet."

"Joe . . . not so fast. Why do we need to meet?"

"Not over the phone."

"Jesus H. Christ . . . OK. Where?"

"Where we met in '51."

"Fifty-one . . . fifty-one . . ."

Wilderness heard the penny drop like a threepenny bit into a pinball machine.

"Jesus, Joe! If you're worried you'll be overheard in Berlin you just picked the most bugged city in Europe. Every fucker listens in on every other fucker!"

"Maybe. But I know somewhere we won't be overheard. Just don't utter the name out loud."

"Sure. Sure. Like old times. I'll bring my cloak and dagger. And I'll be staying at the

Old Soviet Boarding House. Capisce?"

It was slang — spook slang from just after the war, but it told Wilderness exactly where to find Frank.

"Yes. Ten tomorrow morning."

"Do I get to eat breakfast first?"

Wilderness hung up.

# §187

There was a light summer rain falling on the Vienna Ringstraße when Wilderness met Frank outside the Imperial Hotel. Commandeered by the Germans before the war, draped in swastikas for Hitler's stay during the Anschluss, after the war the Imperial had housed the Soviet High Commission for several years — hence Frank's nickname for it. Lately it had been the site of one of the world's most unlikely *liaisons dangereuses*. Kennedy had met Khrushchev here a matter of weeks after the Cuban Missile Crisis. And in an earlier *liaison dangereuse* Wilderness had left a body in a bathroom on the fourth floor in 1955.

Frank looked at the drizzle and turned up his collar. He'd had time for at least one breakfast and belched into his fist.

"This better be good, Joe."

"How was your night, Frank? Hotel still full of Nazis?"

"What makes you think the fuckers ever

left? They run the joint. Just like they run half of Germany. Probably waving the denazification papers you issued to them."

"Very funny. Let's walk to the Metro, shall we?"

"Walk? I walked in New York for you. You think I fucking enjoy fucking walking. I came to talk not walk!"

All the same he followed.

Wilderness fended off his questions all the way to the Prater.

Only when he caught sight of the Ferris wheel did Frank realise where they were going.

"Up there? Again? Jesus, Joe . . . this is so fucking corny."

"Corny but quiet, and you can bet your last nickel it isn't bugged. You might be right Frank. Maybe everywhere in Vienna is bugged, but not the wheel."

The wheel was in poor shape. A shabby symbol of faded glory. Half the cars had been removed — the whole thing looked in need of de-rusting and painting — it seemed as though it had outlived Vienna. Wilderness didn't know how long it had stood here — since some world's fair at the end of another century? — but its age was showing.

Frank was smiling now, as though he'd finally heard the punch line at the end of a strung-out anecdote.

"Joe, Joe, Joe," he said as they car moved

skyward. "Always the cute stunts. Still. I can't complain. I was just the dry-goods guy, minding the store. You were always the one with the overactive imagination."

Wilderness looked at the ground receding, not at Frank. They were five degrees short of the zenith when the car stopped.

"Hey? You pay the guy to do this?"

Wilderness turned, looked at him, and nodded.

"Okay. So what now, is this where you slide open the door and tell me everyone down there is just some fucking ant and ask me if I'd really mind if one or maybe a dozen of them stop moving? If that's the movie we're in, then I want the line about four hundred years of democracy and the cuckoo clock."

"Right now the only thing you have in common with Orson Welles is that you're roughly the same shape, and you're both getting fatter."

"Well, fuck you. Don't bother with small talk and politeness. Get to the point."

"She's not seventy-five years old. She's not Steve's aunt. She doesn't live in that apartment. She's not a retired schoolteacher. She speaks English. She's Marte Mayerling. And she worked on the Manhattan Project and the atom bomb at Berkeley."

Frank sat down with a bump. He wasn't about to deny anything.

He fished around for a cigar in his pocket,

bit off the end, and lit up.

"How did you find out?"

"She's wearing a wig. It slips. Her makeup's OK, but not that good. She doesn't even know where the cups are in what you tell me is her own apartment . . . and . . . I recognised her."

"Jesus Christ."

"Did you think I wouldn't?"

"Joe, I can never be sure what you know. You always seemed to know more than was ever good for you. You recognised her? Now, fuck me, what were the odds against that? What were the fucking odds?"

"There's more . . . the fake passport you gave me to get me through Checkpoint Charlie isn't fake. You told me it was a fake to rope me in. If I'd known it was real I'd've asked questions. And if I'd been firing on all cylinders I might have queried why my ticket to New York was waiting for me at the embassy in Grosvenor Square instead of somewhere like Thomas Cook."

"So? So I fucked up. So what?"

"So you're not retired from the Agency at all, are you Frank? Tell me, did they buy you into Carver, Sharma, and Dunn? As cover?"

Frank just stared back at him, not so much as a blink of assent.

"And this mission to get Steve's 'aunt' out isn't private enterprise, a mission to save one old Jew. It's CIA business, isn't it Frank? It's all legit. You've got me working for the Agency haven't you? What am I Frank, the fall guy?"

"Nah. I wouldn't do that to you. I wouldn't let them, any of them, do that to you."

"So what am I? A *Kopfjäger*? Why do you need me to smuggle an atomic physicist out of East Berlin?"

"We need deniability. You're our deniability."

"What? Some kind of rogue Limey agent doing a job for cash in hand. A fucking mercenary?"

"Exactly."

"So if I got caught that would be the tale?"

"Getting caught's not part of the plan."

"Then you'd better tell me what the plan really is."

Frank sighed, "How long have I got?"

Wilderness sat down opposite him.

"The wheel won't move again till I lob down a coin."

"OK. OK. It's like this . . . we want Dr. Mayerling out. We do not want to be seen to have . . . what's the word . . . effected . . . effected her escape in any way. Clean hands."

"Clean hands if the Russians kick up a stink?"

"No. The Russians won't kick up a stink. They're part of the deal. They want her out too."

"Then why not just drive her out to Pots-

dam and let her cross the Glienicke Bridge?
Why the cloak, why the dagger, why me?"

"Because in the eyes of the world's press
and in the eyes of every other nation this has
to look like she has escaped with the help of
all those idealistic young Berliners we've been
talking about. It needs a touch of heroism, it
needs to look as though it's got nothing to do
with us and above all nothing to do with the
Russkis. All they have to do is go on doing
what they're doing. Turning a blind eye. You
do all the rest. You get her out. The free press
does its dance of joy, and when she gets to
her final destination it's all got nothing to do
with anyone. She is a free individual exercis-
ing her new freedom. The GDR is publicly
outraged, to say nothing of embarrassed. Russia mouths a few protests, but it's all on the
idiot boards. You and those kids in Berlin —
you and the kids and the tunnel are our get-
out clause. No one need ever know. It fits.
It's the perfect scenario. No one need ever
know. You just fade into the background. The
kids take all the credit. No one need ever
know. No one need ever know about you."

"Why not tell me that at the start? Why the
cockamamy story?"

"Would I have got you this far if I had told
you the truth? Besides it wasn't that cockamamy. It didn't look that cockamamy. I still
say it was a long shot you recognising her.
And . . . and it's important the kids think

610

she's just another refugee. If they knew the truth . . . God knows. Would they keep shtum? Would they start boasting before you even got her out? Plan was she makes a statement when she gets there. That was to be the first the kids knew about it."

"Kids I haven't even met yet."

"Right."

"And . . . 'Gets there'? What is her final destination, Frank? Berkeley? Langley? Does America need one more nuclear physicist?"

"No. But Israel does. She's going to build them the bomb, Joe. If it all goes to plan she builds the Jewish bomb. You rescue one old Jew. And you'll be a hero. An invisible hero, but a hero all the same."

# §188

Wilderness dropped a coin. The wheel slowly jerked its way back to the ground.

The drizzle had stopped. The tourists were flocking in the Prater like summer birds returning.

"We should walk a while."

"What is it about the English and walking. Have you guys yet to invent the wheel?"

"Why do the Russians want any part of this?"

"Oh, they got their reasons. You know Russia . . . a problem wrapped in a mess, inside a . . . I forget the rest but you get my drift."

"Tell me or I walk — and I don't mean a stroll in the park."

"Aw . . . fuck. Joe, does it matter?"

Wilderness's look told him it did.

"OK. It's like this. If Israel gets the bomb, its future is pretty well guaranteed. Right? Nobody messes with a nuclear power. That's obvious. Uncle Sam wants a secure Israel. Nobody gets to be president without the Jewish vote."

"Mayerling has agreed to this? After the war she was one of the refuseniks. Wouldn't work on weapons any more."

"Perhaps a few years in the East has changed her mind. God knows it'd change my mind about a lot of things. I'd be grateful for a decent cup of coffee or even water fit to clean my teeth in. She's been there too long. She left England with Karel Szabo when he got out of the slammer in '55. Szabo wasn't a refusenik, of course."

Wilderness thought better of telling Frank anything about the summer of 1955 — once begun it would surely have to end with a dead Russian in his hotel bathroom, perhaps the same bathroom Frank now occupied — and took his potted history as though hearing it for the first time.

"Are they still together? Where is Szabo? In Berlin?"

"No. Odd as it might seem he's right here in Vienna. Has been since 1961. Got out just before the wall went up."

"Then why not get Szabo?"

"For onesers he ain't Jewish, and for twosers . . . he's the refusenik now. If we do this it's Mayerling or no one. And she will do it. America wants her to do it. Like I said, nobody gets to be prez without the Jewish vote."

"So this is . . . presidential policy?"

"It is . . . governmental policy."

"And Steve?"

"A decent guy. Believe me, one of the best . . . who agreed to play a part for us. For us, for his country and for his people."

"Frank, that sounds like a slogan."

"It's true. Steve acted out of one hundred per cent altruism."

"Russia. Let's get back to Russia. Israel gets the bomb. Kennedy gets reelected. What the fuck does Russia have to gain?"

"The persistence of the status quo in the Middle East."

"Wow. Did you read that off a card?"

"Israel stays, Israel thrives. The enmity of Jew and Arab persists. Israel is in our camp, so the Arabs aren't. So long as that opposition persists there is zero chance of peace, zero chance of a major alliance between the Arab states and the US of A. Result . . . Russia keeps a toehold south of the Caucasus. Hell, toehold, ass-hold, both cheeks squatting down on the whole fucking region."

"Oil. It's all about oil."

"At last. What took you so long? Of course it's about oil. We get Israel, the Russkis get the oil. Everybody's happy. Hell, it's not as if we need the oil. We got Texas."

"And the whole deception is simply to convince the rest of the world that Marte Mayerling escaped through the Berlin student network and made her way to the promised land without the intervention of either side. The USA didn't rescue her and the Soviet Union didn't let her go."

"I'm not sure about the 'simply' — but yeah. That's the scam. If it weren't, fuck I'd just give her a passport like the one I gave you and let her walk across. But there's no . . . how should I put it? . . . no illusion of independence in that, and fukkit, no balls to it either. The scam is essential. It can't look that easy. And now . . . this is where you get to tell me you don't do scams any more."

Wilderness stopped with the sun behind him. Frank shielded his eyes.

"No, Frank. This is where I tell you it'll cost you double."

"What? Forty thousand bucks!"

"Now it's fifty. You say another word and it's sixty."

Frank said nothing.

"If you agree, just nod your head. Fifty thousand dollars and I finish the job."

A passing cloud clipped the sun. Frank

614

lowered his hand and looked straight at Wilderness. It was a long pause, but it seemed to Wilderness that he and Frank had looked at each other this way a hundred times before. He would not be the one to break the silence.

Frank nodded.

"OK. Fifty it is. Hell, it's not as if it's my money."

They walked on a while. Frank was breathing heavily. Wilderness stopped.

"There's one more thing."

"I'm glad I don't play soccer with you. You're always moving the wickets."

"Goalposts, you idiot. It's not much and it's in your own interests."

"So?"

"So put your hand in your pocket right now and peel off two hundred dollars."

Frank did not hesitate. A wry, quizzical look on his face as though he was paying for a little extra in a bawdy house with no real expectation of what the new trick might be.

Wilderness took the money.

"That's for my new passport."

"It is?"

"Not getting busted is part of the plan. Right?"

"Sure."

"If the plan goes wrong —"

"It won't."

"It has. Or we wouldn't be here. If . . . then

you don't want me caught with a passport that can be traced to you and will bring the State Department down on both of us, do you? This will buy me a good fake. Nothing the blokes on the checkpoints would spot, nothing that would fool the best Langley has."

"Good thinking, kemosabe."

They'd almost reached the Metro station. Frank's anxieties had eased up and the mindless bonhomie that typified the man was all but oozing from him. He was back in control, the illusion of efficacy. Wilderness would not have been surprised if Frank suggested they adjourn to a bar and get drunk over lunch. But it was time to go their ways.

"One last thing."

"I thought the two hundred bucks was the one last thing?"

"No. That was the one *more* thing."

"How much this time?"

"Nothing. It's Yuri."

"Yuri? I don't get it."

"I keep seeing Yuri."

"You mean in Berlin?"

"Yes."

"You're sure?"

"Of course I'm not sure. It's happened twice now. I catch a glimpse of a man who looks like Yuri and when I catch up . . . well I don't catch up . . . he's gone."

"What does this guy look like?"

"Like Yuri."

"Yuri 1948 or Yuri now?"

"I don't know. Just . . . Yuri."

Frank stuck both his hands in his pockets, rattled his coins — a slight squirm of the torso as though what he was going to say required muscle.

"Joe, how old do you reckon Yuri was in 1948? He was older than us. Had to be forty, maybe forty-five. Now, he'd be sixty. He'd been NKVD. When we knew him he was MGB or whatever. Just supposing he made it into the KGB — and every time they changed the initials heads rolled . . . Old Joe Stalin had a purge, here a purge, there a purge, everywhere a purge purge — Yuri probably collected epaulettes and collar tabs the way my kid brother collected cigarette cards — just supposing . . . there are a lot of possibilities for Yuri at sixty. He made general, and he's a desk jockey in Dzerzhinsky Square — he's retired — he's in a fucking gulag — he's dead. All possible. What's not possible is that fifteen years later he's still knocking around Berlin. You said it. You're not sure. I am sure. You didn't see Yuri."

Frank was utterly serious. Wilderness looked hard at him. The joker, Frank's habitual mode, was not in play.

"On the other hand if you're looking over your shoulder for spooks, keep your eyes peeled for Nell Breakheart."

"What?"

617

"She's still in Berlin, Did you really think she'd be anywhere else? She was forever telling us she was *'ein* fucking *Berliner.'* But you don't need to worry. She's too high up for you. She's Deputy Chief of Staff to the Mayor. In so far as West Berlin has a Foreign Minister, she's it. All those languages after all. She keeps Willy Brandt au fait with all the foreign papers and briefs him on all the foreign muckety-mucks that show up in Berlin. Any day now she'll be minding Jack Kennedy for him. June 26. Fifteenth anniversary of the airlift. To the day. Hell, it's got to be irresistible hasn't it? Another goddamn speech and this time a captive audience. A concrete wall to keep them in has to be one up on locking the theatre doors. Nell'll be there. She'll have her hands full. She won't be hanging around on street corners looking for old boyfriends to get even with or new ones to fuck."

"You know, Frank, you can be so damn crude when you want to be."

# §189

From somewhere Erno produced a bottle of Johnnie Walker Red Label. Wilderness was not partial to neat scotch, but felt he should keep Erno company. Erno pulled a face when he asked for a jug of tap water.

"My God, you buggers make the stuff and

618

you've no idea how to drink it."

He'd thrown open the windows. If he'd had a terrace they'd both be sitting on it.

"You're very trusting Joe. Why do you not think Frank is up to tricks again?"

"I dunno. He could be. But . . ."

"But the money's too good, eh?"

"That I can't deny."

"But the scheme itself, Joe. You had a good word earlier on . . . *cockamamy.* It doesn't translate so well . . . but it sounds wonderful . . . a combination of the marvellous and the crazy. Better than nonsense, short of believable. Very seductive. It would be typical Frank to be caught out by one lie and then tell you another."

"Yeah well. It might be."

"Do you honestly believe his tale about Israel? About the Russians and the Americans?"

"Dunno. But she is Marte Mayerling. As for the rest . . . I'll tell you on Thursday."

"Why Thursday?"

"Because I'm going across. If I'm followed by anyone . . . then it probably is a line Frank made up. If I'm not . . . I'll conclude there's a fair chance he's telling the truth."

"Of course, they can't follow everybody. And with the passport I shall give you, they will be unlikely to suspect you."

"Professional pride eh, Erno?"

"Exactly. You're either going to have to trust

Frank or walk away from it. And somehow I can't see you turning down the money."

"Is this where you tell me I'm a fool?"

"No. We all need money. And I make mine in a market far more dubious than yours. But nobody shoots at me. When we met you were a kid on a roll. The prince of *Schieber*s. I thought you'd make a fortune or die trying. Somehow you did neither. And I think that perhaps you feel the chances passed you by and that Frank, against all your better judgement, is offering you that chance . . . to get rich quick."

"That's what he said."

"And you didn't say 'get thee behind me, Satan'?"

"I'm here, aren't I?"

"Cockamamy," Erno mused.

"So you said."

"But . . . there is a certain logic to it."

"What logic?"

"There are no easy pickings in a stable world. The black market was a gift to men like you and me. The Berlin Wall is a gift — so good for business. If Germany ever unifies I'll be out of work permanently. You and me, men like you and me and Frank . . ."

"Don't forget Yuri."

"OK, Yuri too. Men like us . . . scavengers . . . we make our living at the rough edge of society, and when society has no more rough edges we make zilch. Russia versus the

West. Good for business. Israel versus the Arabs. Good for business. And we, we scavengers, we as individuals are not all that different from the organisations . . . CIA . . . KGB . . . they just pretend to legitimacy. Whereas we are honest criminals. We are highwaymen, they are robber barons. They'll both thrive on the conflict this scheme of Frank's will perpetuate."

"Honest criminals?"

"Not much of an oxymoron. It fits."

"Indeed it does. But in our roll call of absent friends we've forgotten one altogether. Eddie Clark."

"Swift Eddie? Whatever became of him?"

"He's a copper. A sergeant at Scotland Yard."

Erno choked, coughed up whisky. Wilderness thought he might die laughing.

"He's the right-hand man to one of the most famous coppers in the country — Commander Troy of the Yard — and it's rumoured Eddie never leaves his desk except to bet on a horse."

Before Wilderness left for the night Erno set out a driving licence, a passport, and a 7.65 Walther PPK complete with shoulder holster and spare clip.

Wilderness glanced at the passport.

"Reinhold *Schellenberg*?"

"One name is much the same as another when none of them are real. Walter is dead, and if he weren't he could hardly object."

Wilderness flipped the clip out of the handle of the PPK. A Major Weatherill moment. Tooled up again.

"You never cared for guns, did you Joe?"

"I still don't. But dealing with Frank has taught me better. And dealing with Rumpelstiltskin . . ."

"Who? Oh, the little man in green. Your imaginary friend."

"Forget it, Erno. A trick of the light or something."

"Whatever. I have one last thing for you."

Something heavy, wrapped in old newspaper clunked down on the desk between them.

Wilderness peeled back the paper.

A bunch of rusting keys. The keys to the Monbijou tunnel entrance.

"Where did you . . . ?"

"It was January 1949. I got home to find them outside my door. A present from Rumpelstiltskin."

# §190

Wilderness walked up the side of the S-bahn from Zoo Station to the car park. It was used as overspill and was mercifully empty. He hoped it would stay that way.

There was an even layer of tarmac right across. The spot where the tunnel entrance used to be was invisible. He found it by pacing out the distance between two trees which had been there in 1948 and had survived. It was guesswork, but, he felt, good guesswork. With any luck the contractors had bridged the hole rather than attempting to fill it in. A hundred and fifty feet was a deep hole, but then Berlin had been a city of infinite rubble. They might just have tipped the lot down the hole.

It was exposed, visible from the zoo, from the S-bahn, and from across the canal. They'd need cover of some sort. And they'd need a bluff to explain their presence.

They'd be digging in daylight.

He'd bring her out in darkness.

# §191

The palace had gone. A scar upon the landscape where it had once stood. The merest beginnings of turning Monbijou into a park again. No doubt it all waited upon some five- or fifteen-year People's Plan. The Russians had dynamited the Kaiser's schloss years ago as though eradicating all trace of the Reich, any Reich. Wilderness wondered how and when they'd finally disposed of Monbijou. The schloss had been a bit of a monstrosity. Monbijou hadn't. He'd seen it only as a ruin, and still it had been beautiful.

It reminded him of the day he first saw the

pickelhaube kiosk under the S-bahn. Von Jeltsch-Fugger had turned the key and the door had opened up without effort. Just as it did now.

It was untouched. The pulley Fat Stanley had rigged up was still suspended in the shaft. He found the remains of a one-pound coffee packet at the foot of the well, spilled across the stone floor where some rodent or other has sampled it and rejected it, still bearing its USAF PX label.

Nothing had fallen in, nothing had leaked. He stripped to his underpants to cope with heat and dust and walked to the other end in less than half an hour.

The trolley was at the foot of the other shaft, where he had left it in the November of 1948. Its batteries corroded and its axles rusting, but otherwise intact. His spare uniform, coated in a thick layer of cobwebs, was still draped across it. He'd have no use for either.

There was no tipped rubble. He climbed up the spiral staircase almost to the top. The other pulley was intact, and above it a sheet of flat steel had been laid. He reckoned the top of the pulley had been only about three or four feet below the surface. The City of Berlin had capped the hole and covered it with hardcore and a layer of tarmac. They hadn't bothered to explore. They had, as von Jeltsch-Fugger had opined all those years ago, merely done what was asked of them without curiosity.

# §192

In the evening Wilderness met Manfred Oppitz and three other Free University students in a café off the old Potsdamer Platz — a city square now stranded derelict in no-man's-land. It was like Der Kater Murr, it might even have been Der Kater Murr made over. West Berlin at its very edge. He thought that might well be why they had chosen it.

Wilderness had long thought memory as powerful a tool of imagination as anything. But try as he might he couldn't bring the old Potsdamer Platz, the one he and Frank had trod so often, into the mind's eye with enough strength and vividness to impose itself on the sight before him. "Desert" came to mind. The wall compounded by the clearing away of the buildings on the Soviet side. The Potsdamer Bahnhof, bombed into stone lace by the RAF, had gone and along with it almost anything else that had still been standing in 1945. The Russians had made a wilderness, a desert, a Great War no-man's-land in the middle of the city. The Death Strip — a vast, empty space crossed only by the thin steel thread of an elevated walkway. Of course these kids had chosen this place. They wanted him to meet the wall — *Die Mauer* — before he met them. A matter of fact placed squarely before if not between them all. He found he had little or no reaction to it. In '61 he'd watched the goons roll out barbed wire and lay a few breeze blocks in a manner not much above desultory. Now the wall was a solid body, but scarcely better built. The same desultory workmanship pushed to its lazy limit. The artlessness of the jerry-builder. He'd hardly glimpsed it at Checkpoint Charlie, there was so little of it to see. Now, here it was, architect of such vacancy. Ruler of such ruin. A ragged grey line stretching to infinity.

If Oppitz had learnt to smile for the camera his photographs would have done him justice. He had a mischievous grin that would have alarmed any schoolmaster when he was twelve and attract any girl now he was twenty. He was far from the deadly serious Pol Sci student of his photograph.

"Let me introduce you, Herr Johnson. Georg Kies — physics."

A big man, older than the others, his hair already receding, but still, Wilderness would guess, under thirty.

"Friedrich Bochum — chemistry."

A skinny kid, topped out by the moptop haircut that was sweeping England in the wake of the Beatles, and now seemed to be invading the Continent as well. The sort of look that roused retired colonels to apoplexy and might even cause Burne-Jones to raise a disapproving eyebrow.

"Traudl Brahms."

A blonde beauty, peering at him across the top of her spectacles.

Wilderness stared back.

"You are surprised to find a woman in the group, Herr Johnson?"

"Not at all."

"I am the engineer. All these students of politics and science are just empty rhetoric without me."

They all laughed at this, then Oppitz said, "It's true. We'd never have dug so much as a metre of tunnel without Traudl to prevent it all falling in on us."

"Well, I doubt this one will fall in on anyone. It's been there more than a hundred and fifty years."

"You have been down recently?"

"Yes. I walked the tunnel from the East this morning."

Oppitz nodded, Traudl spoke up.

"If you have a tunnel why do you need us?"

"It's been built over at this end. I need help, experienced help, to reopen it. It's long, it runs from Monbijou Park to the zoo end of the Tiergarten . . ."

"Good God . . . that's three kilometres."

"Closer to four."

"And we'd be digging at the zoo?"

"Yes. No more than three or four feet.

Down to a steel plate. Lift the plate — it's heavy, about an inch thick — and the shaft and tunnel below are intact."

"We'd be digging in the open? That would require city permits."

"Just leave that with me. You'll get all the paperwork you need. What I want you to do is get hold of tools, the lifting gear and screening — the sort of hoarding builders would put up around a structure they're restoring. Keeps dust in and peeping eyes out. You'll be city workmen excavating something. Water, gas, whatever fits the story. And I'm sure Frank Spoleto explained . . . he needs your political skills as much as your tunnelling skills."

Kies said, "Just one woman. A drop in the ocean. We brought out twenty-nine."

"I know. Everybody knows. That's why we want you. To ensure everybody knows."

"Why not bring out more?"

Wilderness had anticipated this question. He wondered if Frank had. As far as they were concerned the "one woman" was Hannah Schneider. He'd give them Hannah Schneider. They'd find out later rather than sooner who she really was. And if that blew their chances of using the tunnel again, so be it. But if it didn't? Well, they had ideals — something Frank wouldn't care about even if he understood in the first place.

"There'll be nothing to stop you once this

job's done. The tunnel will be yours. Be discreet about the location and you might get a few dozen out before the Russians shut it down."

"A few dozen? Why not a hundred?"

"They will shut it down, believe me, they will."

Oppitz asked, "Do we have a deadline?"

"We do. The evening of the twenty-sixth. Next Wednesday."

All four heads turned, looked at each other, exchanged quizzical glances.

Oppitz said, "You know what day that is, don't you?"

"Of course he does," Traudl said, a broad smile, teetering on laughter. "Herr Johnson is stealing thunder. We're all stealing thunder."

## §193

"You can take off the wig now, Dr. Mayerling."

She frowned, turned her back on him, removed a couple of pins, tossed the wig onto the sofa and with one hand still ruffling her hair turned to face him.

Much more had altered. The transformation was dramatic. It made him realise that she'd put on a far better performance that he'd given her credit for. An elasticity seemed to return to her body, she seemed to stand taller, and a youthful light had gone on in her eyes — an angry light, aimed at him.

"You know my name? Do I know yours? Or do I go on calling you Mr. Johnson?"

"Johnson will be fine."

"How very . . . how very unequal. Tell me, Mr. Johnson, will I ever be able to trust you?"

"You trust Frank Spoleto."

"That might be because he is Frank Spoleto."

"Of course. What you see is what you get with Frank."

She weighed this one up, unsure of how sarcastic he was being, waited a moment to see if he would relent and tell her his name. When he didn't she picked up the wig and said, "You know, I think I'll hang on to this. Who knows when I might need to be Hannah Schneider again. Hannah Schneider trusted you Mr. Johnson. I do not."

Wilderness thought — all this for a fucking wig? Who lied to whom?

He said, "Well, if you can contain your mistrust we have plans to discuss."

"Do you know when? You will appreciate I need to be prepared."

"Of course, all the packing you have to do."

He could have bitten his tongue. He'd got her back up. That was inevitable once he'd seen through the charade she and Frank had cooked up, but some demon on his shoulder was knifing her. He had to stop. He didn't like her, she didn't like him, and they had to work together.

She was staring at him, as though she would not utter another word until he answered her properly.

"Wednesday next week. As soon as it's dark enough."

"Wednesday? The twenty-sixth?"

She got up and fetched a two-week-old copy of the *Berliner Morgenpost* off the sideboard. Slapped it down in front of him.

### President Kennedy to Speak at Rudolph-Wilde-Platz on June 26

"Are you sure that's the best day?"

"Quite sure. In fact it's a godsend."

"How so? The city will be crawling with secret policemen."

"And none of them will be looking at us."

# §194

Wilderness had Erno forge Berlin city maintenance permits. Oppitz, Kies, Bochum, and Fraulein Brahms would be looking into the matter of a ruptured sewer.

He met them in the car park. Handed out Erno's handiwork and watched as they shrouded the site in dirty white canvas. Admired her nerve as Traudl put her hair up under her cap and strutted about like a workingman.

"You surely didn't think I would let them leave me out?"

"Of course not."

It was a risk, but hardly worth the worry.

Oppitz walked thirty yards out from the hoarding and set down a couple of metal signs on folding legs instructing Berliners not to use the car park while "Public Works in Progress."

"They're real," he said to Wilderness. "So handy to have had them these last two years. You wouldn't believe the natural obedience of my fellow Berliners."

"Believe it?" Wilderness replied. "I'm banking on it."

# §195

Wilderness could face no more of Erno's scotch and took him a bottle of Burgundy — a Gevrey-Chambertin 1952.

"Not Grand Cru or anything."

"When you're rich Joe, when you're rich?"

After the first glass.

"She's taken against me, Erno."

"What did you do?"

"I suppose I exposed her as a con. She doesn't trust me. I think she'd prefer to deal with Frank. Ridiculous, as Frank was the one who set up the con, and she's lost absolutely nothing by coming clean. Except that I rather think she wanted to do this in disguise, be somebody else. As though whatever it is she has to do was done more easily as Hannah Schneider. There was no relief about dropping the mask, she seemed happier with it. It doesn't much matter of course . . . she doesn't have to trust me, she just has to do what she's told. But she trusts Frank."

The wheezing noise he concluded was Erno laughing again. He hardly ever heard Erno laugh in the old days. When he'd stopped shaking, stopped spilling his wine, he said, "When I was at school we read Shakespeare, translated into German of course. I forget the play. *The Tempest* perhaps or *Julius Caesar*. There was a wonderful line . . . *'Ihr Götter, haltet fest auf der Party der Bastarde!'* What would that be in the original?"

"They lost a bit in translation, Erno. The line was simplicity itself . . . 'Now, gods stand up for bastards.' And it's from *King Lear*."

"Well the gods are certainly standing up for that bastard Frank. She trusts Frank Spoleto? That's got to be the funniest thing I've heard since Hermann Göring killed himself."

It came over him in a ripple, the infectiousness of laughter.

After the third glass.

"I was thinking, Joe. When you used to put on your Guards uniform and that plummy voice and go down the officers mess or commandeer a staff car . . . who were you?"

"I've still got that uniform. Who was I? I was me, I was always me. That was the fun, being me and conning them I was someone else. Conning them I was one of them. I suppose I was tinkering with the English class system. You know, Bernard Shaw, *Pygmalion.* If you can get someone to look right and sound right you can pass them off anywhere."

Erno shrugged, sipped at his wine.

"There are other directions. Other reasons."

"Don't quite get your drift here Erno."

"You were a boy. Part of the pretence was that you were a man. Something you would grow into anyway. You were a working-class kid — in so far as coming from a family of thieves constitutes any form of work — and you might one day become what you pretended to be. An officer and a gentleman. You might say that in marrying Burne-Jones's daughter you had turned the pretence into reality."

"Not quite. Burne-Jones did that when he accepted me as a son-in-law. I couldn't do that, make that last move. I could have married Judy and still got rejected. He could accept me, and he did. An officer? I never made it past sergeant. When I went into civvies for him the pay kept going up, the rank never did. Burne-Jones told me rank didn't matter."

"So . . . you are what? The cockney thief made good."

"If becoming Military Intelligence's resident burglar was making good."

"Suppose the journey were the other way around. That you were the brightest of the bright. You streaked through the system. The great and the good in your chosen discipline fought over you."

"I see where you're headed, Erno, but add to the mix that she's female and Jewish."

"I was coming to that. You achieve great acclaim, the Nobel eludes you perhaps only because you are female . . . yet your greatest achievement is a bomb that annihilates a hundred thousand in a few seconds, and has the potential to exterminate millions. A bomb that goes on to become the cornerstone of the post-war world. The international criterion of power. The greatest threat the planet has ever known. Think of Nobel himself — desperate towards the end of his life to be remembered for something other than dynamite. Suppose, even for a few hours at a time, you can slip back to simplicity merely by donning an old frock and a wig. She spent the war in a university in California. The richest place on God's earth. As far removed from Belsen or Auschwitz as one could imagine. If she'd been in one of the camps . . . Belsen . . . Auschwitz . . . would we have any difficulty understanding a lack of identity, a search for identity, or a rejection of identity? All three would be in play. Supposing Marte Mayerling, splitter of atoms, could become Hannah Schneider . . . somebody's old Jewish maiden aunt. Maybe she chose the name herself? Schneider. How many Jewish women from Germany and Poland have earned a living as tailors and seamstresses? Joe, it's not just any disguise. It is Freud's own mask."

"What if Frank chose it?"

"No matter . . . it is what she makes of it. He offers an alias. She makes it into a mask."

"And if she's desperate to be Hannah Schneider . . . why Israel . . . why another fucking bomb?"

"Well . . . we have only Frank's word for that."

Wilderness stared into the ashes. There was always something to be burned at Erno's. The warmest night tinged by a few glowing embers. And it seemed to him that Erno's fire was always a burning of deceptions, his Lenten bonfire of the vanities — this was where the old man got rid of all the evidence. The incriminating letters, the first drafts, the smudged failures. And it seemed that he was looking into the grey dust of months, probably years, of lies and deceit and that the few sparks that were glowing now were merely those he had added himself.

"I won't be asking her that, Erno."

# §196

Erno burnt more vanities. Independent states East and West had hit hard these last few years. The cold war was nowhere near as good for business as military occupation. It was in the nature of things military that there was always a fiddle to be worked — and the beauty of things military is that they were all paid for by the taxpayer. Stealing them was not theft, forging them was hardly a crime so much as a challenge. PX and NAAFI were the initials on the gates of heaven. But the sad truth was that there were not enough fiddles left in the world.

He'd clipped his toenails onto a twenty-year-old page of the *Der Angriff,* and flung them into the stove. He'd got one sock on and was just pulling on the other when he became aware of someone else in the room.

"Joe?"

A woman sat down opposite him. The only light was the light from the burning fire, a flickering golden arc — he could see a pair of shapely legs and the hem of a skirt and little else.

"Joe, he says, Joe. I might have known." And she leaned down, her face half in shadow half out, "You old rogue."

"Nell?"

"I saw him this morning. The porters at the Kempinski brought a car round for him. He got in and drove off. I watched the car until I lost sight of it somewhere near the Kranzler. He still hasn't got the hang of tipping. How long has he been back?"

"Just a few days."

"A few days."

"Maybe a week. You know. In and out. He's been back before. This isn't the first time."

"Just the first time I've seen him. The British sent him?"

Erno had no idea how much to tell her.

"No. He's not with the British any more. He's a civilian these days."

"So, what brings him back to Berlin?"

Erno knew she'd get it out of him, one way or another. He hoped to tell her something of nothing and hang on to the vital detail.

"He's working for Frank Spoleto."

"For Frank? Has he gone mad?"

Erno shrugged.

"You know Joe, Lenchen. Always the chancer."

"Chance? What chance? Erno — tell me everything."

# §197

Nell had her regular Monday meeting with Brandt. The last such before Kennedy's entourage arrived in two days' time. There'd be other, impromptu meetings, but this was the last scheduled meeting before Brandt flew

638

to Bonn to act the role of the most important non-person in the world — just visible in the shadows cast by the West German chancellor and the West German president.

"I have two fears," Brandt said. "An anti-Russian demonstration of any kind — and who knows, Kennedy enthusiasm could well bubble over into that, and we would be compelled to react. Secondly, an escape. Either would constitute an 'incident.' "

"What do we have to lose by an escape?"

"If it succeeds, nothing. Perhaps at the very worst a distraction. If one were to fail . . . neither farce nor tragedy would describe the consequences adequately."

That word again *Vorkommnis*. Incident.

It required no thought — she wasn't ever going to tell him.

# §198

*Wednesday June 26, 1963*
Nell rode in the lead press bus. Just behind the open car that carried Kennedy, Brandt, and Adenauer. They all stood. She wondered if they had tied Adenauer to a post to keep him upright. Next to Brandt — tall — or Kennedy — handsome — the chancellor looked decrepit, a dying tortoise. She turned over Brandt's "It can't ever look like a Nuremburg rally" in her mind. It didn't. It looked nothing like anything ever seen in

Europe. This was America transplanted — a New York ticker tape parade, the uncontainable joy of a young country that did not prize restraint over enthusiasm. Asked how many Berliners were on the streets that June 26, Nell would have replied "all of them."

Shortly after leaving Tegel airport the cavalcade had passed a construction site — every crane had pointed its arm skyward, and every strut was gripped or stood upon by a hard-hatted worker — a metal forest with human leaves.

Bouquets of flowers had been forbidden by the US Secret Service, so the celebration became more and more improvised. Flags at every window, the Stars and Stripes, the occasional flag of Berlin itself and in the absence of any flags just bedsheets, huge, white, flapping bedsheets. And . . . confetti, pink confetti. Shower upon shower of pink confetti. No one had thought to forbid confetti.

Ahead of the presidential car was a trailer of photographers, more than she could count, all with their lenses trained on Kennedy. Nell had had no say in this — she had been content that her route across the centre of West Berlin, around the zoo, along the rebuilt Ku'damm — had finally been approved — but it looked awful to her. She imagined it looked awful to Kennedy, to be looking at a camera lens at every turn of the head, but concluded he was used to it. A life lived in public. He might even like it. After all, he never stopped smiling.

At the Brandenburg Gate the president stopped smiling. A platform had been erected to enable him to see over the wall. Brandt's prediction had been fulfilled as had his fear — the five arches of the gate were draped in red flags — the Russian stunt — utterly obscuring any view down Unter den Linden. The last time Nell had seen this had been in 1938 — but then every red flag had borne a swastika — the German stunt. Today it was a touch, just a touch of a Nuremburg rally. A touch too far. And in front of the gate was a wide yellow placard explaining to the president in English and German that only the East had thoroughly denazified and that the promises of the West had all been broken.

Kennedy passed her as he came down the wooden steps from the platform, from his fleeting glimpse of the East, with not a flicker of a smile. He'd been smiling from the moment the stepped off the plane — but he wasn't smiling now.

# §199

They had thirty minutes rest before the main speeches of the day in front of the *Rathaus* in Schöneberg. Kennedy had Brandt's office. Brandt had hers.

"There's going to be a slight change of plan."

"Slight" in politics never meant slight.

"President Kennedy thinks, and I agree, that his speech should be interpreted by a German, not simply a German speaker. He's asked for a Berliner. He's asked for you."

"What? He's never heard of me."

"Apparently he has. He asked for you by name."

Nell struggled to believe what sounded to her ears to be unbelievable.

"Alright. I don't really have a choice. Do I?"

"Am I forcing privilege upon you, Nell?"

She ignored this.

"We have less than thirty minutes. When can I see the speech?"

"Ah . . . we have a slight problem there, too."

That word again.

"They haven't finished it."

Brandt's delivery was deadpan, conveying nothing of the apprehension he surely felt. Everything planned — from the order of greeting, to the motorcade route, to the choice of hors d'oeuvres at lunch . . . to the text. And now the Americans had begun to ad lib.

"The president's in my office with Mc-George Bundy. They'd appreciate your help right now. But not half as much as I would."

Brandt swept Nell into his office without knocking. Kennedy and Bundy were hunched over the desk with a few scraps of paper and a stack of index cards in front of them, talking softly as though they might be overheard — but then that had been the tone of the entire visit. Public statements amplified by a thousand microphones, private utterances at whisper level — the uncertainty of what was going down to posterity and what was not.

Brandt introduced Nell as "my right hand, my Girl Friday."

Kennedy shook her hand, said, "I've been hearing about Fraulein Burkhardt from Mac for weeks now."

Then, so suddenly she could hear herself breathing, Brandt and Bundy had ducked out and left her to it — and left her to him.

"It's the hook."

"I'm sorry . . ."

"The speech needs a hook. Mac and I agree it should be in German. I don't speak a word, as I'm sure you know. I've been trying to remember that speech Mayor Reuter made during the airlift . . . 'The world should come to Berlin'?"

"Reuter said *'Völker der Welt, schaut auf Berlin.'* People of the world *look* at Berlin. I was there, Mr. President. I heard him."

"You were there? You must have been no more than a girl."

"I was, just a girl."

"So we were thinking of something like, the world must watch Berlin. It just doesn't have the ring . . . it isn't a hook. People of the world, look at Berlin? It's a great line, but I'd feel I'd borrowed it. It's a moment to be original if that's at all possible."

"Mr. President. Does this have anything to do with what you just saw?"

"It has *everything* to do with what I just saw."

"May I see your notes?"

Kennedy sat in Brandt's chair, motioned for her to sit down and handed her the index cards. Nell read them through and leafed back to the third card, the one on which the typed script had been subject to crossings out and scribblings in two hands. This recently, instantly revised version read:

There are many people in the world who really don't understand, or say they don't, what is the great issue between the free world and the Communist world.

There are some who say that Communism is the wave of the future.

And there are some who say in Europe and elsewhere we can work with the Communists.

And there are even a few who say that it is true that Communism is an evil system, but it permits us to make economic progress. Let them come to Berlin.

The anger was palpable.

The tone of the visit was about to change.

"Here," she said. "This is your hook. Say 'Let them come to Berlin' at the end of each statement. Build up the emphasis. I will be translating for you, I shall do my best to be as emphatic in German as you are in English. But the last time say it in German. Just the last. You say. *'Laßt sie nach Berlin kommen,'* and then I will repeat exactly what you said word for word . . . I shall be less your interpreter and more your echo."

Kennedy liked this.

"It has . . . passion."

"It should. I'm passionate about Berlin."

"You're a Berliner, right?"

*"Ich bin ein Berliner,"* Nell said, the metaphorical foot stamping down, the po-face rippling into a smile.

"Would you mind writing that down."

Nell flipped an index card and wrote *"Ich bin ein Berliner"* on the back.

He looked over, said, "Say it again, slowly."

She watched as Kennedy wrote down a sloppy phonetic of the phrase.

*"Ish bin ein Bearleener."*

"I think we're done," he said.

# §200

If pressed Nell could probably have recited Kennedy's speech in either language in full, even years after.

Her ad hoc, instant memory was of the crowd . . .

"Ken-Ned-Dy Ken-Ned-Dy."

Half a million, a million — who could tell? — Berliners on the street.

"Ken-Ned-Dy Ken-Ned-Dy."

At lunch, immediately afterwards, Kennedy had Nell moved up the table. Not next to him, but where with a little leaning and tilting of the head he could address remarks to her. His capacity for chitchat did not surprise or disappoint her. You worked for Brandt you got used to flirting. What stuck in her mind was nothing he said to her, it was a remark to one of the generals, and there seemed to be so many US generals, "If I told them to they'd tear down the wall with their bare hands."

"Ken-Ned-Dy Ken-Ned-Dy."

At a quarter to six Air Force One took off from Tegel and Nell heard the slow hiss as the balloon deflated.

# §201

Nell went back to her office. It felt like one of the longest days of her life. To go home would have been both sensible and impractical.

She rearranged the pencils on her desk in order of length. Brandt had jumbled the pencils. Brandt had left a note.

Can that man never stick to a script? Let me know if the Wall is still there in the morning. WB

To pass without incident — that had been Brandt's phrase. Kennedy had been the "incident," as much as the tanks that had squared off on either side of Checkpoint Charlie two years ago. Kennedy had been the "incident." And she had made it worse. Brandt had sent her in there to keep Kennedy on script, and she'd helped him raise the temperature of the cold war to simmering — *"Laßt sie nach Berlin kommen!"* Perhaps a million joyous Berliners would tear down the wall. Or pigs might fly.

She thought of Reuter's speech, all those years ago.

"Look at Berlin."

Reuter had urged no action on anyone. And, as far as she knew, had never had the arrogance to say it in private either. Still, hundreds had swarmed through the Brandenburg Gate into Pariser Platz, and if there'd been a wall then all Reuter would have had to do was tell them and they too would have torn it down with their bare hands. And the Russians would have slaughtered them.

She sat back in an armchair, put her head

on the rest. It was almost seven o'clock and still the crowds were on the streets. Occasionally a burst of "Ke-Ned-Dy" would come up from the square, as Berlin threw itself a party. She stretched out her legs, closed her eyes . . . "Ke-Ned-Dy Ke-Ned-Dy" . . . and found her mind overlaid the chant with the sounds of an older Berlin . . . of nights punctuated by gunfire . . . of the constant hum and burr of planes low in the sky over Tempelhof and Tegel. And for a while she was back in Grünetümmlerstraße, half-sleeping, half-waking, curled into Wilderness's arm as the sounds of the city drifted into their attic room.

# §202

Wilderness weighed it up. He'd not anticipated quite this situation. The streets were still full of people two hours after Kennedy had flown out of Tegel. It seemed like a million West Berliners were out to celebrate . . .

"Ke-Ned-Dy Ke-Ned-Dy."

Getting to the checkpoint on Bornholmer Straße meant dodging hundreds of people jaywalking and sitting without retaliation as a bunch of teenagers pounded a tattoo on the roof of his tiny NSU Prinz to the beat of "From Me to You" by the Beatles. Da da da — da da — da da daah. "If there's anything that you want" — it might have been the

*Schieber*'s anthem.

"Ke-Ned-Dy Ke-Ned-Dy Ke-Ned-Deee."

Half a dozen times Wilderness braked for kids in the road, and caught the same word over and over again — *Waschmaschine* . . . washing machine. He'd chosen the car to be inconspicuous. It wasn't. It was a tinny rear-engined joke, a washing machine on wheels. One he'd dump in Monbijou Park.

There had been something clinical, almost frail about Checkpoint Charlie. It was just a couple of sheds, and however long it might be there it would always look as temporary as a London prefab. Less ideological boundary than level crossing. The bridge at Bornholmer Straße was altogether different — the real thing. Vast, ugly, dirty. A great metal maw yawning into the sky over rusting railway tracks, bank upon bank of sun-eclipsing floodlights and vicious spirals of barbed wire. Mouth, eyes, teeth — the moloch of *Metropolis*. A fitting place for the meeting of worlds.

At the bridge there were more guards than usual — staring into the West at the distant party to which they hadn't been invited. Noses pressed against the windowpane. But, then, they didn't know what to expect of this day any more than he did. And if they were all guarding the wall there were fewer of them on the streets of East Berlin.

They glanced at his passport, noted down the number of his car, asked the purpose of his visit.

*"Meine Familie,"* Wilderness replied, and they waved him on.

As he passed Wilderness heard one of them say *"Waschmaschine"* and the sound of West Berlin faded to nothing.

"Ke-Ned-Dy Ke-Ned-Dy."

Now not even a whisper.

He'd be grateful for the silence of the East. It was unearthly. A silence that seemed only to amplify his own thoughts. It went with the smell of the East, all those farting Trabants, all those belching chimneys, but for once he'd be glad of it.

# §203

Marte Mayerling was dressed as Marte Mayerling. Standing in the sitting room at Arnold-Zweig-Straße, bag packed, waiting for him. No baggy frock, no ratty cardigan. A neat two-piece outfit in tasteless brown — flat, sensible shoes — a collapsible umbrella she telescoped and shoved in the bag.

"You're supposed to be Hannah Schneider."

"The pretence has no meaning any more."

"It never did have meaning — but it does matter."

"To whom?"

"To the plan — there are people expecting Hannah Schneider."

"People?"

"People willing to risk their lives to help you."

"To help me or to help Hannah Schneider?"

It was pointless arguing. He hefted her bag and took it out to the car. It was a short, silent ride to Monbijou.

He could tell her that the plan Frank had cooked up required her to be Hannah Schneider for a day or so, but he didn't give a damn about Frank's plan.

He could tell her that he wanted time to get clear of the whole cockamamy scheme before her identity was revealed, that he had no intention of ending up as Frank's fall guy — but that was showing his hand. Besides she despised him. He was *ein Menschenhändler* — a trafficker in human souls. She'd never do him that favour.

# §204

It was close to impossible. She'd driven north from the *Rathaus* as far as Hardenbergstraße. The Kennedy motorcade had driven down Hardenbergstraße. It was a mess of confetti and paper strips, and it was full of revellers.

"Ke-Ned-Dy Ke-Ned-Dy."

About a kilometre from Zoo Station Nell abandoned her state-of-the-art VW Beetle and decided to walk. Six men wanted to kiss her before she reached the station, one even picked her up momentarily, swept her off her feet, whirled her around and set her down again without a word and without looking back.

"Ke-Ned-Dy Ke-Ned-Dy."

It would be close to the longest day of the year, but nine o'clock had passed, the day was creeping towards the crepuscular — the station was lit up and the perimeter lights were coming on all around the zoo. Somewhere beyond the zoo was a blacked-out car park she must have passed many times without even noticing it was there.

# §205

Wilderness and Marte Maylering sat on the spiral steps ten feet below the surface at the zoo end. She was impatient.

"We're safe now, surely? We must have passed under the wall half an hour ago."

Nothing was ever safe in the world of Frank Spoleto. Nothing was safe in the shadow of Rumpelstiltskin. Wilderness would not even begin to contemplate "safe" until he'd delivered her into the hands of Manfred Oppitz.

"Trust me," he said to no reaction.

He looked at his watch. It was 9:45. Oppitz was due now, Oppitz was late. He'd even gone through the cinematic farce of synchronising his watch with Wilderness's — something Wilderness had never done in thirteen years as a spy — and still he was late.

Wilderness had said, "Don't be early. I don't want you hanging about attracting attention. Don't be late either, once we're out of the tunnel I want us away."

It occurred to him that Georg Kies was a physics student and would probably know Mayerling on sight, but he'd deal with that when it happened — it was all part of Frank's plot and he'd lost Frank's plot. A simple "shut up" would suffice. He'd hand Mayerling/Schneider up to them in their van and he'd walk away. Make of it what they might.

From above he could hear the honking of car horns, and in a lull the chant reached him again, born on a breeze of intoxicated joy . . .

"Ke-Ned-Dy Ke-Ned-Dy Ke-Ned-Deee."

And it occurred to him that Berlin was in gridlock, and the silly sods were simply stuck in traffic.

"Wait here," he said.

"Why?"

"Just wait. Something's gone wrong. They're late. I'm going up to look."

He stepped out of the awning. Past the steel plate propped up against the mound of rubble they had cleared. Looked around. A couple of rockets bursting in the sky somewhere over Wedding, a swell of "Ke-Ned-Dy" resounding over Tiergarten. It looked as though the party would go on all night.

He stood several minutes staring in the direction Oppitz's van would come from, willing it to turn up, just willing it to turn up before anyone else did.

# §206

Nell could see two triangular municipal signs in the mid-distance, but could not read them in the diminishing light. Only when she drew close.

## Public Works in Progress

A joke description for what Wilderness was up to.

And behind her, monotonous now, irritating, boring . . .

"Ke-Ned-Dy Ke-Ned-Dy Ke-Ned-Deee."

She stood between the signs, watched as a man walked towards her. Only when she saw his right hand emerge from his jacket clutching a gun was she certain it was Wilderness.

The gun was aimed at her now.

"Joe. Don't you know me?"

"Oh Christ, Nell. What are you doing here?"

He didn't holster the gun. It dangled now around his right thigh, his finger still in the trigger guard.

She didn't know what she was doing there.

They stared at one another. Perhaps a

whole minute passed without speaking.

She saw movement over Wilderness's left shoulder. A figure, hunched low, a shadow outlined against the white awning. She raised her hand, pointed and said, "Joe, behind you."

Wilderness turned.

A ragged *Trümmerfrau* had appeared, her head wrapped in a scarf, a billowing skirt, moving in and out of the moonlight shadows, cutting a curious path towards them, clutching a piece of trash she had found — a wooden crutch, or a broken chair.

Then he saw the broken chair leg for what it was. A British Army Sten gun — and as the gun levelled on him he fired twice. His first shot missed, the second lifted the "old woman" off her feet. Then the clip jammed.

He walked towards the body. Dropped the clip, banged in the spare and took aim at the head. The headscarf and the wig had slipped from Yuri Myshkin. It wasn't Yuri Myshkin, it was Rumpelstiltskin. It wasn't Rumpelstiltskin, it was Hannah Schneider. It wasn't Hannah Schneider, it was Marte Mayerling. Marte Mayerling in a ratty cardigan. Marte Mayerling coughing blood, still clutching her telescopic umbrella.

She sat bolt upright, spine straight, legs splayed, a rag doll dropped from the toy-box, and pointed at Wilderness with the umbrella.

"So, this is how you wanted me?"

From the roaring city behind them . . .

"Ke-Ned-Dy Ke-Ned-Dy Ke-Ned-Deee."

And a line from childhood was running unstoppable through Wilderness's mind, ". . . it really was just a kitten."

And Marte Mayerling was rambling too, "So I dress up in rags . . . so he shoots me . . ."

Wilderness said nothing. Stared at the slowly widening puddle of blood emerging from beneath her skirts like the piss stain of incontinence.

"So he shoots me?"

Wilderness said nothing. He stood, the gun loose in his right hand, felt Nell's hand slip into his left, her fingers threading themselves into his, weaving one hand, forming one fist, heard her voice soft and elegiac in his ear.

"Oh my God, Wilderness, what have we done?"

# STUFF

What is this? Book ten, maybe book eleven? Anyway, I'm hoping for a pile big enough to sit on the day I am so broke I have to burn the furniture. Writing most of them has led me to rely upon, rip off, scam . . . dozens of memoirists and historians. Two in particular have gone unacknowledged — an oversight I correct somewhat guiltily now.

Looking at the obituaries early in 2011 I realised that George Clare had died while I was writing *A Lily of the Field,* a novel which learnt a lot from his *Last Waltz in Vienna* (Macmillan, 1980). In 2011 I was at work on this novel, which derives just as much from his second volume of memoirs, *Berlin Days* (Macmillan, 1989). Thus prompted, I decided to look up Madeleine Henrey on the Internet — she had died in 2004. Again I hadn't noticed. If nothing else this ought to teach me to read the *Daily Telegraph* more often. As an old friend once remarked, "nobody dies in the *Grauniad.*" (It's OK. You don't have to read the editorials but if you don't look at the letters from time to time half the gags in *Private Eye* will mean nothing to you. Reading the obits is a treat. Novels in miniature. The one on the late Tony, Lord Moynihan being a classic of its kind. None of them will turn you into a raving Tory, and if they do I will mercifully shoot you.)

Madeleine Henrey wrote over thirty books, mostly as Robert Henrey or Mrs. Robert Henrey. She was French, but wrote in English and it's even been suggested that her choice of noms de plume might be a reflection of her husband's involvement in her work. In particular, and in rapid succession, she produced three volumes of war memoirs depicting life with a small child in a modern flat in Shepherd Market (just off Piccadilly) during the Second World War. They appeared as *A Village in Piccadilly* (Dent, 1942), *The Incredible City* (Dent, 1944), and *The Siege of London* (Dent, 1946). Around 1980 Dent reissued them, edited down, as a single volume, but all editions have long been out of print. They are the most vivid, detailed account of the minutiae of London life during the war that I know of. I've used details from all three at various times and in various books. Perhaps one day they will all be in print again.

George Clare was born Georg Klaar in

Vienna. He escaped to England, was interned, allowed to serve (like so many Austrian and German refugees) in the Pioneer Corps — the regiment of ditch-digging lawyers — transferred to the Royal Artillery, and, when the victorious Allies finally needed German-speakers, posted to Berlin where he interrogated Germans as part of the denazification process. Perhaps because he wrote his books forty years later, they have a much racier, more contemporary feel than Mrs. Henrey's, but George Clare wrote history like a novelist, detail floats down off him like autumn leaves, anecdote rolls out as vivid as yesterday. Who else would bother to record that the Army badge of the British occupying forces (black disc in a red ring) was known as a "septic arsehole"?

He too is out of print.

Every trip back in time yields new discoveries . . . in this case . . .

*Aftermath* by Francesca M. Wilson (Penguin, 1947), a Newnham bluestocking who worked with UNRRA in Bavaria in 1945-46 among refugees and former POWs, and seems to have had the most wonderful ear and memory.

*Hamburg 1947: A Place for the Heart to Kip* (iUniverse, 2011) by Harry Leslie Smith, a working-class lad from Yorkshire who found himself posted to Hamburg as an RAF wireless operator in the immediate aftermath of the war. Again a wonderful ear and memory at work. I came across the book rather late in the writing of this one, but it answered questions about Hamburg that had been dogging me for ages. And whilst Miss Wilson's remarkable career is documented in minute print on the back of her sixty-five-year-old Penguin book, I know next to nothing about Mr. Smith as yet.

*The Answers of Ernst von Salomon.* A former Freikorps soldier whose approach to the 131 questions on his *Fragebogen* is close to complete anarchy. He survived the war, avoided conscription, avoided becoming a Nazi and left a memoir of untold riches for the delving historian. It was translated into English in 1954 and, as with *Aftermath,* I don't think it ever had a second run.

The treatise I ascribe to Peter Camenzind, *Über den Nachweis . . . ,* in chapter 78 was written by Otto Hahn and Fritz Strassman and published in *Naturwissenschaften* in 1939. Almost needless to say I have not read it.

There's a mixed bag of fiction dealing with Germany after the war by both Germans and occupiers. If pressed to recommend just one — and no one is pressing — my choice would be Kay Boyle's *The Smoking Mountain* (Knopf, 1950).

The most readable factual account of Berlin after the war I found to be David Clay

Large's *Berlin* (Basic Books, 2000).

And, probably last, there are also some interesting films made among the ruins: *The Big Lift, A Foreign Affair* (both in English), *Germany Year Zero* (in Italian), and *The Murderers Are Among Us* (in German).

**Paradies Verlassen:** This is fiction. The Femina Club was probably the most famous Weimar nightclub — it survived the war but by 1948 it was a cinema — closely followed by Resi's on the Alexanderplatz, which I first came across in Emanuel Litvinoff's novel *The Lost Europeans* (Heinemann, 1960). Resi's had telephones at every table for the obvious reason, and until I double-checked I had assumed Litvinoff had made up the pneumatic tubes (*Rohrpoststationen*), but it seems Berlin was at the cutting edge of pneumatic technology and had a city-wide tube network. Alas, Resi's closed in 1939 so I invented Paradies, and kept the tubes. With my skool O-level German (grade 9, i.e., total failure, but then the teacher loathed me and me him — miserable bastard that he was), I render *verlassen* as "forsaken" rather than "lost," implying a wilful departure.

**Ernie Bevin:** I don't think he visited Berlin at all during the autumn of 1948, but it doesn't matter. I needed him there so . . .

661

what is real, however, is his utter refusal to meet with any representative of the USSR until the blockade had been lifted.

**The Tunnel:** Also fictional. Berlin may well have been a swamp at one time, but I made up the tunnel and the geology that enabled it. As to geography . . . weeeeell . . . the S-bahn still clips one corner of Monbijou Park. After the war Monbijou was a ruin, today it's highly if dully developed around and under the S-bahn tracks. God knows what it was like in 1963, two years after the wall went up; now it's a row of concrete arches leading to the Monbijou Bridge, out of one of which sticks a steel leg much as I describe. Are there more buried in the concrete? Dunno. I suspect from talking to Berliners that the S-bahn, at this point, was always a series of arches and what I describe as a "steel lattice" was more the norm for the U-bahn surface tracks than for the S-bahn . . . but I stick with it, because it's "moodier" and it fits the plot. Concrete sheds no sparks.

The opposite end of my tunnel would have been somewhere near the pre-war Sportpalast, which was turned into the Tiergarten barracks during the war — I assume to house the flak tower crew. Today, predictably, it's part of the zoo, and a wooden hut stands on roughly the spot I assign to the tunnel shaft, and in said hut lives a rather large pink-headed crane, usually to be found poised on one leg . . . thus . . .

Consider the tunnel to be the historical equivalent of Hitchcock's MacGuffin.

**Ernst Reuter, the Reichstag, the street battles, et cetera:** I've conflated several incidents and at least three of Reuter's speeches in the summer of 1948 into one. The main protest at the Reichstag, and the speech for which Reuter is best known, happened on September 9.

**'Ich bin ein Berliner':** I think the only one of the Kennedy team who laid claim to this phrase was McGeorge Bundy. The historian Andreas W. Daum disputes the claim, but agrees that the president was looking for a phrase equivalent to Cicero's "civis romanus sum." Both phrases, however, are to be found written phonetically on JFK's cue cards for June 26, 1963 — and I think any argument that he was drawing upon a classical education is specious as JFK clearly had no more idea how to pronounce the Latin phrase than he had the German — "kiwis romanus sum." As the park-bench philosopher, the late, great E. L. Wisty used to say, "I didn't have the Latin."

I've no idea who suggested either phrase and the Latin may well have been JFK's own idea — but the most likely way it made it into German is by the intervention of either one of the two interpreters Kennedy had that day, both of whom, in this novel, are displaced by my fictional one. The Americans did indeed request a German as interpreter for the speech at Schöneburg. It may be cheeky to have my interpreter help JFK structure the speech — but what politician since Lincoln has written their own speeches? — cheekier still to think that a woman might have been allowed stand up in front of half a million Berliners and translate for Kennedy.

# ACKNOWLEDGEMENTS
## APLENTY . . .

Gordon Chaplin
Sue Kennington
Elizabeth Graham-Yooll
Sarah Teale
Linda Shockley
Sam Redman
Clare Alexander
Frances Owen
Cassie Metcalf-Slovo
Morgan Entrekin
Peter Blackstock
Briony Everroad
Joaquim Fernandez
Robert Etherington
E.L. Wisty
Ryan Law
Deb Seager
Sarah Burkinshaw
Ulrich Bochum
Jeff Harrison
Cosima Dannoritzer
Claus Litterscheid

Nick Lockett
Aunt Dolly
Marcia Gamble Hadley
David Sinclair
John Sinclair
Bruce Kennedy
Ion Trewin
Jess Atwood Gibson
Sue Freathy
Mrs. Wisby
Anna-Riikka Santapukki
&
Tony Broadbent

# ABOUT THE AUTHOR

**John Lawton** still lives in Derbyshire, England, but writes mostly in the cool isolation of northern Italy. He has written seven Inspector Troy thrillers, two standalone novels, and a volume of history, and has edited several English writers (Wells, Conrad, D. H. Lawrence) for Everyman Classics. Over the years he has worked with Harold Pinter, Gore Vidal, and Kathy Acker. He is devoted to the work of Franz Schubert and Barbara Gowdy.